WAKE

WAKE

A NOVEL

SHELLEY BURR

WILLIAM MORROW
An Imprint of HarperCollinsPublishers

HarperCollins books may be purchased for educational, business, or sales promotional use. For information, please email the Special Markets Department at SPsales@harpercollins.com.

Originally published in Australia in 2022 by Hachette Australia.

FIRST U.S. EDITION

Library of Congress Cataloging-in-Publication Data has been applied for.

ISBN 978-0-06-323522-9

22 23 24 25 26   LSC   10 9 8 7 6 5 4 3 2 1

To my Love and my Joy

ONE

I LIVE IN that house you've seen on the news. We painted it robin's-egg blue the summer I turned sixteen, but in your mind it's white. Two little pink bikes lean against the veranda, and one wall glows blue with the reflected light of a police car. They use the same picture every time there's "news." It's not worth the expense to send a photographer out to get a fresh one. Not when they want the two little bikes and that streak of blue.

Nobody wants to see proof that one of those little girls grew up.

* * *

The sign above the door to the combined general store and post office read PLEASE KEEP CLOSED—AIRCON RUNNING in slanted handwriting, but if the AC was going it was losing against the hazy late-summer heat. Mina remembered the blast of cold air when they pushed open the door as kids—usually when their mother, worn down packing a dozen errands into a single trip into town, agreed to stop for an ice cream. Either the air conditioner had grown too old, or electricity prices too high, or Mrs. Gilligan had hit that age

1

where skin stretched over bone and the hottest day was too cool for comfort. Mina supposed she could ask, but when you asked people personal questions they felt comfortable asking them back.

"You here for your delivery, darl?" Mrs. Gilligan asked.

The General was closer to a convenience store than a supermarket, but it was still the only place in Nannine to buy groceries. Minda had felt awkward the first few times she turned up to collect a package that was clearly a bulk load of dry goods and cans. But Mrs. Gilligan had never commented, never even gave her a sideways look.

Mina preferred the people who did comment. At least when a person sniped to her face, she knew exactly where they stood. The ones who seemed nice could stay a question mark forever.

"It's in the back," Mrs. Gilligan said, pushing herself up off the stool. "I've checked the attached invoice, and there are a couple of items missing." She slid the invoice across the counter. "I do have these all in stock, at the moment."

Mina skimmed the list, hoping it would be the junk food she'd added on impulse. Or the batteries; they could wait another six weeks. But no. The missing items were vital. The canned beans. Two out of the five bags of dried lentils. And the ground cumin.

She drummed her fingers on the counter, doing the math in her head. The cumin was the key to a lot of recipes, particularly the deep pantry rummages she leaned on in the last days of her grocery cycle. Some days she was nearly out, but couldn't face the trek into town. Those days had made her an expert in the sort of cooking that would have made her great- and great-great-grandmothers proud.

The door opened behind her, and a man shuffled in. She studied his warped reflection in the glass door of the cigarette cabinet.

He was tall and broad, wearing a black pullover and cargo pants despite the heat. He had a black knitted cap on, but what she could see of his hair was blond, with the fuzzy texture that might be curls if he used the right conditioner. His face was unfamiliar—an unusual quality here. Nannine was a barely populated town in Central New South Wales, far enough off the highway that no travelers passed through searching for hot pies and public toilets. The seasonal workers at the surrounding farms were all in place by this point in the year.

Mrs. Gilligan straightened her posture, looking at him with an open curiosity that meant Mina wasn't out of the loop on any gossip. He was a new face, and that sent anxiety slicing through her gut.

She walked away from the counter with quick steps. She kept her eyes on the lowest shelves as she passed the man, as if she were fascinated by the cheapest available floor cleaner.

Even though she rarely shopped there, she had the layout of the store, and the location of all her typical items, memorized. Three aisles, six shelves, and a row of fridges and freezers at the back. She was conscious of the man as she moved about. He drifted from one side of the store to another, throwing items in his basket with barely a glance at the shelves. Every time he passed the end of an aisle she was in, he turned his head and swept his gaze over her.

That was normal, she reminded herself. If he was new in town, he would have no idea what was where in the store. And it was human nature to turn and look at the only other person in the vicinity as you passed.

It was normal.

He wasn't watching her.

She grabbed the bag of cumin off the rack and threw it in

her basket, her arm whipping out like she was trying to snatch a live bird from the air.

An anti-shoplifting mirror hung from the ceiling, and in it she saw the man come to a stop at the end of her aisle. He examined the display of chips in front of him, but flicked his eyes to the side, once, to look at her.

She planted her feet and stared down at her basket, dragging in a deep breath. He wasn't the first person to watch her, but this was the first time one of them had shown up in public.

He was waiting for her, waiting until she pushed past him on her way back to the checkout. How long could the two of them stand there, pretending to be interested in their respective displays?

"Sweetheart," Mrs. Gilligan said, her voice warm and low.

Mina startled, her groceries rattling in the basket. Her hyperawareness had been focused on him, so she hadn't noticed Mrs. Gilligan circling around to come the other way.

"Can you get that can of tinned peaches off the top shelf for me? Save me grabbing the step stool."

With her chin, she indicated a shelf where some customer far taller than the diminutive Mrs. Gilligan had changed their mind and abandoned the peaches among the condensed milk. She smiled, the message clear in her eyes. *I see you're upset. Don't forget I'm here.*

Mina smiled back. Say what you want about small towns, but if you're one of theirs they know when to huddle up and raise the shields.

As Mina passed her the peaches, Mrs. Gilligan grabbed them with both hands, squeezing Mina's fingers between the cold metal and the warm skin of her palm. "I've already rung those couple of items up," she said. "I had the codes from the invoice. Want me to put it on your account?"

Mina didn't have an account. The General didn't do accounts; they'd phased them out long before Mina was born. "That would be lovely."

The street outside was washed with sunlight, but so empty. The handful of parking spots in front of the General had been occupied, forcing her to park up the street in front of the pub. There was no sign of the car owners—the pub and the takeaway wouldn't open until eleven, and all the shops in between were long closed. That meant they had probably parked there and left on the train when it passed through on Friday. Nobody parked in the train station car park tucked behind the row of shops, unless they actually wanted to come back to find their car stolen or stripped down to its frame. Everyone knew any vehicle left there would be unattended for at least a week.

Nannine had sprung up to serve farmers bringing livestock to the saleyards and grain to the storage sheds, but now the family farms were disappearing. Fewer people brought loads through, and with the saleyards closed most of them kept going to the next town. The cargo trains blew straight through. The town had faded back to a few essentials, and its primary industry now was stubbornness. Mina felt keenly every window she passed with the curtains drawn or newspaper taped inside the glass.

She considered the petrol station on the other side of the wide road. There would be someone behind the counter there, and a camera to boot. But she dismissed the thought. She was being silly. She didn't need witnesses; she just needed to walk a handful of meters to her car.

She walked fast but didn't run, her keys clutched in her palm with the longest and sharpest of them peeking between her middle and index fingers. Running would be overreacting. Running would be hysterical.

The man had no such qualms. His feet slapped against the pavement, and her heart froze.

"Excuse me," he said, his voice surprisingly soft. The gentle tone jarred against the havoc he was causing inside her.

She came to a stop in front of the old bank building. It was the most beautiful building in Nannine, a classic colonial boom-town folly with sandstone arches and two columns holding up a lintel bearing the date 1871. The windows were covered with wrought-iron bars, and the enormous wooden double doors were bolted shut. The branch was long closed, the tellers all laid off, but the ATM still worked, tucked into a shadowed corner.

"There's a camera," she shouted. "You're being filmed."

"Um . . ." He stopped, looking back down the street as if replaying his actions. "Actually the camera only comes on while a transaction is in progress. But if you want to swipe your card, I can wait."

She wavered. Digging for the card buried in her bag meant taking her eyes off him and occupying both of her hands. Making herself vulnerable.

"Are you Mina McCreery?"

"You know I am," she said.

She'd forgotten her groceries, she realized, feeling so tired. She'd fled with her handful of items and left the actual order she'd come for sitting in Mrs. Gilligan's back room. She needed to go back.

"And Evie McCreery was your twin sister?"

"Evelyn McCreery," she snapped. Mina was happy to accept an alternative to the mouthful of "Wilhelmina," if only as a defense against "Willie," but Evelyn stood firm. "Evie" was an invention by the press, saving space in their headlines and upping the "cute" factor.

"I'm sorry," he said. "I actually knew that."

Of course he knew. She bet he knew enough about her to fill a notebook. And enough false information to fill a second one. Meanwhile, she didn't even know his name.

"Who are you?" she asked.

"I'm Lane," he said, pulling out a wallet. "Lane Holland." He flipped the wallet open to show her his driver's license. "I specialize in cold cases."

"This isn't a police badge," she said. She reached out and took the wallet. A flicker of surprise crossed his face. She doubted many people crossed that boundary, but social mores could suck her dick.

The license was real, as far as she could tell. The address was in Byron Bay. If he'd driven all the way from there to talk to her, he was going to be difficult to shake. She tilted it, and found no sign of scratches or discoloration that would show he had doctored the name. The picture had the same light hair, dark eyes, and solid jawline as the man in front of her.

"I'm not with the police," he said. "I'm a private investigator."

She tossed the wallet back. "I see. So do you already have a book deal? If you're planning to shop one around, you're shit out of luck. There are already two books being pushed out in time for the twentieth anniversary; nobody's looking to buy a third one."

"I'm not writing a book," he said. "I want to lay some ghosts to rest."

"And what makes you think my ghosts need your help?" she asked.

"I have, if you'll forgive me for bragging, quite a record of closing cases everyone else has given up on. You might be familiar with the Tammie Peterson case in Walgett? Or the murder of Bronte and Regina Fermin in Albury?"

She hadn't heard of either of those cases. That softened her opinion of him somewhat. Fame seekers didn't chase after cases that even she, with such a vested interest, had never heard of.

"Three girls," she noted, and let the implication hang in the air between them. "All children?"

"That's my specialty, yes," he said in a tense, clipped voice. "I have a younger sister."

Mina bit back an "ugh" at the cliché. "I suppose you're interested in the reward," she said with a sigh.

"I won't turn it down," he said. "This is my profession, I need to eat."

"Best of luck to you, then," she said. She pushed past him, walking back toward the General.

"Please," he said, drifting behind her like a balloon she was pulling on a string. "I know how much you value your privacy."

"Obviously you don't," she said. She shifted her keys in her hand, pushing the sharp one to once again rest between her fingers like a talon.

He glanced down, eyes drawn by the movement, and fell back but continued to shadow her. "That's why I can help you. Don't you want peace?"

"I've found peace," she snarled.

She pushed through the door, and let it swing closed between them.

TWO

* * *

Mina slid into the driver's seat and hit the fob to lock her doors. She didn't think Lane would follow her home. It was clear he wasn't a threat, just an arsehole. One of many who thought that his fascination with her sister gave him some kind of entitlement. Who cared what she wanted, right? Everything about her life was public property now.

She fidgeted with the keys, thinking. She usually ended up regretting making the trek out to see Alanna at the library. At the outset it didn't seem like much, set off at ten and be there by one, twenty past if she stopped for a chocolate milk at the service station in between. Then it was an hour and a half later and her left knee was starting to ache, and Alanna was still so far away. But for once the idea of going home to a silent house didn't fill her with relief.

The groceries were all dry goods, and would be fine in the back, but driving them all the way to Danby, with its three supermarkets, defeated the purpose of buying them online. Not to mention what they would do to her fuel economy.

Screw it.

* * *

The library had been a source of deep strife within her family for the last five years of her mother's life. Evelyn had loved this library, and so when the local council wanted to "merge" it with another library fifty kilometers away, the Evelyn McCreery Foundation had offered a generous donation to change their mind. When the council proposed to rename it the Evelyn McCreery Memorial Library, Mina and her father had greeted the idea with pleasure. A tangible reminder of something good that had come from her loss would be a great comfort. But her mother had pitched a world-rattling fit at the idea her daughter required a memorial. Not when she could still be alive. She would not even consider a compromise of omitting the troubling word. The notion was offensive—Beverley would know the word was there, whether they engraved it on the sign or not.

Her mother's death had settled the whole argument. Forging ahead once her mother could no longer object felt tacky, and so now the Beverley McCreery Memorial Library bore the name of the one member of their family who was unquestionably dead.

Mina didn't know if this represented a victory for her mother, or a victory for her. When a battle lasts for long enough, it's hard to keep track of what winning would look like.

She wished for a library like the type she read about, cloaked in awed silence, disturbed only by the occasional rustling page. This library was a hub of activity. A father read to two toddlers among piled-up cushions; a group of seniors bickered over a Scrabble board by the bay window; and a young man browsed while his music poured out of headphones that might as well have been speakers.

She kept her head down and slipped through the staff-only door behind the counter.

Alanna Rennold looked up from her work of dabbing glue onto a pop-up kangaroo with a fine paintbrush, smoothing away the evidence of overeager toddler hands. "What's wrong?"

When Mina was fifteen her mother asked her to write a letter to a girl she'd read about in the newspaper. A girl who'd also had a sister disappear. The circumstances were very different—the other girl's father snatched her sister off the street and they were never seen again—but the feelings were the same, surely. Mina resisted the idea; it felt creepy, to her. But her mother had insisted. Imagine if someone who understood had reached out to her in those early, lost days.

Mina didn't get it. Just because she'd experienced pain didn't mean that she knew some secret to managing it. But she'd tried. She sat down and wrote out a letter to this stranger. A letter to her younger self, about what was coming. What came out had no comfort to offer. It was bitter, and it was angry, and on rereading it she was mature enough to realize it belonged in the bin.

So that's where it went, and she ignored any further attempts by her mother to put them in contact. Her mother dropped it eventually.

Then, in the last years of her mother's life, the girl's name started to crop up again. Alanna was so kind. Alanna was so smart. Alanna was so pretty. Alanna liked her makeup tips. Alanna listened to her advice. When Beverley gave Alanna clothes, she actually wore them.

There had been a daughter-shaped hole in Beverley's life, and if Alanna fit, that was none of Mina's business.

They finally met at Beverley's funeral. If there was life after death, Beverley was there laughing her guts out that Alanna was now Mina's closest—only—friend. It was just like her to slip in one last "I told you so" on the way out.

"Who said there's anything wrong?" Mina replied, like her wild eyes and white face might just be a fashion statement. She perched on the edge of the hard couch.

"There's nothing for you on the reserve shelf, and you don't drive three hours to say hello," Alanna said, bowing her head back over the book.

"Two hours," Mina said. "I came from Nannine, not the house. And maybe I missed you."

"Maybe you should friend me on Facebook, then."

"Don't start." It didn't come out playfully, like she'd planned. It came out harsh and ragged, and she couldn't seem to catch her breath to say something else. Shit. Apparently she'd been able to hold it at bay while she was busy chasing off the private investigator, and then driving, but now she was somewhere she felt safe, here came the panic attack.

"What do you need?" Alanna asked.

Mina shook her head. She couldn't force any words out, but she wanted to reassure Alanna it was nothing. It would pass. She was trying to remember the breathing exercise her counselor had taught her. Was it four breaths in, three breaths out, or the other way around? Who'd decided that what she needed in the middle of a panic attack was a math problem?

"Here." Alanna laid her phone on the arm of the couch. On the screen a pale blue circle swelled like a balloon being blown up, then sank back to a dot. "Breathe in as it expands, out when it shrinks. There you go."

Mina didn't love being told what to do by a freaking gif, but there was something peaceful about the animation, and gradually her heartbeat slowed and each breath came more evenly. It reminded her of when her dog Echo fell asleep with his head on her knee, the steady rise and fall of his breathing.

Oh bugger, she was three hours from home and he would be expecting his afternoon feed any minute. At least it wasn't a work day, so she didn't need to worry about getting home to a series of increasingly cranky messages from her supervisor for not logging on. Just the sad eyes of a dog who wouldn't be angry, just unbearably disappointed.

"Can I use this? I need to see if Mrs. Tamm can pop over and feed Echo."

Alanna nodded, but her gaze sharpened. Mina realized she'd just admitted she'd come to Danby on impulse, that this wasn't just a random panic attack during a planned trip. She stepped deeper into the office to make her call, knowing she would get the third degree when she came back.

* * *

Alanna had a cup of tea waiting for her, one of the fussy blends that she collected, judging by the floral smell wafting from it. Mina settled back on the couch and took a sip. Lavender and vanilla. Not her favorite flavor, but familiar and comforting.

"Are you coming to group this week?" Alanna asked.

"No," Mina said. She hated the missing persons support group. There had been an initial spark of something at meeting people who had walked the same mile, but it wore off quickly. She didn't understand where Alanna got the energy to keep telling her story, to keep reliving her trauma with strangers. If Mina needed to talk something out, she had Alanna. "Especially after coming here today, I don't want to make that drive twice in a week."

"Well then, if you're not saving it up for group, are you ready to talk about why you're here? Wonderful as I am, I don't believe you just felt like paying me a visit."

Mina sighed. "I just got myself worked up over nothing. There's some guy sniffing around. He approached me on the street, wanting to talk about Evelyn."

Alanna was quiet for a long moment. She ran her hands over the glossy cover of a Mem Fox book, like the shape of the possum on the cover might hold some answer. "Like, media? Or . . ."

Mina shook her head. "Not media. He claims he's a private investigator."

"Claims?" Alanna repeated. "You think he might be lying? Or he just plays one on the internet?"

"I don't know," Mina said. "It was just a word, I didn't mean anything in particular. He says he's solved a couple of cases."

"What was his name?" Alanna made a show of cracking her knuckles and tipping her head from side to side like she was warming up to wrestle a bear. "I'll look him up."

"Don't," Mina said. "It's over and done with. I told him to pound sand."

"If he's a weirdo, you need to know. Sergeant Starrett will want a heads-up." Alanna spun on her stool and woke her computer up. "Give me a name."

"Lane Holland."

"Oh, that's nice and unusual. Here we go . . . Oh." Alanna frowned at the screen. "Did he look like he'd recently escaped from Goulburn Correctional Centre?"

"What?"

"The first hit on his name is Wikipedia's list of notable prisoners for Goulburn Correctional Centre." Alanna turned the computer screen so Mina could see.

Mina scanned the list. It turned her stomach to see the familiar name slotted between those of a serial killer and a bomb maker. But it was a coincidence. "This Lane Holland would be fifty-eight. The private investigator is in his thirties."

Alanna nodded. "So he's not result number two either, for a guy who died of cancer last year?"

"How many years did your degree take again?" Mina asked. She regretted it the second she said it, as Alanna looked up at her with sharp eyes. Alanna had only finished her library science degree at the end of the year, after six years scraping credits together in between part-time work and family dramas. Mina hadn't meant the joke to refer to that, but that didn't make her foot any less firmly wedged in her mouth.

"It's a process," Alanna said in a bland tone. She kept tapping away at the keyboard. "Well, this one would be the right age, then. Your detective was once literally the poster boy for criminal justice at Charles Sturt University." She shuffled to the side so Mina could see.

A picture of a younger Lane sat beneath the headline REAL STUDENT STORIES. Far from the scruffy man who'd followed her around the store, this Lane looked job-interview-ready in a white button-down shirt, blue tie, and black trousers. *"Four years ago I was told getting into the Federal Police Development Program was a pipe dream,"* Mina read out loud. *"Now it's a reality, thanks to the exceptional programs on offer here at CSU."* She shook her head. "That can't be right; surely he would have said if he was an AFP officer. He definitely said 'private investigator.'"

Alanna shrugged. "He might have bombed out, then. It's a tough program." She clicked out of the CSU archive and continued scrolling through the search results. "Do you have anything else to go on?"

"He gave me some names of cases," Mina said. "One was, um, a girl named Bronte. I don't know if that's like the beach or the author."

"They're both spelled the same, if you ignore the umlaut," Alanna said. "Bronte . . . Lane . . . Holland . . ." she muttered under her breath, and then sucked in a gasp. "Oh fuck, safe search is switched off."

She wrenched the computer screen back, but Mina had already seen the crime scene photos at the top of the search results. She'd already seen the bright blood, the blond hair spread across grass, not all of it still rooted to the girl's head.

Luckily she was sitting down, as the room warped and lurched around her.

"Well," Alanna said, her voice somber. "If he told you he closed that one, he's not a liar. *Police thanked Lane Holland, a private investigator hired by the family, for information leading to the arrest of Jake Frazier . . . previous person of interest . . . confirmed he would receive the full reward advertised in 2008 . . .*" Her voice was absent, more like she was reading to herself than to Mina. "Jesus, the reward was a quarter-million. Does he pay tax on that?"

"I don't know," Mina said. "He didn't look like he was swimming in cash."

"Neither do you," Alanna said.

Mina let that bait go. She'd once put her foot in it badly by claiming that owning a valuable property and being rich were two different things, especially when she could never allow the land to be sold. She wasn't making that mistake again. "There's another one," she said. "Tammy. Tammy Peterson?"

"Safe search on this time," Alanna said. "Oh, Tammie with an 'ie.' Gosh, that's an old case. Doesn't look like it got as much media attention—the reward was much smaller. But there's a write-up on MyMurder."

"No, I don't want to see that," Mina said.

"It's really not that bad. I read an article saying that last year the members raised the cash to pay for private DNA testing on a Jane Doe. A lot of people on there are passionate about finding answers—"

"No one on that forum is trying to find answers," Mina snapped. "They're competing to see who can come up with the most batshit nonsense."

"Alright," Alanna said, although she didn't sound mollified. "In case you were wondering, yes, he's cited as a key person in closing the Tammie Peterson case. This guy seems like the real deal."

"So he's good. That doesn't mean I want him sniffing around," Mina said.

"Why do you offer the reward, if you don't want people trying to investigate?" Alanna countered.

"Plausible deniability, if you ask the internet," Mina shot back.

In truth, the money wasn't hers to control. It was part of her mother's will. Mina and her father might have been able to challenge it in court, but who wanted that headline?

Alanna nodded, mouth pressed into a tight line. The reward money, like so many subjects, was a touchy issue. The New South Wales Police had put up one of the largest rewards ever for information leading to an arrest and conviction for Evelyn's disappearance: one million dollars. Mina's mother had doubled it, offering a further million for any information that led to Evelyn's recovery. Few families had the resources to pursue justice the way they had. The fact they hadn't got it didn't seem to make a difference.

Mina sighed, grabbing a cushion and hugging it to her chest. She did understand. Alanna's family couldn't afford a private investigator, and no one was beating their door down to work for free. Her sister's case had never got the media attention or ongoing interest that Evelyn attracted. She didn't have a mother who was poised and camera ready, or stacks of adorable, high-resolution photos the media could run on the front page. Nobody dissected her case, idly discussing it in the break room or online. If Mina could take her life off like a coat and let Alanna wear it, she would.

But she didn't think Alanna would like it as much as she claimed.

THREE

MyMurder Forums

Subforum: Evie McCreery

Subject: A fun game for Friday

User AgentKHole: I was dicking around on Google Maps, and came up with a new way to amuse myself. Without typing in the address, I tried to find the McCreery property in satellite view, based on the known features (massive house several kms from the road, green roof, circular dam, smaller second residence about a k to the east). It took me an hour and 8 minutes. Can you beat that?

User VolcanicJudo: 45 minutes. The only reason it's so hard is because when you zoom out there's just a sea of red and brown. When I zoomed in close enough to see the houses I had to scroll around endlessly looking for any landmarks at all, let alone those specific ones. It really drives home how isolated the house is (and how absurd it is to suggest it was some kind of random, opportunistic crime).

User LionSong: Mods, how is this not doxxing?

User MODERATOR: What do you want us to do, ban users from
looking at Google Maps?

User WWG1WGA: The address is already out there anyway, you
don't have to dig for it. They ran a commercial farm, there's
reams of old job ads and stock auction notices with their details on it.

User Inspektor: Unfortunately, yeah. Remember that guy who drove
out there and took a selfie in front of the gate like he was visiting
Graceland?

User AgentKHole: Ha, yeah. What happened to that guy? He hasn't
logged on in a few months.

* * *

If you searched for Nannine online, the map that popped up showed
a huge shape that jutted in and out at random. The shape a region
took on when it wasn't designed, but congealed from the results of
squatters and opportunists banding together. The town of Nannine
itself was a little dot in a southwestern corner. Nannine–National
Park Road cut a perfectly straight line across the region, and almost
at the very end of it sat the McCreery property, in the north-
eastern corner.

In the hundred kilometers he drove, Lane counted exactly
three people in the fields that lined either side of the road. When
he was a kid, driving through farmland had meant seeing tractors
rumbling across the fields. Men on motorbikes or horseback checking livestock and crops. People. But here, now, the world felt empty.

"In two hundred meters your destination will be on the left,"
the GPS announced, startling Lane. He'd seen no sign at all he
was almost there, but if he was that close to the gate he must have

passed the boundary fence between the McCreery property and their nearest neighbor several minutes ago. He eased off the accelerator, knowing what could happen to a car that braked suddenly on a dirt road.

He started to pull over onto the broad grassy patch beside the road, then swore and hit the brakes as the car bumped and lurched. He threw on the handbrake and jumped out to check he hadn't done any damage. What had looked like a flat verge actually dropped away to a dry creek bed, hidden by waist-high grass. He was lucky the ground was hardened like concrete in the sun. If he'd hit mud and bogged himself, he'd have had no hope of getting a tow truck out here.

He wondered why the hell it hadn't been mown, or grazed, or back-burned. Neglect, or deliberate hostility toward anyone who might try to stop?

He leaned against his car, waiting for his heart to stop jackhammering. It was barely seven o'clock in the morning but it felt like midday, the sun strong overhead and getting stronger. He'd thought he remembered what it was like out here, the dry heat that sucked everything out of you, but memory couldn't touch the real feeling. Especially when you had nowhere to escape to.

He stared through the strung-wire fence at the flat expanse of red dirt occasionally broken up by clumps of grass or the odd mallee tree. Far in the distance was a timber structure. Not the house—he'd spent enough time staring at pictures of the McCreery home to clock that in an instant—but something much more industrial and rough. A barn maybe?

At first he thought he'd imagined the movement he saw: a long shadow too tall and thin to be livestock or a wild animal.

There was someone walking around the outside of the building. He eased open the car door and took out his camera.

It had been one of his early impulse purchases, when he'd thought he was rich. A DSLR, and a telephoto lens. He was no great photographer, but it was the sort of thing he'd thought a private investigator should have. Since then he'd used it to take far more pictures of couples eating in restaurants or unlocking motel room doors than of murder suspects, but there were bills to be paid.

After a few seconds of fiddling with the focus he could see that the building was derelict, and easily a hundred years old. It was built from hardwood planks, several of them missing, and a section of the roof had collapsed. The side facing the road sported a wooden ramp, leading to a gaping black hole that had probably once had an oversized door, now long gone.

The figure was Mina McCreery, in a flannel shirt and jeans, her long dark hair pulled back under a wide-brimmed hat. She glanced around, checking the area around her, but didn't look in the direction of the road. If she did, she wouldn't be able to see him, but might notice the car. That was fine—if she came to investigate he could have the camera packed away before she got anywhere near him and pretend he'd pulled over to consult his map.

She had a stick in her hand, about as long as her arm and half as thick. It was too crooked to be a walking stick—probably just something she'd picked up. She swung it purposefully as she walked, hitting the side of the building with a force that made the boards rattle. He was too far away to hear, but he'd bet it made a hell of a racket. What on earth was she doing?

He snapped a picture.

She had something in her other hand. A torch, he saw, when

she clicked it on and aimed the beam under the building. She dropped into a crouch and disappeared beneath.

Ah, of course: she was trying to scare off anything that had made a home for itself in there before she went in. That didn't explain why she was under there, though. It certainly didn't look like an operational farm building. Did she have something stored underneath?

His phone buzzed on the passenger seat. He lowered the camera, surprised that he even had reception out here. He remembered traveling through places like this as a kid, the ridiculous things his mother had to do to scrape together a few bars, standing on top of the van on tiptoes, arm in the air, desperately trying to get a message to send. When he saw his sister's picture on the screen he scrambled to pick it up, leaving the camera on the seat in its place.

"Lane!" she said. "How's life as an empty nester?"

"I'm sipping on a mai tai as we speak," he said. He switched the call to speaker so he could slide into the passenger seat and lift the camera again. "How about you? Have you finished unpacking?"

"I finished unpacking pretty much the minute the door closed behind you," she said. "I only own three things. I'm going to have to buy more. There's a whole bookshelf to fill here."

"You could try filling it with books," he suggested. Inside his lens, Mina reemerged, still carrying the torch and nothing else. She brushed off her knees, dislodging a thick hunk of cobweb that drifted away on the breeze.

His sister's laughter died off. "I got my book list," she said. "I visited the university bookshop. I didn't quite realize . . ."

Lane pressed the pad of his thumb to his lower lip. He'd checked some of the prices himself. Visited the website, looked around. Even secondhand, the prices were an order of magnitude higher than he'd budgeted for. And that was on top of paying Canberra rent, particularly the sky-high rates of student housing. For six years that had been the carrot he offered whenever he had to say no to some indulgence, to insist on secondhand instead of new, to say no to nights out and holidays. It would all be worth it when she didn't have to struggle through uni like he had. She wouldn't share a flat with six other people. She wouldn't have to pick any two out of sleep, study, and work. He would cover everything.

And then she went and got accepted into the Australian National University. He couldn't tell her to pass up a place at the country's best university to go somewhere with cheaper rent, cheaper food, cheaper everything. But it cost so much more than he'd anticipated. And the money that had seemed infinite when NSW Police cut him those checks had dwindled fast. He'd already blown through some of it in the months before their mother's death abruptly made him Lynnie's guardian. He'd frittered cash away on stupid shit, drinks and dinners and who even knew what, with all the confidence of a twenty-something man who, having pulled it off a few times, expected to keep doing so. It was a common enough thing—he'd read studies about what happened when people who grew up poor got sudden windfalls, and it wasn't pretty. Knowing it was common didn't make him feel any less embarrassed.

And then had come the expense of raising a teenager, in Byron Bay of all places. He'd opted to go to her, not wanting to take her away from all of her friends and familiar places on top of every other shock she'd suffered, but even in a caravan the cost of living had been eye-watering. His business was feast or famine, and he'd made some bad choices to cover the gaps—payday loans, opening new credit cards to pay the old ones, debt consolidation loans.

He didn't know how big the hole he'd dug himself was, but he knew it was too big to fill with hard, steady work, because he had tried that and kept falling further behind.

He needed a win big enough to wipe it out. Like the two-million-dollar reward for closing the Evelyn McCreery case.

"I've got a plan," he said.

Mina walked around the building, disappearing from his view.

"You're such a liar," Lynnie said. "The job market's strong here, I can get something part-time. Become a barback or a dish pig. But you know, employers always google your name these days."

"Holland's not that uncommon a name," he said. "If your first name pops up in any stories, a single one, tell me and I'll rain fury on them, you hear? It's against the law."

"Calm down," she said. "I'm just homesick and throwing myself a pity party, okay? I've spent so long thinking that getting into uni was the goal, that once I had that letter in my hands I was home free. But it's only the beginning."

"You are home free," he said. "Don't look for a job. I'll buy you the books. Your job is to study hard, become a doctor, and get rich enough to buy me a house in Vaucluse."

She laughed. "That's going to be pretty hard considering this is an English degree."

"You're a smart girl, you'll figure it out."

They fell into a companionable silence, the kind they'd sat in for hours at home, her solving quadratic equations or analyzing *Antony and Cleopatra* at the fold-down table, him flipping through case files on the lounge.

"Are you back in Byron yet?" she asked. "You didn't make the trip in one go, did you?"

"Uh, I haven't headed home yet. I'm going to stay a bit closer to you for a while."

"Oh, you're not going to go helicopter parent on me at the last minute, are you? What are you going to do, join the public service?"

"No, not in Canberra. I'm in Central New South Wales."

She said nothing, stretching past a pregnant pause and into a battle of wills. It confirmed something he'd suspected for the whole six years he'd raised her. This wasn't something they avoided talking about; it was something they refused to talk about. Lynnie was a big talker. She'd talked early and often, a precocious toddler who'd grown into a funny, eloquent young woman. They even talked about their mother, right from the start. They talked about Lynnie's grief. Lynnie talked about her happy memories, and some of the less happy ones. They talked about her schoolwork, her struggles to connect with other kids, her disappointments. They didn't talk about Lane's more complicated sadness. They definitely didn't talk about his disappointment with his work, the way he felt trapped in the wrong part of the country, away from what he really wanted to be doing. It would be selfish to dump that on her.

There was one subject that neither ever broached.

The silence dragged on, and he heard the truth. Lynnie knew what he was up to.

"You're on one of your cases," she said finally.

"I'll probably head home soon," he lied. "This case is the longest of long shots. But dropping you off brought me close by, and I figured a little detour wouldn't hurt."

Was it a long shot, or wasn't it? Some days it seemed so obvious that he was angry at himself for not speaking up nineteen years ago. Other days it seemed absurd that he might hold the missing piece of the most discussed and scrutinized cold case in Australian history.

He hadn't told her yet that there was no home to go back to. He'd sold the caravan, which had netted enough to buy him a few months in which to make a proper go of it. If that didn't work, he supposed he would rob a bank.

* * *

The gate was simple steel, latched shut but not locked, and the fence was a two-strand wire through hardwood posts. The creek bed he'd run afoul of ducked under the driveway via a concrete pipe.

A series of signs hung on the gate. ANYONE ENTERING WILL BE FILMED, read one. NO TRESPASSING, read the other. He paused with his hand on the car door. Entering a property and going directly to the door, with a purpose, wasn't trespassing. But out here, so far from the nearest neighbor, that sign wasn't intended to warn off dog walkers or flower pickers. The McCreerys had aimed that message straight at people like Lane: investigators, journalists, and gawkers. He thought of Mina's voice, the anger in it. But he also thought of the worry in his sister's voice. She deserved to live free of it. So did Mina. He could put things right for both of them; he just needed Mina to give him a shot.

He hopped out and pushed open the gate. It swung away from him easily, no theatrical screeching of bolts or creaking metal. Mina took care of her things, it seemed.

As he turned to get back into the car, he noticed a streak of something red against his bare leg. He brushed it with his fingers, wondering if he'd accidentally pressed up against something that stained. The red splashed over his fingers too. It was a light, beaming from a small white sensor just under the gate hinge. An alert system for cars coming through the gate.

When he was a kid Lane had dreamed of a property like this. He'd leaned against the car window watching houses flash by. Grand stone walls. Bullnose verandas. Wrought-iron gates. He'd imagine what it would be like to live in a home like that. To come back and know it was yours. He built imaginary houses in his head—designed exactly what he would have when his life was his own and he was ready to put down roots.

He drove through the gate, then had to stop and shut it again. As he started his car, he reset the odometer. He couldn't see any sign of the house yet, just the red dirt driveway. He wasn't even sure it was right to call it a driveway. He was on the property, but this was a road. To the left and right were row after row of adolescent trees, about as tall as he was with trunks no thicker than his clenched fist. A corrugated plastic sign hammered into the ground decreed that this site would soon provide foraging for the endangered and beloved glossy black cockatoo. It had cracked and faded after years of harsh sun. They must have planted the trees five or six years earlier—which tracked with the last time the region had experienced enough rain to make it seem like a worthwhile project, he supposed. He wondered how much of a shot the poor things had now.

The road took him up a gentle hill, past the ancient shed built from rough-hewn hardwood logs. Behind it he could see endless wide grassy plains, broken up with patches of mallee scrub, waist-high tussocks of yellowing grass, and patches worn down to red earth. He slowed for a moment, but couldn't see any sign of Mina.

He passed a stockyard that was carefully fenced off but empty, and on the far side of that stood a second woolshed. This one looked to have been built in the seventies or eighties. The steel walls still gleamed in the sun, but it too looked abandoned.

He eased off the accelerator as the road surface switched from hard-packed dirt to redbrick gravel. There sat the house, so strangely familiar. He looked at the odometer, and saw that he had driven almost four kilometers from the front gate.

One of the puzzling aspects of the case was that every tire track around the house matched to a car registered to the McCreery family. Tire track analysis hadn't been particularly advanced in 1999, but the conditions in the McCreery case had been perfect for it. It rained the day before—not much, it never rained much in those days, but enough that any car passing through should have left a mark. If Evelyn was abducted by a stranger, they either walked in or teleported.

An adult could make that walk, if they needed to. But they would have to know exactly where they were going. It wasn't the sort of distance you covered on a whim.

* * *

He parked in front of the house, in a spot partly shaded by an apple tree that was heavy with fruit and swaddled in layers of white bird netting. He sat for a moment in the driver's seat, half expecting Mina to come sprinting up, screaming for him to leave. When he was met with only silence, he got out and climbed the steps. It didn't seem like she was back yet, but her father, Liam, could be at home.

They had painted the house, he noticed with interest—a blue that was strange against the colonial design of the house. He rang the bell but received no answer.

He rang again. Either there was no one home or whoever was there had no interest in opening the door.

He stepped off the veranda and circled around the back of the house. He found himself in a vegetable garden. There were rows of thick timber beds, but only two had anything growing inside. Some kind of vine with large green-and-white leaves the size of his hand spilled out and trailed over the path. The rest of the beds were empty of anything but mulch, waiting for another season, or perhaps just for rain. Lane had never even owned a potted plant, so he had no idea.

"Hello?" he called. "Anyone home?"

He walked along the back wall, counting windows as he went. He didn't peer inside, but it was easy enough to guess what each room was. There was a large picture window, the curtains drawn against the morning sun. There was a little door with two concrete steps leading down to it, surrounded by a cluster of terracotta pots with herbs that even he could recognize—rosemary, basil, mint. Probably the kitchen, then. Next was a high, narrow frosted window—a bathroom. Then a series of three identical windows, also with the curtains tightly drawn. A lounge room maybe, but more likely the bedrooms. Which meant that he was standing within a few meters of the room that Evelyn McCreery was snatched from.

He spun around, trying to think like an intruder. How would he get inside this house? He reached up to see if he could grasp the windowsill. His fingertips barely brushed it. He walked back and tested the kitchen door. It was locked, of course, but would it have been on that night? Beverley McCreery always swore the doors were bolted, but who would have bothered out here?

Getting in wasn't the difficult part, though. The question

was: how did he get out? Beverley and Mina had slept through the whole thing—Beverley just down the hall, and Mina in the same room. There were no fingerprints. Not a drop of blood. No sign of a struggle. In fact, the bed was neat as a pin, the pink patchwork quilt pulled up and smoothed down. How? Had someone killed her inside the house, and crept around cleaning up the evidence while her sister slumbered unaware beside him? Had Evelyn been so disoriented from sleep when she was taken that she was out of earshot before she even realized she should scream? Had he drugged her? Drugged the whole family?

Lane's mind whirled, and he kept walking. He'd always thought that if he could come out here it would all be clearer. There had to be something that couldn't be gleaned from the photos. Evidence that never made it into the newspaper stories, because no one who saw it realized the significance.

He passed a chicken coop, with the chickens lolling in a small patch of shade.

He turned the corner of the house and found another door, and a paved path connecting it to a Hills Hoist.

It was cooler around this side. The heat of the day was cut through with a gentle breeze blowing off the dam.

He was surprised by how close it was to the house. Anyone who had even the slightest interest in the case knew about the Mc-Creery dam, because it was a popular suggestion for where the body may have been hidden. It was strange to suddenly be faced with it in real life. It reminded him of a crater, with steep brown walls, striped with cracks where rivulets had once flowed from the field above. The water came about a quarter of the way up, a duck pond in the footprint of a lake.

Mina was on the far side of it with her back to him, leaning against the fence of an animal pen. She was holding out a handful of something green to a small gray goat, looking completely relaxed. It was a marked contrast to how she'd appeared in Nannine, her body language guarded and tense even before he approached her.

He watched where he was placing his feet as he pushed through the long grass. Something gleamed in the sun and he froze, imagining a double-spring fox trap snapping up out of the undergrowth. But the metallic shine was the brass plate of a memorial marker. He couldn't help himself. He stepped closer to take a look.

Forever in our hearts, it read.

Beverley McCreery
11-12-1962 to 05-18-2013
Finally reunited with Evelyn McCreery
04-10-1990 to 05-01-1999

Lane kneeled down and ran his fingertips over the dates listed for Evelyn. The date for her death was the day after the last time she was seen alive, when the two girls went to bed at 8:00 p.m. It seemed an odd choice to set something in stone—literally—when it was unknown.

Mina twisted around and all traces of relaxation disappeared as she spotted him.

"You're trespassing," she said. She didn't raise her voice. She didn't need to. Not in the quiet of the day.

"I rang the doorbell," he said. "Twice."

"There's a sign," she said.

"I saw it," he said. "It's not trespassing to ring a person's door-bell."

"We're not at the door." She strode toward him, cutting a straight path that crossed the edge of the dam, indifferent to the streaks of white mud that climbed her boots like grasping fingers. He could feel it on his tongue, in his nose, the sweet earthy smell of petrichor.

"After a person drives an hour to visit another person there's nothing unusual about scooting around the back to see if they're home," he said.

"How about we call the local police and see if they agree?" she suggested. "I think you'll find they don't take kindly to people intruding on my privacy like this."

"So the rumors are true, then," he said. "That the local police give you special treatment."

The observation didn't amuse her. She walked past him, leaving smears of mud in the grass. As she passed within his sphere, he noticed her flannel shirt was unbuttoned, and underneath she wore a black shirt screen-printed with a pale face familiar to any child of the nineties.

Wednesday Addams glowered out at him and he bit back a laugh.

She ignored him all the rest of the way into her house, and slammed the door behind her with a thunk of finality. The lock clicked shut behind her.

He picked his way back through the long grass, debating whether he should try ringing her doorbell again or go back to his car in defeat.

He knew she was more right than he was. He'd driven past

the very clear sign and could no longer feign ignorance that his presence was unwelcome.

Pain bloomed in his knee. It felt like an electric shock, the sudden zap of pain from touching an electrified fence.

He stumbled back, looking around for booby traps, homemade security set out to foil unusually persistent trespassers.

Instead his gaze fell on something far worse: bronze scales slipping away through the long grass. He grabbed his knee with both hands, and when he lifted his fingers level with his eyes, twin spots of blood dotted his fingertips. Panic coursed through him.

"Mina," he shouted. "There's a snake. I've been bitten by a fucking brown snake."

He kept walking toward the house, trying to remember what he'd been taught about first aid for snakebites during the hot minute he'd been in the Scouts as a child.

What he recalled involved a lot of staying still on the part of the victim. Clearly that wasn't an option. He needed to get to his car, his phone. And then what? Did he drive himself back to town, to the hospital hours away? Could an ambulance get here before the poison stopped his heart?

The back door opened again and Mina appeared, like an angel. In one hand she held a white home phone, cordless, of the sort he hadn't seen in ten years. In the other arm she cradled a shotgun. The gleam of the stock, the same rich brown as the snake, made nausea rise in his throat.

"Be careful," he said. "It's still out here."

"It's fine," she said, lifting the phone to her ear. "It's my trained attack snake. Part of the security."

"I'm serious," he said. He knew how this looked, and he understood if she thought he was making it up. He'd come into her private space uninvited, and now that he'd been turned away he suddenly needed her help. "I've been bitten, you need to be careful."

"I believe you," she said. "Why do you think I brought the gun? To shoot you?"

He had considered that, yes. "Those guns are illegal, you know," he said.

"Trespassing's illegal," she said. "This is licensed. Now sit down and stop talking. Unless you want to make the poison move faster, you fuckwit."

He sank to the grass, the rough stalks stabbing at the backs of his thighs through his shorts, and tried to hold still. Mina swore into the phone and stepped away, moving back toward the house, probably in search of a better signal. Did those old house phones even run on a signal like mobiles did?

The earth felt heavy beneath him. It was trying to push him away. He did his best to relax, trying to remember if he had really read that too much tension in the body would speed up the venom, his clenched muscles propelling it along like a hand pump. He pressed his palm into the grass. It was rough and scratchy, but beneath that it was soft. It sprang back against his fingertips, yielding and flexible in that way only possible in something alive.

After too many minutes she came back, still carrying the shotgun, but also a blue-and-black tartan rug. She spread it out over the grass and motioned for him to roll onto it. "Relax, please. The snake is long gone; they bite and flee. It's out of venom now."

That wasn't a reassuring thought, given the venom was now in him.

"Am I going to die?" He hated how childlike he sounded,

the genuine fear lacing his voice. He hadn't thought much about what his ideal death would look like, but he knew it wasn't this. He didn't want to leave now, with his affairs in complete disarray. The job he'd come here to do couldn't even be called half-done. It was half-started.

Mina sighed, and crouched beside him on the blanket. "It's not impossible," she said. "But most likely the worst you'll get is a couple of days throwing your guts up and one hell of an ambulance bill. I got through to the hospital: they're sending a plane. You're damn lucky it's available."

"I've got insurance," he muttered, as if that was important.

She shushed him. "Will you shut up if I talk for a while?"

He didn't answer, which he hoped she would take as a yes.

"I looked into those two cases you told me about," she said. "It seems like you really helped those families. But you only told me about the cases you solved, right? There must be lots you failed at."

He didn't classify any of his cases as failures. They were still open. He hadn't given up on them. He just needed to prioritize cases with stronger leads.

Lane stayed silent, staring up at the wide blue sky, searching for a black speck that could be the approaching plane. His knee throbbed, the pain amplified by the images fighting their way to the front of his mind of poison pouring through his veins, climbing his legs. Was it in his groin now? His stomach?

He closed his eyes, making an effort to keep his breathing steady. Hyperventilation would push the venom faster.

"That's it, just stay calm." She reached out and brushed a lock of hair from his forehead, sliding her fingers across his scalp. "Here's what I don't get. There's a lot of people who would want your help," she said. "Why bother me? Is it the notoriety? Are you trying to get your name in the national papers instead of the local ones?"

He didn't answer. They sat in silence, and not a peaceful one, despite her gentle hand on him. He was growing fuzzy around the edges. He kept his eyes open, sure that if he closed them he would drop instantly into sleep.

The plane engine was like a distant drumbeat. It took all of Lane's remaining strength not to burst into tears of relief.

FOUR

LANE WANTED TO scream, but he couldn't, because the wires were holding his jaw closed, and all he could do was hiss against the back of his teeth. Except the wires were gone and he *was* screaming, his throat burning with it. But he could *smell* that he was in the hospital, and the hospital meant the wires.

He scrabbled at the blanket, a white woolen brick wall draped over him. He tried to kick against it, but there was something wrong with his knee. Something was wrapped so tight around it he couldn't bend it far enough to kick out. Was he tangled in the sheets? He wrenched the blankets away, and his fingers brushed the rough weave of gauze. His knee was bandaged.

That wasn't right. He hadn't actually fallen, it was a lie, there was no damage to his knee. He'd hurt his jaw, but that wasn't hurting. It wasn't wired.

He didn't want to be back here. He was past this. There was the pain and then there was the hospital and then he'd been free. He'd escaped.

But that had been a mistake, hadn't it?

"Lane." Lynnie nudged his shoulder with her small, cool hand. "Lane, wake up."

"No. No." He raised his hand to his cheek, tested the line of his jaw with his thumb. "See? It doesn't hurt. I can go."

"Lane?" Lynnie sounded puzzled.

Only it wasn't Lynnie. Lynnie never came to the hospital. He'd escaped, and he left her behind.

He blinked in the low light of the ICU, and the nurse leaned closer. "Can you hear me, Lane?"

"Sorry," he said, blinking again, like he could force his pupils to their normal size. Now she was going to write on his chart that he'd appeared disoriented, and she'd probably start waking him for observations twice as often. Of course he was disoriented: they wouldn't let him sleep.

"You seemed quite distressed when I came in," she said. "Are you in pain?"

Had he actually been screaming, or only dreaming that he was? His throat hurt, but then so did everything else. He shifted his jaw from side to side and clicked his teeth together, checking. "Just having strange dreams. About the last time I was in hospital."

"Ah," she said, her voice sympathetic.

FIVE

MyMurder Forums

Subforum: Evie McCreery

Subject: McCreery family finances

User Inspektor: Can anyone point me in the direction of any articles or resources that shed light on how the McCreery family pays for their lifestyle? They're not running the farm anymore. I suppose Liam gets a pension. Does Mina work?

User LionSong: They do still run the farm, they just got rid of the sheep. They grow stockfeed.

User MODERATOR: Please edit the original post to explain how this question is relevant to the case, or I'll be locking the thread.

User Comet: They made a ton of money from paid interviews back in the day, and Bev's memoir sold a bajillion copies. They don't seem to spend much—if they've invested the money they should be comfortable. They keep it quiet because they know the optics are bad.

User LionSong: How so?

User VolcanicJudo: Losing Evie was basically a lottery win.

User LionSong: Oh, bullshit.

User Inspektor: "They don't seem to spend much." Is that true? I had a look at the electoral roll records for the property, and there were four people listed at the address for the last election: Mina and Liam, and H. & M. Tamm. That's Hendrik Tamm, isn't it—the operations manager? Are they still paying for a full-time employee?

User VolcanicJudo: Huh. M. Tamm would be Margaret. She was the only other adult on the property the night Evie disappeared. And the McCreerys have given them housing and paid her husband a salary for twenty years with no work to do?

User Inspektor: Weird, right?

User VolcanicJudo: Sounds like Margaret knows where the body is buried.

* * *

Mina opened the blackout curtains, which barely changed the level of light filtering into her room. Close to three decades of farm life had stomped out her ability to sleep in past the sunrise. She could have used it—she'd woken up twice in the night, convinced she'd heard the beep of the gate alarm that went off when someone entered the property, but when she went down to the kitchen the system was silent and dark.

She climbed down the loft steps by feel, and made her way along the dark hallway that formed the spine of the house. She brushed the wall with her fingers, sliding over the closed door to the room that she and Evelyn had slept in as children.

She thumped the soles of her workboots together to wake up any spiders that might have crept inside in the night, shook them out, and then pulled them on. From the other room she heard Echo stir in his bed on the floor of the pantry and then come clicking across the kitchen floor.

"You weren't much help yesterday," she said, keeping her tone light. "Did you sleep through the whole thing?"

He picked up on the mild scolding anyway, and whined.

"No, you're right. If I wanted a guard dog I should have got one. You're a good boy," she said, sliding her hand over his yellow head. She was rewarded with the heavy thump of his tail against the back of her legs.

The phone in the hallway trilled. The sound of it usually gave her a little lurch—*What fresh hell is this?* as Dorothy Parker used to say—but there was only one person who was also up and about at this hour and knew it was an acceptable time to call.

"Dad," she said.

"Morning, Minchkin," her father said, his voice hushed.

She closed her eyes and could imagine him at some campground, outside his van in the cool morning air. "Where are you today?"

"Cairns," he said, and it didn't sound like the place was thrilling him. "How are things going at home? Peaceful?"

"Um, yeah," she said. "Yeah, nah, things are good here. Peaceful."

She should tell him. If she didn't, someone else from town would mention it, and then the fact that she didn't tell him would become a whole thing of its own. But the words felt too heavy on her tongue. He was on holiday, he was away from all of this. She could tell him later. "I went to see Alanna the other day."

"Oh, good." His voice brightened, as she'd expected. He was always pleased when she made an effort to perform normal. He wouldn't be as excited if he knew why she'd gone, which was all the more reason not to bring it up.

"What's on your agenda today?" she cut in before he could ask her any questions. The longer they stayed on the subject, the higher the risk she would have to move from half-truths to outright lies.

"Apparently the RSL does a decent big breakfast, then I've booked a glass-bottomed boat tour. They do lunch out on the reef."

"Nice. You'd better see it while it's still there, I suppose."

Her father made a dismissive noise. "From what I've seen, it's doing fine. You'd like it here."

"Mmm." She knew she wouldn't, but it wasn't worth the argument.

"Your mum would have liked it too."

"She went to Cairns, actually. Twice."

"Oh."

"The first book tour, and she gave a keynote at a criminal justice convention, about six months before . . ." Before she got sick.

"Well, who could keep track of all her comings and goings, huh? She was a dynamo."

"Sure."

"So, uh, Hendrik mentioned, uh . . ."

Oh no. Hendrik and Maggie Tamm had been out during the incident with Lane. She'd called their home phone and only got as far as their answering machine, which she hung up on before the beep. But it must have filtered through to them, and from them to her dad. Only one neighbor in a fifty-kilometer radius, and she still had curtain twitchers tattling to Daddy.

"He said he saw you and Echo poking around the old wool-shed yesterday."

"Oh." She stumbled a little, her planned excuses dying away. "Yeah. We were out for a walk."

"Hmm. He said he's run across you a few times. Out walking."

Mina gritted her teeth to hold back a sigh. She supposed she should be glad it had taken this long, considering she'd started up shortly after he left. She hadn't felt able to do it while he was at home, because he would twig to what she was really doing, and then she would catch him giving her that soft, concerned look that she hated. "And?"

"You can't blame me for worrying about you, mate. Wandering around the property on your own, anything could happen, and there'd be no one—"

"Well, apparently Hendrik's keeping an eye on me," she snapped.

"You know it's not like that. It came up in conversation. I'm just saying, there's plenty of nice places to walk the dog that are still within shouting distance of their house. Or you and Maggie could go together . . ."

"I'm checking for weeds," Mina said. It wasn't even a lie, really. She did check for weeds, and in the autumn she'd gathered native grass seed, dragging her hands through the bobbing heads as she walked and stuffing it in her pockets, then spread them on another part of the property the next day. Futile acts, on a property this huge, but productive enough that she didn't have to question if what she was doing was healthy. "It's important that we're keeping an eye out for noxious weeds, Dad. Even just for show. I'm worried that the regeneration work we've done in the front paddocks is making the neighbors nervous. You know that farmers hear that and assume we're rolling out the red carpet for pests and weeds."

"Why do you say that?" he asked. "Has someone said something to you?" What he was really asking was: *Have you been talking to people in town?*

"No, I just hear people complain about it when I'm working. You know, some retiree from Sydney has bought the place next door to run as a hobby, and thinks letting Paterson's curse run riot is getting back to nature."

"We're not hobby farmers," he said, clearly bristling. "And nobody thinks anything of the sort."

They were hobby farmers, but it would be cruel to press that point with him. Her father had buckled under the pressure of trying to search for Evelyn while working the endless hours of a sheep station manager. In some ways that drought had been a blessing—it meant that they were running far fewer head of sheep than they had been in previous years, and so winding down the operation to focus on the search was really the acceleration of a process already in motion. Their mother had accepted her first paid interview to keep them afloat, and then later pursued those opportunities with an aggression that seemed to outpace their actual financial needs. Then had come her mother's book, and the farm never became a necessity again. They were the absolute definition of hobby farmers, growing and selling just enough crops to cover the cost of doing it, while making their real money elsewhere. They didn't have skin in the game like their neighbors, where every turn of the market and change in the weather could make or break the year.

"Whatever. The walk's good for me."

* * *

She left a message on the answering machine at work, calling in sick. She just felt too brittle for it today.

She liked her job, usually. She worked from home, answering

calls for a biosecurity helpline, talking property owners through how to protect their farms, helping them to identify weeds and bugs and blights they'd found, and coordinating response teams when necessary. She didn't make as much as she might have taking her qualifications to a bigger town, or even working locally as a stock and station agent or farm manager, but it paid enough for her needs. Over the years despair had started to creep into the calls, accelerating in recent months as farmers already pushed to the edge discovered one more thing stacked against them. She ended up feeling like a counselor as they poured out their worries, like if they convinced her they were deserving enough she could wave a hand and make it go away. She needed some quiet, not the intrusion of call after call.

Echo walked ahead of her and jumped into the bed of the utility vehicle without needing to be asked. Mina left him there in the ute for a moment, aware of the dog's confused gaze on her back as she walked across the lawn to grab the blue blanket.

She cursed at finding it wet with dew. She was going to need to wash it now. Which was nothing compared to the real problem she needed to deal with. Lane's car was still parked in the driveway.

It was an old Subaru station wagon. She would have expected something flashier, given the money Alanna had mentioned, not something that belonged on a school run. But the reason he chose it became clearer when she peered in the back window. The back seats had been removed and replaced with a wooden platform with a futon mattress on top, strewn with pillows and blankets. Bags were stashed underneath, including an insulated bag that she sincerely hoped didn't have any food inside. If it did, it would have slow-cooked by now and would be completely noxious within a few days.

This wasn't just his car; it was his home and all of his belongings. He would be desperate to collect it as soon as he got out of the hospital—giving him a ready excuse to come snoop around again.

She groaned, trying to figure out a solution that wouldn't throw her whole day off. She had his car key and wallet—one of the paramedics had pushed them into her hands as they loaded him up, and she'd been so distracted she'd accepted them without thinking. That meant she could drive the car off the property. She could leave it on the road. Or push it into the ditch.

No. She sighed. She had a tow frame, and the ute could handle it.

She could have Hendrik make the trip, but going to Danby and back would chew up a whole work day, so it was a big ask. With her father away, she hadn't yet tested the question of whether she was now Hendrik's boss, or if he was still hers. Her father trusted him to make most of the decisions about what needed doing and when. Better for her to return Lane's car herself.

She kicked at the tire tracks he had left in the dirt, as if she could obliterate the mile-long proof of his intrusion with a few sweeps.

* * *

This morning they were going to walk in the northwest corner of the property, where the stand of blue gums grew. She found a reasonably flat, shaded spot for the ute, and pulled the map out of the glove box. She'd sectioned off the property into sections of a few kilometers square, and marked each one off with diagonal lines once she'd walked it. She'd marked the last one off just before Christmas, so a few sections now had lines going the other way.

She whistled for Echo, who jumped down from the truck bed and charged into the deep grass. Her heart crawled into her throat, imagining snakes lurking there, rearing up at Echo's presence. She pushed the fear down. It was a fact of life, living in this part of the world. If she started shying away from the possibility of snakebite, she would never leave the house again.

She popped her earphones in and tucked her MP3 player into the top pocket of her flannel shirt as the shuffle selected Nick Cave's "Jubilee Street."

Suddenly Nick's voice was drowned out by the heavy *chop-chop-chop* of helicopter blades. Mina yanked the buds out of her ears and stared up at the sky, her heart pounding.

The sky was empty, perfect uninterrupted blue. She scanned frantically, searching for the flyspeck that had made the sound, but there was nothing.

She left the buds dangling, trying to narrow down what the hell she was feeling right now. She wasn't afraid. Not of her own home. Was she angry? Anger was such a clean, reliable emotion, but it didn't make a person hallucinate helicopters.

Echo planted his butt on the ground, tipped his head back and howled. That sound Mina wasn't imagining. Echo had alerted. He'd found something dead.

Mina was the closest you could get to an expert on identifying the signs of a clandestine burial without having actual certificates to put on the wall. She'd considered a double degree so that she could study forensic science in addition to agriculture, but her dad had quietly steered her away, fearful of how that would play in the press. If the sister of a famous abduction victim decided to go into law enforcement, that was a story everyone could under- stand. If that same sister decided to become a farmer, but studied criminology and crime scene investigation and the science of body decomposition as a hobby, well, that was creepy.

Her father was very concerned about her being perceived as creepy. His concern did little to prevent it.

Instead, she'd looked up the book lists for the courses she wasn't supposed to take, and sat in quiet corners of the library and devoured them.

The signs to look out for, when searching for a body, were discolored soil, unusual patches of vegetation, and sections of earth that were higher than the surrounding ground, or oddly sunken. Looking at the Martian landscape, the random hillocks and gullies, the patches of saltbush and scrub, she had no idea how any of that could be spotted.

She made her way over to where Echo was still joyfully howling about his find. The bones lay in the shadow of a fallen ghost gum, so bleached by time that the flies took no more interest in them than they would in a pile of rocks or a fallen branch.

One of the legs was broken. It was beyond her skills to tell whether that had happened before death or was a result of scavengers picking the bones over. The tail was curled around the rest of the remains, like a last ditch attempt at protecting itself. Patches of red fur still clung in parts.

A goddamn kangaroo. Mina sat on the fallen tree, oblivious to the flies settling on her arms and neck, and buried her head in her hands.

SIX

MyMurder Forums

Subforum: Evie McCreery

Subject: Unidentified man airlifted from McCreery property with
suspected snakebite

User VolcanicJudo: Did anyone see this article in the Mid-West Post
about someone being airlifted from the McCreery property after
being bitten by a brown snake?

User Waffletoid: Do we really need a thread every time someone
linked to the McCreery family sneezes?

User VolcanicJudo: I think it's notable that there are brown snakes
on the property. Dangerous wildlife has never really been discussed as a possible explanation.

User Waffletoid: Uh, it's Australia, dude. Of course there are brown
snakes on the property. Snakebite is a cause of death, not a
cause of disappearance. If her body was just lying out in the
open they would have found it. If not then, in the nearly twenty
years since.

User VolcanicJudo: They have wild dogs there, right? And pigs?
User AgentKHole: Maybe a drop bear ate it.
User LionSong: Fuck you, Evelyn was a human being. Mods?

* * *

She wanted to follow the path she had followed so many times before, down the hallway, to the left, up the stairs, second door on the right. It would take her to the cancer ward. But instead she walked up to the reception desk. She let her hands drop to her sides, so the greasy paper bag she was carrying would sit out of sight of the nurse. Whenever her mother had asked her to bring something, she would implore Mina to be discreet, not to let the nurses or doctors see that she was smuggling in junk food. They didn't care, but her mother did.

A young man brushed past her, carrying a bouquet of three red balloons. Mina grimaced. She'd forgotten it was Valentine's Day. There were few things more grim than a holiday in the hospital.

The nurse behind the desk was a familiar redhead who she didn't know by name, but who greeted her with, "Mina, what brings you back here?"

"I'm looking for a patient," Mina said. She leaned on the counter, trying to get a proper look at the name tag that was half-hidden in the folds of her scrubs. "He might have been discharged already. His name is Lane Holland?"

"Ah, yes," the nurse said. She didn't enter anything in the computer, which meant Lane's snakebite had caused enough of a stir to be the subject of country hospital gossip.

Was it right to call it gossip when doctors and nurses gathered around the water cooler or in the smoker's garden and discussed interesting or unusual cases? Maybe it was simply networking. Briefing each other on key facts. Perhaps Mina was being uncharitable. "Uncharitable" was her mother's favorite word to describe Mina's way of looking at the world.

"If you follow the purple line painted on the floor here"—the nurse leaned over the counter, her elbow brushing against Mina's, and pointed to the lines on the floor that snaked off in every direction—"it will take you right to him. He's in 4E."

* * *

She found him alone, in a hospital bay bare of any personalization. The three other beds in the room had flowers, crocheted blankets, stacks of books—the usual futile gestures to try to make patients more comfortable. There was nothing on Lane's bedside table beyond a magazine with a Kardashian on the cover. She assumed it was an offering from some sympathetic visitor of someone else in the ward. It hardly looked like the sort of thing he would choose for himself. But, then, what did she know about what he would choose for himself? He'd made nosiness into a profession and had no boundaries to speak of, so maybe reading celebrity gossip was his favorite pastime.

Lane looked surprised, but wary, to see her. He was wearing the same long-sleeved polo shirt he'd had on at her house, and he had a waffle-knit hospital blanket slung over his lap. His bare calves stuck out the bottom, dusted with white-blond hair. She wondered if the paramedics had sliced his shorts away when he arrived at the hospital, if they were in ribbons in a biohazard bin somewhere.

"I brought you a gift," she said. She felt awkward. This was awkward. It was strange to be visiting someone she'd been threatening to have arrested not forty-eight hours earlier. But their mother had raised them with a by-the-book approach to manners. When people go to the hospital, you bring them food and a gift. Mina didn't think that there was a traditional rule for what you did when a trespasser became so dangerously injured on your own property they had to be hospitalized. So she had fallen back on the familiar, and bought him a stuffed animal in the gift shop.

She held it out, half offering, half shield between them.

An expression flashed across his face that she could not read. She supposed she deserved that.

"It's a snake," she added. She was never going to be good at this.

"That's funny," he said, with rather the same tone you would use to humor a toddler's first attempt at a joke.

"It's not the actual snake or anything," she said, as if it could be possible to mistake it for the brown that had felled him, with its purple plush and bright green stripes.

"I'd have preferred that," he said quietly. "I'm sorry, I know this is rude, but I need you to take it away. I've got"—another complicated set of expressions crossed his face as he chose his words—"let's call it a . . . a phobia . . . of stuffed animals."

She faltered, trying to figure out if he was messing with her. He looked away, clearly embarrassed.

"I brought you a burger and chips too," she said, awkwardly stuffing the snake back into her handbag.

Lane looked a lot more interested in that, but he still wasn't brimming with warmth. He grabbed the wheeled table next to the bed and swung it into the mealtime position. He had to slide the remains of his breakfast to one side—scrambled eggs and a damp-looking slice of toast, and a plastic cup of orange juice still sealed with a foil top. Apparently they hadn't changed the menu in five years. It didn't look like he'd eaten any of it, and she didn't blame him.

"Has your family been to visit?" she asked.

She knew that was a mistake as soon as the words were out of her mouth. Of course he hadn't had visitors. They'd have brought him a change of clothes, and something better to read than that ghastly magazine. She shouldn't read too much into that, she supposed. He was far from home. But if she was the one in hospital, her father would have been here in a heartbeat.

He smiled tightly. "My sister's just started university in Canberra," he said. "She's got her own life. I wouldn't dream of asking her to come all this way just to nurse me for a stupid snakebite."

"Is she a mature-age student?" she asked. She thought about going back to school herself sometimes. In the same way she thought about moving to Maui, or renting the house out and joining her father on his gray nomad tour. It was normal, she thought, to mull over all the ways you could tip your life upside down, throw the lever, and steam off down another track.

"No."

That was interesting, given the birthdate on his driver's license put him squarely in his thirties.

"That's quite an age gap," she said. "Is she a half sister? Or do you have more siblings in between?"

Lane shook his head. "No, it's just the two of us."

He pulled the burger out of the bag and unwrapped the white waxed paper around it. It was past its prime after too long sitting on the passenger seat of her ute, but still miles ahead of the scrambled eggs. He spread the paper out flat on the table. His fingers were long, almost elegant. He wasn't a farm worker, that was for sure. He peeled the top bun off and then disassembled the burger with quick, practiced movements—the patty here, the sliced tomato next to it, then the cheese and the fried egg. He grabbed the knife and fork from the breakfast plate and sawed a neat square off the patty, popping it into his mouth and closing his eyes in appreciation.

Mina frowned. Her mother had eaten like that—not in the hospital, but before. She would take every meal apart and eat in tiny controlled bites, so terrified of accidentally overeating. But that didn't seem to be Lane's goal; he ate quickly and with obvious enjoyment, just in tiny pieces.

He looked up at her, noticing her noticing, but didn't say anything.

"I don't want you coming to my house," she said.

Lane laughed bitterly. "Don't worry. I won't be making that mistake again," he said. He shifted his position, trying to get comfortable. A flap of the blankets fell away to show his bandaged knee, the snakebite hidden beneath layers of gauze.

She pulled his car key out of her purse, and set them down on the table. They were practical and impersonal—just a car key attached to a blue plastic tag with nothing written on it. He still recognized them immediately as his, and his eyes widened.

She waved a hand at him before he could say anything. She didn't want him thanking her. She'd brought the car to make sure he would stay out of her hair, not because she wanted to do him a favor.

"It wasn't a real question, but I've realized I do want to know the answer. The real one, not some nonsense about your sister. Why try to force your help on me when so many people would welcome it?" She thought of Alanna, who hummed with anger all the time at being forgotten.

Lane closed his eyes, the space between his brows creasing

like he was fighting back pain. "Because I genuinely think I'm the one who will crack it. And it would change everything for me."

"So is it the money, or the fame?"

Lane didn't answer for a long moment, his eyes still closed. Mina's sympathy receded as she watched him think, watched him try to come up with a pretty enough lie. "The money," he said finally.

That was better than chasing the fame, at least.

"Look, thank you for visiting," he said. "And the food. But they had me up every hour checking for brain damage. Whatever you want from me, you're not going to get it today."

"I don't want anything from you," she said. "And that doesn't make me a bad person."

"Of course it doesn't," he said. "Why would it?"

Alanna thought so, but what did Alanna want? If Mina did accept his help, that would probably just make her friend angrier, one more thing handed to her that Alanna couldn't have.

Huh. There was more than one option here.

She pulled out her wallet, and the white business card she kept in the back. She never used it; she had Starrett's direct line memorized, so she never needed to call the station desk. She fished a pen out of her purse and wrote it on the back of the card. Lane turned it over, running his thumb over the embossed logo of NSW Police.

"When you're discharged, call Sergeant Starrett," she said. "I'll pull whatever strings I can. I can't promise she'll let you see anything related to the case, but you're right. I get special treatment. Luckily for you, you won't even have to travel that far. Nowadays she splits her time between Nannine and running a training program for the Danby police. If you can wait a week, she'll be here."

Lane took it, and gave her a puzzled look. She supposed from his perspective, she had changed her tune abruptly. She gave him the smile her mother had taught her, looking at the bridge of his nose instead of into his eyes, and after a moment he smiled back.

SEVEN

HE BOOKED A "studio apartment" on Airbnb that turned out to be room 1004 in the Danby Motor Inn, but he didn't care as long as the free Wi-Fi worked and it had a real bed. Thanks to Mina, he had his laptop, and his box of files, and a couple of good books. That was all he needed. He hauled them in from the car, stacking them inside the front door. It was funny that what had made his car feel so crowded looked tiny and sad inside even such a small room.

He threw a frozen "man size" shepherd's pie in the microwave, and pulled out his phone, thumbing through his texts and emails while he waited. He deleted a couple of "friendly reminders" about overdue payments, an obvious scam attempt, and an actually somewhat clever scam attempt. Lynnie had sent him a picture of a black swan chilling on the edge of the lake, and he sent back a smiley face and a string of white swan emojis. The story of his own wildlife encounter could wait until she had less on her plate. Like when she'd graduated.

After clearing away the remains of dinner, he spread his map of Australia out on the wobbly kitchenette table. He pulled out the envelope full of little yellow flags, each one marked with a name and date in tiny letters. They had a speck of Blu-Tack on the back so he could press them onto the map. He didn't need to consult his list of where to put each one; he knew them by heart. He probably didn't need the map at all, but there was something soothing about having it out.

When he was almost done, three flags remained. One for Albury, one for Walgett, and one more. He stuck that one on. *Evelyn McCreery, April/May 1999.*

He flipped his notebook open to sketch out a plan for his conversation with Starrett. It wasn't where he'd hoped to start. Starrett likely had a wealth of knowledge, but she was a cop. Any information about the case that she wanted to be made public already had been, and she wouldn't share anything else with him, even with Mina's endorsement. She would have the same interview training he did, and wouldn't fall for cheap tricks.

His plan had been to convince Mina to talk to him. If anyone knew something that wasn't out there in the media or online, it was her. But maybe if he impressed Starrett, Mina would soften.

He scratched out a few bullet points, but it felt like more effort than it should have. Exhaustion was starting to creep up on him, the cumulative effect of an adrenaline spike and crash, followed by endless observations and then trying to catch up on sleep in a rock-hard hospital bed. Even days later, he hadn't had a chance to properly recover.

He sat on the edge of the sagging bed, but he didn't believe sleep would come if he tried to invite it in. Not with his plans for the next day swimming around in his head. Instead, he kicked off his shoes and crawled under the covers.

He pulled his laptop into the empty space beside him. The internet connection was stronger than he'd managed to get on his phone in the hospital, but it crawled.

He went to Facebook first, but ignored his feed, which was full to bursting with nonsense about online games and whichever news articles were getting the whole country stirred up today. He searched "Nannine," to see what groups would pop up. He found a local buy, sell, swap group, and a community noticeboard. He skimmed both briefly, looking for anything of interest. The messages were an even split between people trying to sell things for only a dollar less than they'd paid for them new, and people looking to arrange trades for the latest kids' collectible tat that Woolworths was giving out with every $30 spent.

One person was trying to sell a signed copy of Beverley Mc-Creery's memoir for $15, which had attracted a flock of laughing reactions.

He clicked to write a new post and then paused, wondering if he was taking a risk. He'd only just won Mina's support. His methods were always new to the families he worked for, and often unnerved them at first. He knew Mina had no internet presence and, if she knew the way she was spoken about online, he doubted she would be in favor of going down that path.

But it worked. The key moment that had unknotted the Fermin case came courtesy of a #throwbackthursday picture, innocently shared by a cousin, that had completely upended the timeline as the police understood it. After that, the same evidence told a completely different story, and the police had a confession within a week.

Still. Best be safe. He logged out of his main account and went into his backup account, under the name Leo Dutch. He found the buy, sell, swap group again, and posted a message.

> *Hi*
>> *I'm looking for any pictures taken in the Nannine area on the day of April 30, 1999. In particular, any pictures taken inside the showground or in the Commercial (the Nannine pub) on preview night would be highly regarded.*
>> *I can pay a token amount, but I don't have a huge budget. You'd be doing a real service to the community.*

He hit post, and then refreshed the page a few times, as if he might have been immediately inundated with responses. After a minute one did pop up—from the man trying to sell the book, asking if he wanted it. He laughed, and closed the tab. A watched pot never boiled.

He opened a new tab, and typed "Evelyn McCreery" into the search bar.

Did you mean Evie McCreery? it prompted.

He rolled his eyes, but it didn't matter. Evelyn or Evie, thousands of results appeared in seconds. He'd read all of the major articles before, of course, and watched the videos. But he wondered if he would see them differently, having been to the property, and having met Mina. He clicked on the first result, and grainy nineties news footage fired up of Senior Constable Starrett holding a press conference in front of the McCreery house. It was white, making Starrett's blue uniform shirt stand out starkly in the glare of the gathered media scrum's portable klieg lights.

"We have a search underway for nine-year-old Evelyn McCreery,

last seen at home in Nannine, New South Wales," Starrett said robotically. She looked to be barely in her midtwenties, staring directly into the camera with a look of absent horror and a deep flush on her cheeks. Later press conferences would replace her with a media liaison officer, once it started to dawn on the police how big this thing was going to be.

According to a profile of Starrett in *The Age*, she'd graduated from police training in 1997, then spent nearly two years with the Bankstown police before transferring to a community policing role in Nannine, meaning that she'd barely been in the role for a month before finding herself the lead investigator on Australia's most infamous unsolved crime—a far cry from the quiet life she would have expected when she took the job.

Lane rubbed his forehead. A pressure had started to build up behind his eyes. It wasn't quite a headache, so he didn't reach for the box of painkillers the hospital had sent him home with, but it made him feel even more tired.

The next video auto-played, the famous interview with Beverley McCreery. The interviewer wore an expression of exaggerated sympathy, but Lane could see a hint of triumph in her eyes. The media had fought viciously for the first interview with the family, and the exact payout the McCreerys had received from the successful network was still a closely guarded secret, although it was rumored to have broken records.

Beverley was carefully made up, her blond hair curled as expertly as the interviewer's. The comments below the video kept mentioning this, apparently oblivious to the existence of studio hairdressers and makeup artists. Liam McCreery sat to her left, and between them sat a nine-year-old Mina, silent and sullen. Her chair was off-center, pulled closer to her father, and she leaned toward him like she wanted to climb into his lap. A giant photo of Evelyn hovered behind them, her hands clasped under her chin and her blue eyes wide and bright. By contrast, Mina had her chin down like she was trying to tuck it into her clavicle, and her black hair fell forward over her face.

Lol, why does Mina look like a Japanese horror movie poster? a top-rated comment read.

Because her goddamn sister just disappeared, Lane wanted to scream at the keyboard warrior. He closed his eyes, just for a second, so that he could listen to Beverley's voice without being distracted by the screeching masses. Within moments he'd drifted into sleep.

He didn't know how long he slept—not deeply, and not long enough for the computer to go into sleep mode. The auto-play had kept ticking along, and the algorithm followed its usual path from the mainstream to the amateur to the downright unhinged. He woke up with the room washed in white from the intro of a video, with black text on a blinding white background reading: *PROOF that Mina McCreery killed Evie?*

Lane sat up, fighting confusion. The intro dissolved to some old news footage of a canine unit being led through a paddock—the McCreery property, according to the caption at the bottom, although not the part Lane had managed to visit. A narrator's voice cut in, the tone robotic. Not Starrett's I-thought-the-worst-I-would-see-was-the-occasional-tractor-theft-and-maybe-some-meth-heads nervous monotone, but the mechanical quality of text-to-speech software.

"In 2005 the McCreery family agreed to allow Channel Nine to conduct a new search of the property, including a visit from a team of highly trained cadaver dogs—that is, dogs trained to sniff out buried

bodies. *In exchange for a check from the network, of course, ha ha ha.*" They'd added an echo over the already forced laughter, like they were trying to sound monstrous. "*Now watch this dog.*"

A green circle appeared on the footage, floating over a golden retriever being led in circles around a fallen gum tree in the background of the shot. "*And here comes Mina. She's spotted the dog being walked near that log, and heads straight for it.*"

A figure appeared on the right-hand side of the screen, wearing workboots, jeans, and a white T-shirt. Her thick black braid swung behind her as she strode through the shot, ignoring the dogs around her, her eyes locked on the one circling the tree. Judging by her height and weight, she was maybe sixteen . . . no—Lane did some quick math—she would have been fourteen or fifteen in 2005. She stood in front of the tree, crossed her arms, and snapped something at the dog's handler that the camera hadn't caught. The dog looked up at the handler, tilting its head to the side, and then sat, waiting for instructions.

"*Let's rewind a few frames, before Mina interrupts the dog at work,*" the narrator said.

The video jumped back, and paused on a frame of the dog sniffing the ground in front of the tree.

"*You don't need to be an expert in animal body language to read this dog's mind. Look at the stiff back. Look at the way its ears are coming up. This dog has found something. It was about to alert—until Mina intervened.*"

The image of the dog faded out, replaced by a picture of the fallen gum tree. Words appeared on the screen.

Is this where Evie McCreery is buried?

EIGHT

MyMurder Forums

Subforum: General Discussion

Subject: So many acronyms, halp

User Inspektor: Hi everyone, I'm new to this forum and I keep seeing acronyms everywhere. Some I can figure out from context, but can anyone shed some light on these: WAKE, SKE, TIKE?

User Waffletoid: They're unique to discussion of the Evie McCreery case, although you'll see the last one used as a joke in other subforums sometimes. WAKE stands for "Wednesday Addams Killed Evie," which is used to flag that the poster is a crackpot right up front. SKE means "Stranger Killed Evie" (you'll sometimes see STE for "Stranger Took Evie"). That refers to the mainstream theory that an intruder entered the house and abducted Evie McCreery. "TIKE" means "The Illuminati Killed Evie," and is mostly used to make fun of the WAKEs.

User Inspektor: Wednesday Addams?

User LionSong: Wednesday Addams is what some jackholes in this forum call Mina McCreery, Evelyn's twin sister. Addams Family Values came out a few years earlier, and she bore a rather striking resemblance to Christina Ricci's Wednesday. The press ran a quote from a friend of the family saying that Beverley, the girls' mother, called Mina "Wednesday" as a nickname. People have really run with it.

User VolcanicJudo: Crackpot is a slur. Statistically speaking SKE is the crackpot theory. The vast majority of child murders are committed by a member of the family.

User Waffletoid: And statistically speaking, how many murders are committed by nine-year-old girls?

User AgentKHole: You know, only WAKE and TIKE are acronyms. An acronym is a word formed from the first letters of other words. SKE is an initialism.

User LionSong: I thought you got banned?

* * *

The Danby police station was an unassuming gray-brick building. Aside from the NSW Police sign, and the two flagpoles out the front flying the Aboriginal and Australian flags, it could have been an ordinary office block. He went up the wide concrete steps and through the automatic doors.

Entering a police station always felt strange for Lane. In another world he might have been Sergeant Holland by now, or at least Leading Senior Constable Holland. But he'd made his choices. He'd have had a lot more resources, and security, on that path, and he'd have learned so much about investigation that a degree couldn't prepare him for.

What that path could never have given him was the freedom to choose his own cases. Cases in any jurisdiction. That was key.

So he'd taught himself as best he could. In a way, that had been the reason for his early success. He could apply ideas that were on the bleeding edge, new techniques that were still working their way through layers of approval in the police bureaucracy and might be tried years from now.

The uniformed officer behind the reception desk looked up at his entrance. "Hi there, how can I help you?" she asked, without much enthusiasm.

"I'm Lane Holland, here to see Senior Sergeant Emily Starrett," he said.

"She's not available at the moment, but I can take a message."

"It's alright, Dhvani, he's got an appointment." Starrett stood in a doorway on the other side of the foyer, holding a travel mug with the teabag still in it. She looked rather different from the video. She was more gray at the temples, but also looked more sure of where she was. No longer a wide-eyed newbie stumbling her way through a case with the eyes of the world on her. "Mr. Holland," she said, with unusual warmth. Obviously Mina had called ahead as she had promised, but she must have done far more to smooth his way with the senior sergeant than he'd expected her to.

"It's a real pleasure to meet you, ma'am," he said, making no pretense that he needed her to introduce herself.

"None of that," she said. "Just Starrett'll do fine. Now, I don't have an office here, and the family room's being used, so I've had to pop you in an interview room. Don't read anything into it."

"Honestly, I'll be thrilled with anything," he said. "I'll sit in the loading dock on a milk crate if I have to."

Starrett chuckled. "You're lucky on this case. Parts of our file were already subject to a successful disclosure request under the GIPA Act. It's been redacted, of course, but you can see what was released."

The Government Information (Public Access) Act created a system for members of the public to request the release of information from state agencies, including the police. The GIPA disclosure relating to the case hadn't popped up in any of his research, and it hadn't occurred to him to check the list manually.

"I'll need you to fill out the informal access request, just to cover our bases, but I don't mind letting you have a look before you've jumped through all the hoops. It's nice to see some interest in the case. We're not exactly flush with resources to delve into cold cases here."

"Surely you get a lot of inquiries, though?" Lane said. His fingers itched for that file, but it was clear he needed to let the pleasantries unwind at Starrett's pace.

Starrett half shrugged. "The family has never given up. But they've never been completely cooperative with us, which muddied the waters."

Lane's eyebrows shot up. "You think they lied?"

"Habitually," Starrett said, taking a sip of her tea like she hadn't just blown Lane's mind. "That's just a fact of life when dealing with an addict."

"Drugs?" Lane said. He'd heard rumors Beverley McCreery had a pill problem, of course, but he'd never given them much weight. In some particularly nasty circles, just being a middle-aged white woman of means was enough for people to assume a prescription drug addiction.

"The mother was a real lost soul. Life treated her rough, but that didn't give her the right to ruin her daughters' childhoods." Starrett sighed. "The chain of pain, as we call it."

"And you're telling me this is all in the file?" Lane said.

"Why don't I get it for you." She drained the last of her tea. "I really do hope you have success. Our view has always been that the resolution is clear, but we hit a brick wall."

"You have a theory?"

"I don't want to bias you," Starrett said. "You should read the file and draw your own conclusions. But I'm sure you're aware of the statistics. Most child victims are harmed by a member of their own family. Stranger abductions are exceptionally rare."

He followed her down the hall, his mind buzzing. Did Mina know, when she sent him to Starrett, that the local police weren't actually in her corner?

She led him to a small room a few doors up from reception. It was bare except for a table and one plastic chair.

"I'll be next door in a training room. Let me know when you're finished," Starrett said. He barely heard her.

A white archive box sat on the table. It was smaller than he'd expected. How extensive were those redactions? Maybe she would bring more boxes as he made his way through the contents. Maybe the rest were in Nannine.

He eased the lid open. A white file rested on top, with a column of blue-and-white tabs running down the edge. He laid it on the table with a feeling close to reverence.

He flipped it open, and stopped short. A little girl smiled up at him from the school photo taped to the first page. Her wide-open smile revealed two missing front teeth, and her copper brown hair framed large dark eyes. She was cute, like all five-year-olds, but uncomfortable to look at. Her eyes were unusually far apart, and her small chin made her face look misshapen, like an upside-down pear.

She was not Evelyn McCreery. Even if he hadn't known exactly what Evelyn looked like, he couldn't have made that mistake. This girl was far too young, maybe five or six.

He flipped back to the front of the file, looking at the details he'd skipped in favor of searching for fresh information. This file belonged to Christa Rennold, who had been reported missing five years after Evelyn McCreery. She'd disappeared from her foster mother's front yard on the outskirts of Danby.

He knew this case, in passing. It came close enough to fitting what he usually looked for that he'd read the background. But he'd quickly discarded it. Christa Rennold was one of those frustrating cases where the perpetrator was obvious to anyone, but through lack of evidence or police incompetence no charges were ever laid.

"Well, okay, then," he muttered, opening the file. He didn't know what game Mina was playing, but he could play it too.

* * *

Starrett was reading behind a desk in the empty training room. Rows of chairs were waiting, but there was no sign of any trainees. She seemed happy to tuck her papers in a drawer and give him her full attention.

Her welcoming attitude made a lot more sense now. He'd come in expecting to have to fight for her to give him the time of day, when surely she had spent years fielding questions from journalists and amateur investigators. But that was the McCreery case. This case was under-resourced and largely forgotten.

"If you don't mind me asking, what did Miss McCreery say when she set up this meeting?" Lane asked, sitting in the front row.

"She just shared with me a few of your qualifications, and asked if there was anything I could do to help you look into the Christa Rennold case," Starrett said.

Lane wanted to push further, to ask if she'd specifically said Christa Rennold, or just told Starrett he was interested in any child abduction cold cases they had. And if she had directed him to this case, he wanted to know what Mina's interest was. But clearly Mina had lied to Starrett, apparently to manipulate Lane, and he didn't want to give himself away with too many questions until he knew more.

"Were you involved with this case originally?" he asked instead. "It was before you started working out here, wasn't it?"

She raised an eyebrow. "How did you know that?"

"Mina mentioned it," he said. Probably not the time to bring up the bundle of articles on her he had back in his motel room.

"I came out for the first few weeks," Starrett said. "Given my experience, I get called in for most missing persons cases in this half of the state. Especially abductions."

Lane did a quick estimate of how many cases that was likely to be. Child abductions sat in a strange gray area; they were more common than people realized, but less common than they feared. Most abductions were committed by a noncustodial parent or other relative, and most missing children were located quickly. Stranger abductions were few and far between, and he knew for a fact Evelyn McCreery was the only one in that time.

"How did you rule out a link to the McCreery case?" It made him nervous to drop the name, but it was the obvious question. The handful of articles he'd found on the case had led with that fact. Once the McCreery angle was dropped, so did the media's interest in the case, it seemed.

"Some of that is confidential."

Lane couldn't imagine what they might have used to conclusively rule it out, particularly given the lack of evidence at the McCreery scene. No DNA, no fingerprints. But Starrett seemed completely confident.

Which meant there was something they had held back from the public. Police did that sometimes, to help them identify false confessions by the mentally ill or attention seekers. Withheld evidence from the McCreery case was the holy grail. If he could earn enough of Starrett's trust to wheedle that out of her, it could change everything.

"The possibility was explored thoroughly, but there was no evidence of any link. The abduction sites were hundreds of kilometers apart. We did confirm the alibis of some of our persons of interest in the McCreery case, but it was overkill, mostly done to prevent the press from running with the possibility."

Lane flexed his fingers on his knees at the mention of persons of interest. What he wouldn't do to get his hands on that list.

Starrett continued. "There's no real mystery around who took Christa. The older sister reported seeing their biological father take her. If you've got a part to play here, it's figuring out *where* he took her."

Lane drummed his fingers on his armrest, trying to find the words to ask how the hell the father had got away without it seeming like an attack on the Danby police. "Can you talk me through the police operation, after it was called in?"

She gave him a level look. "A good ten minutes slipped by between the abduction and when it was called in. The older girl, the witness, was only ten. According to the foster mother, she'd fallen asleep on the lounge while the girls played outside. I imagine there was a bit of confusion at first. Ten minutes is a long time, especially if he was driving flat out. They had all officers on alert looking for the car or anyone matching the father's description. There may have been a little too much focus on the former. He dumped the car quite quickly. We think he switched over to one that we wouldn't be looking for."

"That suggests he planned it out, rather than it being an impulsive grab."

"Exactly. He had to wait for the opportunity to present itself, but he clearly had a plan ready to roll. Which means that he was long gone while we were still getting our boots on."

"And since then?"

"Flags on his license and passport. We circulated his picture as a wanted fugitive. Christa appears on missing posters, and there's a reward offered. Not . . ." She sighed. "Like I said, resources are limited. Plus, we're not that far from Cameron Corner, where the three states meet. They could have gone east, or they might be in South Australia or Queensland. He had ties to the Northern Territory. We can ask police in those states to do what they can, but we don't have any control."

He nodded. "The older sister—did she have a different father?"

"Not as far as we're aware."

"A bit odd then, that he didn't wait for an opportunity to take both girls."

"I don't know." Starrett shrugged. "I wish I could tell you that every parent loves their children equally."

Lane knew well enough that they didn't. "The sister would be about twenty-five now, right? Does she still live in the area?"

She sat back in her chair, looking thoughtful. Lane doubted she would give him the contact details of a witness, especially not one who had been a minor at the time, but she'd shown a willingness so far to lean on the boundaries. "The sister is interesting. There was a bit of movement in the case around the time she turned eighteen. The family filed the paperwork to request a coronial inquest, and then withdrew it. Then there was the GIPA request on the file."

"Was there some sort of conflict in the family? The daughter wanted the inquest, and the mother objected?"

"Perhaps. The mother was always a little passive. She never filed to have her husband formally declared dead, although she could have done so years ago. I'm sure it would have made her life easier. But then, with the evidence that he's actively attempting to evade law enforcement, the application might have been rejected."

"Do you think she could still be in contact with him?"

Starrett made an "eh" noise. Either she didn't know, or she'd decided that she'd been too cavalier in what she'd shared, and was done.

* * *

Lane made a beeline for his laptop when he got back to the motel. He'd done a superficial search for the case on his phone, sticking mostly to news articles and Christa Rennold's National Missing Persons Coordination Centre profile. He'd found lately that trying to read things on a phone gave him a headache after a few minutes, so he'd decided to wait until he was back in his room to dig deep.

Just to be safe he grabbed the box of painkillers and swallowed two before he got started.

An email popped up in the corner of his screen, from a PI in Byron who sometimes referred him for jobs she wasn't interested in. Even if he wanted to take on extra jobs right now, he was literally on the other side of the state. But it was an uncomfortable reminder that as long as he was in Danby, his life was all expense and no income. The longer he went without making any real progress toward the Evelyn McCreery reward, the harder it would be to pursue other options. There was still time to back out and place a safer bet.

He flicked it away.

He needn't have worried about finding the sister's name. He searched "Christa Rennold," which brought up the same news articles he'd skimmed earlier. Below that he found a post about Christa on a Facebook page, written by an Alanna Rennold. He clicked through and found himself on the page for a missing persons support group that met monthly in Danby. Alanna Rennold was the page administrator.

Alanna didn't have much on her public profile, but there was a link to her Instagram account, which was open and updated regularly. Most of the pictures were impersonal—book covers, cups of tea, a new dress spread out on a bed. He scanned the few faces that appeared, but couldn't see any sign of Mina in the pictures of Alanna's friends and family.

He scrolled until a message popped up, demanding that he log in to continue. He could, but it didn't seem like he would find anything important, and there was always the risk of accidentally liking a months-old picture.

He clicked in the address bar and deleted Alanna's username, then paused. He knew it wasn't a healthy impulse, but he also knew he was going to do it anyway. He typed the first letter of a username, and the browser helpfully filled the rest out immediately.

The pictures on the page were bursting with color and movement. Bright balloons, bunting, a table heavy with cupcakes and chips and salads, another one covered in gifts in pastel wrapping paper. Alexandra was in most of them, her face lit up with such joy it made his breath catch. His eye went straight to a picture of her in the top-left corner. She was staring straight into the camera, her blond hair tumbling around her face. She held up a knife, smeared with bright blue cake.

It's a boy.

He couldn't identify the emotion he was feeling, but whatever it was he was completely flooded with it. He took a deep, slow breath and closed the tab. Okay. The road was longer than he'd thought it would be, but he had to keep going. There was more at stake here than money.

NINE

MyMurder Forums

Subforum: Evie McCreery

Subject: Christa Rennold

User LionSong: Did you guys know that there's another active missing persons case in the Nannine area? A little girl named Christa Rennold went missing in 2005 about three hours from the McCreery home.

User Waffletoid: Three hours? Casting the net a little wide, aren't you?

User LionSong: Dudes, this is outback Australia. A three-hour drive is like . . . four houses away.

* * *

Alanna Rennold was the only twenty-something woman inside the coffee shop, but Lane thought he could have picked her out even in a crowd of them. She looked uncannily like the photograph of Christa that he had tucked inside the manila folder in his hands. Her hair was neater, straightened to fit an angular bob that framed the same sharp chin and large brown eyes. On Alanna the wide-apart eyes were striking, almost fey, enhanced by precisely applied makeup. She had grown into it. He hoped Christa had too.

She wore a floral dress under a rose-colored cardigan, and had a leather handbag tucked under her chair. Everything was new but looked inexpensive, probably from the Target across the street. The outfit was more formal than seemed necessary for a Saturday morning coffee—most other customers wore shorts and T-shirts.

"Mr. Holland." She awkwardly set her coffee cup aside to shake his hand. She spoke with a smooth tone that was a touch too formal, like he was interviewing her for a job. "I ordered you a coffee. I figured a flat white was a safe choice." She dropped her voice. "They can be slow here."

Lane hated milk in his coffee, but smiled. "Perfect, thank you."

He took the seat opposite her and busied himself laying out his folder and setting up his phone to record their conversation. "Do you mind me recording you?" he asked, enunciating so the app would pick it up. Can't be too careful.

"That's fine." She stroked the rim of her coffee cup with her thumb. "I've brought you something. It's not much. You'll probably think it's . . ." She ducked down to dig in her handbag. "Here."

It was a plastic binder, the sleeves inside bulging with papers. The first few were filled with articles, all of them brief. Most he'd seen during his search the night before, but a few were new—probably from local papers that had never been digitized.

There was a copy of the same kindergarten picture he'd seen in the police file. Another picture showed Alanna and Christa sitting on the edge of a concrete veranda, Christa in Alanna's lap.

Next was a series of age-progression pictures. One of what Christa might have looked like at fifteen, and two recent ones of her at twenty. Alanna must have paid for those out of her own pocket, because they were higher quality than the first sketch, and there were two versions—one with a slim build, and another at a heavier weight. All three progressions appeared to have used Christa's school photo as the base, with Alanna painted over the top.

Next was a painting, clearly done by a preschooler. It was splotched with red and blue, with pictures roughly cut from a toy catalog stuck on. He could picture Christa hunched over it, carefully pressing each piece on exactly the right spot. He remembered how intently Lynnie would focus on her little masterpieces, the tip of her tongue caught between her teeth.

"There's a really clear fingerprint in the paint, just there," Alanna said, misreading his long pause as confusion. She tapped the spot. "The police have her fingerprints, from the scene, but you wouldn't have access to that and I don't know what's useful . . ."

Lane made a thoughtful noise, but couldn't seem to find any words. He tried to remember what he'd thought when he'd first looked at this case seven or eight years ago, searching for likely prospects. How many minutes had he spent before deciding this one wasn't for him? Two? Three?

When Mina pushed him toward this case, the plan had been simple. There was always something he could put forward, some lead that overworked or uninterested police had failed to follow up, or some emerging technique that hadn't existed at the time of the initial investigation. All he had to do was point it out, show Mina she could trust him to get things done. Even if the lead panned out to nothing after a few months, he would already be on the McCreery case properly by then.

But Alanna would be crushed.

The last sleeve was filled with cards, all watercolor flowers and sympathetic words. She'd arranged them in the sleeve so they were splayed open like pinned butterflies, presumably so he could read them without having to pull them out. He flipped the sleeve over to read the personal messages, and was startled to see hand-writing he knew.

"Beverley McCreery sent you a card?" he asked, touching the familiar swooping "B" of her signature.

Alanna's mouth tightened. "She reached out to my mother. It's a small club, you know?"

"They were friends?"

She made a face. "Briefly. They drifted apart again quickly. Beverley was, you know, *Beverley*, and my mum was very much not."

Lane nodded. Beverley's energy had grabbed him from the first moment he picked up her book. She'd been relentless in doing everything she could for her daughter, keeping the world's eyes looking for her. If Deirdre Rennold was as wishy-washy as Starrett suggested, or had chosen to protect her husband over her child, then he could see how any friendship between the two women would have hit the skids. "She didn't like how passive your mother was?"

Alanna looked startled. "No? I don't know. I was ten; I didn't know the gory details. I just know that Mum's entanglements were always pretty brief. I'm assuming a lot here, but it's not like I can ask."

"You're not in contact with your mother anymore?"

Alanna laughed, then cut it off, retreating to a false, tight smile. "I meant I can't ask Beverley. I suppose I could ask Mum." Her own words seemed to surprise her.

"So you had your own relationship with Beverley?"

"Are you winding up to ask about Evelyn McCreery?" Alanna asked, folding her arms over her chest.

Danger.

"Only if it's relevant to Christa's disappearance," he said quickly.

"There's no relevance," she said. "Yes, I was friends with Beverley. Growing up with Mum, my sister was a closed subject. Looking back, I can see how it was painful for her, but as a kid it felt like it made her angry to hear Christa's name. And the last thing she wanted was to be in contact with the police all the time, or have a coroner digging into the details of our life."

"She must have been frightened that she would lose you too," he said.

Alanna looked unconvinced. "Growing up was a countdown to eighteen. I could have my own little flat, and get a job, or the living-away-from-home allowance. She and I would be separate enough that I could start making some noise about it. That . . . didn't turn out to be as realistic as it had looked to a teenager. But I did start to attend a support group, and Beverley was there. She was . . ." She bit her lip, and looked away. "She helped me put in an application to get some of the files opened up to the public, and the request for a coronial inquest. She went way above and beyond what she needed to, especially with so much on her own plate. I think she might have got me my first job at the library too, as a casual. In a town like this, that job gets a hundred applications to every vacancy, and she clearly had clout. The library's named after her now."

"Did your mother ask you to cancel the application for an inquest?"

"Yes, but that's not why I withdrew it. Right as it finally started to get moving, Beverley got her diagnosis. I couldn't imagine doing it without her, not when I'd just started uni as well, and my mum was always in the midst of some fresh drama. Her prognosis was good, at first, so I thought that after a year or two the timing would be better. Instead she died."

"I'm sorry."

"Yeah, well." Alanna looked away. "It was probably going to be more of the same."

"Hopefully I can help with that," he said. "Are you ready to begin?"

"I thought we had. Where do you want to start?" She stared at his phone, where a green line bounced on the screen in time with her words.

Without taking his eyes off her face, he reached out and switched the screen off. "Tell me about your sister."

The tight line of her jaw softened instantly. "Christa was amazing. She was so smart, and fascinated by how the world worked. Once I read her this book about the water cycle, and months later we were standing on the front steps watching it rain—seriously, months later—and she recited the whole thing back to me. About how the water had 'aporated' from the rivers and lakes and now was coming back down as rain. And one time she made me follow this ant. We chased that thing all over the playground for a good hour, watching it search for food and cart it back to the nest. She . . ." Alanna faltered. "I want to tell you more, but I was so young. And I don't have a great memory. We lived together for five years, but when I try to think about that time all I have is scraps."

"That's not uncommon," Lane said. People with unhappy childhoods often struggled to recall them. It astonished him when he met adults who could rattle off the name of their year-three teacher, or wax rhapsodic about a holiday they went on when they were six. If he concentrated hard on remembering what life had been like when he was ten, he got a vague impression of hours spent staring out a car window, a lot of yelling and the sound of a tent peg being struck with a mallet.

"Oh my god." Alanna pressed her hands to her face. "You meant like, what did she look like, didn't you? Hair and eye color and so forth. You don't care about the ant."

"I do," he said gently. "I know her hair and eye color. Brown for both, right?"

"They were more of a hazel," Alanna said, still looking a little embarrassed.

"Good to know. Her eye color is one thing that is unlikely to have changed. Do you know if she ever had any dental work? Fillings, extractions?"

Alanna shook her head. "We only saw the dentist that came to the school once a year. She would have still had her baby teeth, anyway."

"Did she ever chip them? Or break a bone?"

For a moment Alanna looked confused by the question, then understanding dawned. After fifteen years, if Christa's remains were out there somewhere her hair and eye color would be no help to identify them; dental records and healed fractures would be. She closed her eyes and took a deliberate breath, in and out. "She had a broken collarbone, when she was about three."

Lane paused. He'd expected the answer to be "no." Breaks were rare at that age. "Do you know what happened?"

"She fell down the stairs."

Lane studied her face. He'd "fallen down the stairs" a couple of times himself. But if it was a euphemism, Alanna gave no sign of it.

"Tell me what you remember of the day Christa went missing."

"Okay. I . . . um . . ." Her mouth worked, but she didn't seem to know where to start.

Sometimes a broad question helped, and sometimes it was too broad, too big, and people got flustered. He jumped back in. "The file said it was around ten a.m. Where were you at the time?"

"I was inside the house. We'd been playing in the front yard, and I left Christa there to go get a glass of water. I was only gone for a minute."

"The house?"

"You know. You've got the address, all the details."

"I want to hear them from you. You'd be surprised how often files are wrong, or leave out something important. Or how often witnesses think they told police something when they didn't."

"Okay. We were living with Mrs. Stern at the time, in an old miner's cottage on Strickland Street. It was the corner lot, and we were out the front."

"What can you tell me about Mrs. Stern?"

"She was nice. She wasn't one of those foster carers who wants to pretend she's your mother, but she was warm and took care of us pretty well. We were something like the twentieth, twenty-fifth kids she'd had through. Some of them sent her Christmas cards, and she still had them up, months later."

"She's passed now, right?" He'd been disappointed to learn that. It cut off avenues he could explore, based on questions that she couldn't answer anymore. "Did you have any contact with her after you left her care?"

"A little. We weren't close, but she was my first foster mother and I was her last foster child. There was a bond there."

"Did you ever talk about what happened? What she remembered?"

"No."

A disappointing answer, but not crushing. There wasn't likely to be any valuable information there anyway; it would be a memory of a conversation about a memory. Like a photocopy of a photocopy, the edges would have been too fuzzy to rely on.

"How did you come to be in foster care?"

Alanna sank a little in her seat, squeezing herself smaller. "A few weeks before, a trucker found my sister walking by the highway at three a.m. She'd woken up in the middle of the night and decided she wanted McDonald's. I didn't hear her wake up or unlock the front door."

"And your mother?"

"She was at work."

"She left a ten-year-old babysitting? Overnight?"

Alanna looked annoyed. "Did you expect to hear about Mum's excellent parenting choices?"

"I was under the impression you were in foster care due to the drug use."

"Well, something had to happen to prompt them to test her. And once she tested positive for methamphetamines, we were packed off to Mrs. Stern's house. The plan was that we would stay for a month while Mum completed a program, and then they would review the case. Christa disappeared on day eighteen."

"Where was your father?"

A guarded look came over her face. "My father had a fly-in fly-out job; he started just before Christa was born. He would live on the job site for a few weeks at a time. The department tried to contact him when we were taken into care, but the company had no record of an employee by that name."

"He lied about where he worked?"

She broke eye contact and started fiddling with her teaspoon, twirling it in her fingers. "He was definitely working somewhere, because he sent money home as regular as clockwork. But he either gave my mother the wrong company name, or he was working under a fake name. Or both."

"Was there a reason for that?"

"In reality? No. He was just like that. He kept us off grid as much as possible. He paid for everything in cash, wouldn't take out a mortgage, and used a rotating list of fake names whenever he needed to work. I think that's why he liked the fly-in fly-out work so much: it kept his work life separate from his family life, and he didn't work with anyone who knew anything about him."

"You don't have any idea where he was working at the time?"

"What does it matter?" she snapped. Her voice grew deeper, more nasal, as her annoyance came out.

He leaned back in his chair, confused by her hostile turn. "Because if he was living somewhere else half the time, that's a good place to start for where he might have taken her."

She stared at him for a long time, then sighed. "Fine. I don't know where my dad was living, okay? But it was up north somewhere. He told us a story about going swimming with some friends, and having to scramble out when one of them realized a log on the bottom was actually a crocodile."

That wasn't great. If the closest lead was in the Northern Territory or Far North Queensland, there wasn't much he could do.

"And I found a pen in his bag, the last time he was home. It was from a motel in Howard Springs. I remember because he got really mad at me for asking about it."

"Did you tell the police?"

"Yeah. They called the motel, but there was no record of a guest with his name. I mean, duh, but what more could they do?"

"Right. Wherever he was working, your father came back to

town the week before Christa disappeared. He attempted to take Christa from school—"

"He came back from working away and tried to pick his children up from school as he normally would," Alanna interrupted. "The school blew the whole thing out of proportion, calling the police like that."

"And he got in an altercation with the police officer who attended the scene?"

"Like I said, my father has some issues with the government. And he'd just had a shock."

He couldn't help contrasting her words with her earlier comments about her mother—not condemning, but clear-eyed and honest about her mistakes. Yet she was bending over backward to be sympathetic to her father, a man who sounded like he'd been a nightmare long before he progressed to outright child abduction.

"Was that the last time you saw him?"

She looked unimpressed. "No. I know you know that our father approached us twice. He talked to us through a fence at the playground, and once we saw him in the supermarket."

"Did that frighten you?"

"No. It annoyed Mrs. Stern, but he was watching out for his children. It's not a crime."

Lane raised his eyebrows. He could name a couple of crimes that a motivated officer could have made stick—harassment, stalking, intimidation. But even if Mrs. Stern had tried to report it, probably the best she would have got was a vague promise to caution him. Unless the cops were looking for an excuse after he took a swing at one of their own at the school.

Alanna huffed. "Alright, yeah. But he was getting bad advice. A mate told him it would be held against him if he didn't seem interested in visiting us, but talking to the department and scheduling a time to see us with a social worker present . . ." She shook her head, and Lane understood. It would be anathema to a man with that kind of anti-authoritarian streak. "So he thought he should just show up."

"You've had contact with him?" Lane couldn't keep the eagerness out of his voice.

"No. My uncle Dave—not an actual uncle; I think he and Dad went to school together—told me that he was the one encouraging Dad to come see us. He told me when he was twelve-stepping."

"You haven't seen your father at all since he took Christa?"

Alanna's face flushed red. "I didn't see him take Christa."

"You"—Lane wanted to check his snapshots of the file, but that was likely to come across like he was trying to pull a "gotcha"—"you told the police that you did at the time, didn't you?"

She sighed. "I'm well aware that the file says that."

Right. Because she was the one who made the GIPA Act request, she must have viewed the same redacted files he had.

"Is the file wrong?" Unfortunately, that wasn't implausible. Procedures weren't always followed perfectly, especially years ago. The police were far from perfect, and Danby was a small, overstretched precinct.

"I did say that, but I was ten. I didn't understand how important it was to be precise. I didn't actually see her abduction at all—I was inside."

"Was there a window in the kitchen?"

"Yes, but I couldn't see her from the sink. Like I said, the house was on the corner, and the kitchen looked out on the other road."

"Could you hear her?"

She shook her head.

"What could you see?"

"I saw a red car slow right down and turn the corner. A 1995 Commodore sedan."

"That's very specific. Were you into cars at the time?"

"I recognized the make and year because my father drove one."

"Are you saying you saw your father's car outside when Christa went missing?"

"I'm saying I saw a red Commodore. I didn't see a license plate, and I didn't see him driving it, so no, I'm not saying I saw my father's car."

Lane paused, trying to choose his words carefully. "Did you tell the police you saw your father's car?"

She shook her head. "I told them I saw a car *like* my father's car. He wasn't driving it."

He tried not to let any frustration show. Whether it *was* his car or just *looked like* his car was splitting hairs. The police had found his car, deliberately torched. The license plates and VIN proved it was the car registered to her father. "Can you describe the driver?"

"No, I barely saw them."

"But you're sure it wasn't your father driving."

"Mr. Holland, if your father drove past this cafe right now, even just for a moment, you would be able to pick him out, wouldn't you? We notice the people we love."

The idea of Lane's father driving past made his breath catch in his throat. He sipped his coffee to buy a few moments to collect himself. "I take your point," he said. "Then what happened?"

"I took the cups of water back outside, and Christa was gone. The gate was closed, the front garden was empty, and there was nothing in the street. No red car, no Christa. I never saw her again."

"I'm sorry," he said. The words were worthless, but she smiled a little.

"Thank you."

He offered a hand across the table, planning to shake her hand and say goodbye.

She stared down at it, looking confused. "Don't you have more questions than that?"

He pulled his hand back, surprised. "You've given me a lot of your time, and I know it's a draining process."

"D'you . . . do you want to arrange another time? Or if you just need a break, I could take a turn around the park and meet you again in an hour."

He smiled. She had an amazing reserve of empathy, for someone who had been through so much. "I didn't mean it was draining for me. I don't think I need to ask you any more questions."

"What, you're finished?" she asked. Her voice, so warm a moment ago, had gone very flat.

"Yes," he said. Clearly he'd misstepped, badly, but he wasn't going to sit here and put her through the wringer with pointless questions.

"How 'bout I ask you a question," she said. She'd occasionally slipped into a broader accent as they talked, and it was fully out now. Either she was too upset to keep the "professional" voice up, or she just didn't see him as worth impressing anymore.

"Sure."

"I looked into your cases. There were a lot more than I expected, based on what M—" She swallowed whatever she'd been about to say.

Based on what Mina told her, he guessed. If she'd known Beverley, it followed that she knew Mina too, which explained why Mina had sent him after this case. But obviously Mina was an off-limits topic.

"There were a lot more than I expected. It seems like you were all over the country, then suddenly all the cases were in northern New South Wales, southern Queensland. Were you looking for something in particular?"

"I see you're a bit of an investigator yourself," Lane said lightly.

"Librarian, private investigator, they're similar skills."

"Well, I wouldn't say I was all over the country. I always focused on the Murray-Darling Basin, even in my more mobile days."

"Your early cases were all missing and dead little girls. Then the Queensland cases are a grab bag. Men, women, robberies, insurance fraud. And now here you are, back on the road. Back to little girls."

"I was looking for cases that were close to home. My sister was enrolled in high school in Byron Bay, so I needed to be able to get out and interview people, review files, look at the scene, and still be home to make sure her dinner involved at least one vegetable."

That softened her a fraction. A small personal revelation usually greased the wheels, although Lane hated to do it. He hated using his personal stories as currency, carefully selecting one and offering it up as a manipulation tool.

"So this kind of case is what you really want to do?"

"It's good to specialize," he said.

"But my sister never interested you before. Why?"

"I'm here, aren't I?"

"Don't pretend this is the case you want to be working on," she scoffed. "I'm pleased you're here, but not stupid."

He held his hands up. That was fair. "I have specific criteria for the cases I choose. Christa fell outside of it."

"Why? Because the reward is too low?"

"No. It's not about the money, or anything personal about your sister, or how deserving you are of justice. I just didn't think I had any value to add. This case isn't a whodunnit, it's a where-are-they-now. Answering that question would have needed resources I just didn't have."

He didn't have those resources now, either. It would take a full-scale search with thousands of volunteers and a K9 unit. Or access to CCTV footage country wide, and a facial recognition database.

A facial recognition database. Huh. There was an idea . . .

"So you're just like all the rest," Alanna said. She flipped the folder closed and started to tuck it into her handbag.

"Wait." He put his hand on her arm, making her pause. "I'm sorry if I've offended you. I know it must be hurtful to hear the most painful part of your life dismissed like that. But I'm here now, and I promise I'll do everything—"

"You've already proved you won't," she snapped.

Panic rose in him. If she stormed out, then he could say goodbye to any cooperation from Mina. "I don't understand."

"'It's not a whodunnit.' Screw you. Every time, it goes straight to my father. Did you even consider the possibility that she was abducted by a stranger?"

Lane hesitated. The evidence was clear. "Statistically—"

"Fuck statistics!" she snapped, loud enough that a man at the next table with a toddler in his lap turned to frown at them. She glared right back, and Lane held up a hand to bring her attention back to him.

"I'm sorry," he said. "You're right. Of course you're right. I promise you I'll keep an open mind."

"You'll look at everything?" she asked. Her voice was still laced with suspicion, but at least it had dropped back to her normal volume.

"Everything. No stone unturned."

She put her face in her hands and breathed for a moment, in a deliberate way that Lane recognized as a calming exercise. He waited until she was ready to look up at him again.

"Thank you," she said. "I know it's not the case you wanted to work on, but . . ." She stared across the room. On the far wall, the cafe had a community noticeboard, and a Missing Persons Week poster hung surrounded by ads for kittens to good homes and lawnmower maintenance services. The famous picture of Evelyn McCreery took up half the poster, but beneath were passport-sized pictures of other missing persons from the area. Christa was the first.

"It must be hard," he said. "Trying to get attention in their shadow."

"Yeah, well. It's a bit of both. Evelyn makes people look. And maybe while they're looking, they'll see Christa too."

TEN

HE DROVE FROM the cafe to Strickland Street, more to give his mind time to settle than because he expected to find anything. He found the lot easily, but the cottage where Alanna and Christa had lived for eighteen days was long gone. In its place stood a trio of boxy townhouses with their blinds drawn tight.

He took the winding back streets from there to a dirt car park at the edge of a little scrap of reserve, where the burnt-out red 1995 Commodore had been discovered, nine hours after Christa disappeared. No sign remained there either: no scorched earth or scraps of metal.

There were two possibilities—either Gunther Rennold had a second car waiting here, or the two had disappeared into the reserve. The police set up checkpoints at the major roads, but there were too many routes out of town, too many back roads and dirt tracks, and too few police to properly close a trap.

He idled there for a few minutes, staring into the trees like Christa might just stroll out, having lost track of time.

* * *

Back in his motel room, Lane flipped the folder open to the page of age-progression pictures. If that girl was out there, what kind of life was she living now?

She would be old enough for university. Old enough to drive, and drink, and vote, and snap up sale fares to Bali for a weekend away with the girls.

Only she wouldn't have done any of those things—if Lane stuck with the best-case scenario for a moment, and assumed her father whisked her off to some place where nobody knew them, and Christa lived an ordinary, albeit clandestine, life. Without a birth certificate she would have no driver's license. No university admission. No passport.

Lane opened his notebook to a blank page, drew a line down the center, and started a list in the left column. The characteristics he would find in a living Christa. Twenty. Brown hair. Hazel eyes. White skin. Her teeth could have changed, as could her build. He wrote nothing for those. No university education. No car. No history of overseas travel. No Medicare—although men like Gunther Rennold often avoided doctors anyway. No Austudy or Youth Allowance.

Her father was probably an expert at living outside the system—he had to be, to have fallen completely off the map after Christa disappeared, evading not just his wife and eldest daughter, but the police and Department of Community Services.

In the other column, a far harder list to write. The information that Alanna had given him that could be used to match Christa to an unidentified body. Pretty much all he had was the healed collarbone break. The file had listed a height, but he didn't write that down. Families were shockingly bad at estimating the height of their missing loved ones. There had been cases of skeletal remains going unidentified for decades, when it turned out they measured smaller than in the matching missing person's report because she always wore high heels, or he claimed he was six foot when he was actually five-seven. Children, who grew like weeds, could be even harder to get right.

It was a moot point, though, because there were no unidentified bodies that could be hers. If a child's body had been found anywhere within a thousand kilometers of Nannine it would have been national news, because the press would have pounced on the possibility that it was Evelyn McCreery. But the reserve was filled with dense scrub, the kind prone to sudden gullies and deep undergrowth. A person could walk ten meters and be lost forever in country like that. A lot of places to hide a body. Not that he was in any state to go tromping around there looking for one.

What were the actual odds that Christa was alive? Evelyn's body had never been found either, and he didn't consider that compelling evidence she was still alive. If this was a parental abduction, the odds were in Christa's favor. Children had been recovered alive and well years, even decades, after being snatched by a parent or relative.

He opened up Facebook, and the screen immediately filled with nonsense he had no interest in. Lane had ten thousand Facebook friends, and none of them real.

Lane accepted every friend request he received, and sent requests to every person the site suggested, which in turn prompted the algorithm to suggest him to more and more people. Some people also accepted anyone who asked, hungry for people to pitch their business to, too polite to click decline, or too obsessed with seeing their number of friends go up to care that it was a complete stranger boosting their score.

But the richest vein he'd found was the addicts of Facebook games. If he took fifteen seconds to send them imaginary fruit, or new lives, or whatever electronic tchotchkes they needed to progress in their favorite time suck, they were his friend for life. Few people took the time to clear him off their friends list after he stopped responding to their requests.

Very few people understood how vast the social media network's reach was. Sure, recent news stories had spooked the more alert users into unticking whatever privacy settings *Wired* or BuzzFeed told them to untick today. A small handful had even unplugged. But the majority didn't worry much. They needed Facebook to keep in touch with their friends.

"Friends of friends" sounded like an innocuous term. They were the people your friends had vouched for, so they must be trustworthy. It couldn't be that large a group. Unless one of your friends is harmless old Aunt Sally, who plays Apple Pie Mouse Puzzle Quest all day and clicks "accept" on every request she gets. Then your friends of friends could be hundreds of thousands of people. Then your friends of friends included Lane.

He logged out. His cluttered feed disappeared, replaced with an offer to create a new account. He clicked in the box labeled "first name," and typed "Christa."

His Skype burbled. He resized the window so Facebook only filled half the screen, and accepted the call.

The connection was awful. His sister looked like she was trying to talk to him from the other side of a pane of warped colonial glass, but her voice came through sharp and clear. "Hey!"

"Hey. What's up?"

"Does something need to be wrong for me to call you?"

"According to every parent I spoke to while helping you move in, yes."

"Oh my gaaahd, is that your dad?" someone asked with a thick Canadian accent. A girl walked up behind Lynnie and leaned over her shoulder. She had dark hair pulled up on top of her head, and something beside her right eye that looked like green mottling. She leaned in close and the camera sharpened for a moment, showing that it was face paint: a twisting vine with pink roses. Lane assumed she was the flatmate. She was an international student who hadn't arrived yet when Lane left Canberra, so he never got to meet her. Her background check had come up clean, though.

"How old were you when she was born, fifteen?"

"I was sixteen," Lane said. He had no idea what Lynnie had told anyone at university about her family, so he ignored the other question.

"He's my brother," Lynnie said. "Lane, Chelsea. Chelsea, Lane."

"He's cute!" Chelsea whispered.

Lynnie lifted her eyes to the ceiling. "No, you're drunk. Lane, gimme a sec." She got up, and the picture whirled as she picked up her tablet.

While she got herself sorted, he filled in the remaining boxes of the Facebook sign-up with nonsense, and one of his throwaway email addresses.

A moment later he heard her door click shut, and Lynnie reappeared sitting in her desk chair. "So that was Chelsea," she said, pressing her lips together and raising her eyebrows.

"She seems friendly," Lane said, keeping his voice neutral.

He left the profile picture on the account blank, but uploaded Christa's school picture, and tagged it.

"Ugh," Lynnie said. "I thought sharing a flat would be a breeze compared to home. But I'm going crazy. It's like living in close quarters is a skill. I have it, but Chelsea doesn't. She has no idea of all the little things you need to do to keep the machine running smoothly."

"Give it time. Moving across the world for school must be a big adjustment for her."

Lynnie sighed for a long time, to make it clear he was the worst person on the planet.

"Did you do her face paint?"

Lynnie brightened. "Yeah, it's a new design I've been working up. I do a bit most Friday nights, on Chelsea and her friends if they're going out. I charge five dollars a pop, and can do ten girls in an hour. It's so easy I feel like I'm scamming them."

"Chelsea's friends?" Lane repeated, worried. It had only been a few weeks, it wouldn't be odd if Lynnie hadn't made any friends yet, but Chelsea had been in Canberra for even less time.

"Mine too, I guess. I mean, I go out with them sometimes."

"Drinking?" Lane asked, before he could stop himself.

She shot him an unimpressed look that he supposed he deserved for lurching from worrying that she hadn't made friends, to worrying that she was partying. "It's not like my ID is fake, Lane. You remember my eighteenth birthday, right, with the balloons and the cake?"

"Is that alright with your medication?"

"That's between me and my doctor," she said sharply.

Lane held his hands up. It was hard thinking of her as an adult. He'd left home for university at the same age, and certainly hadn't tolerated any attempts by their mother to keep parenting him. But Lynnie at eighteen felt so much younger than he'd been at that age.

"If it helps, I've also booked a couple of kids' birthday parties," she said.

"You don't need to be worrying about that," he said. "Focus on your homework."

He still felt guilty that she hadn't participated in Schoolies week after she graduated. Instead she'd hung around Byron, painting the faces of drunk girls in flower crowns. He didn't want her wasting the first year of uni the same way.

He uploaded the other photo, of Alanna and Christa together. He paused, looking at Alanna's face. The last thing Alanna needed was for the Facebook algorithm to pick it up and suggest a fake account for her own missing sister as a new friend. He pulled up Alanna's account and blocked it.

"Thanks for sending me the money for the books," Lynnie said. He doubted that was the reason for the call, but it was a little more vulnerable than chitchat about her flatmate.

"You needed it," Lane said.

"Did you pick up some insurance work?"

When they lived in Byron Bay, insurance work had been the bread and butter. He wanted to work on missing persons and murder, but the payouts were few and far between. Catching insurance fakers and scammers was more reliable money, but it made him feel greasy. So many of the people he "caught" really were deserving of their money, just not according to the slippery fine print in their policies.

"Yes," he said. She had enough to worry about; she didn't need to know he'd taken the money out of his savings. "Hey, you're about to get a friend request. Can you do me a solid and accept it? The name is Christa Rennold."

He sent a request to Lynnie, and to both his other Facebook accounts.

"Okay. But if my feed gets spammed with those game notifications I'm blocking it, and you."

"It's not for that. Christa Rennold is a cold case I'm working on. I'm trying out a new technique for finding missing persons. You make a fake account for the person, and upload any pictures you have. Then Facebook will send you a notification if the person shows up in the background of other people's pictures."

Lynnie's face twisted. "That's so creepy."

"It's genius," Lane said. He messed around with the page for a moment, refreshing a few times and then accepting the handful of friend requests that had rolled in from random strangers who probably wanted to sell Christa essential oils.

He let the silence sit between them. She would talk when she was ready to tell him what the call was really about. Not rushing to fill silence was one of the most effective interrogation tools in the kit. It was a little disturbing that it also worked so well when parenting, but he wasn't going to look too closely at something that was working.

"So I got a letter," Lynnie said.

Ding, ding, ding.

"Forward it to the police," Lane said immediately. "He's not allowed to contact you." His heartbeat picked up. He hated himself for it, but he felt a spark of genuine happiness. If his father contacted Lynnie directly, then he would almost certainly be slugged with more time on his sentence.

"It's not from him," Lynnie said. "It's from the Salvation Army Family Tracing Service. Someone asked them to track me down."

"Oh." He had a passing familiarity with the tracing service. There was no way they would let someone use them to stalk a victim. Not when there was a conviction on record, anyway. "It could be one of Mum's cousins. Or someone who got an Ancestry membership for Christmas."

"Maybe." She didn't sound convinced.

"If you throw it out, that's the end of it," Lane said. "You don't need to worry about it."

"Sure," Lynnie said, not looking particularly comforted. "I'll talk to you later."

She ended the call, and Lane full-screened the Facebook page again, feeling unsettled. There was a notification.

Keva Saunders added a photo you might be in.

ELEVEN

THIS FOUNDATION MADE Mina's nose itch. She needed to get a different one, something hypoallergenic. She went so long in between wearing it that she forgot, until an hour in when the telltale itch started up again.

The counselor she'd had as a teenager had been fixated on her lack of interest in makeup. He'd seen it not as a practical choice by a girl who spent most of her time outside and alone, but as a deliberate rejection of the world and its norms.

She'd made the mistake of mentioning that the smell of it made her anxious sometimes. Her mother had always applied a little when they were going to appear at a press conference or make a public appeal, to stop the lights washing her out, and now the smell dragged up those memories. She'd thought it would make him drop it, but he'd doubled down, insisting she needed to be freed from this "phobia."

So she always wore makeup when she had a counseling appointment. That was a good half a dozen counselors ago. She'd slid from specialist to specialist. A child psychologist, for obvious reasons. Then one to help her deal with the inherent trauma of being a teenager, then a new one when her mother got sick, then a grief therapist, and now Dr. Zhang, who treated her for a grab bag of conditions with "generalized" in the name.

Dr. Zhang probably didn't care if she wore makeup or not, but he would write "patient appears well groomed" at the top of his notes, and that would set the tone for the whole session. It was only every six months—Nannine didn't have any mental health professionals and so, like for any need more complex than fuel, food, or alcohol, she had to make the three-hour drive out to Danby. For the other eight sessions they spoke over Skype, but he insisted on an in-person check-in twice a year.

She'd read once that it was common for patients to fall in love with their counselors. Dr. Zhang was about her age, good-looking, and smart and attentive. But she isn't in love with him, and she wondered if that meant he wasn't a particularly good counselor. On the other hand, she wasn't sure she'd ever been in love with anyone. Her on-and-off attempts at dating had been neither disastrous nor particularly successful—most fizzled out after a few dates or, at best, a few months. That wasn't enough time to feel safe with a person, and she couldn't imagine falling in love with someone that didn't feel safe.

He tallied the results of the questionnaire that she'd filled out, his face neutral. "You're scoring rather high on anxiety and stress."

She'd known he was going to say that. She'd filled that questionnaire out so many times, it was obvious what result each choice would get. And frankly, she didn't think it said much about her mental health if she was anxious and stressed. It had been a weird couple of weeks.

"Since it's been a few months, I'd like to do a mental state screening," he said. "I'll ask you a series of questions, and you say yes or no. Don't think about it, just go with your first instinct."

"Yeah, I know how it works."

"Okay then. Here we go, lightning round. Sleep problems?"

"No."

"Early wake-ups?"

"I'm a farmer."

He looked up, and for a moment a grin flashed over his face. "I mean earlier than usual, or before your alarm."

"No."

"Stress at work?"

"No."

"Relationship problems?"

What relationships? Her father and Alanna, she supposed. "No."

"Recent bereavement?"

"Not recent, no."

"Irritability?"

"Yes."

"Irrational fears?"

"No." All her fears were perfectly rational.

"Panic attacks?"

She sighed. "Yes."

"Compulsive behaviors?"

The swish of her pen, marking off a map. Dried grass crackling beneath her feet. The weight of a shotgun in the crook of her elbow. "No."

"Delusions?"

"No."

"Auditory hallucinations?"

She took a deep breath, uncertain about what had once been a swift no. "No?"

Dr. Zhang leaned forward, elbows on his knees. "That was a rather long pause."

"I heard something that wasn't really there. A helicopter." She rubbed a knuckle over her nose, trying to stop the itch. "But 'auditory hallucinations' is a dramatic way of putting it. That's a big deal, isn't it? Hearing things?"

"Not necessarily. When was this?"

"A few weeks ago. I was out for a walk." A lie by omission, since she was sure he would find the motives behind her walk important. But she hadn't told him eighteen months ago when she started doing it, like she hadn't told anyone. If she let him pull that thread, who knew what would unravel? She'd layered up so many missing details and half-truths that he was counseling an imaginary person, which was exhausting for her.

"How were you feeling at the time?"

"I don't know," she admitted. "I've been trying to figure that out."

"What do you mean by that?"

"Well, it wasn't out of the blue. There was an incident. A man came onto the property, uninvited, and was bitten by a snake. I had to call the Royal Flying Doctor Service. But they didn't send a helicopter, they arrived by plane."

Dr. Zhang blinked slowly behind his glasses. "Okay. You said this man came uninvited. Did you feel threatened?"

"No, he was just making a nuisance of himself."

"You've said in the past that you don't like having people come to your house. Having someone show up like that must have been stressful."

She paused, surprised. "The way he exited was a bit more stressful than his arrival."

"So when you heard the helicopter, you were feeling concern for him? Fear?"

"Well, I knew he was fine by that point. I think I felt . . ." She wished she'd brought something to occupy her hands. Just talking was too hard. She missed the counseling she'd had as a kid, which mostly involved drawing. "I don't know."

"I have a tool that could help." He riffled through his papers, and handed her a piece of cardboard printed with a brightly colored wheel, with segments divided into smaller and smaller pieces, the name of an emotion written in each one. She'd seen a similar chart before, but that was a simplified version for children, with cartoon faces showing each emotion. This one offered what looked like a thousand choices, and her eyes flitted between them. *Pressured. Resentful. Disrespected. Violated. Infuriated. Ashamed. Abandoned.* "Not a lot of positive emotions on here, are there?"

One slice was rooted in the base emotion "happy," while the others offered six different ways to feel wrong.

Dr. Zhang smiled. "I suppose it's like the fire danger levels. People joke because the second level is 'high,' but there's no real need to split up 'low' into more detail. We don't struggle as much to identify the good feelings."

"I felt bad," she said. What a childish way of putting it. She might as well draw a frowny face for him. "It was my home, and he got hurt there, and I felt bad about that. But at the same time I felt angry at him for getting hurt. He didn't belong there, and he put himself in danger."

"Do you feel like you're in danger on the property?"

"No," she said. "I belong there. He didn't."

"So when people who don't belong come into your home, where you feel safe, then it's dangerous?" He leaned in again, eyes bright, and she leaned back.

"No." She was beginning to feel nauseous. This was supposed to make her feel better, not like she was under attack. "I just know what I'm doing, what to look out for. He's some kind of city idiot, stomping around without a clue."

"Okay." She didn't get the impression he was genuinely appeased, but he didn't keep pushing that line of questioning. "Earlier, you thought it was significant that you imagined a helicopter when the ambulance that arrived was a plane. Why do you think that was?"

Because there were helicopters in the days after Evelyn went missing. Helicopters to search the property, and then those belonging to news channels, taking aerial footage. The steady *chop-chop-chop* had been the soundtrack of those early days.

"I don't know," she said, shrugging her shoulders.

* * *

Mina set out the last chair, and looked up to see Alanna watching her, her face pensive. Mina looked back at the chairs, wondering if the standard eight she had pulled from the stacks against the walls was too few.

It had seemed like a good idea, when she was setting her appointment with Dr. Zhang, to snap up an opening on the same day the support group was meeting. She tried to combine errands that took her far from home, but it was too easy to overcommit and end up exhausted or, in this case, emotionally brutalized.

"How many people are we getting these days?" she asked cautiously. She knew she was potentially opening herself up to more needling from Alanna about her patchy attendance. Somewhere along the line, showing up to the support group had turned from something she needed to something she apparently owed the group. As an old hand, she was there to help out the newcomers, the ones still feeling lost and numb in the weeks and months after filing their missing person's report. She was there so they had someone to look at, to see what kind of emotional stability they could look forward to when their own wounds were twenty years old. She bit back a laugh.

"It waxes and wanes," Alanna said, moving to the side table and ripping open a package of biscuits. "Mum's coming today. The Lu family moved to Perth; they heard from a friend that Christopher might be living there. And Maria Benson . . ." She trailed off—which, knowing Maria, could mean anything had happened to her. "We've had no new starters this year. That's good, of course. It's not like we want to grow."

Mina nodded. That meant she'd put out enough chairs, but Alanna was still staring at the circle with her mouth twisted up. "What's got you so distracted, love?"

Alanna sighed. "Your private investigator called me. About Christa."

"He's not my private investigator," Mina said.

"Oh?" Alanna rolled her eyes. "You expect me to believe he suddenly decided to look into Christa for fun? Because he's chasing the joke of a reward offered by the police? Somebody's paying his bill, and it's not me."

"What, you think I'm paying him?" Mina asked.

Alanna paused, still holding a biscuit in the air above the plate she'd been arranging them on. Her face looked pinched, and Mina realized to her horror that Alanna had thought exactly that.

"I did send him your way," Mina said. "But I haven't given him a per diem or anything."

"Right." Alanna threw the biscuit onto the plate and then upended the bag, so the rest of them tumbled out in no particular order. "I see."

"I thought that was what you wanted," Mina said. "That day I came to see you, you pretty much said—"

"Yeah, you're right." Alanna's tone suggested she thought Mina was a complete idiot.

"Has he done something?" God, what had she been thinking, winding him up and pointing him Alanna's way?

"No." Alanna leaned on the back of a chair and closed her eyes. "He thinks he's found something. He wants to meet me and Mum after the meeting."

"Holy shit," Mina said. She reached a hand out, gingerly, to pat Alanna on the shoulder, then thought better of it. "That's . . . holy shit."

"I know, right?" Alanna said. She took a deep, shuddering breath. "I doubt it's good news. What does good news even look like after fifteen years?"

The library doors opened and she stood up straight, the scared expression sliding off her face in favor of the friendly, welcoming mask of a support group leader. She strode off to welcome the new arrival, leaving Mina alone.

TWELVE

IT HAD STRETCHED Lane's patience to the limits to refrain from calling Alanna back that very same day and telling her what he'd found. He'd tried to take his time and look for more evidence to support his theory, or anything that could disprove it. It didn't help that he'd found nothing, so every day he needed to make a choice of whether to call her or keep looking. He'd decided that a week was appropriate, and forced himself to stick to it.

He was surprised when he pulled into the little car park of the Beverley McCreery Memorial Library and found Mina's ute among the parked cars. She was a three-hour drive from home. He parked next to it, in the only available space, and debated pulling away and circling the block again. His appointment with Alanna and Deirdre Rennold was still fifteen minutes away, so Mina might leave in that time and have no idea he'd been there.

He needed to have a working relationship with her if he was going to crack this case, and giving her another reason to think he was stalking her wouldn't help.

The decision was made for him when someone rapped sharply on the back windshield. He jerked his head up, and found a middle-aged woman shading her eyes so she could peer through the glass at him.

He opened his car door and slid out. "Can I help you?"

"I think that's what you're here for," she said, in a voice incongruous with the rest of her appearance. She was very tidily put together, in a pale green polo shirt with RENNOLD'S LAUNDRY SERVICE embroidered over the right breast. Her hair was braided tightly and pinned around the crown of her head in a coronet. Her green eyes were bright and sharp. Her voice, on the other hand, was a weak rasp, like her words scraped her throat as she brought them up.

"Mrs. Rennold," he said, swinging his door shut. He held out a hand. "Lane Holland; it's lovely to meet you."

"Deirdre's fine," the woman said, grasping his hand and shaking firmly. She patted his hand once with her other hand before letting go. "I'm not whatcha expected, am I?"

"I try not to have any expectations," Lane said, but it was a lie and he could tell Deirdre knew it. He had built up a mental picture of her based on what Alanna had told him, and the information in Christa's file. If he was completely honest, he'd been shocked to learn Deirdre was still alive.

"Guess Starrett forgot to mention I'm fifteen years sober," Deirdre said, rolling her eyes.

"It didn't come up, no," Lane said. He wasn't sure he believed her, but if that was the truth he was impressed. Getting off meth and staying off was no easy feat, and he'd seen plenty of people try.

"Back then they used to say 'you need to hit rock bottom,'

and there's no bottom rockier than your daughter going to foster care and never comin' home again."

Lane nodded.

"I'm sorry that I never called back. I was workin' my way up to it when Alanna called and said ya had some news."

"I understand. Alanna mentioned in her interview that you— that is, you, uh . . ." He fumbled for words that wouldn't come out as accusatory. She'd had a week to call him back. If she had really needed that much time to work up the courage to return an investigator's call, maybe the behavior Starrett had read as passive and uninterested was actually pathological avoidance.

Deirdre's mouth twisted. "I'm sure she did," she said, and turned to walk toward the entrance. Then she stopped, spun around, and stormed back to him. "You ever had a dream that someone you love is gone? That your whole life had gone to shit around you? And then you wake up and it wasn't real, they're safe and alive, and you lie there in the dark and the relief is better than fuckin' . . . anything?"

"Yes," he said softly.

"Every night of my life the opposite happens to me."

* * *

The back room of the library was set up for some kind of meeting, with a circle of chairs in the middle of the room and a picked-over tray of biscuits and coffee urn sitting on a table.

Mina was sitting on one of the chairs, her head bent close to Alanna's. She looked up, and didn't seem surprised to see him. She looked better rested than when he'd last seen her, sitting beside his hospital bed with dark smudges beneath her eyes. She was wearing a touch of makeup today, mascara and a deep red lipstick. It suited her, but there was something unsettling about the unexpected splash of color.

"I thought you were coming to the meeting, Mum," Alanna said, fixing her eyes on Lane but not addressing him. Her reaction to Lane's message had been muted, which was a more common reaction among surviving relatives than people might expect.

"Got enough meetings in my life," Deirdre said.

She went to sit in one of the chairs, but Lane had a vision of them clustered together like a miniature support group, and held up a hand. "It would be useful to have a table. Can we move?"

"Do you want me to go?" Mina asked.

"No, love, stay," Deirdre said immediately, but Alanna considered the question for a long moment.

"I don't mind if you stick around," she said finally.

Mina's smile flattened, and she shot a look at Lane. He sympathized with the awkwardness of the position Alanna had put her in—it wasn't actually a request to stay, just half-hearted permission.

They sat at the table. The three women chose seats on the other side, leaving him feeling like he was addressing a panel. He understood why Agatha Christie's investigators always chose to make these speeches with the group gathered in wingback chairs around a cozy fire. At least the news he was bringing wasn't likely to cause anyone to lunge for the fire poker.

"When I first looked over your sister's file, at Ms. McCreery's request"—he kept his gaze on Alanna and Deirdre, but out of the corner of his eye he saw Mina's lips twitch into a smile that was gone in an instant—"it surprised me that the case isn't more well known. A child disappearing from foster care is a deep black mark on the Department of Community Services."

"Yes, that's been our primary concern too," Alanna said dryly. "The department's reputation."

"Alanna," Deirdre said in a warning tone.

"No, that's fair," Lane said. "I was just trying to say that the lack of attention the case received is frustrating. I think that with more aggressive police work during the critical early days, your family could have been saved a great deal of pain. Because Christa is alive."

It was rare for this job to involve giving good news. He let himself enjoy it, as all three of them stared at him in shock and disbelief. Of course, he hadn't expected them to believe him immediately.

He opened the file and pulled out a copy he had taken of Christa's school photo. "I scanned this picture, and uploaded it to Facebook. The facial recognition algorithm—"

"The what?" Deirdre interrupted.

"Facial recognition. Facebook, Google, and other social media websites use software that creates a face template for every user. It can recognize people's faces and recommend that they be tagged when their friends or friends of friends upload pictures of them."

"Jesus Christ," Mina blurted out. "Now will you stop harassing me about getting an account?"

"Can we discuss that later?" Alanna snapped.

Mina's eyes widened, and she looked horrified. "Sorry. My mouth engaged before my brain."

"Facebook recommended a match," Lane said. "Keva Saunders. A twenty-one-year-old girl living in a remote area in the Northern Territory. Howard Springs, the same town you suspect your father was living in."

"Christa would be twenty," Deirdre interrupted. Her eyes

were glossy, and she pressed her lips together when she finished speaking to try to stop them from shaking.

"Facebook doesn't exactly demand a driver's license or birth certificate when you enter your birthday," Lane explained.

"I don't understand," Alanna said. "I've uploaded every picture of Christa I have to my Facebook account. The panopticon never found her for me."

This was the hard part. "It wouldn't have," Lane said carefully, "if Christa—or Keva, rather—has the two of you blocked."

It was more complicated than that—it had worked for Lane because he had deliberately cultivated a massive network of Facebook friends to use as a resource. Alanna had only a few hundred friends across all her social media accounts, and from what he could find Deirdre didn't have an account at all. But just as he had preemptively blocked Alanna, he expected that had been Keva's first move on signing up for the site. Assuming she knew her true history.

"Why?" Deirdre asked. "Why would she do a thing like that? We love her and she loved us."

"I can't tell you that. Maybe she's worried about Gunther being prosecuted. Kidnapping doesn't go away just because the victim turns eighteen. Maybe it's because he's had years to persuade her that he saved her—that he needed to take her for her own good. Keep in mind you got sober after Christa disappeared. What would her memories of home be like?"

Deirdre's face crumpled, and Lane hated himself. He could have soft-pedaled that more, but not much more.

"Tell me this, then," Alanna snapped, looking ready to flip the table at him. "We were both in that foster home. Why would he snatch only one of us?"

"You keep asking me questions I don't have answers to," Lane

said. "I only have a name. Maybe she can tell you. I can specu-
late, if that helps you. Maybe he had no opportunity. Maybe he
thought you would fight him harder, would turn him in at the
first opportunity. Maybe he . . ." He shrugged.

Deirdre whispered something, far too quiet for Lane to hear.
Alanna was clearly more used to making out her rustling voice,
because she hissed back, "Can we not do goddamn family therapy
with Mina and the PI right here?"

"I can go," Mina said quickly.

"I can go too," Lane said. "I'll let you take this from here." He
took a sheet of paper from the folder and slid it across the table. It
was a grainy printout of two photos he'd taken from Keva's Facebook. In the first, an adult Keva beamed, holding out a glass of
wine. She could be Alanna's twin, minus a few years. The second
was a picture of her looking about six, sitting on the knee of a man
who was a dead ringer for Alanna's father. "If you think this could
be your sister, her contact details are on the back."

Alanna pressed a fist to her mouth, sucking in a breath that
sounded like it hurt. She got up so quickly that her chair shot
backward and hit the wall with a thump, and left the room. Deirdre
jumped up and hurried after her, leaving Lane and Mina alone.

Lane looked over at Mina, trying to think of something to
say to break the tension, but she wasn't paying any attention. She
stared down at the pictures, looking from the child to the grown
woman, her face a mess of yearning and grief.

THIRTEEN

MINA WAS IN a fog as she walked out into the main library. Young Christa's face was so familiar to her, after seeing it beneath Evelyn's for so many years on posters and in the framed picture Alanna kept on her desk. Seeing the same face on an adult woman had set something aching inside her.

Lane followed on her heels, looking almost as bamboozled as she felt.

"Do you want to get a cup of coffee?" she asked on impulse. "It's a long drive back."

"I'm used to long drives," Lane said. "But I never say no to coffee."

She led him across the street to the bakery. "The meringues are good here," she said. "But avoid the vanilla slice. They buy it frozen and present it like they made it on site. The biggest scandal this town has seen since . . ."

Since DOCS lost a little girl in their care, she supposed, the words dying on her tongue. Joking felt wrong in light of the conversation they'd just walked out of.

Lane seemed to read her expression, and offered her a sympathetic smile. "I have to admit I expected that to go differently. I thought there would be happy tears. Possibly even hugs."

"Alanna's sensitive about her dad," Mina said. "She's spent a lot of years fighting people's assumption that he took Christa."

"Give her a while to feel sore about it. Soon enough she'll realize that the other option is—"

Annoyance flared in Mina. Alanna was her best friend, she didn't need to be told how to handle her. "She knows what the other option is. Don't twist this around. Her dad took her sister and not her, and neither of them ever tried to contact her. Being hurt about that isn't the same thing as wishing Christa was dead."

"Of course not." Lane reached the door first, and held it open for her.

"This is good news for you, I suppose," Mina said. She put her hand on the door too, pushing it a little so she was holding it instead. "The reward might not be newsworthy, but it's a decent pay day for only a week's work."

Lane shook his head. "I would need to take this to the police to claim the reward. If Alanna's father is still hiding out in Howard Springs, that would get him arrested. I won't pursue it until Alanna's ready."

Mina stared at him. "I thought you were in this business for the reward money."

"That doesn't mean I'll do anything for a buck. I know how complicated things can get, when it's family."

"Oh?" Mina waited for him to elaborate, but his face closed off. Evidently they'd sailed too close to personal territory, and he was here to rummage through *her* most personal business, not the other way around. She looked down, trying to push away her annoyance. If he'd opened up to her, she would probably be annoyed by that, at him treating her like a free therapist. She was still in that place where anything he did was going to irritate her.

She went to join the takeaway queue, but Lane cut to the left and pulled a chair out for her at the table in the window. She froze.

She wasn't a recluse. She went to the library. She had gone to the hospital to visit Lane. Recluses shuffled around their houses in dressing gowns and watched television from a space cleared among their hoarded possessions. She just . . . preferred not to stay anywhere longer than necessary. Get in, get out, go home.

But the pause had now gone on long enough to become awkward. Lane stared at her, and she stared at his hands, his long fingers splayed over the back of the chair.

"I'm sorry," he said. "When you asked me for coffee I thought you meant that we would sit at the same table. Did you want me to sit somewhere else?"

She'd thought that they would buy their coffees and then part ways, but that was weird, wasn't it? Nobody did that. She pasted a smile on her face and slipped into the offered seat. "Sorry, I was just off with the fairies for a moment."

"Understandable," he said. He draped his coat over the back of the other chair, and stepped away. He returned a moment later with a table number in a metal holder.

"I'm sorry that I didn't give you any warning that I was going to contact Ms. Rennold with my news," he said, sliding into his seat. "It seemed polite, given that you connected me to the case, but I don't have your email address or phone number. And of course, dropping by the house wasn't an option."

"I don't read my emails," Mina said.

"That's fair," he said.

True to her earlier observation, his rush to be as accepting as possible of every word that came out of her mouth grated on her.

"It must keep you very busy, uh . . ."

"Managing the property," she supplied. She didn't know how widely known her daily work was. It had been listed on her Wikipedia page, briefly, until the whole thing was deleted and folded into Evelyn's due to "lack of notability."

"So it does still run as a commercial farm?"

"Kind of," she said. "We're growing sorghum for stockfeed, which covers the rates and the insurance and our operations manager's salary. We grow wheat in the winter, although the crop was . . . not great this year. At least we sold the hay as fast as we could bale it. We're looking at other crops. Hemp, maybe, now that they've lifted the ridiculous ban on selling the seeds for food. But it's small potatoes."

They'd tried agistment, renting out the paddocks to other farmers, out of a hatred of waste more than any need for money. But that meant allowing too many strangers into her bubble. Suddenly the fields around her house were filled with farmhands she had had no part in vetting, and there was nothing she could do about it. As soon as the contracts expired she called time on the idea.

"If you're trying to figure out if we're still good for our half of the reward money, we are. My mother funded it from a life insurance policy, and it's in a trust."

"I know."

The server arrived with a loaded tray. She set a black coffee in front of each of them, and a small jug of milk in the center next to the dish that held the packets of sugar and fake sugar. "Anything else today?" she asked, setting down two plates with meringues shaped like caterpillars, eyes made from Smarties.

"That was all," Lane said. He pulled his meringue closer, and smacked it with his spoon so it shattered.

The server nodded and grabbed the number off the table, tucking it under her arm.

"You mentioned an operations manager?"

Mina turned her meringue so it wasn't looking at her, and broke a piece off the end. "Yep. The crops aside, there's still miles of fencing that needs to be maintained, and soil and erosion to worry about. Not to mention the red tape over our water rights; that's a full-time job in itself. He's got plenty to do." She took a deep breath. Last chance to back out. Letting someone in to poke around the property, laying herself bare to questions, really letting someone *try* to crack this thing, was messy. It was like setting out to clean out a storeroom. For eighty percent of the time it would just be a bigger wreck, and if he couldn't see it all the way through she'd be worse off than when he started. But he'd found Christa. In a week. "You can meet him if you're free to come by on Saturday."

Lane lifted an eyebrow. "I thought I wasn't welcome at the house?"

She shrugged. "I didn't say you could come to the house. Hendrik's house is miles from mine. You'll need to come in through a different gate, and that entrance won't show up on a map search." She snapped her fingers over the phone he had sitting out on the table. "I'll show you how to get there."

He unlocked the phone for her and slid it across the table. She flicked through the icons and opened up the maps app, then plugged in the GPS coordinates of the rear gate. While she worked he picked at his meringue, taking one shard at a time and popping it into his mouth. He wasn't chewing it, just letting it dissolve on his tongue. He'd eaten strangely in the hospital too, pulling his burger apart. He was a big guy, and seemed too solidly built to have food issues. But it was weird. She shot a discreet glance at his knuckles, but couldn't see any sign of scars.

Before the phone finished calculating the route, the screen lit up with a call.

The caller's picture filled the screen, a pretty girl with blond hair and a nervous smile. The caller ID read *Lynnie Holland.*

"That's my sister," he said. "She's probably looking for money." His tone was joking, but the way his mouth tightened around the words suggested it was closer to the truth than he wanted her to know.

FOURTEEN

"THIS ISN'T A great time," he said. He found a spot that was away from the noise of the road but also out of the way of the slow trickle of foot traffic, at the mouth of a little alley between the bakery and a store that seemed to sell only kaftans and alpaca wool throws. He gazed through the glass at Mina. Most people would have pulled out a phone or tablet by now, but she just stared down at the tabletop, lost in thought. Worried about Alanna, he realized, his throat squeezing. He'd come into that meeting so sure he was going to be leaving a feted hero. "Can I call you back?"

"Sure," his sister whispered, her voice raw.

If his throat had felt tight before, it now felt like someone had both hands wrapped around it. "What's happened?"

"It's alright. It's a bad time."

"No, talk to me."

He prayed that she was crying because she'd failed a test. Or some boy had dumped her. Or she was coming out as gay. Anything, anything except the subject he knew she was going to bring up.

"I called the tracing service. The person looking for me was Aunt Beth."

"Beth? We don't have an Aunt Beth."

"Apparently we have a whole heap of family. Paternal family."

Oh, right. Shit. Their father, according to his story anyway, had cut his whole family off when he ran out on them at fifteen. The social worker had mentioned them as a possibility when Lane came back to live with Lynnie, but he wouldn't hear of it. He didn't want her anywhere near whatever cesspool their father had crawled out of.

Mina had glanced up, her eyebrows furrowing as she caught the look on his face. He spun around to face the road.

"Well what does this Aunt Beth want?"

"Apparently she caught religion a couple of years back, and her church is all about forgiveness. Frankly it sounds like the congregation is in some shitty competition. The worse the stuff you sweep under the rug, the holier you are."

"She can forgive whoever she wants," Lane said. "But the only things she can forgive him for are things he did to her. She can't forgive what he did to me. She can't forgive what he did to you. That's our decision."

"Well, that's why she wanted to contact me," Lynnie said.

"Oh, fuck her." Rage rose inside him. "That's third-party contact. Have you spoken to the police? He can't send people to harass you."

"She swears up and down he never asked her. She says she prayed on it and decided to reach out, for my sake."

"Bullshit."

She laughed in a damp little gasp. "Yes." She sounded calmer now that she was getting properly mad. Maybe it wasn't healthy, but anger was often the guide rope that let her pull out of hysteria.

"Well, lose her number, then. Do you want to change yours? I'll call the phone company tomorrow and get them to send you a new SIM."

"There's more." She paused for a long time. Long enough that he would have assumed the call disconnected, if he couldn't hear her heavy breathing. "She told me that she wrote a letter to the parole board to tell them he would have family support in the event of his release. She wanted me to write one too."

Lane took in a deep breath, trying to hold on to his own fragile calm. "I didn't get notice of a parole hearing."

"I'm an adult, Lane. They contacted me."

"You didn't tell me."

"This is me telling you."

Lane pressed a hand to his face. God, he hoped Mina wasn't still watching. "When?"

She paused. "Eighteenth of April."

The week after Evelyn and Mina's birthday, he noted. Today was the seventh of March, so that still gave him six weeks to do what he could. But it was so much sooner than he'd ever expected.

"Can I call you back?"

"I—"

He disconnected the call. He couldn't let her hear him, so hanging up was the lesser of two evils. He stepped into the alley properly and screamed. There was a little patch of red pebbles, and a shrubby tree in a treated-pine planter. He kicked at the pebbles, sending them pinging all over the brick wall of the bakery. He shouted every expletive he knew, a looping chain of *fuck-shit-cocksucking-cunt*. He kicked the planter, sending white-hot pain shooting up his leg. The still-healing snakebite burned like a double-headed match had been put out on his skin, and that brought

127

him back to himself. He collapsed on the ground, sending up a cloud of red dust when his butt hit the pebbles, and put his head on his knees. He breathed in, and out, his throat shredded.

He called Lynnie back. "I'll come to Canberra. I can be there by dinner."

"What are you going to do here except stink up my room?" she asked. Her voice was thick with anger at him for hanging up. "If I want to talk to someone, I'll use one of the cards the floor manager keeps giving me for the campus counseling center. Or I'll go to the women's group circle time. Shave my head and cry it out."

"Look, Lynnie"—he lifted his head, and stared at the brick wall of the bakery—"you have to believe I have a plan, okay? Everything will be fine."

FIFTEEN

MyMurder Forums

Subforum: Evie McCreery

Subject: WAKE: How much does Liam McCreery know?

User VolcanicJudo: I've noticed that whichever camp you fall into—
Beverley killed Evie, or Mina killed Evie—the assumption is that
Beverley knew. If Mina killed her (accidentally or deliberately out
of jealousy, w/e, not gonna rehash it all here), then most people
think Beverley helped cover it up. But what about Liam? He
usually gets ignored because he was in Sydney at the time. Do
you think he knows the whole truth, or did Beverley take the
secret to her grave?

User MODERATOR: Bunch of replies deleted. Read the rule post,
please. Just calling a poster crazy for subscribing to a particular
theory doesn't add any value. If you have counterevidence post
it, otherwise use your scroll button.

User Comet: It's hard to draw any conclusions about Liam. He just kind of sits there in interviews, I'd be shocked if he's said more than ten words on camera.

User Santoro: He has to know. You can keep up an act for an interview, or even in front of friends for a few hours or days, but when you live with a person day in day out you learn who they are damn quick. You can't keep a secret from your spouse for that long.

* * *

"Mr. Holland." Remy, Lynnie's victim support officer, sounded wary when he picked up the phone. "What can I do for you today?"

"I'd like to submit a letter to the parole board, opposing the release of Lane Holland Senior," Lane said.

"And are you on the victims register?"

"Yes, I—" Lane paused. No, he wasn't. He'd been registered as the guardian of the victim, but Lynnie had turned eighteen. She didn't have a guardian anymore. "No. But I understand that the family are submitting letters in support, so I would like to submit one in protest."

"The Parole Authority can only accept submissions from the victim." Remy sounded sympathetic, at least.

"Look, you can't ask her to do that," Lane said. "Lynnie's just started uni. She should be writing essays, not a victim impact statement. She shouldn't have to dredge that poison up again; she barely sleeps as it is. Please, let me write it."

"Mr. Holland, I understand where you're coming from. Now, I would be violating the victim's right to privacy if I discussed the specifics of this case with you. Speaking purely in general terms, the law is very clear that when the victim is alive, an adult, and capable of speaking for themselves, no one else can speak for them. You can help her to write her statement, but you need to discuss that with her, not me."

It was ridiculous. Apparently if Lane wanted to write to the defense lawyer offering his love and support, then that could be considered as evidence, but not the opposite.

"It's not like he never committed a crime against me," Lane said. "Doesn't that count for anything?"

"Yes. If you were a victim of the crimes he was convicted for, you can be added to the victims register and make a submission," Remy said.

Lane knew he was being ridiculous. He knew the law back to front, he knew what he could do here and what he couldn't. But it just seemed so monumentally unreasonable that he couldn't step in and take this off Lynnie's shoulders that he had to try. Maybe there was some loophole he didn't know about. Surely Remy, who worked in the system every day, knew the ins and outs well enough to offer one. "Not this crime, no."

"I'm sorry." Remy did sound genuinely regretful. "If you want to press charges on any other matter, I can connect you to some resources to help."

"Thanks, but no thanks," Lane said. He didn't have any time to waste on long shots.

"Can I offer you some advice, Mr. Holland?"

Please. "Yes," Lane said.

"Barring the absolute worst offenders ruled never to be released, and those are so rare I'd bet you can name all of them . . ."

"I can," Lane admitted.

Remy chuckled. "Outside those extreme cases, prison sentences are supposed to end. You are a young man, and you will live to see him released, one way or another. Parole could be the best outcome. Parolees are monitored, and their movement is restricted."

"Not monitored closely enough," Lane said. If his father was released he would need to be watched twenty-four hours a day. Occasional check-ins for a piss test weren't going to keep anyone safe.

"Still, it's more than he would have to deal with if he served his entire sentence. Then he would be free to return to the community. No transition. No threat of being returned to prison if he's caught violating parole conditions."

"Is that what they're thinking?" Lane asked. "They're going to release him, aren't they?"

"I don't have any special insight into what the parole board might decide," Remy said, and it sounded like bullshit to Lane.

* * *

The two-hour drive back to Nannine gave Lane a solid chunk of time to shift gears. He couldn't let go of the hopeless feeling, but by the time he was halfway, tearing through country roads with AC/DC pumping out of his speakers, he had managed to fold it up and pack it away somewhere inside.

Priority one was to sort out somewhere to stay. On his first night in the town—which felt like a lifetime ago now—he'd slept in his car on the side of the road, and events had prevented him from needing to search further. He'd since tried searching for options online, but a promising website for a motel turned out not to have been updated after it shuttered in 2013, and Airbnb had no listings within a hundred-kilometer radius.

The Commercial Hotel was a brick, two-story pub, the entrance shaded by a wraparound balcony with a bullnose awning.

The windows on the second floor—the ones facing the street, at least—were boarded up.

He was sure that the sign had once read BEER, FOOD, ACCOMMODATION, but now the last word had been blocked out with blue duct tape. That didn't bode well for him.

The inside was a nineteenth-century rabbit warren. The door opened onto a flight of carpeted stairs that were blocked off with a chain across the banister. Down the hall he could see a dining room with chairs stacked against the wall and an unplugged *Big Buck Hunter* arcade game.

The bar was in a small room to the left, and a man stood behind the counter, unstacking glasses from a drying rack. He was maybe a few years older than Lane, with thick black hair and shoulders like a lumberjack. "Eh, hello!" he said, like Lane's arrival was exciting news. "Welcome to the Neeny. I'm Neil."

"The sign says 'The Commercial?'" Lane asked.

"So does the liquor license. But most just call it the Nannine pub, or the Neeny when that's too long. What can I get you?"

"I was hoping to rent a room."

Neil laughed. "Mate, I was in high school when we shut the top floor."

"But the rooms are still up there, right?" Surely the pub had closed the rooms due to lack of interest, not lack of need for the income.

"Yeah, but there's no housekeeper anymore. And it's full of broken pokie machines."

"I'm not looking for a turndown service. If there's still a bed up there and the door locks, I'll take it."

Neil's friendliness faded a smidgen. "No can do. Truth is, back when we rented it out my uncle was living here in the pub. Now everyone goes home at night. If I rented you the room, I'd either have to give you free access to the pub at night, or lock the door at the top of the stairs. And then you'd be stuffed if there was a fire."

Lane jiggled his car key absently in his pocket. "Is there anywhere around that still rents rooms?"

"Sergeant Starrett will generally turn a blind eye to campers on the old showground for a week or two."

A flicker of uneasiness ran through him at that idea. "There must be some option in town. A caravan park? Somebody with a granny flat out the back?"

Neil looked thoughtful, resting his forearms on the bar top and looking past Lane, at the door. "How long were you fixing on staying?"

Lane shrugged. "How long is a piece of string? Hopefully not more than a couple of weeks."

"Even if I were interested in renting out the room—which I'm not—the cheapest I could go would be sixty a night," Neil mused. "Now, young Cherise has a little flat on the books, going for an absolute song. But it would be a minimum of three months."

"Do you know how much she's asking?"

"One twenty, plus a four-week bond."

"One twenty a week?" Lane repeated. "Is it haunted?"

"Probably!" Neil said. "The whole town is. But no, that's just what rent goes for around here. Where have you come from, mate, Sydney or Melbourne?"

"Byron Bay," Lane said.

"Ah. Housing's pretty cheap around here. It's the only thing that is, because it doesn't have to be brought in on the back of a truck. I mean, if you're really looking to stay long term, there's a three beddy over the road that'll only set you back eighty thousand."

"Do you have every listing in town memorized?" Lane wondered if the Cherise he'd mentioned earlier was his wife, or girlfriend, or if maybe Neil just wanted her to be.

"Just those two. Now, are you drinking?"

Lane ordered a beer. He grabbed a coaster and a keno pencil, and did the math while he sipped it. Three months was a huge commitment, especially when he needed to go back to Canberra by the eighteenth of April. On the other hand, if he rented somewhere night by night—and no matter what Neil said, if he knew how much he would charge that meant he was at least considering it—after three weeks he would pay more than if he'd just taken the flat. If he solved the case faster than that he'd have wasted some money, but by that point he'd be two million dollars richer, so what would he care?

He didn't need to decide right away. Another day or two in the car wouldn't kill him while he mulled it over.

"I don't suppose you've got any work going?" Lane asked. That would solve a lot of problems for him. A bit of income, an excuse to talk to the customers without raising any eyebrows, and maybe even access to the records from the night Evelyn disappeared. The closest thing to a census of who passed through Nannine that weekend would be found in the credit card receipts of the pub. "I worked in a pub for a few years in uni."

"I can barely afford meself," Neil said. "'Sides, if we could afford more staff, there's a wait list. But if you're interested in farm work I can give you some names."

Lane made a noncommittal noise. Hoeing weeds and mending fences would certainly give him plenty of time to mull over the facts of the case, but it wouldn't leave him much freedom to chase up leads.

"Is your uncle still in town?" he asked. If he'd lived in the pub years ago, then he'd probably been behind the bar the night it happened.

"Sorta. He's buried in the cemetery over on Church Street."

"Oh, I'm sorry."

"Nah, s'alright. He had a good innings."

Lane stared into his beer. That was the problem with a case this old: key witnesses started to die or drift away. He could have done so much more if he'd come sooner.

"Have you lived in Nannine long?"

"All my life. Both my parents were born here too."

"Do you know the McCreery family, then?"

Neil stopped polishing the glass he was holding. "Yes."

That was a marked change in manner. "You must have lived in town when Evelyn McCreery went missing."

"I must've done, yes." Neil put the glass down and folded his arms.

"I don't suppose you know if the room upstairs was rented out that night?" It was a long shot, but if Neil had known he would take over the pub one day, he might have taken an interest early on.

"No."

"No you don't know, or no it wasn't?" Lane's pulse quickened.

"No, I'm not going to answer questions about Evelyn Mc-Creery."

"Why's that?"

"Because I do know the McCreerys, and I see what happens to them every time there's some new attempt to pick it over. Like that fucking TV special. It's all hope and light at first, then at best nothing comes of it and they're left with all their scabs ripped open and jack shit to show for it."

Lane held up his hands, surprised by the force of Neil's reaction. "Mina McCreery knows I'm here. She's okay with me poking around."

"Bullshit," Neil said cheerfully, and turned back to the rack of glasses.

* * *

Lane had hoped to eat lunch at the pub, but he had a longstanding rule about never ordering food from someone he'd recently pissed off. It was a good rule and he was happy with it.

The takeaway had not changed a single tile since the late nineties. It was a long narrow shop, with chairs against one wall and a long counter slicing the room in two. The menu was written in chalk above the grill and bank of fryers. Pizza, scallops, chips, burger with the lot, fifty cents extra for a fried egg.

The hot grease smelled like home.

He ordered an egg-and-bacon roll from the redheaded teenage boy behind the till, and took a seat. He examined the posters taped to the counter while he waited—a meat raffle at the pub, some garage sales, an upcoming show by a Barkandji artist at the church.

The bell above the door jangled, and a young woman entered, maybe nineteen or twenty. She had dark hair pulled up in a chignon, and warm brown skin complemented by a mauve lipstick. To his complete lack of surprise, her white polo shirt was embroidered with the name B. EVANS REAL ESTATE.

"Hey Marc," she said to the boy behind the counter. He lifted a hand in response.

"Cherise?" Lane asked. He'd imagined someone ten or twenty years older, but it made a certain sense.

"Sorry, have we met?" she asked.

"No. I'm Lane Holland. I don't suppose Neil suggested you come find me in here?"

"Of course not." She laughed and touched her hair, a self-soothing gesture that meant she was probably lying. Or just nervous because a stranger was being weird to her in public.

Still, as a coincidence, it was a stretch.

"Why, are you looking for a real estate agent?"

"I heard you have a little place for rent in town," he said. "But I'm only here for a short time. Do you think the landlord would be willing to go week to week?"

Her cheeks hollowed like she was biting the inside. "The minimum lease is already very generous. I doubt the owner would budge on this."

He was pretty sure what she was leaving unsaid was that week-to-week tenants weren't the sort the owner wanted. Transients and blow-ins, people who might trash the flat and disappear.

"No worries," he said, turning back to the posters.

To his surprise, after placing her order, she took the seat closest to him. "What brings you to town, Mr. Holland?"

"I'm a private investigator," he said.

Marc turned their way. "You're here about the McCreery case, then."

He sounded friendly, but Lane noticed that Cherise's smile faded a little.

"Were either of you around when it happened?"

Marc shook his head with a laugh, but Cherise made a "sort of" gesture with her hand. "My mother was pregnant with me. But my dad worked up at the McCreery farm."

"Really?" Lane leaned forward.

"He was home with my mother the whole night."

"I wasn't implying anything," he said quickly. "It's just interesting to meet someone so close to the case."

"Hardly." She pushed a strand of hair out of her face, trying to tuck it into her fancy updo but succeeding only in getting it to stick for a moment before it flopped back to brush her cheek. "There isn't anyone in this town who isn't related to someone who worked at McCreery's. They were Nannine's biggest employer, until they closed it down a few years after . . . you know."

"That must have been rough on your dad, with a toddler at home."

She nodded slightly, catching her bottom lip between her teeth. "I was lucky, Mum had the real estate, which took a bit longer to dry up."

"I hope you have a plan B, dude," Marc said, putting Lane's lunch on the counter. "You're never seeing that McCreery reward money."

"You don't think it can be solved?"

"Oh, I'm sure it can be solved. But no one came into that house. Solving it means proving that one of the McCreerys killed her. And they're not going to reward you for that."

"Don't, Marc," Cherise said with a sigh. She shot Lane an apologetic smile.

"Don't what? The police have thrown everything at trying to find this 'intruder,' while giving the family a complete pass. Imagine if it had been one of your mob who went missing. You think there'd have been a million-dollar reward?"

"Of course not," she said.

"Or even someone from my broke-ass family. The cops'd've turned our house upside down, searched all our cars, and probably arrested half of us on unrelated bullshit."

Lane scooped up his egg-and-bacon roll. He could point out that the police had searched the McCreery house, and all the vehicles on the property, as was standard procedure. They'd even insisted on digging up a fresh concrete building foundation, despite Liam McCreery's protests that it had been laid weeks before Evelyn disappeared. Nothing was found.

SIXTEEN

LANE PARKED HIS car under a tree at the showground. There were going to be parts of the day when the inside became dangerously hot, even in the shade, and he was probably going to need to wait until long after sunset before he would feel safe locking himself inside to sleep. But that was fine. He didn't plan to spend any of his time lounging around at "home."

He was going to need access to the shower block, though. The town didn't have a gym or a public pool, and he definitely couldn't just douse himself in body spray and hope for the best.

The shower block was the same as every public amenity in the country—brick walls, a corrugated-iron roof and a hand-width gap between the two that meant there were almost certainly possums up in the rafters. There was a galvanized-steel gate at the entrance, held closed with a chain and a combination padlock.

He examined the lock. Most padlocks could simply be busted open using a trick he'd learned with a pair of wrenches. He had a whole set in the car, in case he ran into trouble on a remote highway or back road. But he was camping illegally, and sooner or later the local cops would be by to move him along. The odds of him getting in actual trouble were low, but went way up if he went around smashing locks open. If he could get it open without damaging it, then he had plausible deniability. Maybe someone just forgot to lock it. And if it wasn't locked when he found it, how was he to know he wasn't supposed to be in there? It was a public bathroom, wasn't it?

The lock was old, which was good. Most locks had security flaws, and the older it was, the better the odds someone had already figured them out. He turned it over to find where the brand name and model number were stamped, and plugged them into YouTube. The top result was a video of someone picking it using seven different methods. Lane was going to chew through his data plan in a heartbeat at this rate, but that was a problem for tomorrow. He had an answer within three minutes.

On the first dial he carefully tested each number. As promised, on the correct number the dial moved minutely further than it had for the other nine. The first digit in the combination was 1. On a hunch, he tested 9 as the second digit. People frequently used significant years in their life when they had to pick a four-digit combination. As expected, 9 had the extra wiggle room. That meant the third digit was probably between 5 and 9, as people born in the 1940s were increasingly rare. He spun the dial to 9, planning to work his way down, but to his surprise he felt the extra wiggle. He tested 8 and 7 just to be sure he wasn't imagining it, and then locked it in. He spun the fourth dial to 9, again intending to go in descending order. The lock popped open.

1999.

Creepy.

His flip-flops echoed on the concrete floor. He moved cautiously, checking the shadowed corners for unwelcome shower buddies. He doubted he would survive two snakebites within a few weeks of each other.

The water was cold, but the day was hot enough it didn't matter. He tipped his head back and let the water hit his face. He lathered himself up with the three-in-one soap he always kept in the car—body wash, shampoo, and conditioner.

It felt good to wash away the funk of too long spent in the car, but something new settled in its place. The prickling weight of the too-familiar. This felt like a routine he'd left behind a long time ago, and part of him expected to walk out the door with his wash kit under his arm and find the show setup in full swing outside, like the past nineteen years were just some flight of his imagination.

* * *

On the first proper day of the 1999 Nannine Show, Lane woke up beside a fire, one tenacious log still smouldering and pouring out smoke that the wind had redirected straight into his face. He groaned and rolled over, pulling the flap of his swag over his head.

He pressed a button on his watch to light up the numbers. Eight a.m.: way later than he'd expected. Usually on show days the clatter of setup woke him, but he'd somehow slept through it.

"Lane!" someone bellowed. "Wakey wakey, hands off snakey." That was the preferred greeting of Billy, who was the show employee in charge of wrangling the others.

"I'm awake," Lane shouted back. He didn't sit up.

"Is yer dad about?" Billy asked. His shadow fell over Lane.

Ah. So Billy was checking in, trying to catch them out. "Nah. Mum gave him the boot in Danby," Lane said. He held Billy's gaze steadily, because people could tell you were bullshitting if you looked away when you did it. "After . . . you know." Lane himself didn't actually know, but it made him feel grown up to pretend he knew exactly what had happened the night his father was tossed out of the show.

"Ah," Billy said. "Don't you worry about that stuff, lad. It's all bullshit anyway."

Lane sat up. The showground was eerily quiet, and he couldn't see anyone pottering around, making breakfast or packing up their campsites for the day. "Where is everyone?"

"Out front of the office. Word is a kid's gone missing on one of the farms. The SES are looking for volunteers to help search."

"Oh," Lane said, blinking. The smoke had shifted again, and he shuffled across to get it out of his face. "Is that going to mess us up?"

"Eh, I wouldn't worry. Sometimes kids wander off. She'll turn up soon enough. But we might find the morning a bit slow. A lot of people are headed that way instead."

"Okay." That wasn't good. They needed a solid day. Not just enough cash to get to the next town, but further.

"Anyway, when you meet up with yer dad again, tell him I haven't forgotten about the money. Even if he's leaving the outfit, I'll see him, and he'd better have it."

* * *

Lane rolled up his swag and threw it in the luggage compartment under the van. Show nights were his favorite, when the camp was set up and he could sleep outside, like the whole world was his backyard. He didn't like to go into the van on those mornings. Going straight from the swag to their stall space and then back to his swag let him stretch out the feeling of having all the space he could ever want.

But Mum needed to know about the search.

He hoped his dad was still sleeping, maybe passed out enjoying his "weekend off." He peered into the bedroom, and saw Mum asleep facedown, her short blond hair the only thing visible between the pillows and the blanket. The space beside her was empty.

He looked around the rest of the van, like he might have just not noticed his dad in there when he opened the door. There was barely any space for a person to be hiding. The kitchen table, benches, and most of the floor were stacked with cardboard boxes that needed to be moved out to the stall site before the show opened.

The sink was empty. Mum had washed the plates, forks, and cups from dinner and stacked them in the dish rack, but there were no added breakfast dishes or coffee cups. His father couldn't function without a cup of coffee right after waking up.

Hmm. Maybe he'd got sick of hiding, of lurking in the van out of sight of the show manager who had banned him, and cleared out early.

As if in answer to his hopes, he heard the rattle of the luggage compartment opening and closing again, and a moment later his father strolled in the door. Lane scanned his face quickly, then relaxed. His father's posture was loose, and he had a grin on his face that went all the way to his eyes. Maybe the time off was agreeing with him.

"Morning!" his father said, heading straight for the sink. He washed his hands, and then turned to the cupboard to pull out the instant coffee.

"Did you go out?" Lane asked, trying to sound interested, not accusatory.

"Just the pub, just the pub."

Lane glanced out the van window. The pub was right by the showground, over the fence and through a patch of trees. It made sense that his father might have thought he could risk it. Slip out under cover of dark, slip back in when everyone was busy setting up for the day. But it frustrated Lane; he and his mother needed the two days of work, and his father was willing to risk getting them kicked out for a beer.

"How did preview night go?" his father asked.

"We've had better," Lane said. They'd done quite well, actually. The attractions that catered to men had done more trade, since the camp was full of workers from the nearby farms, though there had been enough families to make the night worth his while. But he and Mum had agreed to make out to his father that the weekend was a bust, so they could shave some cash off and hide it.

"Oh yeah? Give any prizes away?"

"Just one. I had a set of twins come through, and it was obvious they weighed the same, so I threw the second guess. Cute kid, Shirley Temple type. I figured her carrying around a prize would be good advertising, but not much came of it." Another lie—the girl's over-the-top glee had made three other families stop to see, and then have a go.

His father stopped stirring his coffee and turned around, still smiling. Lane shrank back instinctively, but his father just clapped a hand on his shoulder. "You're a good lad, Chip."

"Thanks." Lane paused, wondering if he should tell his father about Billy and the search, but decided against. He would try to get Mum alone later, and they could discuss how it would affect their plans, then tell his father. And like Billy had said, she'd probably turn up before they opened.

His father picked up his coffee cup and sauntered toward the bedroom. As he passed, Lane saw something gleam on his shoulder. A hair, far too long to be Mum's. On impulse, Lane reached out and plucked it off, grabbing the dangling end so his fingers wouldn't brush his father's shirt. Mum had already decided they were leaving; there was no sense in piling on one more hurt.

* * *

Lane propped his car door open and slung his damp towel over it to dry. He leaned against the bonnet, the warm metal comfortable after his cold shower.

The showground looked smaller now that it was empty. That seemed wrong—surely the crush of tents and vans and jostling crowds should have made the space feel smaller, not bigger. But when the show was set up, Lane had to wind back and forth through laneways and side alleys to get anywhere, and the way it was sectioned into zones for different activities made it feel like a miniature city.

Some things about the town had obviously changed, the ebb and flow of nearly twenty years. But other things were simply different from his recollection—bigger, or smaller, or laid out differently. Human memory was infamously flawed. Which was why he tried not to think about that hair, or what color it had been.

SEVENTEEN

THE ROUTE THE app calculated to the second gate was completely different from the way he came that first time. It was roughly the same distance from the town, but the two gates were so far apart that it directed him onto a different road, an old two-lane highway that curved back and forth. He passed no other cars.

His phone beeped to indicate he had arrived at his destination. Lane had expected something nondescript, but he found a double-width gate and an enormous truck-turning circle, although one that was clearly no longer used, judging by the weeds poking up through the gravel. The posts for a sign were still bolted to the fence, but the sign itself was long gone.

As Lane slowed down, a man stepped out of the shadow of a gum tree with a trunk so thick it must have predated the property. He was about a foot shorter than Lane, with narrow shoulders and blond hair turning white. He unlatched the gate and swung it open, then indicated for Lane to drive through.

Lane scanned the driveway, expecting to see a ute or maybe a red postie bike parked somewhere, but there were no other vehicles. He rolled down his window. "Can I give you a lift to the house, mate?"

The man pulled the gate closed behind him. "The walk doesn't bother me," he said. There were still traces of Eastern Europe in his voice, but layered over with enough broad Australian twang to suggest he'd been in the country for decades. Lane guessed that he was in his late fifties to midsixties, but he'd never been good at pegging the age of country men. Some of them got to sixty and simply stopped aging. Others hit forty and immediately circled the drain.

"I wouldn't mind you showing me the way," Lane admitted. It wasn't manly to ask for directions, but he was beginning to understand just how massive the property was. The last time he'd been here had been disastrous enough to require a hospital admission, so he wasn't willing to take any chances. He could admit that to himself, just not anyone else.

"It's not possible to get lost," the man said, but he strolled around the car and slipped in the passenger door. "Straight ahead. The road doesn't branch before you reach the house."

"Are you Hendrik Tamm?" Lane asked. "The operations manager?"

"Yah." Hendrik nodded. "And you're Lane Holland, the private investigator. Wilhelmina—Miss McCreery—has told me about your work."

"How long have you worked for the McCreerys?" Lane asked.

"Thirty years," Hendrik said. He lifted a hand and pointed through the windshield, to where a green corrugated-iron roof had just popped above the rise of the next hill.

"So you were here when . . ."

"When the other Miss McCreery went missing, yes sir. Though not *here*. I was in Adelaide to meet a cousin who had just arrived in the country. Flew out on the Friday morning." Hendrik stared down at the bush hat in his lap. "That's been a heavy weight to carry. I should have canceled my trip when Mr. McCreery had to go away the same weekend. My wife was alone in our house that night, and Mrs. McCreery all by herself in the big house with two little girls. It wasn't right."

The Tamm house, while not the "big house," was still bigger than any home Lane had ever lived in.

"There are millions of households out there with no men living in them, Mr. Tamm. Very few of them experience abductions."

Statistically speaking, women and children were most at risk when the man of the house was at home. But that didn't seem like a helpful thing to say to Tamm.

"Right," Hendrik said, looking more annoyed than comforted by Lane's words. "Thank you for the lift. Miss McCreery is waiting for you; I'd best get on with my work."

Mina was indeed waiting for him, leaning against the white wooden fence that bordered the front garden, chatting to an older woman who was hacking at her shrubs with an enormous pair of shears. She parted ways with the woman by leaning over the fence and hugging her, so the woman had to hold the shears awkwardly to one side and hug her with the other arm.

There was a clear performance to the way she had asked him to come in the back way, to sending Hendrik out to manage the gate when he could easily do that himself. She wanted to show him that there were people on the property with her, people who would hear a shout.

He wondered if she carried the other half of Hendrik's guilt: anger at being left undefended that night.

"As you can see," she said, "it's really not possible to show you the entire property—short of a helicopter, and we're just not the sort of beef baron family that can afford one of those."

"That's alright," he joked. "I've seen it by air once already."

She didn't even offer him a pity laugh. "Didn't exactly have a window seat, though, did you?"

She walked around the side of the yard, and reached for something leaning against the fence. He took an instinctive step back when she lifted the same shotgun he'd seen on the day of his snakebite and cradled it in the crook of her elbow. "I'm happy to show you whatever you think you need to see. Outside."

She started walking down the dirt road and he followed, falling into step on the opposite side of her from the gun, so the barrel was pointed well away from him. It wasn't that he'd never dealt with firearms. He'd clocked up plenty of hours on the firing range, before his abrupt exit from recruit training. But he wasn't used to the person he was questioning having one while he didn't. And there was something unsettling about her casual manner with it. Like it was just a toy, like the one he used to shoot rubber ducks in the sideshow alley.

As they walked along the track, Lane become aware of a rhythmic thumping somewhere to the left. Sticks snapped and leaves rustled. Mina seemed unconcerned by it, but stopped walking and turned in that direction. After a few moments a large dog burst out of the scrub, bearing a stick almost as large as himself.

"What have you found?" Mina said, her voice low and affectionate.

The dog tossed his head, bringing the stick over to the road. One end of it dragged on the ground.

Mina put a hand on the dog's head and scratched behind his ears. "This is Echo," she said.

This could be another warning, Lane supposed. A friendly reminder that in addition to the Tamms there was also a dog. He thought of the joke that had sprung to her mouth so easily the first day he'd come here. Her trained attack snake. Had she been alluding to real skills found in Echo? It didn't seem likely, in such a bundle of friendly energy. But Lane had seen dogs turn on a dime. Bundles of joy and love turned into vicious, single-minded machines when the object of their affection was threatened.

He'd never much cared for dogs.

The course of the walking took them up a gently sloping hill, and gradually the trees fell away to reveal an open grassy area. At the crest of the hill stood an old steel windmill. It was still today, and possibly had not turned for many years.

Mina came to a stop at the bottom of the windmill, and stared up. It was maybe thirty feet high, with access to the top granted by an old welded ladder about half the width of a man.

"Are you afraid of heights?" she asked.

"No," Lane said, wondering if he was about to regret that assurance.

"Just stuffed animals, then?" Mina asked, a smile quirking at the edges of her lips.

Lane stifled a grimace. Most people thought he was joking, and he understood why. That put him in a double bind—those people often thought it would be a hilarious next step in a shared joke to surprise him with them. The people who didn't think he was joking were even worse, because then they knew an embarrassing thing about him, and it was a rare human being who could avoid pressing at a weak point they had found.

"It's sturdier than it looks," Mina said. "You can't see the entire property from the top, but it's damn close. As a first step it's not a bad option. Unless you have a better idea for where we could start?"

Lane's preferred place to start was an interview with any surviving witnesses. He was pretty sure that the only way to get that was to climb the damn ladder.

"Lead the way," he said.

She slotted the gun onto two hooks that had been welded onto the side of the tower as a gun rack and then headed for the ladder, grabbing a rung about half a foot above her head.

"Are you just going to leave that there?" Lane asked.

"What exactly are you worried about?" she asked. "Do you think someone's going to stroll up and take it?"

"It doesn't seem safe," he said.

"Look, I get it," she said. "You read in the rule book that I'm supposed to keep it in a locked safe, unloaded, with the ammunition on the moon. But that shit just isn't practical for farm life. You've seen that things can get hairy out here. It needs to be at hand, and loaded. And yeah, I need to put it down occasionally. Once we're done here I'll take it home, unload it, and lock it in a safe. If that's not good enough, if me hauling it around is making you uncomfortable, you're welcome to leave the same way you came in."

"No, it's fine," Lane said. "Of course you need to make some compromises."

She stared down at him, like she didn't believe he was really going to drop it, then gave a brisk nod. She climbed at a rapid pace, practically leaping from one rung to the next with the grace that came from doing something your whole life.

He climbed with considerably less ease. The creak every time his foot hit one of the metal rungs ran through his entire body. He was glad Mina was above him on the ladder and not below. If he panicked and needed to go back down, at least he wouldn't suffer the indignity of asking her to make room for him to flee.

After a few minutes Mina's feet disappeared from above him, as she pulled herself up onto the platform.

She walked to the edge and placed both hands on the railing, seeming oblivious to the way the tower swayed ever so slightly in the wind. Lane was not oblivious.

"We keep it maintained to use as a fire tower," Mina said.

He sagged at the knees as he made his way toward her, squatting against the surprisingly strong wind.

"You don't need to do that," Mina said. "You can just walk around. Look." She skipped backward a few steps, and splayed her hands out in a jazzy gesture.

"That wind is stronger than I expected," he explained.

"Have you ever in your entire life been knocked over by the wind while walking?" she asked. "It's not any more likely up here."

She'd chosen the location well if her intent was to have the upper hand in the conversation.

Lane made it to the railing, and for a moment was struck silent by the view laid out before them. He'd seen aerial photographs of the property, but something constrained by the edges of a computer screen couldn't do it justice. The sheer scale was breathtaking.

He could see the two houses, that green corrugated-iron roof of the Tamm house, and the matching roof of the big house. He could see the dam, round and bronze like a fresh-minted penny dropped in the landscape. The gardens curled around the big house like a pair of green hands cupping it. Beyond that the landscape stretched forever, in a hundred shades of brown. Paddocks that would once have supported thousands of sheep stood empty, dried out, and forgotten.

Mina followed his gaze out to the horizon, and it was clear she could tell what he was thinking. "People think we're crazy, like we're leaving millions of dollars on the table by refusing to run a full-scale operation. But we weren't even the first farm in the area to destock. We were barely turning a profit, and it was taking more than my dad had to give."

"But the other farms that destocked, most of them would have sold the land, or at least let some paddocks go when they weren't using them, right?" Lane was cobbling this together from what he'd gleaned from his research, playing at understanding the industry.

She looked at him like she saw right through it, which was fair. "Yeah, that's true. In another life, we would have sold most of the property off. Let some multinational scoop it up and roll it into a factory farm. Just kept the house, maybe a couple of hectares to run as a homestead. Which is essentially what we've done. Our farm is the forty acres around the house, and the remainder just happens to have our name on it."

Lane didn't comment that "the remainder" was in the order of thousands of acres. "Why, though? You must see why people find it odd."

She leaned on the railing, staring out at the endless plain of dirt and scrub. "We got as far as a buyer coming out to look, once. He was very excited and had all sorts of grand plans. Massive extra dams, more buildings, an efficient new internal road layout."

It took Lane a moment to understand. The unimaginable

horror of selling up, knowing that one day soon they might get the call that a bulldozer crew had turned up Evelyn's remains.

Or, worse, never getting the call, and wondering if she'd been ground to dust by oblivious machinery. The idea was too awful to hold in his mind, and he pushed it away.

His face must have been an open book, though, because she nodded. "Regardless of what my mother thought, the most likely explanation is that she's buried out here somewhere." She lifted both her hands, palms to the sky, to indicate the endless stretch of the property. "Until we find her, selling is out of the question."

"What do you mean, 'what my mother thought'?"

Her face shuttered instantly. It seemed the subject of Beverley was a no-go, if he wanted to keep the conversation flowing.

"What about you, though?" he asked instead. "Have you ever thought about moving away, starting again somewhere else?"

"It's not like I've never left. I tried it twice. The second time even went reasonably well. I managed to stay away long enough to get my degree."

Assuming that she went directly to uni from high school, that would have been about seven years ago. Beverley had been dead for five years, so it was likely that any plans she had after graduating were derailed by her mother's diagnosis. Not that he could ask to confirm.

"The first time didn't go so well?"

"How is any of this relevant? We're talking about things that happened years after Evelyn disappeared."

She always used those words. He'd noted it with interest when reading the few interviews she'd given: "Evelyn disappeared," not "Evelyn was abducted." It was a neutral way of saying it, shying away from a painful expression. But it also made it sound like she saw it as something Evelyn had done.

"I'm just interested."

"It's not that interesting. I didn't come home because I couldn't hack the real world, or whatever it is you think . . ."

"I don't think that," he said quickly. "Look, you're far from the first person to come home because shit hit the fan."

"Okay, no," she said. "Yes, I came home when Mum got sick. But I would have come home anyway. The funny thing is, no one would think that was weird if it wasn't for the Evelyn thing. Our family has worked this land for generations. Did you know that Nannine—the town, that is—doesn't have a natural water supply?"

"No?" Lane wasn't clear on the relevance.

"It's too far from the Darling River or the lakes; it runs entirely on man-made dams and bores. When it was being built, water was brought into the town on a dray. That dray was driven by a McCreery."

He didn't have any response to that, except to boggle that the town had ever been built at all. He couldn't relate to feeling so tied to a place. Especially in a country like Australia. What was a few hundred years, compared to tens of thousands?

"If anything, leaving would be letting the past hang over me, not staying."

He let silence fall, waiting to see if she would add anything more. Instead she seemed happy to let it linger.

"This view really is incredible," he said finally.

"My dad used to tease us," she said, "that when the show was in town you could see the lights from this tower." She looked away, lost in memory for a moment.

Lane laughed. "Surely not." Nannine Showground was an hour's drive away. The view was good, but not that good.

"Yeah, he was just being a dad. We believed him, and were so disappointed every year when he wouldn't let us climb up here to see." She sucked her bottom lip between her teeth and shook her head.

Lane rested one hand lightly on the railing, but he couldn't bring himself to lean his weight on it the way she did. The imp of the perverse whispered to him that he could just swing his leg over it and jump off, if he wanted to. "You went to the show on the night Evelyn disappeared," he said.

She side-eyed him. "You know that we did. You know the timeline."

"Is everything I've read true?" he asked.

That got him a small smile. "Of course not," she said.

"Then I'd like to hear the story from you," he said.

She was quiet for a moment. Contemplative.

Down below Echo whuffed, a deep throaty sound, and took off. He was a streak of yellow against the green. Chasing rabbits, probably.

"So," he prompted, "you went to the show on the Friday night."

"Yes. We dropped our father off in town around five, and he drove on to Sydney. I think he was sitting on some livestock industry committee. Nothing came of it, so it's hard to remember. Obviously he turned around and came home first thing Saturday morning." Her face grew serious as she dipped deeper into memory. "Since we were in town already, Mum took Evelyn and me to the show. On the first night they have cheaper entry, kind of a preview. Most of the rides weren't running, and of course none of the concerts were on. It didn't really matter; we were going to go to the show again in the morning. We were supposed to compete in Miss Junior

Showgirl." She picked at the railing, breaking away specks of rust. "Mum had to sign a form for us to be in the competition, so we went over to the show office in one of those . . . those temporary on-site things. What are they called?"

"Demountables," Lane said.

"Right, yes. We went to the show office in a demountable"— she enunciated the word—"and dropped off our forms. Mum took a picture of us holding them up, so she could bore our grandparents with it at Christmas. You've seen that picture, right?"

Lane nodded. "Did she take any others?"

Mina shrugged. "Probably; she was always snapping away with the damn thing. I felt like I spent my whole life posing. She used to say, *If you're not in the picture, people will wonder if you were even there!*"

"It would really help me to see any pictures you have of that day, or the days leading up to it."

"I'm sure you've seen them all," she said. "Mum gave a lot of them to the news, and whatever she didn't give out or sell ended up in her book."

"The pictures that would be most useful to me would have been difficult to sell. Publishers would have passed on pictures with a lot of people in the background. Getting releases from everyone captured isn't worth the effort."

"Oh." She stared down at Echo and chewed on her bottom lip.

After a few moments of awkward silence, Lane said, "Don't worry about it." So much of her life had been splashed on the news, or detailed breathlessly in Beverley McCreery's memoir. If she couldn't stand to give up the few private pictures she had left, he understood. "What happened after you left the show office?"

The tension leaked out of her shoulders. For a moment

she flashed him a look that was both relieved and grateful, but she looked back down immediately, like she hadn't wanted him to see it. "Evelyn suggested stopping at one of the food trucks to get a hot dog or some hot chips. Mum had a go at her, asked her what she was doing participating in Miss Junior Showgirl if she was going to eat like that. But we got the hot dogs anyway. Then we stopped by the sideshow alley. One of the game booths was up and running, the guess-your-weight booth. Mum took us over there, because she was like that."

Lane looked away at the mention of the guess-your-weight booth, worried that his face might give something away. At the time it hadn't been a significant enough encounter to stick in his mind. He hadn't even known they went to the show until it was mentioned in the papers a few days after his family left Nannine. He didn't realize he had met them until he read Beverley's book, and found himself there on the page.

Mina took in a deep breath and let it out, shaking slightly. "I suppose that was convenient, really. When it came time for Mum to fill out the missing person's report, we knew Evelyn's exact height, because the Showgirl forms had required it. And we knew her weight, because the boy running the game booth put it on the scales after his guess to see if she won a prize."

"I'm sorry—can you just explain the guess-your-weight booth to me?" Lane was intimately aware of how it worked, but didn't want to get into the habit of letting her skip things because he was already familiar with the story.

"It's just one of those tacky show things," Mina said. "The carnie—"

"Show worker," Lane interrupted reflexively.

"What?"

"Carnies are American. They like to be called show workers or showmen here."

"Um, okay." Mina gave him an odd look. "The showman running it looks you up and down and tries to guess your weight. If he's within a kilo, he's the winner and he keeps your money. If he's off, you're the winner and you get one of those . . ." She trailed off and looked at him.

"A stuffed animal," Lane said with a small laugh. "It's alright, you can say the words. I'm not going to jump off the tower in terror."

"I just wanted to be sure." The smile she gave him suggested that she had been under no illusion that he needed her to be that careful.

"He was right on for me, but Evelyn won a prize. I think it's possible he just threw it, because we weighed exactly the same at the time. We were nine-year-old girls; there's not that much room for variation."

"Were there many people around?"

Mina frowned. Lane looked out to the horizon again, pretending to be fascinated by the silhouette of a hawk wheeling above the trees, and let the silence build on her.

"Not as many as there would have been on Saturday, but a few. The weight guesser's booth didn't have anyone waiting, but there was a handful of people at the stall next door—mums and kids lined up for the face painter. I wanted to go there next, but Mum was worried about me ending up with a rash on my face."

"Did your mother speak to anyone while she was waiting?"

"Not really." Her voice grew harder and angrier. "I mean, there was this one guy who was all, 'Hey, how much for the little girl?' and my mum was like, 'Oh, I can give you a discount if you buy them both,' and then he was all, 'I only want the blond, the brunette is too hideous.' You know, boring grown-up small talk. I wasn't really listening."

Lane brought his gaze back to Mina's face. Lynnie could be like that. Whenever a subject was painful for her, she would crack a joke so dark it stopped Lane's breath in his throat. "Is me asking about the show upsetting you?"

"Everybody obsesses over the show. I know what people think."

Lane hesitated. "What's that?"

She laughed, small and bitter. "Because we were signed up for the Miss Junior Showgirl competition, people think that's why she disappeared. The people who think she did disappear, that is. They think that because my mother took us there that night, that was as good as chumming the water for pedophiles. It doesn't matter that they've seen pictures of us that day. Doesn't matter that they know we went in goddamn jeans and T-shirts. They hear those three words and their minds go straight to *Toddlers & Tiaras*. Big hair and makeup and children pursing their lips for god knows who in the audience."

"I think the word 'showgirl' makes people think of that movie. Their minds jump straight to sequins and nipple tassels."

That got a real laugh from her, and she crossed her arms over her chest as if protecting herself from the exposure she was imagining. "You can tell who's never lived in a country town by what they think. Every girl in my class was planning to be in the competition that year. We were bored. There were a handful of TV channels. We could barely get internet out here and what we did get was slower than the mail. So yeah, we signed up for Miss Junior Showgirl. We put on a Sunday school dress and we answered some interview questions. Those of us who could play an instrument would play instruments and those of us who couldn't would pretend we could dance. Then we would get a photocopied certificate of participation to pin on our noticeboards and we'd go see who won the jam prize at the CWA tent."

She looked away with a small smile on her face, lost in nostalgia for a day that had never come.

"Do you remember anyone approaching you, while you were walking around? Maybe someone offered you something, or asked for your help?"

He breathed in, his hands flexing on the railing. He needed to pull back, because he was getting dangerously close to trying to goad her into giving the answer he wanted to hear: *Why yes, we were approached by a showie who seemed a little too interested in us. He looked a lot like an older version of you, come to think of it.* Witnesses had shockingly fallible memories, and with the right emotional state and the wrong question they could remember things that had never happened.

She looked frustrated. "There were a lot of people there, most of them strangers. I don't remember anyone who seemed significant."

"Did you go anywhere, after leaving the show?" He restrained himself from adding, *Like the pub?*

She shook her head. "We went straight home, and then Mum packed us off to bed. Next thing I knew it was morning, and . . ." She raised her fists and mimed an explosion.

* * *

Getting down was far worse than climbing up. Mina slid off the platform and back down the ladder with ease, but Lane was as ungainly as a walrus sliding off a rock into the sea. Sticking his foot down into the void felt impossibly wrong, and he was glad that Mina couldn't see him digging his fingertips into the metal platform as he kicked around in search of the top rung.

On the ground, Echo greeted Mina as if he'd been waiting years for her to return from a war. Mina returned the enthusiasm, petting between his ears and down his thick-furred neck.

"Is Echo a trained sheep dog?" Lane asked. Even seeing him roll on the ground begging for belly rubs, the possibility that he was a barely restrained weapon worried him.

"He's a cadaver dog," Mina said.

EIGHTEEN

"WHAT?" LANE SAID.

"He's a cadaver dog," Mina repeated. "Well, half of one. Very few of them make it all the way through the program. That's how I got him. He found out he's a crappy cadaver dog but he's a wonderful Echo."

"That's amazing," Lane said. He didn't sound like he was amazed. The few people whom she'd told about Echo's origins had found it creepy, but she'd expected Lane to be interested. This was his wheelhouse.

Why should she care? She wasn't fishing for Lane's approval, showing off her private cadaver dog and her private crime scene.

Mina slapped her thigh to get Echo's attention, and started walking. Lane followed.

"I loved the dogs," she said.

They came to a small clearing beside the road, and she walked over to a fallen spotted gum tree. The tree had split in some wild storm long before she was born, the larger trunk shearing off. The second, smaller trunk held gamely on, thin and twisted but still

165

tapping into enough nutrients and water to bloom each year. It was showing signs of stress now, with a ruff of green epicormic shoots growing near the roots. They did that when the top of the tree might die, as a way of holding on.

The bark was smooth, worn smoother after years of use as a bench. She sat down, and Echo scrambled up into his usual spot beside her.

Lane stood in front of her with his hands in his pockets, obviously waiting for an invitation to sit. She didn't offer.

"I didn't understand," she said. "Not properly. I was nine. They were dogs. I thought they were cool. You could call it a bright point. Not that there really were any. Maybe a comfort is a better word. I just know that the day the dogs came, Mrs. Tamm let me sit in her garden at the table with a cup of tea and I saw the handlers as they passed through the area behind their house."

She peeled a long piece of bark away, then turned it over and over in her hands. "The dogs seemed so happy," she said. "So full of purpose. I was obsessed. I read all of the books on them I could get from the local library system, and watched every documentary I could find."

Lane nodded. "I went through something similar," he said. "A fascination."

Not like hers. God, she hated it when people who couldn't possibly understand her lived experience tried to pretend they did. But what she said was, "I imagine you must have, to be in this line of work now."

She left a space for him to tell her more, maybe share a little of what had prompted him to study criminology. Why he had pursued this path, instead of being sworn in as a police officer.

But he smiled blandly back at her, until she gave up and continued her story.

"When I was fourteen, we got an offer from a TV network to do a special. It had been five years, and Mum had just put out a new edition of the book, so interest in the case was high. They wanted to conduct a new search of the property, using dogs hired from a private company. I understood what they were really doing, by that point. That they wanted to search for Evelyn's body." She snapped the piece of bark in half and let both halves fall to the ground.

Lane watched her without any sign of confusion, meaning that he had seen the video. Wonderful. He'd probably seen all the videos, and read the books, and listened to the recording of her mother phoning the police as calmly as if she were ordering a pizza.

Why was this suddenly news to her? He was an investigator on the case; of course he'd researched it.

"Mum wasn't particularly keen."

"Really?"

She understood why that startled him. Her mother wasn't usually one to turn down media attention. "Mum didn't"—she paused, surprised at how difficult she was finding it to tell this story—"Mum didn't like stories that focused on the possibility that she's buried on the property somewhere. She was worried that if people assumed that was true, it would close them off to other possibilities. She wanted people to be looking for her, not thinking of her as dead."

She glanced up at him, looking for any hints of skepticism. The conspiracy theorists had a different interpretation of why her mother tried to steer interviews away from that topic. If Mina got even a whiff that Lane gave those theories credence, she would make sure he left screaming. He just looked back at her with a small furrow of concern between his eyebrows, and she relaxed a fraction.

"But I begged her to accept. I was excited. I was just as in love with the dogs as I had been before. I knew all about how they worked, so I would know what to look for this time."

She closed her eyes, remembering the energy of that day. Back then, everything new they tried had a glow of possibility. Even her mother had perked up as the cameras and microphones started to arrive, and she'd buzzed around with mugs of tea and tray after tray of scones.

"Are you okay?" he asked.

"Yeah." She kicked her heels against the tree trunk hard to blow the fog out of her head. "Have you seen the old footage of that live broadcast of Geraldo Rivera opening a safe that belonged to Al Capone?" she asked.

Lane shook his head. "Organized crime has never been my particular interest."

"Not enough little girls involved?"

"Ha ha."

She'd expected him to push back harder. Maybe she'd been trying to wind him up a little. But he was getting what he wanted, and any taunt or challenge she threw at him was going to roll straight off his back. She sighed, and picked up her story again.

"It damn near ended his career. Massive fanfare, weeks of promotion talking the whole thing up while live on air, and then the big moment comes. The safe crackers finished their work, it swings open and the thing's empty. It's the cautionary tale the television producers whisper to each other. In our case, the network had already started promoting their Evelyn special. The amazing access they were being given. The chance to investigate afresh. Then the cameras started rolling, and disaster struck. They found nothing."

Echo's ears picked up, and he slid forward, rear still planted on the spot beside her but his front paws sinking into the layers of leaf litter and bark so he could nose through the debris, hunting whatever small creature's movements had caught his attention. She laid a hand on his back, causing a small, startled yip.

"One wonderful thing I learned about working dogs is that they love to please their handlers. I noticed that one of the handlers wasn't following the correct protocol. He was taking the same dog to the same patch again and again and again. Dogs aren't stupid. Even an impeccably trained dog knows if his handler keeps returning him to the same spot he wants an alert. He was trying to get the dog to show a false positive so the network would have something to run in their promos. I was fourteen years old, I wasn't trained in media management. All I really saw was a man being unfair to his dog. So I stepped in. And that's the footage that the network ran in their promos."

Lane looked sympathetic, but also confused. "Why are you telling me this?"

"Because you must be wondering about it," she said. "And because I don't get many opportunities to tell my side of that story. Mum's publishing company sent a flak—a PR person—to try to smooth it over, and he insisted that any attempt to address it would just prolong the story and make things worse. In a way it was good. Mum never forced me to do another media appearance."

More than that. After that episode, her father woke up from the fog he'd slipped into, and started to side with her when she wanted to withdraw, instead of assuming her mother knew best.

She might even have had a few years of peace, if the world hadn't found a new way to intrude.

"But the theory that I killed her started to take off," she said. "Or that our mother killed her, and I helped hide the body. There was a scattering of them before, of course, but they were hardly a majority."

"They're far from the majority now," Lane said.

"It depends where you're taking a sample from." Mina looked away from him, scanning the little clearing. "Anyway, I suppose the point of bringing you here was because if you've done any research on the case you know that this is where her body is buried." She smiled. "At least according to the internet."

NINETEEN

THEY WALKED THE property until the sky started to glow pink. They were within sight of the house—the main house—by that point, but Lane didn't mention it. She had made it clear that he wouldn't be welcome inside.

Mina stopped, and pointed to an empty field beside them. "That's where the slab was."

She led him over, ducking to slip between the gap of a two-strand wire fence. Lane hooked his finger under the top wire and lifted it up to give her more clearance, which she ignored.

There was nothing but empty dirt where the slab had been.

"Why didn't your father continue with the build?" Lane asked, nudging a clump of sod over with his toe.

"Would you have?" Mina asked. "If Dad did any construction or landscaping work for the rest of that year, the masses would have been howling for it to be torn down and checked. Besides"—she stared across the empty lot, seeing something he couldn't—"the slab was because Dad was planning to build a third house on the property."

"Why?"

"For guests, he said. But I think he'd hoped . . ." She sighed. "He hoped that the two of us would grow up and get married, and one of us would move into the Tamm house once Hendrik moved on, and the other would take this one. And we'd all run the farm together."

He tried to see what he was sure she could: a twin of the Tamm house, a little garden, blond children playing on a swing. "Tell me about your sister," he said.

She shot him a sideways look. "I've done nothing but all day. My throat's sore with it."

"You've talked about her disappearance all day. I'd like to hear about her."

He knew instantly that it was a mistake. She just stared at him. Her throat bobbed as she swallowed, and then she turned and walked toward the house.

He caught up to her. "I'm sorry," he said, expecting to be told to piss off again. She didn't answer, but didn't object to him walking beside her.

* * *

At the house Mina stalled, her hands in her pockets. Lane wondered if she was torn between the polite thing, which was inviting him into the house for a cup of tea, and the sensible thing, which was to bid him farewell.

Whatever was going on in her head, she settled on the latter. "I can give you a lift back to your car, if you'd like."

"Thanks," he said.

As they crossed the yard a shiver went through him, and he

kept his eyes glued to the ground, looking for the snake. "Did you ever see that brown again?"

"No," she said. "You must have scared it off."

"The poor thing," he said, rolling his eyes.

She smiled back at him. She paused for a moment, under the apple tree by the door. The apples were all gone, as was the netting, so the season must have ended. Summer had slipped by so fast. She reached up into a thick patch of leaves and twisted, pulling out an apple. "Missed one," she said. She turned and held it out to him. "Want it? I have literally a hundred; I'll be eating apple butter until Judgment Day."

The apple was warm in his hands, like it had been baked in an oven. But the flesh wouldn't be soft, and he knew from bitter experience that trying to bite down through the skin would put too much strain on his jaw. "Thank you," he said, slipping it into his pocket.

"It's nothing." She sighed, and slapped the trunk of the tree. "Though if we don't get decent rain this winter I doubt it will survive next summer. I can't justify watering it."

He didn't know what to say to that. The apple felt heavier in his pocket, possibly the last one the tree would ever produce.

She stopped at the back of the ute and, to his relief, clipped the gun into a holder bolted to the floor of the tray. He climbed into the passenger seat and rubbed his knuckles across his jaw, which had started to ache, like just imagining eating the apple had been enough.

The shadows had grown deep. The ute easily chewed up the miles between the two houses, so much faster than it would have been to walk it. The ground that flashed past his window was uneven, loaded with trip hazards in the form of loose rocks, abandoned branches, irregular ditches, and gullies. Not to mention the snakes.

It would have been tough going at dusk, and even tougher in the full dark of a late night. But it would be doable with any decent torch, like the heavy rubber-coated one that he had camped with as a teenager.

As Mina pulled away he turned and stared up the long dark road, trying to see if any light from the house was visible. It wasn't.

* * *

Lane unlocked his car, and when the light inside came on a woman behind him called out, "Good night, Mr. Holland."

Mrs. Tamm sat on a swing on her veranda, a bowl in her lap.

"Actually," he said, "do you mind if I talk to you for a moment?"

Mrs. Tamm gave a little hum. She pulled a pea pod out of the bowl and snapped it with a practiced gesture, running her thumb inside to pop the peas out. Lane had no idea people still did that when peas were ninety-nine cents a kilo frozen. "I've given plenty of interviews, and never had anything useful to say."

"Still," he said, "there are only two people alive who were here that night."

"Two or three," she said.

"You mean Evelyn?" After so much time speaking to Mina, who always seemed so sure her sister was dead, it was jarring to remember that her being alive was a real possibility. A horrifying possibility, but a real one. Christa was alive, after all, although she'd been abducted under very different circumstances.

Mrs. Tamm laughed. "I mean whoever took her. Perhaps he's dead, but probably not."

"Well, I would love to interview him. And maybe something you know could get me closer to that."

"Okay." She put the bowl aside and folded her hands in her lap. "Come, sit."

The swing screeched beneath him as he sat down. He pulled out his phone. "Is it alright if I record?"

"That's fine. What would you like to know?"

"You were the only other adult on the property that night, weren't you? Can you tell me what you remember?"

"I don't remember very much. I dropped Beverley and the girls off at the house, and came back here—"

"You drove them home from the show?" he interjected.

"Mm-hmm. They rode with Mr. McCreery as far as Nannine, and hitched back with me."

"How did they seem with each other?"

"They were tired. Evelyn was keyed up, in that way some kids get when they need sleep badly. I don't think Mina said a single word the whole ride, and she fell asleep so soundly her Ma couldn't wake her up when we arrived. She had to carry her in."

That wasn't how Mina had told it. She'd said, *Mum packed us off to bed.* Could she have slept through the entire bedtime routine, and turned her assumptions about what had happened into a memory?

"What about Beverley and Evelyn, what did they talk about?" He thought about Mina's description of her mother picking at Evelyn's food choices. Had that been the seeds of a full-blown fight between the two, while Mina slept unaware?

"It was twenty years ago. That car ride wasn't as memorable as the next morning, my mind hasn't clung on to it in the same way," Mrs. Tamm said. "I think they talked about Mr. McCreery, what he might bring back from Sydney." She paused. "Beverley seemed very irritated by that, that Evelyn was acting spoiled."

"Did you go into the house?"

Mrs. Tamm pursed her lips. "I was her employee. The dynamic wasn't exactly *Upstairs, Downstairs*, but we weren't friends either. I never went into the house."

"Even after driving them more than an hour home?"

"A drive I was going to take anyway, in a car the McCreerys paid for. If you're probing for some secret animosity between me and Beverley, you'll be disappointed."

"So if you didn't go into the house, did you come straight back here? Did you notice anything out of the ordinary?"

"Yes, and no. Everything was as it always was. I went straight to bed; I was tired from helping put up the marquee for the Country Women's Association. I slept like a log."

"You didn't hear or see anything at all?"

"No." Mrs. Tamm pursed her lips, staring out across her garden at the trees that blocked the view of the main house.

Lane waited, and after a moment she gave a little shrug. "I might have woken up at one point. Back then we had an old German shepherd named Lars. He got up in the middle of the night, started running up and down the hallway, dancing around the way he did when Hendrik got home from work of an evening. I thought for a moment maybe he had come home, and I went into the kitchen in case he wanted the kettle on, but there was no one there. Lars was an old dog; he'd started to get soft in the head. We had to put him down about six months later."

"Did you go outside?"

She waved him off. "I waited a minute or two, feeling silly, and then went back to bed. I was out like a light again in ten seconds, and slept through to seven, when Beverley knocked on the door to see if Evelyn had come to my house."

"Did Evelyn do that often?"

"No, never. I think by that point Beverley had started grasping at straws in her search. She was on the veranda wringing her hands and talking about how she'd checked the house and the garden and the dam and the tree house. But she was so odd about it. Calm, but not an in-control calm. She seemed . . . uninterested. Not like she was missing a child, but bored, as if one of the girls had lost a doll and she was going through the motions of looking for it. I remember thinking that I was more worked up than she was. I had to take over, and suggested that we each take one of the farm bikes and check the fields."

That wasn't an uncommon reaction, to be eerily calm in the face of a devastating trauma. Too many people had lived their lives shunned by communities that expected the sort of dramatic shouting and garment-rending they'd seen on television and the big screen. The actual numbness that suffused people was read as coldness. Guilt.

"Where was Mina?"

Mrs. Tamm frowned. "You know, I don't know? Back at the house, I suppose. Poor mite. Once the police arrived, I brought her back here, and we made lemonade scones. I meant to make them for the cake stall at the show, so I had all of the ingredients. I never went, obviously."

The police must have taken an hour to arrive, assuming they left immediately. A long time for Mina to be left alone, under the circumstances. "Who called the police? You or Beverley?"

He knew, of course. He'd found a recording of the call online, had listened to it over and over like it was his new favorite song. Beverley seemed nonchalant, repeating the address and that her daughter was missing, with the same calm that Mrs. Tamm had described.

"Beverley," she said. "But I made her call. She wanted to check the back fields first; she thought for sure Evelyn would turn up and then she'd be embarrassed when the police arrived. I insisted that she call first, and when Evelyn turned up dispatch could radio the police and tell them to turn back. But Evelyn didn't turn up. And . . ." Her fingers clutched the bowl. "It was so obvious how green poor Starrett was. She had this checklist, you know? For a missing girl Evelyn's age."

Lane nodded. He was familiar with it.

"Most of the questions were just ridiculous for a place like this, like: How many of her friends live within walking distance? How many relatives? She just kept working through it. Could she have walked to her school? The school was an hour's drive away. That's about when reality crashed in on poor Beverley, and she started screaming that someone had to have taken her. So I decided to scoot Mina back here."

"How did Mina seem, while you had her here?"

"What do you mean? Do you want to know if she was acting like she murdered her sister?"

"If she was, that would be helpful to know," Lane said, trying to hold back his irritation. He wanted to know if Mina had seen something she wasn't telling. He wanted to know if it was possible the answer has been locked up in Mina the whole time. But ultimately, he just wanted to hear about Mina and how she'd spent that morning. Something about the casual, almost surprised way Mrs. Tamm had mentioned forgetting about her had got under his skin.

"She seemed like a confused, frightened nine-year-old girl," Mrs. Tamm said. "Although there was one weird thing."

"What's that?"

"She wanted to know if she would still get to go to the show."

TWENTY

THE DAY LANE received his check for solving the Peterson case, he also received a phone call from a Department of Community Services social worker. The two events weren't connected, but it felt like they were. He'd done something great and been rewarded for it, and so the universe needed to sweep his legs out from under him and then kick him in the stomach.

The poor social worker had to break the news to him that his mother had been killed. A drunk driver took a corner too fast and wiped her out walking home from a night shift stocking shelves at the supermarket. His twelve-year-old sister was at home asleep, being watched over by a teenage neighbor. The social worker, trying to get his sister delivered into the hands of a guardian before she woke up, got in touch before the police. She was so mortified that he ended up soothing her, while the news of his mother's death buzzed in the back of his head like a song playing in another room.

He drove through the night to make it to Byron Bay before sunrise, and was sitting in the kitchenette waiting for Lynnie when she crept out of her bedroom in *Hannah Montana* pajamas.

He didn't expect her to recognize him, and was braced for a fearful reaction. He'd been the sun and moon to her until she was three, then had all but disappeared. Until she was six, he'd dropped in for the occasional afternoon visit, when he was on uni holiday and their father was occupied elsewhere. From six onward, he was gone entirely. He didn't even know if they still had pictures of him.

Instead, she'd lit up and threw herself at him, locking her arms around his neck like she did as a toddler. "Lane! Oh my god!" Then her excitement ebbed, and she threw a glance toward their mother's bedroom door. "Does Mum know you're here?"

He'd had hours behind the wheel of the car to practice his speech, but his jaw locked up. "Let me take you out for breakfast. Where has the best pancakes?"

"We don't really go out for breakfast . . ." she said. "The chippy does a decent egg-and-bacon roll, though."

He bought them both an almost-decent egg-and-bacon roll, took her to the beach, and then finally worked up the courage to drop the hammer.

She'd looked stunned for a moment, then confused. "She's supposed to volunteer at the tuckshop today," she said. "Are you going to do it?"

"Mate," Lane said gently. "You're not going to school today. I'm sure the tuckshop will be handled."

"Oh," she said in a small voice, and then she cried. Lane had hugged her awkwardly.

The early hours of grief made it difficult to figure out what was important and what wasn't. Coming to terms with the way the plans for the day had changed could loom as large as the questions of how the rest of your life would work, all jumbled in with the primal roar of "No!"

If nine-year-old Mina wanted to know if they were still going to the show, that didn't sound cold to Lane at all.

* * *

Lane pressed his thumb to the space between his eyebrows. The pressure was back, but that didn't automatically mean a headache would follow. If things at the edge of his vision started to glow white, that was the signal to pack it in and crawl into bed, or a world of pain would descend. Just the pressure meant he could keep working for a while. He really needed to make a follow-up appointment with a doctor, but he didn't want to take up a precious slot in the twice-monthly clinic that the Royal Flying Doctor Service ran. It could wait until the next time he had reason to go to Danby.

What he really needed was to stop pretending he was still a teenager who could camp in the back of his car for weeks on end. He resolved to call Cherise at the real estate as soon as the office opened in the morning. Things were coming together here, and he could afford to settle in a bit.

He kicked his boots off and climbed into the back, into bed, propping his pillow against the driver's seat so he could sit up and work.

With Mina and Mrs. Tamm interviewed, there was only one witness left—and she couldn't speak. But Beverley McCreery had spoken more than anyone.

He pulled the book out from a pocket of his duffel bag. It was his second copy. The first he'd bought for a dollar at the Violet Town op shop. It was just another stop on their endless loop through the basin, and his stomach couldn't handle cutting the boredom with another pie or bottle of Coke. He'd read it in the car, keeping the book in his lap so that no one would see the cover. He wasn't ready to admit to himself why he knew it would cause trouble, but he kept it hidden anyway. He'd placed his other hand on the edge of Lynnie's car seat, her tiny hand wrapped around his thumb. Sitting like that made the top of his shoulder ache, but it kept her calm, which kept their father calm.

That copy had fallen apart somewhere near Wagga, three or four loops later. This copy he'd bought brand-new at a signing event in Danby. It was the fifth-anniversary reissue, with three new chapters and twenty-five never-before-seen pictures. The event was small, with only a handful of people showing up on a rainy day.

He'd absolutely buzzed with questions as he read the book. He'd filled the margins of the old copy, the lost one, with penciled queries and comments. But then he got to the front of the line. Beverley McCreery had looked up at him and smiled with lips painted brick red, but she'd looked so tired around the eyes. So human. All at once, it was like Lane forgot how to speak English. Her smile faltered, and she glanced to the side at a young woman glued to her phone—not Mina, probably a handler or assistant from the publisher.

"Sorry," Lane said, and pushed his book across the table to her.

"Who should I make this out to?" Beverley asked. She had the same accent as his mother, a Victorian twang, but ironed out. She might have had elocution lessons, or a strict parent or grandparent trying to hold on to the family's British accent. That's where his mother's voice had come from, his ten-pound-tourist grandmother who'd somehow expected Australia to be London with sunshine.

"Lane," he said, and then spelled it to be safe. He wondered if she'd asked his name the first time they met. Not many people did.

"Is it a gift?" she asked. "Want me to write anything special for her?"

"Uh, no." The polite smile was starting to make his jaw ache. He didn't know if it would do that for the rest of his life, or if he was straining some hairline crack that still hadn't knit together. "Lane is me."

"Oh." Her face fell in embarrassment. Or dismay. "Are you here on your own?"

She glanced down the line, and he took her meaning. Most of the people clutching books in the line behind him were women her own age, and a handful of men. The only other teenage boys had obviously been dragged along, and stood staring into space with their hands jammed in their pockets.

"I'm in my first year at university—criminology," he said quickly. "I'm hoping to join the AFP one day."

"Ah." She opened his book to the title page, and wrote something with a practiced hand. "My daughter is interested in studying that," she said, and then her smile flattened into a grimace, like she regretted saying it.

"It's a great course. If she's got any questions I'd be happy to—"

"My daughter has no shortage of acquaintances in law enforcement," she snapped, and then softened it with, "Anyway she's just started high school. I'm sure next week she'll want to be an astronaut."

* * *

Huh. Lane had forgotten that. Mina definitely never got a degree in criminology, unless she'd done so very quietly. Had Beverley mistaken her daughter's preoccupation with detector dogs for a general interest in becoming a cop? Or had Mina's research on the dogs been part of a wider interest? Lane didn't see how he could ask, not without explaining how he knew about it in the first place, and opening himself up to way more questions than he could comfortably answer about just how long he had been following this case, and why.

He cracked the book open. The copy was a mess, flagged with so many neon-colored tabs that he'd had to give up on putting them down the side, and had started a layer across the top.

He easily found the page where she described the night before Evelyn's disappearance.

> *I wish that I'd known then to savor such an utterly normal evening. We came home, and I made dinner for the three of us—not that unusual, as Liam often spent the weekend away on business trips, or over in the workers' quarters on the other side of the property when the farm was busy. I reheated a minestrone soup for dinner . . .*

Another story. Mina said they ate at the show—hot dogs, over her mother's objections. And Beverley had Mina awake, like Mina's story but unlike Mrs. Tamm's. It didn't matter, not really, but if Mrs. Tamm had the right of it then Beverley and Evelyn had spent some time alone together.

God, it didn't matter. He scrubbed a hand over his face. Whether they spent that time together, or apart, or asleep, or awake, or up on the roof throwing rocks into the dam, it made no difference. It didn't tell him anything about who came to the house that night.

He flipped back to the section on the show itself. It was frustratingly brief.

After saying goodbye to Liam, we stopped by the preview night of the Nannine Show. I took the girls over to where the Miss Junior Showgirl competition would be held, so the space wouldn't be unfamiliar and frightening the next day. Evelyn won a toy at the guess-your-weight booth in the sideshow alley, and then we stopped by the Country Women's Association tent. Mina wanted to go see the woodchopping, but there wasn't anything running there until the next day.

There was nothing. No information. A three-hundred-page book, and she spared three sentences for what could be the most critical part of the whole case. Mina remembered barely anything, Mrs. Tamm even less.

He pulled out a photocopied map of the showground, thanks to the Greater Danby Heritage Library's ephemera collection. He spread it out and traced a pencil line from the front gate to the main stage, the sideshow, the CWA tent, the woodchopping, and back to the front gate.

No. He erased a section, and redrew it. Mrs. Tamm had driven them home, which meant that despite Beverley's recollection in the book, the CWA tent must have been the last stop. Maybe she'd liked the flow better the other way. It made little difference, except that the most rational path had them going through the sideshow alley twice.

He would have to show Mina the next time he saw her, to see if she remembered doing that. He tapped the doubled line with his pencil, leaving little tick marks on the page. While the girls were winning at the guess-your-weight booth, had Beverley struck up a conversation with anyone in the line? Maybe complained to another mother about being home alone all weekend in that isolated house?

Had someone noticed a beautiful woman and her sweet daughters and followed them through the dirt roads of the showground? Did they encounter his father, roaming the showground, where he wasn't meant to be?

He opened the front cover. He'd done it so often there was a soft part where his thumb had pressed into the cardboard a thousand times. On the title page, Beverley's swooping handwriting said,

Dear Lane. Someone knows something. Is it you?

TWENTY-ONE

MyMurder Forums

Subforum: Evie McCreery

Subject: Age-progression photographs

User Brava89: So I'm a graphic designer by trade, and I have a side business touching up and manipulating photographs. Mostly wedding and prom pictures, sometimes commercial stuff like covers for self-published writers.

I've been dabbling in trying to teach myself some age progression techniques for a few months now, and thought I'd practice on a picture of Evie McCreery.

What do you think? I used pictures of Beverley and adult pictures of Mina for reference.

User Comet: Why would you use pictures of Mina? Everyone knows they looked nothing alike.

User Waffletoid: Drumroll. Are you going to turn out to be a "Mina killed her sister because she was jealous Evie was more attractive" crackpot, or a "switched at birth/one of the twins wasn't their biological daughter" crackpot?

User AgentKHole: Does anyone else think age-progressed Evie is kind of hot? And by "kind of" I mean smoking hot.

* * *

The little perspex door of the roadside mailbox was propped open, unable to close due to the package inside. Mina tugged it out warily. She'd ordered nothing, and her birthday was still weeks away. Best-case scenario, some well-intentioned creeper had worked out her address and sent her something. Worst-case scenario, they weren't well intentioned.

It was a padded envelope, marked with the stamp of the Beverley McCreery Memorial Library remote librarian service. She knew it existed—she paid its bills—but she'd never volunteered to use it. She and Alanna had an understanding that she was happy to make the long drive once a month to pick up the books she'd reserved, if Alanna was going to be on shift at the time. She ripped the top off the envelope and peeked inside, just to be sure. She was greeted by the unmistakeable heft of *Call of the Reed Warbler*, which she'd reserved a few weeks back.

Apparently Alanna had quietly signed her up for library by mail. She sighed. She didn't think Alanna was angry at her for meddling—she'd never been the kind to hold her tongue when she was upset. But the message was still clear. She didn't want any unexpected visits from Mina while she was working through her feelings about the "Keva Saunders" situation.

It was half past eight by the time she got back to the house, a reasonable enough time to call someone. Alanna usually started work at ten, so she would be awake but not yet rushing around getting dressed. Mina popped on the headset she used when taking work calls, and wandered into the garden while it rang. She couldn't do that while she was working, since most calls had her jumping between databases and government websites and phone directories, but it worked well enough for a casual conversation. She sat on the edge of a raised bed, and yanked out a clump of spurge she had missed the last time she weeded.

"Hello?" Alanna said. She always sounded wary on the rare occasions Mina called. She'd explained once it was because Mina's number came up as private, and calls from private numbers were always bad news when she was growing up.

"Hey, it's me."

A magpie came in to land on the bed opposite her with a great whoosh of wings. One for sorrow, Mina thought. A lone magpie was a bad omen, because they were such social birds. They usually came at least in pairs, so a lone magpie meant something had happened to the other one.

The others would be along shortly. There were seven in the flock that lived around the house, and they were smart enough to know that if she was in the garden then an easy meal was about to appear.

"Oh, hey." This was the point in the conversation Alanna's voice usually warmed, but she still sounded like she expected bad news any minute.

"I, uh . . ." There was a flutter and a thump as a second magpie arrived, and then a third. Three for a girl. "I just wanted to let you know I got the book you sent."

"That's good. I'm sorry, your RMB has been inside the delivery area for years, I don't know why you were never told."

Mina had known, but she just said, "Oh, yeah, thanks." She

spotted a caterpillar on a pumpkin leaf and tossed it onto the path. The three magpies descended on it at once. "How have you been?"

Alanna's laugh wasn't any warmer than her voice. "It's been a weird week. We managed to get a phone number for Keva, and we got as far as her voicemail. Mum says that the voice on her message sounds just like mine, but I don't hear it. She never called back, though. I tried again, but the call won't connect."

"I'm sorry."

She was sorry, but it was a mixed-up kind of sorrow. It had become such a mundane problem, the kind they saw often in the support group, where the missing person was alive and well but didn't want to be found. Sometimes Mina privately agreed with the person's decision, having met the parents looking for them. But this situation was different. With time and patience it could be worked through.

They exchanged small talk for a few minutes, but it was obvious Alanna was just going through the motions. Mina let her go with a sigh.

As she headed inside the last four magpies descended, pecking at the soil she'd disturbed. Seven for a secret. Not that it mattered. They weren't even the right type of magpie.

* * *

She tried to shake off the unsettled feeling as she worked through her list of chores. She had no right to it. This was good news. Unimaginably good. So why was dread settling in her stomach?

She didn't know what her friendship with Alanna was if they didn't have this in common. They didn't share many interests, and while they'd supported each other through family dramas, relationship ups and downs, and work and school stress, the fact that they had both experienced something extraordinarily rare was the underpinning of everything. That had to shift now. If Alanna had Christa back in her life, then she and Mina wouldn't be the same anymore. Alanna's support of her would become sympathy. Pity.

Mina didn't consider herself a particularly good person, but that couldn't possibly be what was bothering her.

The chickens didn't come running like they usually did at the sound of Mina unlatching their gate. Her first thought was of the snake, that it had slipped in during the night and made off with all of them, but then she spotted them crowded together at the base of the wattle tree at the edge of the enclosure. They squatted close to the ground, wings out and beaks ajar, clearly struggling with the heat. Hattie, the enormous brown-and-white Brahma who ran the flock, looked over at her like she was personally responsible.

"Buck up, ladies," Mina said. She emptied her bucket of water into their shallow stone water trough, and a couple deigned to stroll over.

One of them was the bravest of her last clutch of chicks, now in the awkward teenage stage of too-long legs and scruffy heads. She looked thoughtfully at its knobbly red comb, which seemed to be growing bigger than those on the other chicks. She'd suspected for a while that one was a rooster, which she didn't have room for. She was just waiting for him to start crowing.

She didn't love the fussing around that was involved, the plucking and the cleaning, but she was looking forward to fresh chicken. She hadn't made a proper roast chicken since before her dad had left on his trip. It might be a bit depressing on her own, though. Maybe she could offer to bring dinner over to Hendrik and Maggie's place one night. Or she could make it the next time Lane came out to see something on the property. She could put the table out on the veranda.

Mina paused, letting the empty bucket swing in her hand. Where had that thought come from? She still wasn't sure that she'd made the right decision; feeding him was the last thing she should do.

She'd let him in and let him ask his questions. She couldn't undo that now. If she'd stood firm, he would have given up eventually and searched for fame and fortune elsewhere. Now Lane knew there was a door in her wall, and if she tried to close it again he would never stop trying to get back through. The only way out now was to see it through.

She'd gone back and forth at least three times on his request for her personal photographs. Some moments she felt like she might as well give them to him, they were hardly precious memories. Then the clock would tick and it was just as clear that the request was outrageous and she couldn't imagine handing them over.

Her mother's files were impeccable, a holdover from when she'd first arrived to work as the farm's bookkeeper. Even her personal papers—like day care artwork and Christmas cards—were organized by year, right up until the year that she entered the endgame of her cancer fight. Everything after that point was jumbled in an IKEA document box, which Mina would get around to sorting through one day.

She opened the filing cabinet drawer marked 1995–1999. The hanging file for April 1999 was open a few inches, like her mother hadn't bothered to push it closed after the last time she delved into it, looking for some treasure she wanted.

Or had been asked for.

Mina pulled out the yellow envelope of photographs and slammed the drawer shut.

* * *

Mrs. Gilligan was out the front of her shop, taping a notice to the window about the pub's upcoming meat raffle. She lit up when she spotted Mina coming her way. "Hello, dear. I hope you're not expecting a delivery; I don't have anything for you."

"No, that's alright. I'm looking for someone. Do you remember the man from a few weeks back who gave me a bit of a fright in your store?"

Mrs. Gilligan looked stricken. "Why? Has he given you trouble again?"

"No. It was all just a misunderstanding, really."

"Oh, thank god," Mrs. Gilligan said, with considerably more relief than the situation warranted. "You see, I've been worried you would be angry when you found out."

"Found out?"

"I've rented him the upstairs flat."

"That's great!" Mina was surprised at just how pleased she was to hear that. She was happy for Mrs. Gilligan, of course. The FOR LEASE sign had been on that flat for as long as she could remember, as much a part of it as the iron railing with its chipped paint and the heavy beige door. Getting some cash flowing in for it must have been a huge relief.

* * *

Lane opened the door wearing a white T-shirt and sleep pants, even though it was well after 10 a.m. She'd never seen him in short sleeves before—she'd wondered if he was covering up scars, or poorly thought out tattoos, but the skin of his arms was un-marked, paler than the skin on his hands and face but otherwise ordinary.

His mouth was already open in greeting, but when he saw that it was Mina he stopped, and blinked once like his brain needed to recalibrate.

"Mina. What brings you here today?"

"I decided to bring you those . . . photographs." The wind nudged the door open another inch, letting more light seep into his flat. The poster on the wall behind him resolved into a large map of Australia, a continuous line snaking around the eastern states in blue highlighter, with little forests of paper flags marking particular locations. To the left of it were dozens of photos and printouts, pictures of Nannine and the showground. Each photo had a Post-it stuck to it, but she couldn't make out what was written on them.

On the other side, the wall was nearly completely covered with photographs of Evelyn. The famous last picture, the two of them in the dusty lane at the show. Mina had her arm draped over Evelyn's shoulder, and Evelyn had her hand pressed to Mina's, jelly bracelets stacked from wrist to mid-forearm like a Spartan bracer. Beside it he'd taped a picture of a snapped jelly bracelet in an evidence bag.

Beneath that was the picture most news stations used when they wanted to show Evelyn: her dressed up for the Christmas concert, her face framed in giant blond curls from their mother's old soup can–sized rollers, and her blue eyes rimmed in too-heavy mascara. Their mother had frozen in the bathroom doorway when she saw how much Evelyn had on, but it was too late to scrub it off and still make it to the school on time.

His flat was like the funhouse mirror version of her own home, festooned with her own family photos. They were all publicly available, of course; her mother had handed pictures out to the press as freely as a grandmother passing a packet of holiday pictures around the dinner table.

The picture of the evidence bag wasn't even real—a journalist had ducked out and bought a jelly bracelet and photographed it in a sandwich bag when the detail leaked about the crime scene unit finding a broken one on their garden path. The bracelet they'd found had been purple, while the one in the picture was green. It had always struck Mina as stupid anyway. Those things snapped constantly, and Evelyn had lived in the house. Of course there was evidence of her everywhere.

"Are you okay?" Lane asked. He looked over his shoulder, taking in what she was seeing. He turned back, looking sheepish. "I'm sorry. I know it's not great, having the case board visible from the door. Anyone who knocks could potentially see it. But I only have this room and the bathroom, and I don't want it to get water damaged."

"It's fine," Mina said. "What does the blue line signify? On the map."

Lane's smile faded. "Nothing," he said, shifting his gaze so he was staring directly into her eyes. "It came printed that way. I'm reusing a free map I got from a tour company, and that's their travel route."

Mina looked at him. It was a pretty blatant lie—the line was too uneven to be printed, and he'd added pushpins that clearly followed the line. But Lane didn't break, and just smiled blandly. "Thank you for the pictures," he said, holding out a hand.

"No problem," she said, which was a lie. She still wasn't sure she had made the right decision in handing them over, but it was done now. "Do you need anything else?"

"If you've got some time, maybe you could talk me through them?"

"They're pretty self-explanatory," she said. "But yeah, I've got a little time."

"Actually, if you could do me one favor . . . Do you think we could do it down at the pub?"

She laughed. "I don't care if your flat is messy, Lane."

"Er, it's not that." He ran a hand through his hair. "I think it would help if some of the locals saw us having a drink together. A lot of them won't talk to me."

She laughed again, louder. "What? Country towns can be weird about newcomers, but this isn't a regency romance, Lane. Being properly introduced isn't going to make a difference."

"I'm serious. Nobody will answer any questions about the case until they know you're okay with it."

"Nobody in Nannine cares what I think," she said. "But if you insist, fine. You're buying."

He relaxed visibly, and stepped away from the door to let her in. "Thanks. Just give me five minutes to change. Can I get you anything? I've only got instant coffee at the moment, and, um . . . water."

"I think I'll wait for the beer."

He disappeared into the bathroom, and she took a closer look at his wall of photographs. The writing on the Post-its turned out to be the names of people in the photographs. A lot of them were either her current or former neighbors. She picked up a pen he'd abandoned on the bedside table, and filled in a couple of names he was missing.

"Where did you get all these pictures?" she asked, when he came back out of the bathroom in a Henley and a pair of jeans. She didn't know how he could stand being covered from wrist to ankle when the weather was still so warm, but he didn't seem bothered.

"Here and there. Some I found in people's public albums online, and others people have given to me when I asked. Not as many as I'd hoped. I'm trying to identify everyone who was in the area that weekend."

"Oh," she said. She touched one photo that had jumped out at her as not like the others. It was all the way to the left, separate from the others, so maybe Lane had already picked up on that too. A man with close-cropped blond hair smiled at the camera, but looked irritated at being asked to pose for the picture. "Someone steered you wrong with this one. It wasn't taken in Nannine. This here in the background is a banana plant; there's no way one of those could survive out here."

"I know," he said. "That's a picture of my father, actually."

"Oh!" she repeated, embarrassed. "Of course. You look a lot like him."

"I know," he said, not sounding pleased. "Shall we go?"

TWENTY-TWO

NEIL'S GAZE WENT to Mina first, and his smile broadened from customer service polite to something warm and genuine. It faded when he noticed Lane with her. He looked between them, clearly trying to get a read on the situation—checking for signs that Lane was giving her trouble. Or that they were on a date.

Lane wondered which possibility would bother him more.

He looked at Mina, wondering if she was aware, but she was more focused on making her way to a table. He headed to the bar, since it was his shout.

"What can I get you?" Neil asked. He kept his eyes on Mina, over Lane's shoulder.

"Carlton Draft, and whatever the lady's usual is," Lane said. He wondered if it would help to assure him there wasn't anything going on. Probably not.

* * *

Mina had opened the envelope and laid a couple of photos out on the table by the time he brought the drinks over. They were

198

a time machine. There were a handful of famous pictures associated with the McCreery case, and a mountain more for anyone dedicated enough to look for them. He had, and he'd committed every millimeter to memory. These ones took his breath away. The half-assembled rides at the showground. The spaghetti strap tops and peasant skirts, button-down shirts open over T-shirts, frosted tips and unironic fedoras. It almost seemed like Beverley had been more interested in photographing the crowds and the show layout than her daughters. It was exactly what Lane needed, but it was unnerving. He flipped through picture after picture of rows of marquees, rides with straggly queues forming in front of them, girls and boys trying their luck on the sideshows. Beverley had been out for an evening with her children, snapping pictures for her family, but the girls were barely in them.

"Didn't you say she insisted on you being in every picture?" Lane asked.

Mina frowned down at the pictures. "Usually, yeah. But keep in mind these are the leftovers. Most of the good ones of Evelyn have been taken out and used."

That was a good point. But still, it sat wrong.

He flipped to the last picture, and Mina's face beamed up at him. It was odd to see her looking so happy, without the guarded look she always wore.

It startled him when he realized that Evelyn was also in the picture, standing next to her sister with her eyes closed. He had been drawn instinctively to the more familiar of the two faces. When had that happened? When had Mina become more familiar to him than the face splashed over TV screens for nearly twenty years?

A mobile phone jangled on the other side of the room, making him jump. A man with thick gray hair pulled back in a ponytail dropped his pool cue and grabbed the phone, then silenced it after looking at the screen.

A moment later, the phone behind the bar began to ring. The two men standing at the pool table with the first man laughed.

Neil picked up the phone and, after listening briefly, said, "No, he's not here, Syl. I haven't seen Reg all day, but I'll let him know you called if I run into him."

The man, who must have been Reg, gave Neil a little salute and resumed his game.

Mina shook her head. "So which of these ratbags did you want to talk to, anyway?"

"I just need some general goodwill," he said. "Although it would help if you put in a good word with Neil."

"Alright," she said, flicking her hair over her shoulder. "Oi, Neil!" she shouted, cupping her hands over her mouth.

"Y'know I don't do table service," Neil chided, but he strolled over anyway. "What's up?"

"Sit with us a minute—my friend here has some questions for you," Mina said, which was not at all what Lane had intended. He'd thought they would have a drink together, obviously friendly, and then he would come back later to ask his questions. Instead, Neil was pulling up a chair, looking at Lane expectantly.

"Uh, yeah," he said. "It's regarding Evelyn."

"I'd gathered," Neil said. He glanced at the pictures on the table, then looked back at Lane.

Mina took pity on him, and placed a gentle hand on Neil's forearm. "How's your mum, Neil?"

Given a brief reprieve, Lane grabbed a coaster, and pulled a pen out of his pocket to plan out some questions. Even so, he couldn't help watching Mina out of the corner of his eye. Her tone was light, but the set of her shoulders was tense.

"Great!" Neil beamed at her. "She's none too happy that you haven't been by the General lately, though."

Lane paused in the notes he was scribbling. Apparently Neil's mother was Mrs. Gilligan, which cast his suggestion that Lane rent the flat in a new light. Lane was almost certain Mrs. Gilligan was his landlord, given the interest she took in the condition of the flat every time she popped around.

"I've been busy."

"Hmm," Neil said, glancing at Lane. "Anyway, if you've got questions you'd better fire away. I'm the only one here this afternoon, so I can't hang about too long."

"Were you here in the pub the night Evelyn disappeared?"

"Only until eight," Neil said. "Show weekends were big business days for the pub, but not the sort of nights you want kids around. I was helping wait tables, but once the dinner rush ended I headed home. Mum can vouch for that, if you're checking my alibi."

"I'm not," Lane said. "How much do you remember about that night?"

Neil looked up at the ceiling, thinking. "It was nineteen years ago."

Most people would round up to twenty, Lane noted. Clearly Neil felt an emotional connection to what had happened, which bode well for how much he was likely to remember. "Did you or your uncle take any pictures in here that night?"

Neil shook his head. "Mate, I dunno what kind of pubs you're used to, but the Neeny doesn't take pictures on a Friday night."

"Alright." He'd known it was unlikely, but you miss every

shot you don't take. "Since you were here, do you recall if the room upstairs was rented out or not?"

Neil looked at Mina, and seemed to deliberate for a moment. Then he stood up. "I'll be right back."

Mina relaxed visibly as he walked away, sinking back into her chair like the interaction had exhausted her. She frowned, catching Lane watching her. "What?"

"Are you okay?" he asked, pitching his voice low. "You don't seem comfortable. You don't have to do this if Neil makes you—"

"What? No. Neil's lovely." She stared down at her drink. "I've known him all my life, why would I be uncomfortable?"

That was the question, wasn't it? This was Mina's local pub, full of people who knew her, and yet she was clearly working at appearing relaxed. "Do you come here often?"

"It's a bit of a drive."

"Everything is. How often do you leave home?"

"Often enough," she snapped.

"Is it because we're talking about Evelyn?" If it was getting to be too much, he could come back and talk to Neil later without her.

"If I didn't want to talk about her, I wouldn't have come to your flat," she said. "I didn't drop by to be social."

Neil returned before Lane could put his foot in it any further. He laid a red leather ledger open on the table, on top of the pictures. "Here's the reservation book. The room was rented, but the person just paid for the room and didn't use it."

"Are you sure?" Lane scanned the page, but all the notes were in some kind of shorthand.

"Yeah. Look, my uncle made a note here. He charged them less because he didn't have to clean the room."

"Really?" Lane perked up. "Does it say who the customer was? Do you have anything else—a credit card, or check-in paperwork?"

It was circumstantial, but if he had paperwork showing his father had rented the room, proving he was in town, and that he hadn't actually stayed, he could take that to Starrett. It would be enough to persuade her to investigate him as a serious suspect, at least.

"They paid cash, and we've never had any paperwork. That was part of the reason we stopped doing the accommodation. If someone trashed the room, we were shit out of luck, and getting set up to keep a credit card on file was a lot of bother."

"But you've got a name," Lane said, trying not to let impatience creep into his voice.

Neil hesitated, and looked at Mina again. "No," he said. "My uncle hasn't noted a name. Just the letter H."

H for Holland? Lane drummed his fingers on the table. Was that enough? No, he needed more.

"Why would someone pay for a room and not use it?" Mina asked.

"For the parking space," Neil explained.

"Ah," Mina said.

"What parking space?" Lane asked. His father hadn't needed to park a car that night; their car had been on the showground. That was one of the things he struggled to square with his theory that his father was responsible. He would have needed to get from Nannine to the McCreery property and back, and Lane was certain their car never moved. He'd slept two feet away from it that night.

Neil jerked a thumb to the back wall. "The pub used to have a car park. Out the back, with a wall so you couldn't tell from the road who was at the pub. I tried to turn it into a beer garden when

I took over—bloody awful idea. I'm halfway through converting it back."

"Of course," Mina said. "So if someone knew they had to leave their car in town overnight, it would be worth the cost of a room to have a secure parking space."

"Somewhat secure," Neil said. "We were always clear the cars weren't our responsibility. But it's better than the train station, eh?"

Mina laughed, a little too loud to be genuinely amused, while Lane stared at the reservation book, like he could make that letter resolve into a full name through force of will.

* * *

"Why are you so interested in the room?" Mina asked, as they were packing the photos back into the envelope. "It's one room; there were tons of people camped out at the showground."

"Just a half-baked theory," Lane said. "Probably nothing."

She looked at him, clearly annoyed by his evasion, but didn't say anything.

"Do you want to get some lunch?" he asked. He was hoping that she would extend another invitation to the property when they parted. Maybe even invite him to the house. But that wouldn't happen if they left things on a sour note. "I was going to grab a pizza."

He'd been planning to heat up instant noodles in his flat, actually. Takeaway for two wasn't really a great choice if he wanted his money to keep stretching, but needs must.

"Nah, I need to get home and feed Echo," she said.

"Maybe next time?" he suggested, and cringed internally. God, he sounded like a teenager trying to get a girl to come to the blue light disco with him.

But she gave him a small smile. "Yeah, maybe."

204

* * *

There was a private message waiting for him when he returned to the flat. It was from someone outside of his friends list—he had to approve the message before it popped up—clearly in response to his request for photographs.

Meryl Ramsey: *I've got pictures. None with the McCreery kids in them, but taken at the showground that day, like you asked. Some at the pub too.*

A thrill went through Lane. He'd had only a handful of replies to the request. Any pictures taken that day would be buried in drawers or on rolls of undeveloped film. Most of them had probably been consigned to the rubbish bin a decade ago. Of those who had offered up pictures, none were taken at the pub, only the showground.

Wonderful, he sent back. *Do you have them scanned? Can you send them to my email address? It's public.*

The little bubble indicating that she was typing appeared, then disappeared several times. Finally a message popped up.

They're not scanned. I've only got the negatives.

Shit. Where would he even find somewhere that printed photos from negatives these days?

Lane clicked through to Meryl's profile. She was about Mina's age, and had attended Nannine High School, although she had mistakenly listed it under "graduate school." Her job was listed as "#BossBabe at HevinScent," a multilevel marketing candle company that had suckered his mother when he was a teenager. He was surprised to see it was still kicking around.

Another message from Meryl popped up. *You said you can't pay much, but that does mean you will pay, right?*

Meryl couldn't meet during the week, because she had young sons she didn't want to bring with her. They arranged to meet at the church, which ran a small op shop that sold coffee and cake on a Saturday morning, the closest thing Nannine had to a coffee spot.

Mrs. Gilligan stood behind the till, filling out the newspaper crossword in pen.

"Morning, dear," she said, folding the newspaper over and straightening up. She'd warmed up to him considerably. She'd been frosty the first few times he popped into the store for bread and milk, but it was hard to hold a grudge against a reliable customer.

"Don't you get a day off?" Lane asked. He looked at the menu, chalked on a sandwich board in an uneven hand. Coffee, tea, hot chocolate, lamingtons, hot cross buns. Good lord, was it really time for them already?

"If I took a day off I'd spend it here anyway," Mrs. Gilligan said. "This way I get all the gossip and I'm helping the church out. We're fundraising to replace the church roof, you know."

"Be careful who you hire for that," he said. He'd known a couple of blokes who'd made a decent living from the old-fashioned roofer scam.

"Yes, I watch *A Current Affair*," she said. "What can I get you?"

"Just a regular coffee, please."

"The CWA ladies have been experimenting with a vegan lemonade scone, if you're hungry," Mrs. Gilligan said, punching the coffee order into the till slowly. "It's not on the menu yet, but today's attempt was rather passable."

"I'm not vegan," Lane said.

"Oh?" Mrs. Gilligan sounded surprised, although she'd seen him buy full-cream milk often enough. "I thought you came from Byron Bay?"

Okay, Mrs. Gilligan was definitely his landlord. Only Cherise at the real estate and his landlord would have seen the previous address on his form, and he doubted that even in a town as small as Nannine that information was interesting enough gossip to be passed around. "There are a handful of omnivores living there."

"Ah. Milk in the coffee, then?"

"No, thank you. But one sugar, please."

Mrs. Gilligan disappeared into the kitchen, where he strongly suspected they had a pod machine stashed.

He took a seat at a table with two chairs. It was set up next to the open door, with a view of the sandpit out the back. Beyond the small play area lay a wide yellowing lawn, and then the town cemetery. A few ostentatious Celtic crosses loomed over a cluster of moss-covered headstones. The more recent graves sat closer to the church, one black marble lettered in gold, one wooden temporary marker, and a broad patch of markers the size of his palm, with brass plates marking where cremated remains were interred. He was reminded of the brass memorial he'd stumbled over beside the McCreery dam.

Mrs. Gilligan put his coffee down on the table. If it was pod coffee, then the church had also sprung for the milk foamer attachment, because a puff of foam floated on top, with a design of a spindly tree.

"I took an evening course over at the high school," Mrs. Gilligan confided.

The doors of the vestibule clacked, and a woman strode in. She had thick red hair in a twist on top of her head—too red to be her natural hair color, but it suited her. Her eyes were hidden behind round sunglasses, and she wore a cream cotton wrap dress, with a messenger bag slung over her shoulder. It had a clear plastic front, with little pockets to store samples of each candle scent. Her profile picture was apparently a few years out of date, but it was definitely Meryl.

She looked Lane up and down, her disappointment clear. Obviously she'd hoped for a television executive or location scout in a thousand-dollar suit.

"Thanks for coming," he said, ignoring the way her mouth had settled into the shape of a cat's arse.

"Mmm," she said. "So, what's your deal? Are you making a TV show or something?"

"No."

She looked disappointed again, but she pulled out the chair opposite him and sat down. "A podcast?"

"No. I'm not writing a book either." Lane pushed the milk coffee across the table, like he'd ordered it for her. "Coffee?" Clearly, despite what his message had said, she'd made the trip into town in the hope there was serious money on the table. Hopefully a free drink would buy him a few more minutes of her attention.

She stared at it for a moment, like she was going to refuse, then shrugged and pulled it closer. Lane would have turned it down, if their positions were reversed. Accepting an open drink from a stranger you met on the internet was the sort of thing he'd warned Lynnie against while helping her move into her flat. But that was none of his business.

"Did you know the McCreery girls?" he asked, leaning back in his chair.

Meryl shrugged with one shoulder. "They were in kindergarten when I was in year six. Everyone was excited when we heard there was a set of twins enrolled, but then they showed up and it turned out they couldn't do any Enid Blyton–style twin-swapping pranks." She ripped open a stevia packet and poured it on her coffee. It sat on top for a moment, then punched a hole through the patterned foam. He wondered if he should have mentioned the sugar already in it.

"Did you finish year twelve?" he asked.

"Yes. And if you're asking if that means Wilhelmina and I were at school together for another year, no. She was enrolled—when I was in year eleven we had to sit through an assembly about how we needed to respect her privacy, and how phones would now be banned from school grounds even during breaks, in case any of us tried to flog some blurry pic of her to *New Idea*. Then she never turned up, and it was dropped."

"There must have been talk, though."

"Well, my girlfriend Sarah's mum was on the P&C, and she said that Beverley McCreery wanted her at the same plummy boarding school she went to, and she was on the waitlist until just before the school year started. But we saw Wilhelmina around with her mum sometimes, shopping or whatever. Way too often for her to be just back for school breaks. The private schools have different holidays, but not that different."

"Nannine High would have been difficult for her," he noted. "That's a long trip, twice a day every day."

Meryl rolled her eyes. "You think the rest of us lived next door to the school?"

Still. Lane was building a picture of a lonely, disconnected adolescence for Mina. Some form of homeschooling, stuck on a farm with only a handful of remaining employees, with any foray out into the world requiring an hour-long drive. *Governess??* he wrote in his notebook. If Mina didn't have a private tutor, then she probably learned by correspondence, receiving packets of material in the mail and sending them back for marking. A method like that meant all communication came with several weeks' delay, with no possibility of the teachers keeping an eye on her emotional state or offering her a sympathetic ear when she needed it.

Isolated, perhaps, but not necessarily alone. Liam McCreery had always worked close to home, but would have had far fewer duties with operations closed down and barely any employees to manage. And Beverley made her living writing her book and conducting interviews, work she almost certainly did from the house. How often was Mina, their sole remaining daughter, even out of their sight?

Lynnie once told him that she'd had to fight their mother to be enrolled in public school, like the girls she played with in the caravan park. His mother had argued that the correspondence had worked fine for him, her brilliant big brother who aced his criminology degree. There had been no reason for it, no benefit beyond her desire to keep her little girl where she could see her. But it wasn't school that hurt her.

If the McCreerys had kept Mina home out of fear, there was a deep irony there, given that the house was where the danger had been.

Meryl unzipped her bag and pulled out a yellow envelope, the old kind that photographs came in when they were printed. The logo on the front was for Nannine Chemist and Photo Shop, a store that now only existed as a fading sign a few doors down from his flat. "I managed to find a few that were printed after all," Meryl said. "But most of them are still just negatives. I dunno where the photos went. They probably got chopped up during Mum's scrapbooking phase."

"Do you know anywhere around here that can print from a negative?" Lane asked. Did anywhere in Australia still do that?

"Oh!" Mrs. Gilligan yelled from the kitchen. "The op shop has a negative projector!"

"A what?" Meryl said.

Mrs. Gilligan appeared in the doorway, looking absolutely thrilled and completely oblivious to how obvious she'd made it that she had been eavesdropping on their entire conversation. "Like a slide projector. You put the negative in and it projects the picture up on the wall. I'll go get it."

She bustled into the shop next door, and returned a few moments later with a white box similar in size and shape to a shoebox. She put it on the table between them, and it made a solid clunk. "How's that for perfect? I never thought we'd find a home for it. And only twenty dollars too."

Lane blanched. He didn't even know if there was anything of interest on the negatives. On the other hand, it was certainly cheaper than whatever it would cost him to send them away for processing—and, more importantly, it was fast. "Thanks," he said, pulling out his wallet again.

"So you do have some money," Meryl said, resting a hand on the envelope.

"If these pictures lead to a break in the case you would have a claim to the reward money," Lane said.

Meryl rolled her eyes with her entire head. "I've got five pictures. How about you pay a hundred dollars each, and I'll throw in the negatives for free."

Lane's eye fell on the familiar HevinScent logo printed on her bag. "What if I buy a couple of candles in exchange for the pictures and the negatives?"

Meryl perked up. That had her attention. "If you buy six candles, I'll make Provisional Diamond this month and qualify for additional training."

"I'll buy three," he said. He was doing her a favor. His mother had made Provisional Diamond once, and it damn near bankrupted her. It wasn't like a promotion, which once achieved was yours from that point on. If you reached a level, you had to keep up that level of sales to stay there, and sliding back down the ranks had the stink of shame. So the next month, when she fell short, her "upline" convinced her to buy enough product herself to meet the minimum. She could hold it as inventory and sell it later. But that meant she was even further behind the following month. She ended up with a mound of credit card debt, a cupboard full of candles in a home with zero available storage space, and got to go up on stage at the annual convention (tickets $399 they didn't have) to collect the chintzy "diamond" pin she'd essentially bought. The stone fell out on the drive home.

"Deal," Meryl said. "That'll be a hundred and forty-nine dollars forty-seven. I can take cash, or I have an app on my phone if you need to use a card."

Lane nearly choked on his own tongue. The products had been overpriced when his mother was all in, but $49.99 for a lump of soy that smelled a bit like fresh linen or sandalwood? Not to mention that, unless the terms had changed dramatically, Meryl would keep only six percent of that, whoever snookered her into the scheme would get two percent, and the rest would go to the company.

He counted the cash out of his wallet and Meryl watched him, her face going thoughtful. He braced for it.

"You seem like a tough negotiator," she said. "Have you ever thought about going into business for yourself? I know what you're thinking: *Where would I find the time? I don't have the skills. Who can afford the start-up costs?* But what if I told you that for ninety-nine dollars you could have everything you need to be up and running today? You could have your first commission check by dinnertime."

It took a lot of willpower not to laugh out loud. He admired the chutzpah, if nothing else. Three minutes ago she'd been desperate enough to meet her minimums to trade something potentially worth seven figures. But sure, she would be letting him in on a life-changing business opportunity. "No, thanks."

Meryl looked a little deflated, but also somewhat relieved. "Okay. If you ever want to take the first step on your freedom journey and start your own small business, give me a call." She slid a card embossed with the HevinScent logo across the table.

Lane wanted to snap at her that the only person on a freedom journey was the HevinScent CEO, who owned a private island he bought by scamming money out of desperate women like his mother. But he didn't want to be cruel to Meryl. What were her other options? A retail job in the shuttered chemist? Waiting tables at the one pub in town? It wasn't like the McCreerys were still hiring farmhands.

* * *

The instructions for the projector weren't in the box, but it was easy enough to figure out. Once he plugged it in and switched it on, it threw a square of yellow light on the wall of his flat, and he fed the strip of negatives into the slot at the bottom. The colors were inverted, and the people who appeared on his wall looked like ghosts with glowing eyes and mouths, but it would work enough to decide if it was worth getting prints from the negatives.

The first picture was a gem—the photographer had captured

the ticket counter, including a poster for the show and a rack of newspapers being offered free with ticket purchase. The poster was the correct one. More importantly, a quick internet search confirmed that the newspaper headlines were also the ones from that day, reporting on a political scandal that would soon be forgotten as a much bigger story gripped the nation. That confirmed that Meryl had her years right, and these pictures really were taken the day Evelyn disappeared.

He adjusted the settings until the projection was as large as he could get it, and counted the people in it. Four. Two in the foreground: a young Meryl and a similar-looking little boy who might have been a brother or cousin. Two in the background: a show worker with his back turned to the camera in the middle of setting up a marquee and a uniformed council worker wheeling two large bins down a path.

He noted down a brief description of each person and moved on to picture number two.

Meryl and the unidentified boy again, this time sitting at a table with a plastic tablecloth, showing off matching chicken schnitzels on enormous white plates. A beer advertisement hung on the wall behind them—the Ramseys must have gone to the pub for dinner. A better choice than a dagwood dog at the show.

He checked the next picture—another taken at the show. That was better than any metadata you could find in a modern digital picture. If this picture was on a negative strip between two taken at the show, it must have been taken that weekend.

He went back to the pub picture to look at the people eating their meals in the background. Lane's breath froze in his throat. A small man sat at the table behind them, bent over his meal, his hair a pale halo. Nineteen years may have passed, but he recognized the man immediately. To be sure, he grabbed Beverley's book from his bedside table and flipped to the glossy pages in the center with photographs, and found a picture of Liam McCreery and Hendrik Tamm, the operations manager, at work on the farm.

Even in negative, the man in the background was unmistakably Hendrik: who had told Lane—and the police—that he was in Adelaide that day.

TWENTY-THREE

THE WALK FROM his flat to the police station was only a few blocks. Lane walked with his hands in his pockets and the negatives and projector in a bag that sat heavy on his shoulder. He almost turned back several times. These pictures shredded Hendrik's alibi. He'd said that he flew out to Adelaide on Friday morning, but there he was that night, tucking into a steak and chips. A fake alibi wasn't enough for a conviction, but it was more than enough for Starrett to take him in for questioning. If Starrett couldn't get him to crack, then for a case this high-profile an expert would be sent from Sydney, and if the operations manager had been involved in Evelyn's disappearance, sooner or later they would prove it.

Once that happened, Lane was a millionaire.

He tried to feel joy at the idea. It would take time, of course, possibly even years before they got a conviction. After that he would need to go through the grimy process of actually getting NSW Police to pay out the reward. But he was confident it would happen. Giving them a new suspect after the case had been becalmed for nearly twenty years was huge.

Lynnie's university degree would be paid for. He could cover her rent. He could buy her a flat. A house. A mansion.

If their father was released, Lane could take her away. He could move her again if he found them. As many times as needed.

But no amount of money could make her feel safe. Not if their father was out.

Sharing the world with their father was like sharing a caravan with a huntsman spider. He'd be happiest with it dead, but barring that he only felt safe when he knew exactly where it was. Right now he always knew where his father was, and Lynnie got a letter once a year confirming it. After he was released, it didn't matter where Lane took them to live, or how much money they had to help them hide. They wouldn't know where he was, and that would torment them.

He just felt hollow. He'd wanted the money, but more than that he'd wanted to pin this on their father. He wanted someone else to write the victim impact statements. He wanted the courts to understand that his father should never be released.

He paused for a moment at the corner. He didn't have to take this to Starrett. His father had a parole hearing coming up, and surely just the suspicion that he was a person of interest in the Evelyn McCreery case would be enough. All he had to do to create that suspicion was prove that his father was in Nannine on that weekend.

But not if Hendrik confessed first.

He shifted the bag to his other shoulder. This evidence had waited nineteen years. How much harm could it cause to wait another few weeks? He could leave the case open until he found proof his father was in town, let that kill the parole application, and then bring this photo to Starrett. He could have everything.

And in the meantime, Hendrik would go on living on Mina's property. Lane started walking again, feeling revolted at himself.

* * *

The Nannine Police Station was as different from the Danby station as a building could get. The entrance was shaded by a veranda with a wrought-iron balustrade, nestled between two wings of red brick, the corners capped with white stone. Still, it had a similar air about it. Something about the business of policing sank into a building.

Someone had attempted to plant a wonga wonga vine to train up the veranda posts. He could tell this not from the plant, which was long gone, but from the plastic nursery pot marker still sticking out of the dry dirt.

He rang the buzzer. After a moment the lock clicked, but no one appeared at the door. He pulled the screen door open, and as soon as it crashed closed behind him Starrett called from somewhere in the back, "Who is it?"

He was relieved she was here. He was sure his resolve would have crumbled if he'd arrived to find the station empty, or someone else on shift. "It's Lane Holland. We met a few weeks ago, in Danby?"

There was a long silence, which made sense. He wasn't sure she'd even known he was in Nannine now.

"Just come straight down the hallway, I'm in the tearoom."

The hallway was quiet, in the way all old buildings were, the outside noise smothered by real double brick. The tearoom, by contrast, was awash with noise. A TV mounted to the wall was tuned in to a football game, although which code exactly was beyond Lane's limited knowledge.

Starrett was standing beside a hot-water urn, stirring sugar into her tea with a spoon that she kept clinking against the sides of her mug. "Hello again, Mr. Holland. How are you going with the Christa Rennold case?"

It jarred him to be reminded that, as far as she knew, he was still actively working that case. He needed to follow up with Alanna; he'd just been juggling too many other priorities in the two weeks since their meeting in the library. "Nothing to write home about on that one, I'm afraid."

So he was already lying to her. Not an auspicious start to a difficult conversation.

"I'm sorry to hear that," she said. She reached into a high cupboard and pulled down a mug for him.

"I think I have something for you on the Evelyn McCreery case, though."

She paused in making his tea, dropping the teabag into the mug but pushing it aside without adding any water. "Do you now."

Lane didn't blame her for the drop in enthusiasm. With a multimillion-dollar reward on the line, she probably dealt with people reporting pointless or unfounded information all the time. "Before I show you anything, can I ask a question?"

"I'm sure you're capable of it," she said, leaning back against the counter and folding her arms. "My mother used to say that. She was an absolute stickler for using 'may I?' properly."

"Right," Lane said. If she was trying to put him on the back foot by quibbling with his grammar, it was a bad strategy. He was too confident in what he had for her. "May I ask a question?"

She gestured for him to go on with a little twirl of her hand.

"How was Hendrik Tamm's alibi verified?"

Now he had her attention. "Hendrik Tamm, the operations manager? He was ruled out very quickly. He was out of town. He didn't even get home for several days after Miss McCreery was reported missing."

"And he proved that how, exactly?"

Starrett left the tearoom in no particular hurry. A few minutes ticked by, during which Lane couldn't figure out what to do with his hands. He clenched them, put them in his pockets, tapped the edge of the counter. He didn't know what he wanted her to come back with. If she returned with an airtight alibi that explained the discrepancy—perhaps after nearly twenty years Hendrik had become confused about when he left, and given Lane the wrong information—then his father was still in the mix as a viable suspect. If she came back with something he could prove was a lie with the negatives in his bag, then he was a millionaire.

Starrett returned with a few stapled-together pages. "He showed us his tickets for a flight that left on the Friday morning. He also had credit card transactions throughout the week at Adelaide businesses."

The sinking sensation in Lane's stomach at least clarified his own feelings. He hadn't wanted it to be Hendrik. "Did any of your officers call the airline and confirm he actually boarded the flight? Did he have his boarding pass?"

That earned him a sharp look from Starrett. He was flying dangerously close to criticizing how she'd conducted the initial investigation. "The record does show we asked him for a boarding pass, but he says he threw it out on the plane. He had no reason to think he would still need it after he landed. Given the amount of proof he had that he'd spent the time in Adelaide, it seemed reasonable."

So no, no one had called the airline. Which meant the ticket proved nothing but that Hendrik had paid for the flight. He could have changed his flight dates after printing the ticket—the most likely explanation, given the card transactions—or sold it to someone else, or even just eaten the cost to bolster his alibi.

Lane bit back a sigh. This happened too easily in big investigations. An overwhelmed officer working their way through a long list of possible suspects is too quick to cross someone off the list, because they want to clear them and move on to the next person. Especially in those critical first hours after an abduction, when the odds of finding the victim alive plummeted by the minute. Once Hendrik had been ticked off, his alibi never got rechecked. Dozens of people would have seen Hendrik in the pub that night, but if they'd been assured by the police he was cleared, with no specifics, how were they to know they'd seen something important?

He pulled out his phone, and opened the file he'd saved of his conversation with Mrs. Tamm. "When I spoke to Mrs. Tamm, she said something interesting. Apparently the night Evelyn disappeared their dog woke her up in the night, reacting like he'd heard Hendrik's car pull onto the property."

"That's extremely flimsy, Mr. Holland," Starrett said. "I remember that dog. Sweet, but dumber than a half-brick."

"It's a lot more compelling once you've seen photographic proof that Hendrik Tamm never got on that flight." He pulled the envelope from his bag, and slid it across the counter to her.

Lane had known a lot of cops in the course of his career, and the one thing he knew was that they didn't last long without developing an excellent poker face. Showing too much emotion was a weakness they couldn't afford. So when Starrett's mouth fell open in dismay, just for a moment before she caught herself, it affected him as much as if she'd screamed out loud. It was safe to assume she was replaying the past nineteen years in her head, of Hendrik's presence in the background, friendly interactions, the same pleasant helpfulness he'd feigned when Lane met him.

"At the very least you can arrest him on perverting the course of justice. That will buy you time to build the case against him," Lane said.

"I don't need you to tell me how to do my job, Mr. Holland," she said, without much heat. She still seemed a touch shell-shocked. "I can take it from here."

TWENTY-FOUR

THE ALARM SYSTEM chimed once to indicate that a car had passed the first gate. Luckily Mina had just wrapped up a call, and was nearly done logging the details. She changed her status in the system to "busy" so it wouldn't put another call through to her, and laid her headset on the desk. She would probably get a stroppy message from the shift manager, since she was only ten minutes from her scheduled end time, but she could deal with that. She wasn't expecting Lane, and she trusted him not to try to push his way in again, so if he was on his way without warning there had to be a reason.

She ducked up to the bedroom, and shucked off her jeans and T-shirt. She pulled a sundress out of the cupboard and threw it on. Her bare feet would be fine; she could pull on her boots by the door if Lane wanted to see something on the property.

She paused by the mirror on the front of her wardrobe and ran her fingers through her hair. Then she stopped. What was she doing?

Mina walked back to the front of the house, feeling foolish.

Maybe she should let Alanna set her up with one of those profiles on that app she was always talking about. She needed someone in her life who hadn't been brought into it by Evelyn.

A sharp rap sounded at the door. Mina peered through the peephole in the door, and then opened it with unconcealed surprise.

Alanna stood on the veranda, looking more casual than Mina had ever seen her in a polo shirt and jeans. Mina couldn't remember the last time she'd seen her friend in something other than the neat pinstriped shirt and black slacks she wore behind the library desk.

"Hi," Alanna said, looking sheepish. "Sorry for just showing up, but my grandma always said an apology's not worth anything if you don't do it in person."

"You don't need to apologize for anything," Mina said, stepping back to let her in. It felt weird to have her at the house. They may have been friends for years, but she always went to Alanna.

"I basically ghosted you for three weeks," Alanna said. She stepped inside, looking around the kitchen with wide eyes.

"I'll make some tea," Mina said, not wanting to argue about it anymore. "You take one sugar, right?"

"Any chance of honey?"

Mina nodded. "It's from a shop, though, so there's a fifty-fifty chance it's corn syrup."

Alanna chuckled. "You ought to get your own hives going. You've got the space for it."

"With all my free time," Mina said. She'd thought about it, though. It was one less thing she'd need to source from town, and a good hive would kick her vegetable garden's productivity into high gear. One more excuse never to leave.

They fell into an uncomfortable silence while Mina fussed with pouring the tea leaves into the pot and filling it with water.

She wrapped her palms around the pot as she waited for it to steep, enjoying the warm, solid feel of it. She usually found small talk slow and sticky, but Alanna had always filled in the gaps by bringing some basic social competence to the table. Now she just sat on a stool and looked worried.

Mina pushed the tea across the counter, hoping that Alanna was planning to cough up the real reason she'd showed up here.

"I've put in for annual leave," Alanna said, and then took a sip of the tea like she was hoping it was laced with rum. "I'm going to the Northern Territory, and I'm going to see Keva."

"Oh," Mina said. "Have you managed to talk to her on the phone, then?"

"No," Alanna admitted.

Mina grimaced internally. So she planned to ambush her sister in person. Like Lane had done to her, the first day they'd met. But that had all worked out, hadn't it?

"I was wondering if you would, uh, consider, um . . ."

"Watering your plants?"

"Coming with me."

Mina swallowed her mouthful of tea painfully. "To the Northern Territory?"

The idea filled her with dread. Alanna wanted her to travel all that way, to get tangled up in the Rennold family's heartache? They were friends, sure. Close friends. Best friends. But did that mean Mina had to do something like that for her? It reminded her of the support group. She'd jumped into it expecting to get help, and it had rapidly evolved into expectation and guilt. "What about your mother?"

Alanna shrugged. "I think it would be better if I went first. If it is . . . if there's something to it, we'll work our way up to Mum later."

"When?" she asked, hoping she already had some excuse. Not that she had anything on her calendar except work and farm chores.

"I'd hoped to go immediately, but my boss couldn't get someone to cover me. The earliest she would approve was the first and second week of April."

"That's still really soon," Mina said. She glanced at her wall calendar. God, the first of April was less than a week away. "I'd be gone for my birthday." She winced hearing that out loud. As excuses went, it was weak enough to be insulting. But she was shocked at the visceral "no" she felt at the idea of going so far from home. What if that was the week that . . . what? What did she think could happen while she was gone?

"Good! We could celebrate it properly. Let's do one of those sunset tours of Uluru. We'll drink champagne and heckle the people climbing."

"I can't just leave here," Mina said. "There's so much to do every day. I have Echo, the animals . . ."

"Couldn't the Tamms help you out for a while?" Alanna drew in a shaky breath. "I'm not sure I can do this alone."

Before Mina could muster another attempt at an excuse, the alarm system chimed again.

"What's that?" Alanna asked.

"There's a sensor on the gates; it goes off when someone drives up," Mina said. "It must be Lane."

Alanna's eyes widened. "He comes to the house?"

"Not inside. But I've been letting him look around. He helped you, after all."

Alanna looked unsure. Before she could say anything, the alarm went off again—the double tone, which meant someone had driven in through the back gate, near the Tamm house.

Then again. *Ding-ding, ding-ding.*

"I think it's broken," Alanna said, flapping a hand at the panel on the wall like she was trying to shoo cooking smoke away from a sensitive smoke detector.

"No," Mina said, feeling like a balloon was expanding in the back of her throat. "That's four cars. One coming up the driveway, and three coming up the back road."

Someone knocked at the door, hard enough to rattle it in the frame. Alanna jumped to her feet, and Mina hurried to peer through the peephole.

Sergeant Emily Starrett was standing on her front veranda. She wasn't wearing a uniform—just a pair of smart pressed pants and a white shirt—but, then, she rarely did.

She had a grave expression on her face. It was the expression of someone with bad news. Mina's mind immediately flew to her father. His caravan overturned in a ditch somewhere between Cairns and Townsville. A wild thought went through her of just leaving the door closed, of letting the moment of not knowing extend forever. She took a deep breath and opened it.

"May I come in?" Starrett asked.

"Of course." Mina stood aside. She should offer her biscuits, get another pot of tea going. But no words came out. She just looked at Starrett, waiting for the crash.

"There's been some new information come to light," Starrett said. "I have officers coming in through the other gate."

"I know," Mina said. She could hear her own voice but didn't feel like she was in the conversation. She felt like she was watching it from far away. Alanna moved to stand beside her, close enough that she could reach out and wrap her arms around her if she needed to. She knew that move from support group: moving in close to someone who was getting worked up so you were there if they needed to reach out. She wasn't that person.

"We're going to take Hendrik in for questioning," Starrett said gently.

"Hendrik?" Mina repeated.

"Someone has presented us with compelling evidence that Hendrik was in Nannine on the evening of April the thirtieth, 1999," Starrett said. "It's circumstantial at this point, but the fact that he would lie and maintain that lie for twenty years . . . it's highly suggestive."

"Excuse me," Mina said. She turned away from Starrett and walked quite sedately down the hall into the guest bathroom. She very nearly made it to the sink.

But only nearly, and she vomited all over her mother's blue slate tiles.

When her stomach was empty she made it the rest of the way to the sink. She splashed water over her face and washed out her foul mouth.

Someone touched her lightly on the shoulder. She turned, expecting to find Alanna hovering, but it was Starrett.

"Can I help?" she asked. Her motherly concern brought a sense memory back, of Hendrik's wife Maggie fluttering about her like a protective mother bird.

"They sent me to the Tamm house," she said, her voice croaking. "For a few days. They thought it would be less traumatic, while the police were here. While the crime scene unit worked. I slept in his house."

Starrett's eyes met hers in the mirror, looking like her heart was breaking. "I'm sorry," she said. "I should have . . ." She trailed off.

Anger whipped through Mina. Of course she had nothing

to say. Whatever evidence Hendrik had to support his alibi clearly couldn't have been interrogated too closely. Now Starrett, for all her motherly concern, needed to shield her department from the fallout. Needed to avoid saying anything that could open them up to a lawsuit.

She needn't worry. Mina's father could sue if he wanted to; Mina just wanted it to be over. She didn't want this story to have a third act.

TWENTY-FIVE

LANE PULLED OUT the pins holding his notes to the wall, letting the papers and photographs flutter to the floor. He packed the pins carefully back in their box. The papers he would shred and put in the recycling bin when he was finished. There was no point holding on to them. His car had no space to spare for sentiment.

He ran his fingertips over the map, tracing from one flag to the next. He thought all roads led here, to Nannine, but it was just another bad hunch.

When he solved the Fermin case there hadn't been room for any disappointment about being wrong, not in the rush of winning and sudden wealth. There'd been a twinge when the Tammie Peterson case also didn't go the way he'd hoped, but he'd known that was a long shot. His father had been fifteen when Tammie was killed, which was possible but unlikely. Besides, he'd thought he had nothing but time.

Now he had a few weeks. If he moved on to another case right away, maybe he could get somewhere in that time. There were some with warm leads, and some where he already had a few contacts that would help him get rapid traction. But if he only had one more shot at this, he had to be sure it was one that his father had been responsible for. Up until a week ago, if anyone had asked him which case was the most likely prospect, he would have pointed confidently to Evelyn.

His jaw burned and he focused on unclenching his teeth, forcing the muscles to stop jamming from panic.

He moved around the small flat, half finishing half a dozen different tasks. He threw his toiletries in a plastic bag, then left it sitting on the sink when he remembered he needed to move his clothes from the washing machine to the dryer. As soon as that was humming, he moved into the kitchenette and started sorting the foods that could travel, like canned soup and bags of pasta, from the foods that would need to go in the bin.

He was being ridiculous. He should just go to Lynnie, today. He could stay with her until the hearing, do the best he could to help her feel safe, and if it didn't go their way, they could leave. The reward money was enough to get one of those rich arsehole visas for the US or Europe. His father wouldn't be able to leave New South Wales until his parole period was up, and a lot of countries would never let him in with his record.

But his father coming after them wasn't really what he was afraid of.

And there was nowhere he could take Lynnie where she wouldn't have to face her bed at the end of the day, where she wouldn't be listening for the sound of her doorknob turning.

The dryer dinged and he startled so hard he knocked his shoulder on the wall. He dragged his duffel bag into the bathroom, rolling his shoulder to ease the ache as he went. He threw the clothes in, the warm fresh shirts and shorts mixing with winter clothes he'd never needed to unpack.

He dragged the zipper closed, letting out a slow breath in time with the movement. The warmth of his clothes soaked through the fabric of the bag, where he'd pressed his palm against it for balance. He clenched his hand into a fist, suddenly burning with the urge to destroy something. He drove his fist into the side of the bag, but it just slid away from him across the glossy tile floor. He pressed up out of his crouch and kicked, his foot connecting with the bag with a muffled thump. He booted it into the living area.

A noise made him look up, and he nearly jumped out of his skin. Mina stood framed in his doorway, the late afternoon sun behind her.

He paused, staring down at the bag between his feet. He was aware of his breathing, too fast and too ragged for a casual afternoon of packing.

Mina looked him up and down, and then her gaze came to rest first on the duffel bag, then on the blank wall. He remembered the look of disgust on her face when she first saw his flat, first saw the way he had her sister on display. Now she looked equally horrified to find it gone. He couldn't win.

"Why are you packing up?" she asked.

"I . . ." He hadn't expected to have to do this. He'd been planning to leave a note with Starrett, since the only other way to say goodbye was to drive out to the house, and he'd assumed she would be bemused that he'd even bothered. "I have to go."

"You can't," she said, and he was surprised by the strain in her voice. "It's so far from over. This is only the beginning. Hendrik hasn't confessed, and we still need to find the . . . body." She paused, swallowed. "Her body."

"That's a job for someone else," Lane said. "I can give you some names of forensic specialists, if the police want help, but in my experience they'd prefer I get out of the way."

"I don't want you to leave," she said. She seemed as surprised by the words as he was.

She probably believed it too.

"Do you want to come in?" he asked, for want of something better to say.

He realized it was a mistake as soon as she stepped through the door. Without the glare behind her, he could see that the skin beneath her eyes was tight and flushed deep red, like someone had pinched the apples of her cheeks and twisted. He didn't have anywhere to sit, so he had to guide her to the end of his bed, which doubled as his lounge.

He went into the kitchenette and filled a glass with the slightly coppery tap water. "I'm always happy to keep in touch after my cases are done," he said over his shoulder. "If it's needed."

A handful of the families did keep in token contact with him—an email at Christmas, the occasional New Year text. Most shook his hand firmly and forgot about him. They didn't keep in touch any more than they would keep in touch with a builder who replaced their skirting boards, or the dentist who maintained their braces. He was in their life for a specific purpose and then moved on.

"I'd like that," she said, accepting the water with a brief, weak smile.

Lane rubbed his hand over his chest. Whatever this was, he couldn't do it. Until yesterday, he'd thought he could help Lynnie and Mina at the same time. Now those paths were diverging, and Lynnie had to come first. "I'll let you know how I get on, eh? If I have anything to tell you, I guess I can put a notice in the *Mid-West Post*."

It wasn't a good joke, but it didn't have to be to try to ease the tension between them.

She picked up his phone off the bedside table. "You could have found my number if you'd tried. The press have always managed it."

Of course he could have. It would have taken minutes. "I'm not going to call a number you don't want me to have."

"Huh." She smiled down at his phone, and then hit "save." "There."

He took the phone back, feeling strangely honored. He doubted there were many people in the world with that number saved.

She took a sip of the water, and seemed a little more together. Her face had lost some of that pinched look.

"Not that I mind the visit," he said, "but did you need something specific?"

"I was feeling jittery, so I thought I would go see Alanna at the library," she said. "But I was driving past your street and"—she stared down at her water—"I thought I might as well stop in and talk about the money."

He knew that was a lie. Unless her family's lawyer was completely useless, Mina would have been warned not to discuss the money with him, for fear of a slip of the tongue being upheld as a legally binding promise. This wouldn't be his first reward payout, although it would be the first of its size, and he doubted the process got less contentious as more zeroes were added.

"Of course," he said. "When will your father be back?"

"Starrett only just got a hold of him," she said. "I was terrified he was going to find out from the news. His flight lands at eleven, then it's a couple of hours' drive."

"Oh god, the media," Lane said. "When is Starrett making a statement?"

"She's trying to balance keeping it under wraps—so Dad doesn't get mobbed at the airport—with trying to get ahead of any leaks. She'll probably put out a statement tonight, and then they'll send trucks to get footage for the breakfast editions." She closed her eyes, and something in him lurched. "You can't imagine what it's like having them camped out at the gate."

"Stay here," he said.

Her body language stiffened, her hands clenching into fists on her knees. He held his hands up. "Not with me," he said quickly. "I'm leaving. This flat will be empty. You might as well use it."

"You're just going to walk away from a flat you're still paying rent on?" She frowned. "Is there a warrant out for your arrest or something?"

"No." He sighed. Why not just tell her? If Evelyn McCreery had just proved to be another dead end, then he wouldn't be tainting the case anymore. And there was comfort in knowing that Mina would probably respond with something withering and rude, not with pity.

"After I graduated from uni, I went straight to the federal police training program," he said. From the look on her face, this wasn't a revelation to her. It was interesting to get confirmation that she had dug into his background and credentials. How much had she found? "But when I was about halfway through, I was woken up and told I had an urgent phone call."

As if summoned by the words, his phone went off, and his heart jumped in time with the noise. They both turned to look at it, buzzing on the bedspread beside him, and probably both had the same thought: was someone calling him because they'd heard his name on the news?

He grabbed it, expecting to see his sister's picture, but another familiar number lit up the screen. Alanna Rennold.

"Lane," she said, as soon as the call connected. "I've just had a hysterical phone call from Liam McCreery. Mina's not answering the home phone and, well, it's not like I can call the Tamms. I know it's a big ask, but do you think you could drive—"

"Mina's here." He switched the call over to speaker. "What do you mean Mr. McCreery called you? He's in the air right now."

"You might want to check the news," Alanna said. "I'll give Liam your number," she added, and disconnected the call.

He turned to grab the remote to the old television that had come free with the flat, the sort of miniature flat screen that stores often gave away when they sold full-sized ones. Mina beat him and bashed the power button. Luckily, the TV was tuned to a twenty-four-hour news channel, not to what was in the DVD player.

To his surprise, the screen wasn't splashed with Evelyn's picture. The story onscreen was a doping scandal in sport, but a headline scrolled into view at the bottom: BRISBANE–BROKEN HILL FLIGHT TURNED BACK AFTER TAKEOFF DUE TO DISRUPTIVE PASSENGER.

"Oh great, that's just what we need," Mina said. "Dad stuck in another state."

The news anchor's smile froze for a moment and his posture changed from "daily grind" to "oh shit, here we go."

"We're going to return to that story later. The passenger who forced a Qantas flight to turn back to Brisbane Airport fifteen minutes after takeoff has been identified as Liam McCreery, the father of Evelyn McCreery, who disappeared from her home in

Central New South Wales in 1999. A representative for the Nannine Police has called a press conference for five fifteen, and we will be crossing to that during our evening program."

The news transitioned into the Evelyn McCreery package the station had on file, and Lane switched it off.

"Shit. Fuck. Goddamn it," Mina said, her tone flat even as she emptied what had to be her entire repertoire of curses at the television. "Son of a . . . this trip was supposed to be Dad's chance to get away from this garbage."

"I thought staying put was how you got away from it," Lane said.

That actually got a laugh out of her, which made him proud, even though that hadn't been his aim.

"There is no getting away from it," Mina said. "The shadow is there whether you set up a goddamn picnic underneath it like my mother or if you try to run away from it like my father. No matter which way you go, you're still responding to the shadow."

Lane's phone rang, and he tossed it to her without even looking at the screen.

"Dad," she said, a little plaintive. She wasn't trying to put on a show for Lane anymore.

Liam McCreery's voice rang tinny in the room. The phone was still on speaker.

"Sweetheart." McCreery's voice was shattered. His breath came ragged. "Hendrik didn't kill your sister, Mina."

"He's been lying to us for twenty years, Daddy," Mina said.

"So have I," McCreery said. "I know that he didn't hurt your sister, because I can account for his whereabouts for every minute of the night that she went missing. I'm so sorry. I'm sorry. So sorry."

Mina's face went completely still. "You've been lying about where you were that night too?"

"No, sweetheart—"

"Stop calling me that!" she shrieked.

"Alright. No. I was where I told you I was. I was in Sydney when your mother called on Saturday morning. We both were."

Relief flooded Lane. The police would need to verify that— presumably more thoroughly than they had checked Hendrik's first alibi—but if McCreery was telling the truth, then the case was wide open again.

"You need to understand, Mina. What was I supposed to do? You and your mother were already dealing with something so unbearable. And me too. How could I have struck another blow? I know that the truth would have made no difference to the investigation, because neither of us were anywhere near the house that night." His voice shook with emotion. "Hendrik had mailed his credit card to his cousin, so if his wife checked the account she would see purchases in Adelaide like she expected. He showed those to the police. If he hadn't, if we'd told the truth, the police would have wasted so much precious time looking into us, and it would have broken five people's hearts. It was the right thing to do, Mina."

The words came out smooth as cream, despite his obvious distress. Lane wondered how many times Liam had practiced that speech, not just today but in the past twenty years. How many times he had whispered it to himself in the dark.

"Thank you for telling me the truth," Mina said. Her voice was detached and she stared at the wall, at a hole left by one of his pushpins. "You need to call Starrett immediately, before she starts her press conference."

Lane sat on the bed, feeling like his legs were going to buckle beneath him. To his shock, Mina leaned into him. She was so much warmer than he'd expected her to be, pressed into his side. He slid an arm around her back, and squeezed her shoulder with his hand.

"Okay, sweet—okay. The airline found me a seat on the next flight. I'll be with you tonight."

"I think it would probably be best if you stayed where you are," Mina said, still in that detached voice. "I think that's the right thing to do."

TWENTY-SIX

MyMurder Forums

Subforum: Evie McCreery

Subject: The press conference that wasn't: theories, rumors, what
we know

User Inspektor: The whole thing is pretty weird, though. I was all
settled in with a cup of tea waiting for it to start—I can't remember the last time I watched free-to-air television, I had to scan
for the channel—and then just nothing. Not even an explanation
of why it was canceled.

User VolcanicJudo: The newsreader seemed embarrassed as hell.
My guess is they heard the words "Evie McCreery," got excited,
and shot their load too early. The "news" probably turned out
to be, like, a press release for a new edition of Bev's book.

User Waffletoid: I don't think so. They said the press conference
was organized by the police, not the family. Something happened, and then they pulled the plug at the last minute. If you
look at the comments on **this** article, there's a user who lives in

240

Nannine, who says word around town is that there's a private investigator reworking the case.

* * *

Twice Lane had received midnight phone calls that sent his life skidding off course. The first was when he was a police cadet, holding on to his place in a punishing training program by the skin of his teeth, and looking forward to a bright future with a guaranteed salary, annual leave, and a retirement plan. Then he was shaken awake in the middle of the night and sent to the office to answer the phone.

"Lane," his mother said, her voice so despairing that he was filled with the immediate, dread conviction that something had happened to Lynnie. "Lane, Daddy's been arrested."

"Your father?" Lane said, still barely conscious. His grandfather was in a nursing home in Young. He couldn't imagine him committing a crime.

"No, *your* father. Dad."

His immediate, shameful thought was to wonder if this was going to fuck his career before it even started. It would, but not in the way that he thought in that moment. "What for?"

"Car theft." She sniffled. "He took a BMW from a restaurant parking lot. But the police are saying he found the owner's address in the glove box, and they're threatening to stick him with attempted burglary too. Apparently he had a street directory open to the right street on the passenger seat."

"Shit," Lane said, scrubbing a hand over his eyes. Frankly, the man going to jail would probably be the best thing that ever happened to his mother, but she didn't need to hear that right now. "Did they give him a lawyer?"

Stealing a motor vehicle, with his previous good behavior bonds, would net him three years, minimum. Maybe more, especially if the burglary charge held up in court. That would be good; it would give Lane a few years to work as a police officer, sock away money for the two of them, work on getting his mother some counseling. This was good. This was great.

"That's why I'm calling," she said. "You know Dad has always managed the money—"

That was a euphemism for "he keeps every cent in an iron grip so I can't scrape together enough to get away from him." "I can't send you money to pay for a lawyer, Mum. I don't have it."

"Shut up and let me finish," she snapped. She fell silent for a moment, and he could hear her crying. "I'm sorry. Don't hang up, baby."

"I'm not going to hang up," Lane said, feeling like an arsehole. "What is it?"

"I went into his laptop, trying to find the banking passwords. I dug through his files."

"What did you find?" Lane asked. Wind rushed in his ears.

"Pictures," she choked out.

"Is he having an affair?" Lane asked hopefully. Please let them be pictures of an adult woman. Or an adult man, that would be fine.

"Lane," his mother wailed, and he knew that they weren't.

Lane felt like he had stepped outside of himself and was watching the conversation from the corner of the room. "It's going to be okay, Mum."

"I should just delete them, right?" his mother asked, dropping her voice low.

"What? No!" Panic coursed through him. "Do not delete them."

"He's already going to jail, baby. We don't need to deal with this. Surely it would just hurt her more, getting it all dragged through the court system?"

Lane saw it all play out at the back of his mind. His mother deleting the pictures, telling herself it was Lynnie she was protecting, not their father. He would go to jail, and after three years, maybe two with good behavior, he would step back into the light. And she would be there in the car park, with Lynnie in the back seat, because surely serving his time had set him straight?

She'd seen him literally break his own son's face—*her* son's face—and managed to forgive and forget. She would forgive him for what he'd done to Lynnie too. He couldn't let her. She didn't have the right.

"Don't do anything," he said. "Just stay where you are. I'll drive to you. I'll sort it all out, okay?"

"You can't leave the barracks, surely," she said, but her voice was relieved. Someone was going to take care of this for her.

He hung up the phone and sat in the dark office with his hands on his knees until they stopped shaking. Then he picked up the receiver and dialed the number of the New South Wales police.

* * *

He liked to think that the remaining six years of her life were peaceful. She moved Lynnie up to Byron Bay, and they stayed in one place for longer than she'd rested anywhere in her life. He liked to imagine them eating toasted marshmallows on the beach at sunset, Lynnie spending her nights sleeping peacefully with the window open, his mother sitting at a table out the front smoking her last cigarette of the day with a sea breeze on her cheeks. He needed to believe those were happy years. He didn't know for sure, because his mother never spoke to him again after the officers showed up at the door looking for the laptop.

But it was worth it. Because six years later he got another call in the middle of the night, from a social worker calling from the emergency room of Byron Central Hospital. His mother had been hit by a drunk driver while walking back to the caravan park from the supermarket. And if Lane Holland Sr. had only gone down for car theft, he would have been out of jail and ready to take that call.

* * *

Lane lay awake, every lump in his mattress feeling like an iron ball trying to bruise him. He regretted mentioning the phone call to Mina. It had churned it all up, and now here he was feeling the weight of every wasted passing day. He rolled onto his side and watched the clock change on his phone, minute by minute, until it hit a reasonable hour to get up. As soon as the clock ticked over to seven, his phone started buzzing in his hand. Like Lynnie had been doing the same thing in Canberra, waiting for it to be an acceptable time to call.

He pushed down his guilt at not having called her in a few days. As they counted down to the hearing, he should be reaching out to her far more often. But he hadn't trusted himself not to blurt out what was going on with Hendrik Tamm, and now he didn't want to burden her with the disappointment of losing the reward money. He reminded himself that there was nothing to be disappointed about. This was progress. A layer of dishonesty had been stripped away, and who knew what could become clear as a result?

"Hey you. What's up?"

"Nothing, I just wanted to chat," she said, and then breathed in with the audible shake of someone who had either just finished crying or was about to start.

"It's okay if you're not okay," he said.

"I am okay," she insisted. "Busy. It's nearly exam time, can you believe?"

"Wow, really?"

"Mm-hmm."

"How are you feeling about it? Do you think you'll go well?"

Her voice was steadier now. "I think so, yeah. I'm really enjoying my classes. It's easier than high school; I only have to take courses I actually want to do, so no more math."

"Yeah, I remember it being like that in first year. I hope you're not working too hard. Are you getting enough sleep, eating properly?" He was strolling up a dangerous path there, coming at a serious question sideways.

"It's all good. Hey, weirdest thing," Lynnie said. "While I was out shopping, I ran into that girl you thirst-follow on Instagram."

"I have no idea what that means," Lane said. He quickly googled the term, and immediately regretted it.

"The blonde," she said. "It was super weird to see her here in Canberra."

"It's not that weird; she lives in Yass. And I'm not 'thirst-following' her. Don't be gross."

"Will you relax? As long as you're not messaging her offering to buy pictures of her feet, you're fine. You're allowed to have your weird little crushes. I'm an adult, we don't live together anymore, you don't have to keep pretending you've never heard of sex, much as I always appreciated that."

"I wasn't . . ." Lane sighed loudly. "What even is this conversation?"

He knew what it was. It was her trying too hard to keep it breezy, and him matching her.

"I don't look at her page because I'm into her, okay? It's complicated." He swallowed the embarrassment. He had no idea he'd been doing it often enough for Lynnie to not only pick up on it, but recognize Alexandra out in public.

"Although it is a tiny bit gross, because she's, like, my age. You were already in high school when she was born. You could be her dad." Lynnie paused. "Oh god, you're not her dad, are you?"

Lane pinched the bridge of his nose. "No."

"Because I don't know anything about what your life was like back then, except that you and Mum and . . . except that you all traveled a lot. You could have kids all over."

"I am completely certain I don't, and if I do, Alexandra isn't one of them."

"Good, because when I saw her she was looking at prams."

"What were you doing in a baby store?"

"I was in Target, looking for a real coat, because the one I brought from home is apparently decorative. Womenswear and the baby stuff are right next to each other."

Was it really already time for a coat in Canberra? He supposed it would be starting to cool off, especially for someone used to balmy northern weather. Here the change in seasons had been barely perceptible—it had gone from scorching to just hot. "Were you able to get one? Do you need money for more warm stuff?"

"No, I'm fine. I've got it covered," she said.

They chatted about nothing for a few more minutes, and then she begged off to go get breakfast. He stared at his phone for a long time after, wondering if the conversation had made either of them feel better.

* * *

"Hey, mate," Neil said. He poured a beer before Lane had a chance to order, and set it on the bar top. "You must be feeling pretty rough, huh? You went from two million in the hand to nothing." He whistled.

Lane forced a smile. He'd actually managed to put that out of his mind for a few hours. "It's never in the hand until it's actually in your hand. There's a long road from calling something in to actually getting the reward, and even once they've got a conviction it's a knock-down drag-out fight with the police to actually get them to pay out the reward. I was never thinking of it as my money."

"Still. And you wouldn't have had to fight Mina; she'd have done right by you."

Lane shrugged. The nicest person in the world could turn nasty once money was involved, and Mina wasn't particularly nice to begin with. "So, I'm guessing that Starrett questioned you, given that what happened isn't supposed to be public knowledge."

"Yeah. Don't worry, I'm not going to spread the story around."

"Yes, you're good at keeping secrets, aren't you?"

Neil held his hands up. "Fair."

Lane traced the logo on the beer glass with his thumb. "Did you know that the 'H' in your reservation book stood for Hendrik when we asked, or did you put that together when Starrett showed you the picture?"

"A little from column A, a little from column B. I didn't know. I knew that he used to rent the room sometimes, and I suspected. But I never thought it meant anything in relation to Evelyn."

"Well, you were right on that count." Lane sighed. "So it's just part of the job, huh? You help men hide things from their wives."

247

The smile slipped off Neil's face. "You mean like with Reg and Syl?"

"Yeah. No. I mean, it's all just hilarious, isn't it? A woman calls here worried about her husband, and you help him blow her off. It keeps him here buying drinks from you, I guess."

Lane should go. He'd had a shit couple of days and had barely slept on top of it, and he wasn't actually angry at Neil for lying to him; it just felt good to needle him.

"Let me tell you something about Reg, mate," Neil said. "This summer he had to cut his herd size down so far he started sending his breeding stock to slaughter. That bloodline is his life's work, and he can't keep 'em fed anymore. And now he's done that, there's no coming back. Even when the land recovers, he won't have the breeding stock to recover with it. He's sixty years old. He's fucked. It's a good sign to see him here, surrounded by friends. Better than him drinking at home by himself."

"Why not tell his wife that, then? Let them work it out between themselves like adults."

"Hey, if you don't like how I run things, you're welcome to open your own pub."

The words were dismissive, but he was still looking at Lane like he was worried he was about to have a breakdown. Lane wondered if Neil had some sort of savior complex. After all, he'd been quick to white-knight Mina the day he and Lane met, and he was telling himself a story where lying to Syl made him a hero.

Lane sighed. "Did your uncle do the same thing?" he asked. "Cover for punters when someone called for them?"

Neil nodded. "He was pretty old-school."

"Would he have done the opposite? Told a woman her husband was here when he wasn't?"

"Yeah, a bit of that went on. I won't do it myself; I can't stand cheaters."

"I don't suppose you remember if anyone called that Friday night? Preview night?"

"Straight back on the horse, huh?" Neil chuckled, but it was more uncomfortable than amused. He wavered for a moment, and Lane thought he might be about to get chewed out again. "Beverley didn't call, not before I left. Answering the phone was one of my jobs for the night."

"Did anyone else call?"

"I dunno, mate. The Friday night . . ." Neil shook his head. "I remember every moment of Saturday morning. My mum waking me up and telling me Evelyn had gone missing, my dad taking off to help with the search. The whole town had this awful air, with everyone on edge. I think most people who lived in town at the time are the same, it's printed on their brain. One of those 'where were you when?' moments. But the Friday? I didn't know it was important at the time. It's a blur."

It was the same story, again and again. Nobody was paying attention, because they had no reason to think that any tiny detail might turn out to be important one day.

"Do you remember who was in the pub?"

"There were a lot of strangers that night."

"What if I showed you pictures? You could tell me if anyone seemed familiar." Lane would have to set that up carefully. Just showing Neil a picture of his father and asking if he was present wouldn't hold up under scrutiny, and could bias him for future questioning. He could get a couple of pictures of random men, and one of his father, and set it out like a photographic lineup. If he did that and Neil still pointed to his father as someone who was in the pub, it would hold up. Then he would have a witness, proof his father was in town.

"Look, it was so long ago . . ." Neil looked genuinely sorry to say no.

Neil wanted to be the hero, a dark part of Lane thought. He wanted to help Lane. He wanted to help Mina. That would make him so easy to manipulate. It could be as simple as a question phrased in a leading way. Or he could show him a picture of his father now, and come back in a few days to do it all properly. He could—

A door behind the bar opened—Lane had assumed it led to a storeroom or cupboard—and Liam McCreery shuffled out. Lane straightened, surprise chasing the idea away.

Apparently the pub did have rooms to rent, for the right person. But, then, that door didn't lead upstairs. Liam had left it open, revealing what looked like a sitting room furnished with a garish upholstered tub chair and a wood-veneer coffee table. Lane would be willing to bet those were the rooms that Neil's uncle had lived in, back when he ran the pub.

"Good morning, Mr. McCreery," he said.

He was taken aback by how old Liam looked. Lane didn't know exactly how old he was, but he'd been older than Bev, so he was at least in his late sixties. His dark black hair had turned to steel wool, and his barrel chest had faded away. He had narrow shoulders and skinny arms, his elbows and wrists jutting out like his body wanted to be bigger. Lane supposed it was a shock because Beverley had become frozen in time when she died just shy of her fiftieth birthday, and subconsciously he had expected Liam to stop aging too.

"Morning." Liam rubbed the back of his neck. He looked a little disoriented—it was well after eleven, but Lane suspected he'd just woken up. With the week he'd had, Lane didn't blame him for having a lie-in.

"Lane Holland," Lane said, offering a handshake.

"You're the young man who was on the phone." Liam shook his hand and Lane relaxed a fraction.

"I'll sort some coffee, eh?" Neil said, and headed into the dining area.

"Does Mina know you're in town?"

"That depends entirely on whether she's listening to my messages or deleting them." Liam slid onto a barstool. "Has she said anything to you?"

Lane thought carefully before answering that. If Mina wasn't ready to talk to her father, then it would be a terrible move to act as a back channel for him. But if he shut that down firmly, Liam would lose interest in talking to him.

Over in the dining area, Neil turned a little, obviously interested in finding out exactly how close he and Mina were.

"I haven't talked to her since our conversation with you," Lane admitted. "I was planning to call her soon."

It wasn't an offer to say anything on Liam's behalf, but the man's expression warmed, and he looked so hopeful for a moment that Lane felt like an arsehole.

"I'm worried about her," Liam said. "Her birthday is coming up, and she's so alone with all of this."

"You lied to her for nearly twenty years," Lane said. "It's only been a few days—let her process it."

"Nearly thirty years," Liam said ruefully.

"Mr. McCreery—"

"Liam is fine, son."

"Liam, do you think I could ask you a few questions?"

"Depends what they are." Liam glanced over at Neil, who was coming back through with Liam's coffee.

"Would you like to move?" Lane picked up his beer, and indicated a table tucked in the back.

Liam hesitated for a moment, and then nodded.

Once they were settled at the table, Lane pulled out a small spiral-bound notebook. He'd palmed one of the keno pencils at the bar. He would have preferred to pull out his phone and record, but he was sure that would scare Liam off entirely.

"I'm not going to pry into your relationship with Mr. Tamm—"

"We don't have a relationship. I mean, we haven't for a long time. Ever since . . . ever since that weekend, he's been my employee. Nothing else."

"Even after you closed down the sheep operation?"

"Are you asking if he's been on the payroll as some kind of kept man? Or do you think he's blackmailing me?"

Lane paused, wondering if he'd stepped in it already. Of course there was no reason to think Liam was oblivious to the rumors that swirled around his family, just because he'd always stayed stoic. "I have seen people online suggest that the salary is your way of paying him off, yes. And while Starrett has managed to keep a lid on this new information so far, if the truth got out it would only feed that assumption."

"Right, the fucking internet sleuths." Liam's face twisted, and Lane could see Mina in his expression. "Yeah, we probably could have saved some money by laying Hendrik off. But we were still growing grain, and we couldn't just let the equipment and build-ings for the sheep operation go to rack and ruin. We wanted to keep our options open, especially once Mina decided she wanted to farm it one day. Someone had to keep things running until she was old enough."

"What about you?"

Liam's knuckles tightened on his coffee cup, and he didn't answer.

"Did you ever consider selling?" Lane was mostly curious to see if his answer would differ from Mina's.

"Plenty of times. I even had a buyer out to see it once, thinking that a real offer might sway Bev. She hit the roof." Liam chuckled. "I think that was the only subject she and Mina were ever united on."

"Beverley wanted to stay?" That surprised him. Between her media appearances and book tours, it seemed like Mina's mother had spent most of her time away from the property.

"She, uh . . ." Liam swallowed. "She was worried that if we moved, Evelyn wouldn't be able to find us. She forced me to keep the same phone number for the same reason, even after journos started getting a hold of it."

Lane knew that was a common worry for the families of missing people. In the vanishingly unlikely event that Evelyn was alive, she wouldn't have had any difficulty making contact with her parents. But anxiety didn't need to be reasonable to be powerful.

"Anyway, what are we really here to talk about? I assume you're not angling to buy my farm." Liam forced the joke, clearly uncomfortable straying into such emotional territory.

Lane chuckled. "I can't imagine anything I'd be worse at than farming. No, I was hoping to clear up some of the timelines of that Friday, now that everything is out in the open. Who was where, when. I know that Hendrik had an early dinner here. Were you with him?"

Liam nodded. A tiny choice, Lane thought. If they'd chosen their seats differently, so Liam ended up in the photo and Hendrik sat just out of frame, this would all still be a secret. The most random things, impossible to predict, made all the difference.

"Did you talk to anyone here in the pub, or notice anything unusual?"

"No." Liam shifted in his seat. "We kept to ourselves. I was in a hurry to get on the road."

"Why was that?"

"Hendrik was getting cold feet. He mentioned that he was worried about leaving Bev and Maggie home alone. It didn't make sense—Bev was tougher than he was—so I figured it was just guilt eating at him. If he got cold feet and went home, that would have been impossible to explain. He was supposed to be in another state. So I wanted to get going before he freaked out anymore."

"When did you leave? Did you stop anywhere else first?"

"Around five thirty, and no, we headed straight to Sydney. I was an industry representative at a meeting with the Department of Agriculture, meaning I was supposed to spend the weekend on conference calls while they bullshitted us about levies. I only made it as far as the hotel. There's piles of evidence supporting that—I'd kept my fuel receipts for the taxman, and the hotel receptionist made a statement that I checked in at midnight and took breakfast at five."

"That's not much time to sleep," Lane remarked.

"I slept a bit on the drive, since I had Hendrik to spell me."

Lane did the math quickly, drawing a little box in his notebook and scribbling out the numbers. Nannine to Sydney was about seven hours—six if there was no traffic and a driver blew through every town at a hundred and twenty clicks. Sydney to the McCreery property was closer to eight hours, and anyone trying to speed the last leg would almost certainly wipe out on Nannine–National Park Road, which was barely maintained.

Evelyn and Mina went to bed at 8:00 p.m, according to Beverley's statements and the book, and Mina woke and discovered Evelyn missing at 5:00 a.m. Even if for some reason Liam checked into the hotel then immediately left Sydney to return home and hurt his daughter, the fastest possible trip would have him arriving at the house hours after that.

What about Hendrik, though? Could Liam have had Hendrik impersonate him in Sydney, while Liam secretly remained behind in Nannine?

It didn't seem likely. Back then, Liam was an imposing figure with dark hair, while Tamm was slight and fair. Within days the McCreery family had the four most recognizable faces in Australia, so even if they had managed to snow a receptionist, he or she would have noticed quickly that the guest they'd met wasn't the same man.

He stared down at the paper. Or maybe it was a perfectly valid theory that he didn't want to give credence.

"Why did you drive so far, instead of flying?"

"When you live in this part of the world, an eight-hour drive stops seeming like a lot. Besides, have you ever flown Regional Express, in one of their tiny prop planes?"

"No, but I rode in one of the Flying Doctor Service's planes a few weeks ago."

Liam nodded. "Ah yes, that was you, wasn't it? Well, I don't know if the experiences are comparable, but I assure you the drive is preferable."

"While we're talking about planes—Hendrik bought a plane ticket to Adelaide. That seems an expensive step, just to cover an affair."

"After he booked it, and showed it to Maggie, he exchanged it for a later flight. The plan was for him to spend the weekend in Sydney with me, then I would drop him at the airport on my way home, and he would actually go out to visit his cousin for the rest of the week. But then Beverley called, and all plans went out the window."

"It seems like taking your operations manager on a business trip wouldn't have raised suspicions. Can you tell me why you went to such lengths to hide that he was with you?"

Liam was quiet for a long moment. Lane realized he was probably the first person, outside of Hendrik, who Liam had spoken to openly about this. He could wait a few minutes for Liam to find the words.

"Beverley was . . . the word 'jealous' is on my tongue, but that's wrong, that's wrong. 'Jealous' implies she was irrational, when she was right: I was stepping out on her. She picked up the signs, you know? I was more cheerful, I started caring whether my shirt was clean and my trousers still had knees in them when I headed out of a morning."

"All the classics," Lane said.

Liam's expression turned sympathetic. "You've been there, huh? A wife or girlfriend?"

Lane laughed a little. It was a reasonable assumption, but the idea of him having a wife sat oddly. That wasn't for the likes of him. "I've just done a couple of infidelity cases in my time. How sure are you that Beverley knew?"

"We never talked about it. She didn't make any accusations, or throw any lamps. But I'm sure she knew, because it was clear she knew it was Hendrik. She was suddenly so interested in the goings-on with the farm, when she'd always busied herself with the house and volunteering with the CWA. She'd drop by the shearing shed unexpectedly with scones, or bring the girls out to watch us sink fence posts."

Lane thought of the pictures Beverley had taken at the show, trying to capture the crowds and corners. She'd been looking for her husband. If she'd picked up on his attempts to give her the slip for the weekend, it was a logical jump to think he was actually headed for the weekend long party at the campsite in the showground. If she'd gone for a pub dinner like the Ramseys did, she might have found him.

Instead she went home. He could imagine how agitated that left her, and based on what both Mina and Maggie Tamm had said, she'd been letting it slip out at the girls as bickering and barbs. Then she'd been alone with Evelyn, twisted up with anger at their father, while Mina slept.

No. Lane pushed away the thought. Beverley's love for Evelyn defined the rest of her life; she was no Medea.

"If she knew the two of us were going to Sydney together alone, she would have tried to turn it into a family trip instead." Liam's eyes, already red from the emotions the discussion had churned up, grew wet. "And if she had, then everything would have been different."

"Or all four of you might have been killed by a semitrailer on the drive home," Lane said. "It's easy to believe that if you could just change one thing then you would have lived a perfect life with no pain or loss. Life would have just found some other way to kick you in the shins."

"Oh, mate," Liam said, his voice warm but rough with tears.

Lane had to look away for a moment, focusing on the corner of the table until the constriction in his throat eased. "What about before the pub?" Lane asked, forcing himself to keep his voice brisk. "What do you remember of that Friday, before you left home?"

"I don't think I know anything useful," Liam said. "I woke up at five, as usual. The girls and Beverley were asleep when I left the house. Show day was a local public holiday, and we'd encouraged the men to head into town for it. So I did a couple of things that morning that I'd usually have one of the fellas do, then went back to the house to pack. We had lunch, then I sat with the girls for a while to spend time with them before I left and give Bev a break." He smiled to himself. "Evelyn was trying to convince me to bring her back a Furby from Sydney. Finally it was time to head off, and Beverley announced that she and the girls would ride with me as far as Nannine, so they could go to the opening night and get their paperwork in for the showgirl competition. That was silly, of course—she could have enrolled them on the day of the competition—but . . ."

"But she wanted to check if Hendrik was in the car with you," Lane guessed.

Liam mimed a golf swing. Hole in one. "I managed to slip away and let him know to meet me in Nannine."

"You weren't worried she'd catch you at the pub?"

"Call it a calculated risk. The Neeny could get pretty raucous during show weekend." He looked around the silent pub with something close to a smile on his face. "Plenty of families were fine with it, but Bev would never have brought the girls in."

Lane's pen skittered to a stop. "Can I ask an odd question?" he asked, his throat dry. "Was there anything in Hendrik's ute with the farm's address on it?"

"What?" Liam scrunched up his face, obviously racking his brain. "I imagine so. It was a farm ute; there'd have been a log-book. Probably some mail too—we used to pick it up whenever we were driving past."

It wasn't just Hendrik who had been taken out of consideration by his fake alibi. It was his car, and the tracks it had left on the property.

It was like one of those logic puzzles with the fox and the hen and the bag of grain. Three cars and four adults, all flowing to and from the property, separating and recombining in Nannine. One car, Liam's, went to Sydney with two drivers. One car, Maggie's, went from the farm to Nannine and back again.

And one car, Hendrik's, was left here at the pub, unattended. A car the police believed was parked at an airport in another city.

TWENTY-SEVEN

* * *

Mina laid the map of the property down on the dashboard and
marked today's section off with sharp, hard strokes. She always felt
an extra spark of hope on significant days. It would be so narra-

tively tidy for her to find Evelyn's body on her birthday, or on the anniversary, or on Christmas morning, that her mind twisted itself into thinking it was actually more likely. The comedown added a bitter kick to already difficult days.

There was a message waiting. That had to be her father. He knew exactly when to call to get the machine, the coward. She hit the button to send it to saved messages.

She went into the kitchen, where she had left a white tea light sitting on a saucer. She preferred to do this outside in the flower garden, but the region was in a total fire ban this year. She struck a match and lit the candle, and then threw the match in the sink.

"Well, Evelyn," she said with a sigh. "Happy birthday. I hope you'll forgive me if I don't sing."

Twenty-eight, goddamn. She couldn't picture it. She'd seen age-progression pictures, of course, but they were as much a guess as any image she could conjure up. Would Evelyn have grown up as a copy-and-paste of Beverley, the way she had looked as a kid? Would their father's features have asserted themselves as she grew up, the way that Mina had come to look more and more like him as the years passed? Maybe she would look like neither of them. Maybe she would have embraced lip fillers and implants, or neon hair dye and piercings.

She wished that their birthdays and the anniversary were further apart. With only three weeks in between, there wasn't time for the emotions stirred up to subside before they got hit by the next one. During those weeks, the three of them had always become their worst selves. Her father collapsed in on himself, shuffling around the house in silence as he battled depression and, as she now knew, crippling guilt. Her mother would be gripped by a fervor, awake half the night clattering away on her keyboard, writing blog posts

261

and articles and emails to every media outlet she could think of. And Mina would become acid-tongued and selfish, goading the both of them in hopes that one or the other would snarl back.

But this year they would both be gone.

Not that it would make this year an easy one. She couldn't even look forward to the relief of the anniversary being over for another year, because that would be day one of the lead-up to the twentieth anniversary. Which meant articles, and books, and TV specials. Calls for comment and journalists on her doorstep.

The phone rang, startling her.

Her machine picked it up, and before she could turn off the speaker, Lane's voice said, "Hi, Mina." He sounded a little surprised, like he'd suspected the number she put in his phone would turn out to be fake.

She picked up the phone. "Hey."

"Hey. Hello," he said. There was a pause as he shifted gears from the message he'd been about to leave to normal conversation. "I was just calling to wish you a happy birthday."

For Pete's sake, wasn't he supposed to be a crack investigator? "It's not my birthday."

Lane was silent for several beats. "It's the tenth of April."

"Yes," Mina said. "Today is Evelyn's birthday."

"You're twins," Lane said, then sighed as he spotted his mistake. "Ah, I see. Evelyn was born before midnight?"

"You got it," Mina said.

"I'm sorry."

"Don't worry about it," she said. "It means I can mark Evelyn's birthday, and any . . . feelings it brings up without losing my own birthday in the process." That wasn't strictly true. Whether their birthday was on the same day or six months apart, she doubted the feelings would be different. Her birthday was just another special event with an Evelyn-shaped hole in it. "We loved it as kids; it gave us each a special day. My mother was never very happy about it."

"Because it meant cake for breakfast two days in a row?"

Mina laughed. "Because it was an annual reminder that she'd had the worst of both worlds. She gave birth to Evelyn, then had me by emergency caesarean section half an hour later."

"Ouch," he said. "Can that happen? Really?"

"Afraid so," Mina said. "It's extremely rare—it only happens in three percent of twin births. Quick, ask me how I know the exact number off the top of my head."

"Frequent reminders, huh?"

"At least the rarity factor took some of the sting out of it. The obstetrician brought all the student midwives to see her while she was in recovery. She would have been in her element."

"It must have been frightening for her, though. If she had to have an emergency C-section, then you could have died."

Mina hadn't really thought of it that way. Her mother had never treated her like something precious she'd almost lost. They'd all been lucky, she supposed, that they'd been born in the nineties, in a properly equipped hospital. Fifty years earlier and things would have gone very differently, especially for a mother living on a remote property. Although it didn't feel right to think of the three of them as *lucky*.

"So if your birthday was the eleventh of April 1990 . . . that was a Wednesday."

"Congratulations, detective," Mina said. "You cracked the secret code. Yep, Mum called me Wednesday because of the different birthdays thing, not because she was so bitterly disappointed by my looks."

Hardly better, though. Instead of a jab at her coloring, it was just years of needling blame for an event she had no control over.

"Evelyn loved it, of course, because she got to be full of grace while I was stuck with woe," Mina continued.

"I'm afraid you've lost me."

"You don't know that old poem? Mum loved it, because she was born on a Monday and so was fair of face. Monday's child is fair of face, Tuesday's child is full of grace, Wednesday's child is full of woe . . ."

"What's Thursday's child?"

"Is that your birthday? Thursday's child has far to go."

"Oh, that's true enough. Let me check my sister's birthdate, she loves these old superstitions." Lane went silent, probably scrolling through a calendar app, and then sounded disappointed. "Another Wednesday."

"Ah. Well, I hope she avoids the woe," Mina said.

"Does anyone?" Lane asked.

"I suppose it's theoretically possible. Tossing a coin and getting heads every time is as probable as any other combination. Maybe there's someone out there who slides through life always getting the best possible outcome."

"Well, I'm sorry for the mistake. I won't make it again. Let me take you out," he said. "To say sorry, and for your birthday. I'll buy you a drink."

"Ooh, a free drink. And I only have to drive an hour to get it." Mina laughed.

"Sorry, that was a strange suggestion," he said. He sounded worried about something, a worry that seemed out of proportion to the situation.

She felt bad. Why was her first impulse always to be so damned bitter?

"Anyway," he continued, "I'm sure you've got plans for your birthday."

She made a dismissive noise. Her important plans were to take her usual morning walk, and then get drunk and eat cake by herself. On impulse, she said, "How about this: why don't you come to the house tomorrow?"

TWENTY-EIGHT

LANE PULLED IN beside Mina's ute, in the same spot he'd parked the first time. He gathered his things from the passenger seat. He'd brought a bottle of wine, one that was decent but not expensive. He'd hovered in front of Mrs. Gilligan's small selection for nearly half an hour, trying to find the exact right bottle of wine, one that would look like he hadn't gone to too much trouble picking it out.

He'd been relieved when she turned down the suggestion of meeting at the pub. The words had been out before he remembered that her father was there, and if she still didn't know that, he would have had to tell her. The less involvement he had in that situation, the better.

But he wasn't sure what it meant, that she'd invited him here. Were they celebrating Mina's birthday with a drink, or was he finally here to inspect the house? The crime scene.

Mina opened the door in a yellow sundress, with her hair scraped back into a high ponytail and a touch of pink on her lips, which did nothing to lessen the ambiguity.

"You made it in okay," she said. "No snakes today."

"I trust your training of them," he said. "And I'm welcome today."

She chuckled. "I just put the kettle on. Can I get you a cup of tea?" Then she dragged her gaze down his body and saw the bottle of wine. "Or we could day drink. That works."

"You are . . . you did . . ." he fumbled.

"I'm messing with you," she said. "Come on in."

Her yanking his chain again didn't help with the feeling that it was dangerous to step through the door. He knew they'd moved past her game of seeming to help him only for it to prove a trick, but there was still a part of him on edge. Like this might be a hidden test, and she would rage at him for expecting to be offered entry to the private space she guarded so fiercely.

The house was more or less what he had imagined based on the outside. Heavy floorboards. No floating floors installed from a Bunnings flat pack or linoleum cleverly designed to look like real wood here.

The entryway opened immediately into the kitchen. It had a generous-sized gas stove next to a deep farmhouse sink. On a separate island Mina had set out a teapot and two cups.

She pointed to a stool and he sat himself down awkwardly. He wanted to ask who else she'd heard from today. Had her father made a call? Had she answered it? But the words stuck in his throat. He knew he wasn't responsible for the way all of Mina's relationships seemed to have imploded since he arrived in town, but knowing you weren't responsible and not feeling responsible were two entirely different things.

"I've brought your mail," he said, putting the short stack of letters he'd found in the roadside mailbox down on the counter.

She raised her eyebrows. "Messing with my mailbox without permission? You commit a lot of casual crimes for a man of the law." She riffled through the stack. She threw most of it aside, but lingered over a postcard that showed a woman standing in a waterhole in what looked like Kakadu.

"I don't know that I'd describe myself that way," Lane said.

"Of course," she said, her eyes brightening the way they always did when she was about to say something awful. "Because you dropped out of the police academy, didn't you?"

"The Federal Police Development Program," he corrected. "Yes."

Mina watched him for a beat, to see if he would tell her more, if he would pick up the thread of the story he'd begun to tell her in his flat, then sighed and looked at the wine he'd brought.

She tucked it under her arm and disappeared into the pantry. She returned with two glasses, a corkscrew, and a different bottle, a Hunter Valley shiraz with a sleek, minimalist label. He lifted himself from the chair to offer to open the wine but she deftly jammed the corkscrew in and uncorked it in the time it took him to open his mouth. She poured two glasses; not the generous sloshing that most people would serve, but a precise legal standard glass of wine.

He wondered where that skill had come from. The precise measuring—and by eye at that—screamed professional. "Did you tend bar at uni?"

Lane had, for brief stints. He was never very good at it, especially since until he took the job he barely knew drinks other than beer existed, but it was good training in the art of listening, which had served him well.

"No. My mother . . ." She sighed, probably debating if she wanted to answer him or brush him off with a joke. He was growing familiar with that specific pause from her. "Her mother, my grandmother, was a near professional thrower of dinner parties. She read the works of Emily Post and June Dally-Watkins the way most women in her position would read the Bible. She made sure my mother knew the rules too."

"She went to finishing school, right?"

"Finishing school," Mina repeated, rolling her eyes. "She went to a boarding school outside of Melbourne. A lot of rural girls do."

"Did you?"

"What, you don't have that in your notebook?" She took a sip of her wine. "No. We tried it; it went badly."

"What does that mean?"

"Is this one of those things where you know what happened, and you're testing to see if I lie to you?"

He hesitated. "There are rumors. But no, I don't know what happened."

"You've met me. I don't exactly make friends easily. The first year was okay. The other girls were nice to me, but mostly because they'd all been given a lecture about how a terrible thing happened to me and so they needed to be nice."

"What changed after the first year?"

"I told you already. The TV special. Suddenly the rumor was going around that maybe a terrible thing didn't happen to me. Maybe I *did* a terrible thing. And you don't have to pretend to be nice to someone who did a terrible thing. Anyway!" She pasted on a bright voice. "After that little crash and burn, I guess my mother thought it would help to give me the same training. Social graces and deportment and all that bullshit. I even had a deb ball." She gestured with her chin to a picture on a little shelf above the sink. In it, she was perched in a white satin gown on the edge of a little chair, her face professionally made up and her chin resting on a white-gloved fist. Beside her was a boy in a tuxedo, with one hand on her shoulder.

"Who's that?" Lane asked.

Mina shrugged. "I think his name was Gerald. He's not a person of interest, if that's what you're wondering. He was the son of one of my father's friends. They moved to Nannine when I was eleven, twelve."

"I see," he said. Next to the picture, looking quite deliberately placed, was a framed photo of the two girls in communion gowns. Again wearing little white gloves and silver jewelry. That picture created a palpable absence in the first picture of a girl who should have been there in a white dress.

"So I know all the rules. I know how to set a table and which royal is expected to curtsy to which and how the rule changes when their husbands are present. I would find socializing quite easy if everybody else knew the rules and played by them too."

She took a larger sip of her wine. "Evelyn took to it more naturally. People loved her, and not just because she was pretty. She was so friendly. She liked to talk to strangers." She said the word "liked" as if it were shocking. "Even before, I was never outgoing. Evelyn would make friends, and they would just be my friends too. I didn't make any friends at university."

"What about Alanna?"

"She came later. I inherited her from my mother, really. They were friends first."

Lane put his glass down, and looked at Mina carefully. She seemed off-kilter. Open in a way that he wasn't used to. The pale skin of her neck was flushed. "Were you drinking before I got here?" he asked.

"What of it?" she asked. "It's my birthday. If you can't have a shower beer on your birthday, when can you?"

"I'm not judging," he said, and paused a beat. "Did you say 'shower beer'?"

"Yes." She laughed. "Cold beer, hot water, there's nothing better. Again, it was just the one. It's my birthday. Don't go haring off about me being an alcoholic."

"I wasn't planning to," he said. But he wasn't sure he should be talking to her if she wasn't entirely sober.

"Here, catch up," she said, leaning over and pouring another serve of wine into his barely touched glass.

She had a point. He picked it up and took a gulp. They were just celebrating her birthday, he decided. There was nothing un-ethical about that. "You know, I didn't make any friends at uni either," he said. "It's not unusual."

"Oh?"

"I left home at eighteen, and my family didn't give me any support, financially. I couldn't afford to retake classes if I failed them, and I had to work to live, so there wasn't much time left over to head out with the boys."

He'd hoped to connect with her, but he'd misjudged. She pulled her head back, like he'd snapped at her.

"Yeah, alright," she said. "I know, I should be grateful I didn't have to scramble for money as a student."

"That's not what I meant."

"Oh." She looked down at her glass. "I'm not good at this. I never have been and I never will be. Evelyn would have been so good at it. The attention, the interviews. Mum said so once, when I was having a sulk in some green room, not wanting to go on camera. I don't even remember what show it was. 'Evelyn wouldn't behave like this. She would want to help you.' It's not exactly the same as saying she wished I'd been taken and Evelyn left . . ."

"But there's not much daylight between them," Lane said.

"Yeah, she was a cunt and a half," Mina said with a sigh. "But I loved her." She put her empty wineglass down on the island with a dull clink.

Lane sipped his wine to give himself a moment to decide how to respond to that. She still didn't know that he'd met Beverley. She still didn't know a lot of things about him, about his history with Nannine. She was being so honest with him, in a way he knew was rare for her, and the vast swath of information he was hiding from her meant that any response would be essentially a lie.

"Cake?" she asked.

"Please," he said, as eager as she was to row the conversation back to shore.

She went to the fridge and pulled out a Tupperware container. The cake was a dense chocolate, topped with whipped cream and strawberries. The slice she cut him was as tall as the span of his hand, and just looking at it made his jaw ache.

"Could I get a fork?" he asked. It looked soft enough, but he didn't know for sure his jaw could handle picking it up and just taking a bite, and he didn't want to embarrass himself.

She gave him a small smile, and he wondered if she'd done that on purpose. After all her talk about June Dally-Watkins, it seemed odd not to give him a spoon.

She opened a drawer and passed him a small silver cake fork. "I've noticed that you tend to cut up things that most people would eat in one go," she said. "Is there a limit to how far you can open your mouth?"

"Did you make that whole cake to test that theory?"

She rolled her eyes. "I made this cake because it's my birthday. But I'm right, aren't I?"

"You're close."

"Close only counts in horseshoes and hand grenades," she said.

"It's not the opening that's the problem, but the closing," he admitted. "I've got almost no bite strength, because my jaw is more metal than bone."

"You had it reconstructed?"

"I had a nasty break when I was a teenager." He caught her eyes and held them. "I fell down a flight of concrete steps."

"Hmm." She took a bite of her own slice and chewed thought-fully. "You always look me right in the eye when you lie. Did that take a lot of practice?"

He stilled. It wasn't surprising that she was quick to pick up on attempts to manipulate her. Everyone learned what they needed to survive. "You had your training, and I had mine."

"Ah." She went back to eating her cake, but looked at him expectantly.

It wasn't going to work on him. He could handle silence just fine. But she had shared, and if she woke up tomorrow embarrassed that she'd made herself vulnerable, he could lose her trust entirely. "You remember I said earlier that I moved out of home at eighteen? My father broke my jaw. And my left eye socket, but that's had fewer long-term effects."

"I'm sorry," she said softly.

"It's fine. The upside is that I never saw him again. I had to sneak around for the next few years if I wanted to see my mother and sister, though. He, uh . . ." Lane pushed the cake away and reached for his wineglass. "He got it into his head that a teenage boy shouldn't be so close to his toddler sister. He was fine with it when I was doing half the nappy changes and making bottles in the night so the two of them could sleep." That had been self-preservation before it turned into love—their father was a nightmare when he was tired. "But then suddenly we were too close, and he went off on me."

Projection, Lane knew now. Scum always thought other people were just like them, saw their own sins everywhere they looked. Or maybe he'd been deliberately laying the groundwork to point the finger at Lane if he ever got caught. He'd certainly tried it when he was arrested, claiming Lane could have taken the pictures the police found on his computer. The accusation hadn't gone anywhere—it was obvious from the start that he was just a hit dog hollering—but coming as it did right in the middle of Lane's AFP training, it poisoned that well. At least that had made the decision to quit easier.

"I . . ." He paused, surprised by the emotion in his own voice. He wanted to stop, but it was hard to stem the flow of words once they got started. How often had he used that to his own advantage? "I left. It was hard, but I survived. I spent years trying to get Mum to leave too, and she was always almost ready. She just needed a bit more money, a bit more time. I knew Lynnie wasn't safe there, and I put my safety above hers."

Mina stared at him, her eyes wide, and he wasn't sure what he saw there. Disgust?

"Can I use your bathroom?" he asked, jumping to his feet. He almost sent his stool clattering to the floor, and grabbed it at the last moment. He needed a few minutes to pull himself together again.

"Sure," she said, her voice so quiet he needed to lean in to hear her. "It's the middle door in the hallway."

* * *

Her bathroom was as nice as the rest of the house, with blue slate tiles and an old clawfoot tub. He sat on the edge and focused on the details around him, trying to distract himself enough to calm down. The fittings were all in the gold electroplating that had been popular in the nineties, but in good nick and obviously high quality. He would bet that Beverley had redone the room shortly after she and Liam got married.

It occurred to him that letting him in here was a remarkable display of trust. For all she knew, he was going through her bathroom cabinets right now. Best not to hang about too long, then. He flushed the toilet for appearance's sake, and washed his hands.

Mina was standing in the hallway when he came out. He glanced into the kitchen and saw that she'd cleared the plates and glasses away. He looked back at her, prepared to be dismissed.

"I suppose you want to go to the bedroom now?" she said instead.

* * *

To his relief, the "bedroom" proved to be a small sitting room, with a leather recliner and a shelf bursting with books, all of their spines cracked, sometimes even missing. It was a stark contrast to the case full of pristine books visible from the kitchen, each one carefully selected to look good and never be read. This was a comfortable, well-used room of the kind that most fine houses had—the one that guests never saw, that never needed to look good.

It took him a moment to connect it to the crime scene photo he had taped to the wall above his computer desk. They'd repainted the walls, replaced the curtains. And, of course, the twin beds were gone.

"We left it as it was for about a year," Mina explained. "Like a time capsule. In case Starrett needed to come back and check any details, not because we wanted to. Well, I think Mum might have left it for longer if it was up to her. Dad insisted on redecorating; he didn't want to live with a shrine. So we turned it into this."

"Wow," Lane said. He felt humbled. In a very real way, letting Lane into this room was a far more intimate gesture than leading him to the room where she slept now. "May I look around?"

"I didn't bring you in here to admire my book collection," she said.

"Not that it isn't impressive," Lane said. In different circumstances he'd have gladly thumbed through her full set of Pratchetts and Anne McCaffreys.

He moved to the window first. It was an old-fashioned wooden frame, with a thumb lock and no screen. "May I?"

"Just do whatever you want," Mina said, settling in the chair.

He heaved the window open, and the metal runners groaned as the pane lifted. "Did it do that back then?"

She nodded. "Nineteen years hasn't helped, but that's a drop in the bucket compared to how old that window is."

"Would that have woken you?"

She shook her head.

Lane closed the window and opened it again, listening to the ruckus it created. "You know," he said gently, "no one would think anything of it if you heard something, and you were frightened. You were nine—freezing and closing your eyes and pretending you were asleep would be perfectly normal. No one would judge you."

"I promise you, plenty of people would judge me," Mina said, her jaw tight. "But I didn't hear the window open, or close. I didn't wake up. I was a heavy sleeper. Not like Evelyn."

Lane raised an eyebrow. "Evelyn was a light sleeper?"

Mina nodded. "The sound of a leaf falling would wake her up, especially when it was hot."

"I've never seen that mentioned before."

"My parents could be funny. They lied sometimes, about things they thought made them look like bad parents. Most of it was in their own heads; no one cared. But Evelyn's sleep problem was one of them. They thought her weird sleep pattern would make them look negligent, or just ruin their 'perfect family shattered by one tragedy' branding, or whatever."

"Do you think that's why you"—Lane searched for a word that wouldn't leave her justifiably offended—"why you were left undisturbed? Evelyn woke up and you didn't? Dealing with two kids would be tough."

"I like that theory better than the one where he chose Evelyn because I was just too ugly to kidnap."

"You're not ugly," Lane said. "And you weren't then either."

Mina laughed. "Relax, I'm not fishing for reassurance. Trust me, I'm aware that I'm not the hunchback of Notre Dame. But I know that Evelyn was more conventionally striking. Mum made no secret of the fact she thought so. If we'd lived in a city, she'd have probably had Evelyn in Kmart catalogs."

Lane leaned out the window and peered down at the ground below. It was a reasonable drop—not enough to injure someone, but enough to be jarring if he jumped. Climbing up the other way would be a stretch, but probably easy for someone a few inches taller than him. Or someone who had a stepladder, or who pulled over a handy object.

"Don't waste too much time fussing with the window," Mina said. "It's a dead end."

"You think it's been picked over by too many people already?" Lane asked. "I'm not going to find anything?"

Mina didn't answer, staring down at her hands folded in her lap.

Something flipped inside Lane's stomach. "Mina," he said gently, "why is the window a dead end?"

"You always do that voice with me," Mina snapped. "Like you're trying to coax a kitten you just got from the pound out from behind the refrigerator. Miiiina . . . Miiina," she mimicked.

An apt metaphor. Mina had something to tell him, but if he spooked her she would flatten herself out and jam herself even deeper somewhere he couldn't reach.

"Sorry," he said, trying to keep his voice neutral. He opened the window again, slowly, trying to ease it up without making any noise. If anything, slowing down made it screech louder. He leaned on the sill, looking out at the red-brown paddocks, broken up by patches of trees. A single blade of the windmill peeked over the top.

"This must have been a great bedroom," he said. "It's got an amazing view, and it's nice and big."

"We always complained about having to share it, though," she said. She looked sad, and he wondered how often during the first nine years of her life she'd wished on a star or a dandelion to have a room to herself, only to have her wish granted in such an awful way.

"I never had a room of my own," he admitted.

She looked up, immediately interested. "Isn't your sister much younger than you? You must have had a room to yourself until she was born."

He shook his head. "I didn't have a room at all. We lived in a campervan, and I racked in the space above the bed of the truck. I'd climb down of a morning and be right in the kitchen."

"A campervan? Like the one my dad has? They're tiny!"

"Our model was bigger than average. But I'm guessing we crammed more stuff into ours than your father does." He shut the window with a screech.

"I suppose the people matter too," Mina mused. "There's no house big enough if you share it with an arsehole."

"That's true," he said. He and Lynnie had got along fine in an even smaller caravan. "Was this house big enough?"

"My sister and I didn't hate each other," Mina said firmly.

"What about your mother? She and Evelyn argued that night, didn't they?"

"They squabbled a bit at the show. I don't know."

"Because you were asleep, right? You didn't see Evelyn at all after you left the show."

"Yes I did, I—" she frowned. "How did you know I was asleep?"

"Mrs. Tamm. So you were asleep, but you also saw her? When?"

She looked panicked. "You're not one of them, are you? You don't think my mother killed her? Or that I did?"

"No," Lane said. "I don't believe that."

"Why not?" she asked. "There's plenty who do believe it. Aren't you just a tiny bit curious? Ten percent? One percent?"

"Zero percent," Lane said. "People want mysteries to have earth-shattering resolutions. You should see how many elaborate theories fell apart when the Golden State Killer was caught. People wanted him to be a mastermind, not just some angry, violent man whose red flags someone should have acted on. With Evelyn, they want the twist ending. They want it to be someone whose name they already know. You didn't kill Evelyn. It's ridiculous."

Mina closed her eyes, taking in a deep breath. When she opened them again her lower lashes were damp. "You do think someone killed her, though."

"I don't think she got a great job offer in Sydney and left without saying goodbye," Lane said. "And the only two options are that someone took her and killed her, or someone took her and kept her alive. And I find the latter too terrible to contemplate."

Mina nodded. "I remember just before my mother died, those women were found in Cleveland—the ones who were trapped for ten years." She pressed her knuckles above her left eye. "I'm blanking on their names."

"I know who you mean," Lane said. "That was, what, 2012?"

"It was 2013. We were watching the news in her hospital room, and my mother was so happy. 'See?' she kept saying. 'See?' She died wanting to believe that Evelyn was locked in someone's basement somewhere, and I just . . ."

Lane put a hand out, tentatively, and touched her shoulder. He expected to be shrugged off, but she leaned into the contact. He wondered when was the last time she'd had any kind of physical affection. "I'm sorry."

"My mother thought I was a monster for hoping she's dead, but I do. I hope she's dead." She let out a long, damp sigh that rattled her chest. "My idea of a fairy-tale ending is this: one day, Echo and I are out walking and I stumble across her remains. I want her to have died of natural causes. A snakebite, or maybe she fell and hit her head in the dark. I want her to have died fast and without fear or pain."

"That doesn't seem possible," Lane said. Saying it gently wasn't an option now that she'd asked him to knock that shit off, so he said it bluntly.

"Bodies are harder to find than people think," she said. "Especially in rough terrain. There have been . . ." Her voice cracked a little. "There have been plenty of cases where bodies turned up in areas that had been searched already. Sometimes multiple times."

"No, not just the missing body. How is it possible? She was asleep in bed. How do you get from here to her dying of natural causes somewhere out there?" He pointed to the window.

Something shifted and hardened in Mina's eyes. "I told the police and the press that the last time I saw her was when we went to bed at eight p.m. Our mother read us two chapters of *Black Beauty*, one for each of us, clicked off the light and I never saw Evelyn again. But I did. She woke me up—I don't know when; probably a bit after midnight, knowing her pattern. She wanted to walk to the windmill and see the lights from the showgrounds. I told her to piss off and went back to sleep. And I never saw her again."

The blood rushed in Lane's ears. "She wasn't in here? She could have been anywhere in the house? Anywhere on the property?"

Mina nodded. "I suppose so."

"Why would you keep that a secret?" The words exploded from him.

"I don't see what difference it makes," Mina said. "Keeping quiet about it couldn't have affected the investigation that much."

"Have you considered making that your family motto?" Lane asked.

"Don't you compare me to my father," Mina said, pushing up to her feet.

Lane stepped forward, squaring up to her. "Every investigation, including mine, has started from the assumption that this room is ground zero. The impossibility of slipping a girl out from under the nose of her sleeping mother and sister. The lack of tracks and footprints around the house. No fingerprints, no fibers, no stray hairs. That's why it's so fascinating. If it's not true, then everything changes."

She stared at the floor, and winced like every word was stinging her. "Inside, outside, it doesn't matter."

"If it didn't matter, why wouldn't you just say something?" Lane fought to keep his voice level. "Why not tell the truth?"

"I didn't want to make my mother angry," she said, in a small voice. She had that pinched red look under her eyes again, but they were dry.

Lane was completely lost. "I understand that when you were nine, but surely once you were an adult you saw—"

"I said no," Mina snapped. "I said no, and so she went alone. If I'd been with her, then maybe I could have gone for help. Maybe whoever—whatever—it was would have been scared off by two girls instead of one. If I'd said yes, she might be alive."

Oh.

"Hey," Lane said. He put his hands on her upper arms, and again she relaxed under his hands. "You're not to blame here. If you'd said yes, you'd be dead too."

TWENTY-NINE

IT WOULD BE so easy to tilt her chin up and let something start. If she tilted her head back and looked up at Lane through her lashes, he would lean in and kiss her, as surely as a light coming on at the flip of a switch.

Exchanging childhood traumas and then making out: wouldn't that be exactly her brand of fucked up? Her love life could be one more area where Evelyn slipped in and took over. Like cotton bush, and just as toxic.

She sighed and rested her head against his upper arm, closing her eyes. She was amazed how good it felt to not be carrying the secret anymore. It was a tiny thing, but it weighed so much.

Lane seemed to sense the moment's charge ebbing away. He released his grip on her arms. She missed the contact, but didn't chase it.

"Take me to the windmill," Lane said.

"You've seen it already," Mina said. "It's the one we visited the first time I invited you."

She hadn't made a conscious decision to take him there. It had seemed like a sensible idea. It was true that you could see almost the whole property from the top. But in hindsight, she could see how the windmill had loomed large in her mind, as if some part of her had wanted Lane to confirm her secret hopes.

"I know," Lane said. "Take me there. Show me the path she would have taken."

"Alright," she said with a shaking voice. "Her bed was on this side, and I was over there. So she'd have gone this way." She led him toward the hallway.

She followed Evelyn's ghost down the hall, toward the mudroom in the back. Lane trailed a few feet behind her.

"Are you sure she would have gone to the back door? What if she wanted something from the kitchen?"

"She would have had to pass Mum's room to get to the kitchen, and Mum always slept with her door open. Evelyn might have gone that way, but I think the back was more likely."

She opened the door to the mudroom. Her mother would be horrified to see her bring a visitor in here—it was the kind of backstage, lived-in area that always needed to be carefully shielded from view. Firewood was stacked against one wall, and along the other wall was a low bench with shoes and boots jumbled beneath it. Above, a row of hooks burst with coats, hats, and scarves. The gun safe was bolted to the floor in the corner. She considered getting the shotgun out, since they were going to walk so far, but it had freaked Lane out the last time he saw it. She decided to leave it alone.

She reached for the Maglite that sat on the windowsill. It was still only midafternoon, but sunset snuck up on her at this time of year.

Lane put a hand on her elbow. "Was that there back then?"

"Yeah, we've always kept a torch here," she said. "Not this specific one—they last a long time, but not that long."

"If she went out at night, wouldn't she have taken it with her?" he asked. His voice sounded odd.

"I suppose so." She stared at the torch. When had they replaced it, exactly?

"Was this room photographed by the crime scene unit?" he asked. "I've never seen pictures of it."

"I don't know," she said. "I wasn't here when the photographer came through. I think my mother has copies in her files."

He turned around without asking her to show him the way, and headed down the hallway. Suddenly she was the one trailing after him, in her own house. "Is this the office?" he asked, pointing to the closed door to the guest bedroom.

"No," she said. "Go back to the kitchen and I'll bring you the pictures."

She went into the office, glad for the moment to catch her breath away from his sudden enthusiasm. She knew that if she asked him what the hell was so important about the torch he would just brush her off. She leaned against the closed door, considering going back out and asking him to just leave. But she'd brought him here to investigate, hadn't she? Why did she want to push him back out for trying to do it?

She found the pictures in seconds, thanks again to her mother's impeccable filing.

Lane was literally on the edge of his seat when she returned to the kitchen. She felt suddenly very stupid for her earlier belief that something was unfolding between them. He'd never looked at her the way that he looked at the envelope of pictures in her hand.

He opened it with the excitement of a kid ripping open a packet of trading cards, and laid them out on the counter. She poured another glass of wine to wash down her queasiness at watching him arrange them. There were her childhood toys, her *My Little Pony* sheets, Evelyn's bike helmet discarded on a side table. In the picture of the bathroom, a pair of tiny pink panties dangled from the towel rack.

"There!" Lane said excitedly, jabbing his finger at the picture of the mudroom. The windowsill was bare. No torch.

"But what does that mean?"

"I've seen that torch before," Lane said.

Before he could explain further, his phone rang. The bright spark disappeared from his eyes. "I have to take this," he said. He shot her an apologetic smile and slipped out the front door.

She waited for him to come back, but after a few minutes his car started, and she watched through the window as he drove away fast enough to send a plume of dust swirling into the air.

THIRTY

"HEY, LYNNIE, WHAT'S up?" he asked, trying to sound bright and casual. They would see each other in person in a couple of days, so he could be with her when the parole board made its decision. He hoped she was just calling to ask him to bring something, but this close to the hearing the sight of her name lighting up his screen opened a deep pit in his stomach.

The way she drew a breath in told him this wasn't going to be a social call. "They're going to let him go."

"Lynnie, honey, it's okay," he said. "I promise you, I'm not going to let that happen." He stepped away from the door, worried about Mina hearing him from inside. "I've found something, okay? It's not enough, but I've got a hold of the thread now and I just need a few more days—"

"No, for real. The parole board approved his application."

Shit, she must have had a nightmare or something. "The hearing isn't for a week."

"No," she said, almost too soft for him to hear. "The hearing was today."

"No." He couldn't possibly have got that wrong. She'd told him the eighteenth of April, there was no way . . . "You gave me the wrong date?"

"I'm sorry." She was crying now.

Lane reached out and pressed a palm against the trunk of the apple tree to hold himself up. How badly had he screwed up as a guardian if she felt like she had to lie to keep him away from the hearing? Did she think he was going to make a scene? He thought he'd done well at the job of keeping a lid on his own feelings, of not ever making it about himself. Apparently he hadn't.

"I'm an adult now," she said. "I thought I could . . . you shouldn't always have to drop everything to come take care of me."

"Honey, no. No. It's not a burden. Not when it's for you."

Panic coursed through him. He was supposed to have more time.

"I should have made the statement," she sobbed. "This is my fault."

"No," he said. "It is not your fault."

"What if he hurts someone else, and I could have stopped him getting out? It was just a letter. Why am I too weak to write one letter?"

"You will never be responsible for something he does. Never." He closed his eyes, wanting to punch Mina's front door. Why was he here? Why had he listened to Lynnie instead of driving back to Canberra the second she told him about the parole hearing notice? "How long until he's released?"

"Seven days."

He could work with that. He was so close. "Do you have someone who can be with you tonight? I'll get there as soon as I can, but I need to take care of something here." He glanced at his watch. Four p.m., which meant he would make it to the police station before they closed, if he absolutely floored it.

"Chelsea's here," she said.

That would have to do.

* * *

The security door to the police station was locked this time, and Starrett came at his buzz with a wary look on her face. It was a far cry from the open welcome he'd received at his last visit, but he couldn't blame her. He'd brought little more than chaos since he arrived.

The incident with Hendrik Tamm hadn't just been a mess; it could easily have embarrassed her and the rest of the force for their mishandling of the alibi. That axe still hung over her, ready to fall if he, or any of the others in the know, went public with the full story.

If he'd come to her the day he arrived in Nannine and told her the truth, everything would be different. But he'd wanted more. He'd wanted to be the one to untangle it.

He'd wanted to be sure he'd get the money.

Now he needed Starrett's help, and he didn't have any extra evidence to justify the time he'd kept her in the dark.

She led him not to the tearoom, but to the interview room, and sat in the interrogator's chair.

"I haven't been entirely upfront with you," he said. "I have a personal stake in the case."

Starrett's face didn't change, but she leaned back in her chair and crossed her arms over her chest. "What kind of personal stake?"

"I was here in May 1999. My family was in Nannine. I was fourteen years old, and I worked for the show with my mother.

She, my father, and I were staying at the showground the night Evelyn was taken."

Starrett stood up and left the room, shutting the door firmly behind her. Minutes ticked past, and he wondered if she had disappeared into the next room to watch him through the two-way glass. He kept his eyes on the table, trying to look well intentioned.

She reappeared with a folder. He actually looked at the file name this time, and saw MCCREERY, along with an ID code that showed it was one of many. Finally, the real McCreery file. She turned the folder so he couldn't see what was inside when she opened it. A good strategy. Never let the subject know exactly what you know.

"I've never been on this side of the table," he joked. It came out like he was trying too hard to be cheerful, which he was. "Do I need a lawyer?"

Starrett peered over her glasses at him. "Are you asking for a lawyer?"

"No." He couldn't afford to lose the time it would take to scare up a lawyer. "I haven't done anything wrong."

"Mm-hmm." She put a piece of paper down on the table. It was the list of show employees, each of them marked with a series of symbols that he assumed only the investigating officers could interpret. "It took me a minute to find you. Lane Holland, born 1983, running the guess-your-weight booth. No criminal record, alibied by another employee, never interviewed. It didn't even occur to me to search the file for your name."

Lane would have searched for it, if their places were reversed.

"And here's your mother." She pointed to Sharon Holland, born 1961. Two of the symbols beside her name were the same as Lane's entry, and one was different. So the star next to Lane's meant "never interviewed," and the star inside a circle next to his mother's name meant "interviewed." "No entry for any other Holland. Does your father have a different last name?"

"His name is Lane Holland too." Arrogant bastard, saddling his son with the same name. "But he was here."

Lane paused. Maybe he should get that lawyer. But if she was inclined to press charges, it was his mother who had committed a crime by making a false declaration, and she was far beyond the reach of prosecution. "He wasn't supposed to be onsite. He'd been banned a few weeks before, and my mother told the show organizer she'd given him the boot too."

"Why was he banned?"

"I don't know. I was just a kid."

That was true, in that he didn't know the particulars, but he still knew. You could tell a fourteen-year-old that his dad was accused of stealing. You could tell him about a DUI, or that he'd got mad and thrown a punch, or that he'd been late one too many times. But when you said, "That's not for you to worry about, it's all bullshit anyway," there were only a few crimes that it could be.

"I see." She shuffled a few papers, pausing for a moment to read one. "But he hadn't actually left?"

"He was supposed to hide in the campervan. We just needed one more show to get some cash together, and we were going to go find a different outfit. But he left during the night and came back in the morning. He said he'd been at the pub, but that was impossible. It closed at eleven, and the only room was rented to Hendrik Tamm. He was unaccounted for between then and about eight the next morning."

She smoothed it away almost immediately, but he clocked her grimace at the mention of Hendrik. He wished he didn't have to mention him, but he did. "You know Hendrik Tamm left his work ute at the pub that night?"

"Yes, and I know it was still there when he came home. Don't you think he would have reported it if his ute had been tampered with?"

"Only if he'd noticed. Drunk fifteen-year-olds stealing cars for joyrides leave evidence of tampering. Nineties cars didn't have all the security features that come standard now. I know how to start one with a pocketknife." He faltered, and pasted on what he hoped was a charming smile. "I mean, when I tried it as a purely educational exercise with the full permission of the car's owner, it was surprisingly easy. And that's without the sort of tools a habitual car thief would have."

She looked thoughtful, but not as impressed as he'd hoped. She tapped the list of names. "If your father is not on this list, then your mother must have signed a statement that the two of you were the only ones living in your campervan."

"My father had an active warrant. She was worried that he would be arrested, and the show manager would find out, and we wouldn't have been allowed to work the remaining two days. He painted a pretty dire picture of him stuck in a lockup and us on the road with fifty cents to our name and not enough petrol to get to the next town." He slipped into the broad accent his father spoke in. "'Gawd, Sharon, it's not like I had anything to do with it. It won't affect the search any.'"

"What was the arrest warrant for?"

He leaned forward. "Car theft."

Starrett got up and left the room again. She was off to run the name, he supposed, and confirm that he was telling the truth.

His phone buzzed on the table. The number that came up

was private, so he let it ring out. Whoever it was didn't leave a voicemail.

Starrett stormed back in. Her face was still impassive, but she threw herself heavily into her chair. The distrust had become a storm of anger beneath the surface. "Your father is not in prison for car theft."

"It's a disturbing file, I know," he said. "And it only tells half the story."

The car theft charges paled in comparison to what the police had found on his laptop, and what came out during Lynnie's forensic interview. As far as he knew, the police saw no connection between his initial arrest, and the far more serious crimes discovered in the fallout.

"The night he was arrested, he'd stolen a car from a couple having their anniversary dinner at a restaurant. He was originally charged with attempted burglary, because he was on his way to their house with their keys in his hand. But I don't think he was planning a burglary. The couple's six-year-old daughter Alexandra was home with a babysitter."

Starrett's expression didn't change at all. Silently, he begged her to take the pieces he'd laid out—Hendrik's ute, Evelyn, the stolen car, Alexandra, Lynnie—and piece them together the same way he had.

But under the harsh fluorescent lights, it all sounded ridiculous. All the nights he'd lain awake thinking about it, it had seemed obvious. But it was a chain of maybes. He was sure his father had taken Evelyn because he was sure he'd been planning to abduct Alexandra. And he was sure he'd been planning to abduct Alexandra because he was sure he'd taken Evelyn.

"Alexandra's twenty-one now. She's about to have a baby."

Starrett sighed. "What kind of game are you playing, Mr. Holland? You didn't think any of this was worth mentioning when you came to me. About the Christa Rennold case, I might add."

He had no real answer for that. "Please. He's going to be released in a week's time."

"I take it you don't want that to happen." Her face softened a fraction. "I understand if you're worried about retribution. I can help you apply for an order of protecti—"

"I don't care if he comes after me," Lane snapped. "Let him. Listen to me. He has been locked up for fifteen years, away from everything that's ever brought him joy. What do you think a man like this is going to do when he gets out? He'll go for a beer, get a McChicken and large fries, and then go on the hunt for someone to hurt. I hope it *is* me. The best-case scenario here is that it's me. But I don't think it's going to be me."

Starrett flipped open another file, with no care for how much of the contents Lane saw. Inside were stacks of documents, each with an envelope paper clipped to the front. "They've slowed down recently, but we still average three a year. Letters from people convinced their father killed Evelyn. Or their brother. Or their grandfather. Their son. All of them genuinely believe it. This country is full of men with violent histories, who were itinerant farm workers in the late nineties, or long-range truckers, or just unemployed and untraceable at the time."

"How many of them have proof their accused was right here in Nannine that day?"

"Do you have proof of that? A photograph? Something from your father admitting he was here? Another employee of the show who can corroborate your story?"

"No. But I saw him. My testimony is evidence."

"Your testimony will be colored by the fact that you are clearly desperate to stop your father's release. He'll be able to point to your mother's statement that he was not here. A statement that she never felt the need to retract, even after his conviction."

Lane could feel it slipping through his fingers. This was his last chance, and he couldn't get her to listen. "There's one more thing. Growing up, we had a Maglite torch. I still remember the feel of the thing in my hand, it was so heavy. It lasted for years, and when it finally died I looked the brand up, wanting to get another one. It cost hundreds of dollars. I know that doesn't seem like much, but that was mad money for us growing up. Paying ten dollars for a new torch would have stretched us. But somehow my father came home with one. I swear I never saw it before May 1999. And Mina McCreery told me they lost one the night Evelyn disappeared."

Starrett looked at him, her mouth twisted in frustration.

The revelation of the torch had been enough for him. It had made it all click into place, convinced him he wasn't crazy. But now, speaking it out loud to Starrett, he could see how little it actually proved. He couldn't get her to see the same picture. She hadn't been there. She hadn't seen the way his father had smiled whenever he used that torch.

"Mr. Holland"—Starrett's voice was like ice—"what you are offering me is testimony contradicting another witness, and testimony that you saw your father with an expensive torch. An expensive torch that was not reported missing in the original crime scene catalog."

"Mina only realized—"

"Yes. In the course of your investigation, Miss McCreery has suddenly remembered a missing torch that might link your father to this crime. Because you inserted yourself into this investigation while concealing that you are a person of interest. Have you ever seen a defense lawyer piss himself with excitement, Mr. Holland? Because if I try to prosecute based on anything you've said here today, you will." Starrett slammed the folder closed. "Get out. And I don't just mean out of this station. You need to get out of this town and away from that family before you cause any more damage."

THIRTY-ONE

MINA FISHED A fork out of the drawer. She scooped a chunk straight off the cake and jammed it in her mouth. Fuck it, she was alone and it was her birthday.

The skin on her neck was prickling, a flush crawling its way up. She took a deep breath. She'd never had a panic attack inside the house before. She wanted to run upstairs, lock her door, and climb into bed. But she was supposed to feel safe in the house. The sphere she could handle kept getting smaller and smaller, and if she retreated to her bedroom now, maybe she would never come back downstairs.

She had a prescription, for moments when her anxiety was spinning out of control. She stepped into the bathroom and opened the medicine cabinet. She'd set a marble inside, balanced against the door so it would roll out and catch Lane if he tried snooping. Evidently he hadn't, because it clattered down now, spinning in circles around the sink and then coming to rest in the plughole with a death rattle.

She reached for the box, then hesitated. She'd been drinking, and the two didn't play well together. Fine. Fuck.

She went back into the kitchen and poured herself another glass of wine. Might as well kill the bottle since it was open.

It was good that he'd left, she decided. If he'd stuck around she'd have done something stupid.

She should have just gone to the Northern Territory with Alanna. She could be there right now, the two of them watching the sun set over Uluru. No, that wasn't right. The territory was half an hour behind, not ahead. No matter what time it was, Alanna was probably out there with her sister right now, washed in golden light.

She fumbled for the postcard Lane had brought in with him. There wasn't much to it—just Alanna's pretty, looping writing. *Happy birthday. Thinking of you.* She must have bought it as soon as she landed and dropped it in the postbox at the airport for it to have arrived on time. Alanna was so fucking thoughtful. She'd been so understanding; of course Mina couldn't be expected to leave after everything that had happened.

It was pretty funny that her mother had ever thought Mina would be the one to help Alanna.

She should open that awful bottle of wine Lane had brought, she mused. Since she was already three-quarters of a bottle in, this afternoon was probably the only time it would be drinkable.

It was a little weird that Alanna hadn't called yet. She emptied the last of the first bottle into her glass, pondering this. But, then, once Christa opened the door Mina would have become the last person on her mind.

She could look at the pictures, she realized. Alanna was always snapping pictures of this and that and posting them online. Apparently Christa liked to do that too, judging by the pictures Lane had of her. She could just look and see what Alanna was doing.

She went to her computer. It was old, but functional—enough for her to work from home and her father to do whatever he did for his self-managed super fund. She used it occasionally to buy things online and order groceries. She had an app on it, designed for parents trying to keep their kids out of Pornhub, that blocked any other site. It was meant to add one more layer of difficulty to dissuade her on the dark nights when getting online and just having a quick look seemed like a good idea. It was just to give her time to think it over.

It took a lifetime to boot up, long enough that she wondered if it had kicked the bucket. But it got there, and within a few minutes she had entered the password that switched off all the controls.

It took her a couple of tries to remember how to find Alanna's Instagram page. In the end, she resorted to typing Alanna's full name into Google, and then it was the second result.

The first was a thread on MyMurder.

She gritted her teeth and scrolled past it, opening the Instagram result. She braced for a parade of everything she was missing out on—waterfalls and cocktails and selfies of Christa and Alanna pressed cheek to cheek. She found nothing. The most recent picture was dated a week ago, the day Alanna left, of a #LoveOzYA anthology sitting on top of a black suitcase, a boarding pass sticking out of it as a bookmark.

She back-buttoned out and leaned back in her chair, dizzy from the sudden loss of momentum. Or possibly just from the wine.

She definitely shouldn't look at the MyMurder link.

It was a terrible idea. She would sit up all night reading every scrap of nastiness she could find about herself. She would spend the next week feeling like she needed a shower, even while she was in the shower.

She clicked the link.

MyMurder was an internet relic: an Australian crime forum that had launched at just the right time, and been caught up in the rising tide of attention and interest brought by her sister's disappearance. The forum had never needed to move on from its early 2000s aesthetic, so it was like a time capsule. Users started threads, and the responses appeared one under the other in a single flowing conversation. Each user had a little box to the left of their message, with a user picture, name, and a little string of text that the user could set themselves, with a quote or brief bio. Most chose pictures not of themselves but of their pet cases, so it looked like a group of famous murder victims had gathered for a postmortem chat. Mina swallowed against the nausea.

The thread was brief—the original post was a few sentences on Christa's abduction, mentioning Alanna by name, and a link to an article Mina had read before. Only two people responded: one criticizing their foster mother for leaving them unsupervised in the front yard, and one arguing that Gunther's actions were understandable because the family court hates fathers and couldn't be trusted.

Underneath was a heading: "Today's most active posts." Mina's eye caught on her own name.

Is anyone here because they have skin in the game, or are you all just creepers like me?

I know Mina McCreery in real life.

Mina felt like she had stepped out of herself and was now standing behind the chair, watching her hand move to click the thread open. The user, "LionSong," had set off an impromptu question-and-answer session with the other users. She read the answers rapidly, looking for some error, some repeated urban legend, some work of fiction that would prove that this person was lying. That the person was a troll. Then she could just pretend she'd never found it. If there was anything to be done about the trolls, her mother and father would have done it a long time ago. Her mother's solution was to ignore them. The trolling was just proof people were listening. Do more interviews, write more newspaper articles, have another teary-eyed picture published in the women's magazines. Her father had encouraged Mina to make herself smaller. Stay out of the interviews. Stay home from school. Stay off the internet, stay on the farm, and sooner or later they'd lose interest.

It was nineteen years later and the other users had jumped at the bait within moments. The questions ran the gamut from the easily googled to the downright hostile. The answers were short, peevish, and one hundred percent accurate.

One user asked a question about Mina's Miss Nannine Showgirl costume. *Does she wear it around the house like Miss Havisham?* It would have been funny if it wasn't about Mina. Her mother actually had pulled Evelyn's Sunday dress out of the cupboard all the time. Mina would find her in their bedroom, sitting on the floor in front of the window with it crumpled in her lap, just staring silently at the wall. Once Mina had gone and sat next to her. Her mother tipped over like a collapsing tree branch, pushing all of her weight onto Mina, and sobbed, *I want my daughter back.* She'd been ten. She never approached her mother again.

There never was a costume, LionSong replied. *She wore the same dress she wore to church every week. All the girls did. It wasn't some* Toddlers & Tiaras *shit.*

Mina's stomach lurched. The wind blew in her hair, and she felt the metal floor of the windmill sway under her feet. She'd said exactly that to Lane, hadn't she?

THIRTY-TWO

LANE STUMBLED OUT into the sunlight. He had to lean against the post as a wave of nausea crashed over him. He squeezed his eyes shut, hoping he wasn't about to puke his guts up all over the bare dirt where the wonga wonga vine had been. Starrett would probably come out and charge him with vandalism if he did that.

Goddamn it, he should have asked for that lawyer. Talk about haste not speed.

Okay. Okay. He needed to think. Starrett needed more evidence. Maybe he could talk to the other employees of the show again. There had been people up and around when his father came back on the Saturday morning. Surely someone saw him. Lane just needed a little more time. He could do this.

His phone buzzed in his pocket. Again, the number on the screen was private. He debated answering it for a moment. A private number had a good chance of being a debt collector, but it could also be someone from the court calling about his father's release. He hit the green button. "Hello?" he said cautiously.

"Lane."

"Mina, hey, I need to—"

Mina's voice cut across his, as heavy as stone. "I know."

Shit. Starrett must have called her the second the door closed behind him. "Look, if you just let me—"

"No. I don't want to hear some half-arsed explanation, Lane. I trusted you. You know how I feel about—" She broke off, dragging in a painful-sounding breath. She started to cry.

"Mina, please—"

"If I ever see you again, I'll file for a protection order. Fuck right off, Lane."

The call cut off.

* * *

As he drove away from the police station, the white aura descended. A headache was about to rip through his brain like a screwdriver in the eye. He pulled off the road, parking on the lawn in front of the church. He was barely a kilometer from his flat, but he didn't trust he could safely drive there. This couldn't end with him wrapped around a tree.

He pulled out his phone and texted Lynnie to let her know he wasn't going to make it. The message was probably nothing more than a collection of random letters, autocorrected into word salad, but she would get the gist. That he was letting her down, like he always did.

It was fitting that he would sleep his last night in Nannine crammed in the back seat of his car, just as he'd spent his first nights.

THIRTY-THREE

THE NEXT MORNING Mina got to her ute after her walk and realized she had no recollection of anything she had seen. She had walked, she knew, because her legs ached and her trousers were covered in grass seeds, but her head had been so full of snatches of what she had read playing over and over that she had just gone through the motions without paying any attention. She put the shotgun away in the rack in the tray, and got into the cab. She tucked the map away without marking the section off, and then sat with her hands on the steering wheel, trying to collect herself. She needed someone who could help her make sense of this. Usually that was Alanna, but with her away there had to be someone else. Deirdre? Starrett? Her father?

She wanted her mother.

She took the turn onto the road too fast, and the back wheels of the ute slid sideways in the dust like a stone skipping over water. Out of instinct she slammed her foot on the brake, the worst possible move. The skid deepened and the sky whirled in the windscreen. She shot straight off the road, with no curb or verge to slow her down, and bounced down into the drainage ditch. Her seatbelt bit into her hip and shoulder, and her head careened to the side and smacked against the window.

The ute was tilted at a sickening angle. She waited, listening to the hiss of the engine, to see if it would tumble further, all the way over. Once she was confident it had come to a complete stop, she unclicked her seatbelt and scrambled out, running up the slope of the ditch to the side of the road.

She pressed her fingers to her temple. She might have an ugly bruise for a few days, but she didn't think it was bad. There was no ringing in her ears, no floating splotches in her vision. She slid her hand over the back of her neck, checking for tender spots.

Fine.

She looked over the ute. It was significantly less fine, but nothing a panelbeater couldn't fix. Unless there was damage to the undercarriage she couldn't see.

She counted her options. She was literally at her own front gate, but walking back home would take her an hour. She could fish the satellite phone from the glove box and call for help, but she could walk home in the time it would take anyone to drive out to her. The day was still relatively cool—she hadn't felt the need to switch the air conditioner on in the ute. In a few hours the temperature would start to climb toward 30°C, but for now neither option was dangerous, just uncomfortable.

She was about halfway up the farm road when a car horn beeped, and she looked up to see Alanna coming in her little gray Corolla. Alanna frowned when she saw her, and pulled over.

"Are you okay?" she called, opening her door. "I saw the ute."

"Oh, peachy," Mina said, scrubbing a hand over her face. It felt hot against her hand, and she was willing to bet it was red and splotchy, the way it always was when she got too worked up. She had probably looked like that even before the accident. "I was bored, and decided to spice things up with a little off-roading."

"You want me to call a tow truck?"

Mina looked up at that with genuine surprise. Danby wasn't that far away in the grand scheme, but it was another world. "No way. Tow trucks won't service this area, and if they did it would cost a ransom. Can you run me up to the house? I'll come back this afternoon with the tractor, haul it home myself."

She slid into the passenger seat. Alanna shot her a sidelong glance as she pulled back onto the road. She'd clearly noticed that Mina was in an absolute state, far more than made sense for a minor accident, but for whatever reason she wasn't calling her on it. Mina appreciated it.

"Why are you here? Shouldn't you still be up north?"

"My flight landed last night. I'd wanted to stay longer, but I had to go with the cheapest fare. Plus, you weren't with me, and those extra days were meant for us to celebrate your birthday."

Right. If only she'd agreed, she'd be waking up in a hotel nursing a hangover right now, instead of feeling like she'd let Lane turn her inside out.

"I did call ahead," Alanna said with false cheer. "But it just went straight to your voicemail. I figured driving out was a safe bet—if you're not at home you're in Nannine, right, and I'd have seen your ute on the way through."

Mina felt a strange twist at how accurate that was. "Clever."

"Did you get my card?"

"Forget my birthday. What happened with your trip?"

"Well, I spoke to Keva," Alanna said. Her blank tone said a lot more than her words did.

"Oh," Mina said. "Oh, honey. Are you sure?"

"A hundred percent," Alanna said. She sucked a breath in through her front teeth like she was trying to stop herself crying. "They showed me her baby pictures. Hundreds of 'em. She and her mum were surprisingly nice, considering they've been dodging my calls and I just bowled up at their front door sobbing about my long-lost sister. Which she is, but"—she scrubbed at her eye with the back of her wrist—"the wrong one."

"Seriously?"

"Seriously." Alanna pulled the car up in front of the house and cut the engine. "Dad had a whole fucking second family out in the Northern Territory. Keva's four years younger than me and a year older than Christa."

"Was he there?"

Alanna shook her head. "Nope. They haven't heard from him either. Probably fucked off and started a third family."

"Oh my god. I'm so sorry, Alanna."

Alanna shrugged with fake nonchalance. "Well, back to the drawing board, I suppose. Think I could borrow your pet private investigator again?"

Mina laughed bitterly. "Keep him. If Lane Holland tries showing up here again, he can talk to my shotgun."

"What the hell happened?"

Mina wasn't sure how much to tell Alanna. She didn't want to tell her about the birthday drinks, or the aftermath, or the weird stew of feelings she'd found herself in as he pored over the photographs. "I found out he was online, sharing my personal business to anyone who'd pay him attention."

Alanna went pale. "What do you mean?"

"I went on MyMurder and—"

"I thought you never looked at that," Alanna interrupted. "You seemed pretty torn up about it."

"Yeah, well, it's a good thing I looked or I'd still be rolling out the red carpet for that slippery fucker. Some of the shit he's written on that forum is so personal, so invasive, I want to throw up. He had me fooled that he was a decent guy when he has to be a sociopath or something. I'm going to need to take out a restraining order."

"It can't be that bad," Alanna said quietly.

"Not that bad? *Not that bad?*" Mina shouted. "Listen to this one." She grabbed Alanna's phone from the center console and tried to pull up the forum.

"Hey, don't just take my phone," Alanna said, snatching it back. She jerked her chin toward the house. "You want me to go in there and start rummaging through your underwear drawer?" She tilted the phone so Mina couldn't see, and tapped away at the screen. "What username am I looking for?"

"LionSong," Mina said. "With a capital S."

Alanna blanched, like there was something particularly awful about the name, but before Mina could ask, Alanna pressed the phone back into her hands. Mina scrolled through, holding up the phone so Alanna could see, her stomach churning even on the second viewing. She'd let him inside her house. She'd told him so many things that no one knew. How quickly would those details pop up on MyMurder now, especially with Lane freed from trying to conceal whose account it was?

She'd come so close to sleeping with him. One sidelong, hopeful glance, or one step forward during the moment that she was wavering, and she would have. She spun in her seat and opened the car door, sure she was going to throw up.

"Those comments look alright," Alanna said. "What's on the first page is mostly pushing back against crazies, and defending you."

Mina counted her breaths until the acid taste subsided from the back of her throat. "It's the secrecy," she said. "Every post could be about how wonderful I am, but it would still be creepy to be running to a forum to talk about me every day." She went back to the phone and scrolled down to the message she'd been looking for. "But they're not all defending me. Listen to this. Another user asked, *What's something most people get wrong about Mina?* And he writes, *It'd be faster to list what people get right. And a lot of the typical myths get chewed over a lot here. So here's one that bothers me—a lot of people think Beverley disliked Mina, and Mina constantly chased her approval. The truth is, while their relationship was awful, most of the venom was from Mina's side. After Beverley died, Mina let* Woman's Day *print a statement from her saying, 'We made the decision to cremate my mother, and spread her ashes here at the property. My mother knows the truth now. I only hope that some part of her remains have come to rest with Evelyn's.' God, I'm sure that statement had everyone skimming the mag in the supermarket queue scrambling for their hanky. But if you know Mina, if you know how she talks about her mother, you realize there's enough acid in that statement to etch glass.*"

Mina stared at the phone. She'd told Lane about that anger at her mother, but not until her birthday.

Alanna paled as the words sank in. "That is true, though," she said softly.

"It's my truth," Mina said. "It belongs to me. Not to the fucking internet."

"I . . ." Alanna reached out and took her phone back. Her fingers shook as she switched the screen off, and Mina felt like her heart was being dragged down her chest into her stomach.

"It's you," she said.

Alanna looked for a flicker like she was considering denying it, like she might fight the accusation. Then she nodded. "I didn't start out planning to talk about you," she admitted. "I guess you didn't go right back to the earliest posts, because I joined to talk about Christa's case, to see if anyone had any interesting ideas or suggestions. But the case has no name recognition. It's not a brand. My threads got a handful of hits, maybe a comment or two that didn't really say anything. And when people said awful things about you or Evelyn, I would comment and push back." She flexed her fingers on the steering wheel. "And any post about Evelyn got ten times the attention of my earlier stuff. And then I went to see Keva. I'd started to believe, a little bit, that maybe I could have Christa back. I started to hope. And so"—her voice cracked in a ragged sob—"I got drunk and I started running my mouth online, or whatever you call it when there's typing involved. If I could just get some goddamn attention, maybe they would look at a post about Christa."

"But you knew," Mina said. "You knew how much I hated that site. How much this would hurt me. You're supposed to be my friend."

"You are my friend," Alanna said. "I love you. But I love Christa more."

"Oh my god." Mina pressed her palms to her face. "Oh my god, I completely flipped out on Lane."

"That's your takeaway here?" Alanna asked, her voice rising. "For fuck's sake, Mina, you know he doesn't give a shit about you, right? He doesn't care about Evelyn. He didn't care about Christa."

"He got closer to finding her than anyone has in years."

"No, he didn't. He stirred up a whole bunch of crap for my

family, got my mother all worked up about Christa coming home, and stopped returning my calls the second you started answering his. Christa and I were just heads he could step on to get to you. And not because he cares about you so damn much." Alanna was fully shouting now. "You think you're so distrustful, but all he needed to do was hold your hand and pat your cheek and you've fallen all over yourself. And all he wants is the money, and his name on the news."

"Are you seriously going to lecture me about who really cares about me?" Mina snapped. "About who's just using me for attention? I'm sorry, okay? I'm sorry that Keva isn't Christa. I'm sorry that my sister disappeared during a quieter news cycle than yours did. I'm sorry we didn't have to compete with the Olympics for airtime. I'm sorry my family was so goddamn photogenic and had high-resolution photos to give the media. If you haven't noticed, it hasn't made a damn bit of difference."

"For fuck's sake, Mina, Christa's case got buried because of your mum," Alanna snapped.

Mina reeled back. "What?" Alanna and her mother had been friends. Where had that come from? "What, you think she killed the story so it wouldn't distract from Evelyn? My mother could work the media, but she didn't have that kind of pull. That's ridiculous."

"I don't mean like that. Look, I've only just found out myself. Deirdre and I got fucking deep into it when I got home. Your mum reached out to mine when Christa was taken. That's pretty much how the support group got started. But then your little stunt with the dogs—"

"It wasn't a stunt. He was—"

"Not the point. The point is your mother had just seen all that blow up in your face, and was beginning to see that she'd created a beast she couldn't control anymore. And it was eating you alive. So instead of hyping Christa's story, my mother did everything she could to let it die. She thought the police would work on it quietly, and Christa could come home without any media circus. But—"

"No," Mina said. "No, that's . . . No. My mother never regretted any of it. She died sure she'd made the right choices. She left a will doubling the reward money, to create more headlines. She made me promise on her fucking deathbed I'd help with a new edition of her book."

"I've always . . ." Alanna took a shaking breath. "What happens in the group's meetings is supposed to stay confidential. Your mother attended for a long time, long before I ever met you. She was my friend before you were. And she did regret it. She was so sorry about what it did to you. But at the same time, she genuinely believed Evelyn was still alive. And if she was, then every time she spoke to the media, maybe Evelyn saw it. It was the only way she could talk to her daughter."

Mina stared out the windshield, her eyes burning. "I need to go. I'm sorry, you've come a long way, but I need to go." She got out of the car and slammed the door behind her.

* * *

She called Lane, and went straight to his voicemail. She hung up the phone without leaving a message, and it began to ring immediately. She answered, hoping it was him.

"Miss McCreery," Starrett said. "I'm calling to let you know Lane Holland came to the station yesterday."

Oh. That made sense—Mina wouldn't hear his explanations, so he'd gone to Starrett to plead his case.

"Don't worry about it," Mina said. "It's all a mess, but it was a misunderstanding."

"A misunderstanding?" Starrett repeated, sounding completely confused. "I don't see how—"

Mina just wanted to crawl back into bed. "I'm trying to sort it out, okay? It will be fine."

"Mina," Starrett said, her voice serious, "I'm concerned about his behavior. Don't speak to him. If he shows up at your property, call me immediately."

"What's happened?" Mina asked. Starrett wasn't prone to dramatics, so whatever Lane had said at the station went far beyond a miscommunication about some forum posts.

"There's been a development in Evelyn's case. We're pursuing a new line of inquiry."

"Oh." Mina tried to muster up a spark of interest, some excitement, but she just felt terribly tired. After the past few weeks, it was hard to believe that any development involving Lane could come to anything.

"Please," Starrett said. "Stay away from him."

THIRTY-FOUR

LANE TURNED ON to the road leading to the McCreery property. After packing up his flat, he'd set out that morning planning to see Mina, hoping to plead his case for forgiveness one more time. Maybe she would listen in person. But as the miles of trees whipped past him, a new idea started to take shape. The time for this investigation was over. What was he going to find on the property, nearly twenty years after the fact, that would be any more compelling than what Starrett had already rejected? Any DNA was long gone, and any fingerprints had been wiped away a thousand times over. If he kept questioning witnesses, any testimony he got would be tainted. No, the investigation was over. He needed a Plan B.

Lane pulled up in front of Mina's gates. He'd intended to leave the car here, go on foot to avoid the sensors and get what he needed by stealth. But he didn't need to. Mina's ute was on the other side of the road, completely unattended.

* * *

Canberra was too many colors all at once, the buildings too tidy and freshly painted. The trees and grass were too green, after the muddy browns of Nannine. Even the brown of the autumn leaves was the wrong shade. These trees weren't dying; they were resting.

Lynnie threw herself against him. He stumbled back, tired from the long drive after an awful night of sleep.

"Hey," he whispered. This reminded him painfully of the first time he'd driven through the night because she needed him. It was going to be the last time. He was going to make it the last time.

She made him up a bed on the lounge, with a throw cushion for a pillow and a knitted blanket. "We're not supposed to have guests in these apartments," she said. "But I think they'll let it slide under the circumstances."

She chose to dance around the reason why he was there, hinting and alluding if she needed to speak of it. He was happy to go along with that, both because it was what she needed and because it removed any risk that she would want to talk about their plans for the immediate future.

* * *

Her quiet weeping woke him up. He checked his phone—around 3:00 a.m. He stepped slowly to avoid making any noise, and peered through her open bedroom door. She had a pillow clutched to her chest, and was curled around it with her shoulders hunched and her head down. The sound of her crying was only barely audible even in her silent room, but he'd spent so many years tuning in to it.

"Lynnie?" he whispered.

She didn't answer, didn't react. She was still asleep, trapped in some dream that she would never tell him about. He stepped back from the door. She'd asked him not to wake her when she had the dream, no matter how distressing it was to watch—that left her awake and frightened in the dark, trying to get back to sleep. If he let it pass naturally she would wake up in the morning completely unaware anything had happened.

Well. He couldn't be sure he would get another opportunity to do what he had to do. He slipped into the flat's kitchenette, still walking as quietly as possible. Lynnie had a pile of papers accumulating on the end of the counter, the same place she'd always dropped them at home. She would get the mail, open it on the walk inside, and then leave whatever it was on the first available flat surface until Lane nagged her into tidying it all away.

He riffled through the papers, trying not to read anything more than was absolutely necessary to confirm it wasn't the letter he was looking for. That way he could kid himself that he wasn't invading Lynnie's privacy.

The letter from Aunt Beth was at the bottom of the pile. He didn't read it—he didn't have the energy to get angry again tonight. He just skimmed it, looking for what he needed: the contact information for their father's lawyer. He folded it up and jammed it into the pocket of his pajama pants.

He moved into the bathroom and opened the medicine cabinet, wincing as the door squeaked. He felt like an absolute heel rummaging through her tampons and toothpaste, but if he couldn't stomach this level of unethical behavior, the next steps in his plan were a joke. He pushed the doubts aside. He found her medications on the highest shelf. He put her antidepressants back immediately. It was the sleeping pills he was after. He opened the box, and slipped one blister pack inside the cuff of his sleeve.

He turned around, and Chelsea was leaning against the doorframe watching him.

He barked out a curse. "You scared the crap out of me," he said, forcing out a self-deprecating laugh. "I'm not used to having a third person in the house."

"Me neither," she said, eyeing the box in his hands. "Are you having trouble getting to sleep?"

"Yeah," he admitted, running a hand through his hair in embarrassment.

"I'm not surprised." She looked sympathetic. "Those will take ages to work, though. You want something stronger?"

"Excuse me?"

"You've been driving half the night, and you're stuck on that awful lumpy futon," she said. "I'm not surprised you can't sleep. But those are slow-acting. You want something that can knock you out right away, or you'll just be finally getting to sleep when we're up clattering around with the coffee maker." She disappeared back into her room, and returned with an American-style pill bottle. "I used these for my flight, and they'll expire before I fly back. No sense letting them go to waste."

"Thanks," he said. He wasn't sure he was comfortable with Lynnie living with someone with such a cavalier attitude toward controlled substances, but that was the least of his problems right now. He took the proffered pills, and tucked them into his pocket beside the letter.

"Your sister's a great roommate," Chelsea said. "A bit quiet, but such a sweetheart. I'm glad you're here to help her."

* * *

The week passed like a dream. After months in a town where the pub's Friday night meat raffle was a cultural highlight, he was glad to let Lynnie take him on a tour of her favorite restaurants, and the ones she'd only visited in daydreams. She seemed to accept his splashing money around as an attempt to buy her happiness in a terrible time, and didn't question it.

He spent the time with the expectation—hope, maybe—that someone would stop him. His heart jumped into his throat every time he looked up from a bowl of laksa or beef massaman to see a police cruiser sliding past the window. He was sure that Mina had noticed by now that the shotgun was gone.

While Lynnie was in class, or at her appointments at the campus counseling center with a woman whom she had thoughtfully pronounced "not a complete moron," Lane drove to the city's single gun range and learned to fire the shotgun. By the end of the second session his hands had stopped shaking when he lifted it, and by the middle of the week he was almost comfortable with the routine of lift, aim, fire. On the way out that day, he stopped by the little shop and bought a set of earplugs.

* * *

Lynnie's phone buzzed on the table, a private number showing on screen. The three of them were eating lunch at a beach-themed Mexican restaurant, and the buzz of music and voices faded away as she said, "Hello?" followed by a distinctly more downbeat, "Hi, Remy." Chelsea took her other hand, and laced their fingers together, which Lynnie didn't even seem to notice as she listened to whatever Remy was saying.

When she hung up the phone, Lane stayed silent, giving her space to share in her own time. Chelsea wasn't in on that plan, however, and asked, "Is he out?"

"Tomorrow," Lynnie said, her voice flat.

"Hey," Lane said. "Did you see the sign when we drove past

the cinema by the lake? They're doing a movie marathon tomorrow. Every Marvel movie, in order."

"You hate those movies," Lynnie said. She didn't look even a tiny bit fooled by his story—he'd been on his phone for half the week, frantically looking up activities that might distract her when the day came. But there was a tiny spark of interest in her eyes too.

"Well, maybe you and Chelsea can go. I'll spring for those fancy seats."

THIRTY-FIVE

MINA STARTLED AWAKE. She'd been dreaming that she and Evelyn were playing at the antique dollhouse they had in their room. But Mina was herself, long-legged and broad-shouldered, and the only way they could both sit in front of it was if Evelyn climbed into her lap.

She sat up and reached for the jeans draped over the back of her chair, and then remembered her crumpled ute. She couldn't drive it out to the scrap of property she'd planned to walk today.

She felt suddenly, intensely vulnerable. She was alone on this enormous property, with no vehicle and no one to hear her if she shouted. The Tamms had finished packing up their house and disappeared a few days before her birthday. She hadn't evicted them. Maggie Tamm had sent a note on floral letterhead announcing that they would be vacating the operations manager's cottage as soon as possible. The whole thing made her feel awful. That was their home. But she hadn't done anything to them. It wasn't her fault.

They had left Hendrik's farm ute behind, the one her father paid for as a perk of the job. It was parked in their driveway, with the keys on the kitchen counter, according to a second floral note

Mrs. Tamm had left in the roadside mailbox the day they moved out. She could walk over to their house and take that ute, get on with her routine. But if something happened to her on the walk, if she fell and turned an ankle, or the brown snake came back, or she took sick suddenly, then there would be no one to help her. No one for a hundred kilometers.

She lay back down.

She had an appointment for a Zoom counseling session. She filled out Dr. Zhang's preappointment questionnaire to show that she was the picture of mental health. She was sleeping a totally normal amount. She was still engaging in all her usual activities and taking pleasure in them. She didn't feel hopeless at all.

She wouldn't have got away with it in person, or with a sharper counselor.

"You're speaking more slowly than normal," he said. "And pausing a lot. Is there anything—"

"Sorry? I didn't hear that." The connection was crystal clear. The property had unusually reliable internet for the area, since they'd sunk plenty of money into a satellite dish so she could work from home. But Dr. Zhang didn't know that.

"I said, you're speaking more slowly than normal, with a lot of interruptions—"

"So are you. I think the connection might be bad."

She hung up the call, and then after a few minutes sent him an email saying that she'd been trying to call back but couldn't seem to get through.

* * *

On the fifth day after her crash, Mina paid an extortionate call-out fee to have a mechanic come look at the ute. He beat a dent out of a front panel, checked the engines, fuel lines, and brakes, realigned the wheels and declared it largely unscathed. She didn't invite him in for a cup of tea. She imagined her father would sigh in disappointment at that, but it didn't matter. He'd heard her loud and clear, and she hadn't come downstairs to find the message light blinking in days. Alanna hadn't called either. Or Lane.

Just like she'd always wanted.

The next day, Mina didn't go out walking.

THIRTY-SIX

WHY HAD THEY built such a beautiful prison? Peel away the barbed wire fences and Goulburn Correctional Centre belonged on a postcard, with its red bricks, sandstone arches, and belltower.

There was a part of Lane that really thought seeing his father again in person would drop him dead on the spot, like his father had a gorgon's eye. Instead, his father strolled out of the gates in a cheap shirt and old pants, a little scrawnier but still entirely human. He swept his gaze across the car park and saw Lane, and Lane survived.

"Chip," Lane Holland Sr. said gruffly.

"Don't call me that," Lane snapped. The goal here was to be friendly and conciliatory, but that was a step too far. No.

"Whaddya want me to call you, then?"

The son you never see, Lane thought, but he just shrugged like he didn't really care. "Lane's fine. It can't be that weird."

"Alright." His father looked him up and down. "You came together okay in the end, huh?"

Lane forced a smile. His father meant it literally. The last time they saw each other in person, Lane had been an eighteen-year-old blubbering mess, one hand holding his jaw together and the other hand trying to stop any snot from getting mixed in with the blood.

He opened the passenger door, gesturing for his father to get into the car. When his father's eyes widened he worried that he'd made a mistake, that the gesture was too fawning to be believed. That his father would figure out that the child lock was on, and the door could only be opened from the outside.

But his father climbed in without hesitation. "I didn't expect the full red-carpet treatment," he joked, then his face grew grave. "I didn't expect you to come at all. My sister Beth said she wrote to you, but you never replied."

Lane never got a letter, but then it was probably moldering in the letterbox of his old Byron Bay address. "I was surprised," he said. That wasn't a lie, at least. "I thought we had a few years yet."

"I was surprised too," his father said. "But time served and good behavior, and I guess the intervention of our Lord Jesus Christ, and here we are."

"Amen," Lane said. He pulled out of the parking lot and drove around the corner, away from the closed-circuit monitoring that covered every inch of the jail. "What do you say we stop for a pie?" he suggested, pointing to the pie shop. The veranda was empty, with no truckers or frazzled traveling families tucking into a hurried lunch at the tables. Most importantly, there were no cameras. He'd checked, while picking up an egg-and-bacon roll for breakfast.

Lane Sr.'s eyes lit up like he'd been offered the throne of England. "Oh, I could murder a pie." He rubbed a hand over the stubble on his chin, where patches of white circled his mouth. "The closest we ever got in there was that snap-frozen garbage."

The shop had its own little car park, and Lane pulled in to the space tucked behind a jacaranda tree. He stepped out of the car and tipped his head back, staring up through the green leaves at the patches of blue sky. This was it. The last moment to be the person he'd once thought he was. After this, there was no going back.

He went inside, and returned with two steaming pies and two bottles of Coke. He passed one to his father.

"Cheers," Lane Sr. said, unscrewing the cap. If he noticed that the seal on it was already broken, it didn't stop him from tipping it up and taking an enormous swig.

THIRTY-SEVEN

THE ALARM BEEPED once. Mina was upright before she was even fully conscious, and sat blinking in the dark. Had it actually gone off, or had she dreamed it?

Echo shifted at the end of the bed, lifting his head up to check why Mina was awake. She'd moved his bed from its usual spot in the pantry up to her room, and after a few days that had mysteriously turned into him sleeping on her bed. He became alert and made the low whine that meant he wanted to bark, but knew he wasn't allowed.

Shit. A car really had come through the gate, then.

"Shhh," she whispered. "Good boy. Stay."

Whatever was going on, the last thing she needed was for Echo to be in danger. She grabbed her jeans from the back of her chair and pulled them on under her sleep shirt.

She headed for the back door. It could be Starrett again, or someone lost on an unfamiliar road, or shitty teenagers out drinking and looking for someone to bother. But something told her to get her gun, go back to her room, and then pull the loft stairs up behind her.

The mudroom light was an old CFL that needed half a minute to warm up. She jammed her feet into her boots in the dark. When the light finally came on, the door to the gun safe was ajar. She pulled it open, but knew what she would see. She had never, ever left the door open with the shotgun inside.

Cold washed over her. Was someone in the house already? No. There was no way someone had driven up, broken in, cracked the safe, and hidden in the two minutes since the alarm had beeped.

When had she last seen the gun? She'd been off routine all week, only leaving the house for the most essential chores. So she'd last had the gun out the day after her birthday. She'd put it in the bed of the ute when she finished her morning walk, and it must have still been there when she ran off the road.

Alright. Alright. It was in the ute.

She opened the back door. She could hear the car now, but couldn't see it. Whoever it was had the lights off and was crawling up the drive at about ten kilometers an hour. She crept around the side of the house, nearly sagging with relief when she got to the ute.

She felt inside the bed. Her fingertips brushed over cool metal. A folded tarp. The curve of the ten-liter plastic water container she kept for emergencies. A shovel. Finally she found the gun rack. It was a contraption bolted to the bottom of the bed, like two large alligator clips that held the shotgun in place.

Usually.

"Fuck," she hissed.

The sound of the car wheels changed as it passed from the dirt road to the gravel of the front yard. She ducked behind the ute, dropping to the ground so she could watch from between the wheels.

It was Lane's old Subaru.

Lane pulled up in front of the house; he clearly hadn't seen her. He walked around the front of the car, leaving his door ajar so the light inside stayed on, and dragged something from the back seat. An oversized duffel bag, like the one she'd seen in his flat?

No.

Lane heaved it to the ground, where it moved on its own. It was a person. Their head rolled to the side and then lifted slowly, like they'd been asleep. But from the way they moved, there was more to it. Their hands were definitely bound, and maybe the feet as well.

Lane turned back to the car and pulled out a much more familiar shape. A gun. Her gun?

She pushed herself up to a squat and took a shuffling step back, her balance precarious. She needed to get to the back door, get to her phone, call Starrett.

But an old man's croaking voice called out. "You there! Girl! Please, help me!"

Shit. From his position on the ground he could see her as easily as she could see him.

Lane froze. "Mina?"

Mina said nothing, and took another step back. If the old man hadn't called out to her she might have made it, but if she ran now Lane would be on her in seconds.

"It's okay," Lane replied. "I know this looks bad, but I'm going to fix things. I was trying not to wake you up."

"Fix things?" the old man said. "He's crazy. Help me, please."

"Who is this?" Mina asked.

"The man who killed your sister," Lane said, at the same time that the man on the ground said, "His father."

THIRTY-EIGHT

LANE PULLED HIM to his feet. His father sagged the other way, trying to sandbag him, but those years stored in a cell like a sack of potatoes had robbed him of all the strength he'd once used against Lane.

The look Mina gave him was strangely calm. She pressed her lips together, inspecting first Lane's face then his father's. "Shall I put a pot of tea on?" she asked, then cackled at her own joke with an edge of hysteria.

"You have to help me, lady," his father said. "He's had some kind of psychotic break."

Mina looked uncertain, and her gaze flicked again to the house.

Lane hated that he'd frightened her. She didn't deserve to be caught up in this.

"Let me tell you a story," Lane said. "About a man, his wife, and their son. They traveled the country in a caravan, scraping together a living at regional shows. The mother painted faces and hawked shitty candles. The father ran the guess-your-weight booth, until he fucked up enough to get banned by management, and their son took over."

Mina made a small noise.

"I'm sorry," Lane said. "I didn't think keeping it a secret would affect the investigation." He looked her straight in the eyes as he said it, because it was a lie. He knew the investigation would have gone differently if he'd piped up that day on the windmill, if he'd said he was there. It would have opened the door to a thousand questions, and she'd have looked at him with even more suspicion than she already had.

"The father was an endless storm of a man. The mother and her son were going to get away from him, after one more show. But it was a bust. On Saturday, the big money day, the news broke that a little girl had gone missing. Hardly anyone showed up, and everyone who did was in a somber mood. Except one man."

He pulled on the cable ties binding his father's hands. "This one had some kind of road to Damascus moment during the night. He woke up as a ray of goddamn sunshine. The family drove off together, away from that sad little town. You want to tell her what happened next?"

"I don't know where you're going with this," his father said. "You need help, son."

"With his newfound positive attitude, the mother decided to give their marriage a second chance. They even had another baby. A beautiful girl. What did you name her?"

"We named her after your grandmother."

"My grandmothers were named Gwen and Maeve. Try again."

"A great-aunt or something, then, how should I know?"

"Nope. Mum told her you picked the name out all by yourself. You were so insistent. She tried to spin it like you were just being a loving and involved father, but I could tell it made her uneasy. But she never went against something you wanted, did she?"

Lane's father looked at Mina. "Please. If you go in the house, he won't hurt you. He hates me, he always has, but he doesn't have the balls to hurt you."

"Tell her what you named the baby!" Lane shouted.

"Evelyn," Lane's father said. "We named her Evelyn."

Mina's face collapsed. She pressed a hand to her mouth and closed her eyes, and her shoulders lurched a few times like she might throw up. "Are you the Lane Holland from Goulburn jail?"

"You want to tell her the story of what got you sent there?" Lane asked. "You think you could still talk her into helping you, if she knew?"

"I should have drowned you in a bucket," Lane Sr. said, his voice resigned.

"I used to daydream about murdering you in your sleep," Lane shot back. "The pain I could have prevented, if I worked up the guts."

The gentleness in Lane made his father so angry. He wanted someone in his own image, to drink and start fights with. When Lane had grown up into a man who would rather help his mother in the cramped little kitchen, or sit with his sister and build cities out of Duplo, his father couldn't stand it. It gave Lane a small amount of pleasure, to know what his father saw as weakness was the only reason the man was still alive.

"So instead you're trying to spin this fantasy about Evie Mc-Creery. She was in the news all the time when you were fourteen, fifteen. You obsessed about this stuff when you should have been sneaking *Playboys* into the toilet. It's crawled into your brain and fucked you up, son."

"No," Lane said quietly. "End of the line, Dad. Tell the truth."

"Lane," Mina said. "You've got a gun. A confession's not going to be worth anything."

"You're right," Lane said with a sigh. He lifted the gun. "If you want to live, take me to her body."

Something changed in his father. Lane had spent his whole childhood as a weathervane, tracking those changing winds for his own survival.

"Okay," Lane Sr. said.

"It's a trick," Mina said. "He's just trying to survive, Lane."

"Maybe so," Lane said. "I need you to drive."

Mina quailed. "Lane—"

"If I leave you here, you'll call the police. If they come before he takes me to the body, then this is all for nothing. He'll be released, I'll be arrested, they'll never get anything out of him. The only way this ends is if I force him to show us the body. Or I kill him."

"Okay, I won't call the police. I promise."

He didn't know if she was lying, but it didn't matter. If she didn't call the police, then people would wonder why for the rest of her life. He couldn't do that to her. "I need you to drive."

"I can't." She held up her shaking hands.

"You can," he said softly. "You don't have a choice. The only other option is for you to sit in the passenger seat and hold the gun. If you drive, you're my second hostage. If I drive, you're an accomplice. Get in the ute."

THIRTY-NINE

MINA WIPED AWAY the tears that had gathered in the frog hollows under her eyes. She hadn't cried in so long that it was almost a pleasure to feel the damp on her fingertips.

"Take this road," Lane Sr. said, raising his bound hands to point at the main carriage road of the farm, toward the Tamm house.

It was a trick, she knew it. Lane seemed half-mad. A baby name and a shitty father's strange, changeable moods didn't add up to much. She didn't know where this night would end—with violence, certainly, but against who?—but she knew it wasn't leading to an answer.

They drove past the windmill, then down the dark road that passed the clearing with the old felled gum tree. Mina's heart climbed into her throat as the headlights washed over the trunk, and Lane Sr. shifted minutely beside her. But they said nothing, and the ute rolled on past the Tamm house.

Lane was silent in the passenger seat, rubbing the wooden stock of the gun with his thumb. He kept the end pressed to his father's chest, angled so that if the bullet passed through him it would hit the seat behind. It would be difficult to fire from that angle, awkward and slow, but Mina appreciated the effort to protect her.

That meant he didn't plan to kill her. Not planning to didn't mean he wouldn't, of course, once this already pear-shaped night went truly wrong. He was going to kill his father, that much was obvious. She didn't know if Lane Sr. was directing them somewhere in hopes of enacting a plan to save his own life, but once it became clear that he couldn't give Lane what he wanted, she didn't expect Lane to pay much attention to where he was shooting.

"Out the gate?" she asked. She thought of all those mornings spent searching the property.

"Out the gate," confirmed Lane Sr. "And then left."

In the back of her mind, she heard the alarm ding in the house as they drove through.

Left took them west, which was another way of saying nowhere. To the west was a melange of Crown land—land so overgrazed and dirt-packed it wasn't worth the cost of rehabilitation—and neighboring farms that weren't really neighbors but food factories tended by robots and drones. If they went far enough, they would hit the national park. In other words, Lane Sr. was leading them into an entirely uninhabited patch of the country, away from any traffic or passersby that might be able to help.

He was leading them exactly in the direction a man would go if he needed to hide a body.

Even so, she was sure it was a trick. The thought repeated in her mind. *This is a trick, this is a trick, this is a trick.* With every repetition her heartbeat slowed and her breathing evened out. She shifted gears, picking up speed on the familiar road. Her father had taught her to drive on this road. She could hear him, the way his voice lifted whenever he was nervous, saying, "Slow down, Minchkin. You don't want to go this fast on a dirt road."

If she died tonight, he would think forever she was still angry with him.

She eased off, although it ached to do it. She wanted to go faster, to get this over with.

Lane Sr.'s dark eyes narrowed every time they passed a gate—which wasn't often—but he let each one slide behind them.

Finally, Mina broke. "Lane," she said, "it's been twenty years. Even if—" No, she wasn't going to question his theory. The safe path was to pretend to be all in. "It's been twenty years. These farms have changed hands, been merged, subdivided. He's not going to find it."

"It's the next right," Lane Sr. interrupted.

The next right was barely a road. They rattled over a cattle grid, and the ute sank into two ruts so deep Mina could have taken her hands off the wheel. She slowed to a crawl, and Lane Sr. swept his gaze over the side of the road, like he was searching for a vacant spot in a crowded car park.

"That tree," he said, pointing to a wattle tree that listed over a barbed-wire fence. "It was smaller, but that's the one."

Something snapped loose inside Mina's chest. She coasted to a stop in the middle of the road. She leaned over the steering wheel and started to cry again, heaving sobs that shredded her chest.

"You stay here," Lane said. She had her eyes squeezed shut, so she didn't know if he looked over at her with concern, if he hesitated before opening the door. She chose to believe that he did. The door squeaked open, and Lane Sr.'s warmth was gone from beside her.

"I'll show you the precise spot if you let me dig," he said, his voice low.

"You think I'll fall for that?" Lane snapped.

"If you want to spend all night searching, be my guest. But you never were much good at digging, were you, boy? Or lifting, or kicking, or anything that made it worth having a son."

Lane laughed. "You think that button's still attached to anything, old man? I want nothing more in life than to be a disappointment to you."

Mina looked up, scrubbing at her eyes. The two Lanes glowed like ghosts in the light from the ute, trying to stare each other down.

"Use your brain, boy," Lane Sr. said. "If you take the shovel, where's the gun? You can't hold both. Are you going to make the girl do it? Force her out of the car at gunpoint and make her open up her own sister's grave? Because I've got to say, it wouldn't disappoint me to see you do that, Chip."

Lane made an enraged, animal sound and swung the shotgun, whipping his father in the face with the barrel. The older man staggered back and lost his balance, unable to steady himself with his arms, and tumbled to the ground.

"Fine!" Lane snapped, standing over him. He stomped back to the ute. Mina turned to watch through the back window, but he didn't look at her as he dragged her shovel out of the back. He circled to the open passenger door and pulled her multi-tool out of the glove box.

"Lane," she said. "Don't do this."

"It's fine," he said. "What's a shovel against a gun?"

A lot, if the shovel was in the hands of a killer and the gun in the hands of a compassionate man. But was either of them a killer?

Mina jammed on the hazard lights and stepped out of the ute. It was unlikely anyone would drive up this road in the middle of the night, but if they did the ute was safer where it was visible, as opposed to pulled onto the too-narrow shoulder.

Lane finished sawing through the cable ties, and his father rubbed his wrists. "I never thought something could make me miss handcuffs," he joked.

"You don't need to talk anymore," Lane said. "Dig."

Lane Sr. heaved himself to his feet, groaning and grumbling. He walked over to the wattle, and Mina stepped back, keeping him out of her personal space. He winked in a way that made her sick to her stomach, then pressed his back to the tree trunk. He took a measured step away, then another. Three, four, five, six, seven, eight, nine, ten. If this was a performance, it was an elaborate one.

He marked a spot in the dust by dragging a cross with his toe. He picked up the shovel, rolled his shoulders, and sliced the blade into the crumbly, sun-bleached earth.

Lane's face hid nothing. He'd come so far and risked so much on the belief that he was right about this, but as he watched his father dig he crumbled.

"Lane," Mina said. "Give me the gun." He couldn't be trusted with it. He was too emotional; he could do anything.

"No," he said in a low moan.

"It's getting heavy, right? Let me hold it. Go sit down."

Lane looked her directly in the eyes. "No. I can handle this."

Later, it would be this fork in the road that kept her awake, not what came after. Would things have gone differently if she hadn't spoken? If she hadn't dragged his attention to her, forced him to look at her, would it have gone better? Would it have gone worse?

If someone had asked her to imagine the sound of a person being struck with a shovel, she would have conjured something wet and fleshy. Surely the human body being brutalized would be the focus. It shocked her, then, that the sound of the shovel slamming into the small of Lane's back was so metallic. It was like a stubborn car part being whacked with a wrench. Lane gasped and stumbled forward, his knees buckling.

The gun dropped from his hands and hit the dirt.

The warm, comforting fog of dissociation that had been keeping Mina calm blew away as she watched it rattle to a stop. She had no idea if it was loaded—surely it was loaded—but it was cocked, with the safety off. It was a top-of-the-line gun, supposedly drop safe, but her breath still turned to glass in her chest.

It lay still, casting a shadow much bigger than itself in the glow of the headlights. Lane straightened up with a low animal groan.

They both reached for the gun. Maybe they all did. Mina had no idea what Lane's father was doing. She didn't have time to look. Mina got there first, but not fast enough to stop Lane from closing his hand around the stock. She gripped the barrel firmly and yanked. Lane hissed in pain and let go.

Swinging the gun into the firing position was second nature. It belonged in her hands. The barrel wobbled as she trembled, but she told herself it didn't matter. If she could face down a feral pig, she could handle this.

To her horror, she couldn't see Lane's father. While the two of them tussled over the gun, he must have slipped out of the circle of light from the ute and into the shadows. He couldn't be more than a meter or two away, but where? Behind the ute? Behind her?

With a shovel.

If she turned away from Lane, he could wrestle the gun from her and they would be back where they started. If Lane's father was inclined to attack her, they would both be at the mercy of an extremely dangerous man.

But was he?

Lane's evidence that his father had killed Evelyn was shaky, bordering on delusional. He had been obsessive from the start, pushing and pushing whenever she'd said no. He'd seemed so understanding, so empathetic, but then on her birthday he'd lost interest in her pain the moment he got whatever it was he'd been looking for. Like a switch flipping. That was the sort of thing a sociopath did, wasn't it? Was this just an elaborate plan to get rid of a man he clearly loathed, in a way that might stir a jury's sympathy? He'd had no trouble using Alanna as a stepping stone, why would Mina be different?

"Here's what we're going to do," she said, proud of how even her voice was. "You're both going to plant your fucking feet and stay where you are. I'm going to get the satellite phone from the ute and call the police. Got it?"

Metal gleamed out the corner of her eye. The blade of the shovel caught in the headlights as Lane's father moved toward her.

She swung the gun and fired.

Lane said something, dropping to his knees like it was him she had shot. His words were lost to the roaring in her ears. Lane Sr.'s chest was a mess, his white shirt soaked with blood like he'd been rolling around in it. He was still breathing, but each breath gurgled like his lungs were filling up with blood.

If he was innocent, he wouldn't have moved, she told herself. She was going to get the police. The only reason he would move was if he needed to prevent that.

That meant he was dangerous, right?

"Please," she said. "If you killed her, please tell me."

Lane Sr. smiled, and the gurgling sound fell silent.

She didn't know how long she sat there, staring at the smile on his face, before Lane put a gentle hand on her shoulder. She jumped and shrieked, and Lane shushed her like he was trying to soothe a spooked dog. "Everything's going to be okay," he said.

"I killed him," she said.

"No," Lane said firmly. He put a hand on the gun, and this time she let him ease it away from her. "Do you have water in your ute?"

"Of course."

"Then go wash your hands. Up to the elbow. Have a drink of water. Change your shirt if you've got a spare. I'll handle this."

"Wash my hands?" She looked down at them. There was no blood on her anywhere.

"The gunshot residue," he said. "They probably won't even test your hands, but better safe than sorry."

She walked over to the ute and opened the tap on her ten-liter water canister, scrubbing her hands as instructed. The fog was creeping back in, wrapping its protective arms around her. She cupped her hands to let the water flow in, and drank. Behind her a shot rang out.

"Lane?" she screamed, spinning around.

He stood at the fence, the gun aimed into the grassland beyond. "Gunshot residue," he said again, and then leaned the shotgun against the fence post. He approached his father's body staring at it like he expected him to spring back up like a horror movie villain. He crouched down, sucking in a breath in pain, and picked up the shovel.

Mina closed her eyes. After a moment, the hiss and scrape of dirt being shifted began again.

She had just shot a man and now they were going to bury him beside an abandoned back road and then . . . what? Shake hands and agree to never speak of it again?

The sound of shoveling stopped, and Lane swore softly under his breath.

"Mina," he said.

She didn't want to know. She didn't want to see. But she turned, slowly and painfully, and peered into the hole at the doll-sized human skull he had uncovered.

FORTY

MyMurder Forums

Subforum: Evie McCreery

Subject: Lane Holland

User Comet: I have a theory about Lane Holland. We now know, from the pretrial reporting, that Holland was the snakebite victim on the McCreery property in February. Everything in his history suggests he was a stand-up guy—a model student, an AFP trainee, a private eye whose past clients speak glowingly of him. He dropped everything to go home and raise his little sister after their mother died. I don't think it's a coincidence that only a few weeks after the bite he began behaving erratically and then spiraled. Has his lawyer requested he be examined medically? It sounds like a traumatic brain injury.

User Inspektor: The guy meticulously planned out a kidnapping and murder. That's not a TBI, that's a psychopath. I think the apple didn't rot far from the tree.

User LionSong: Where did you guys get your medical degrees?

User VolcanicJudo: Just so you know, I donate $1 to his GoFundMe every time one of you jack-offs uses the word "psychopath." Lane Holland is a hero. He took out Australia's worst serial killer since Mr. Cruel.

User Inspektor: Uh, Lane Holland Sr. doesn't qualify as a serial killer. Minimum's three.

User VolcanicJudo: Oh please, you know they're going to find more.

* * *

Lane's lawyer's immaculate gray suit was the same color as the table. Everything about William Magala was immaculate, from his neat squared-off nails to his precise taper fade. It jarred compared to the scruffy edges of the men he'd been around for days, who had been snatched away from their usual grooming routines or had never had much of one to begin with.

Magala was also disconcertingly young, a few years out of his University of Sydney honors degree, but that was the only reason Lane could afford him. Within hours of the news of his arrest breaking, a link had started circulating on the internet, fundraising for his defense. Magala's first act as his lawyer was to insist he decline the money, to avoid getting tangled up with laws around the proceeds of a crime. But it didn't matter—he had waived most of his fees in exchange for being the lawyer of record on the Lane Holland trial. It was the sort of case that would have instant name recognition for the rest of his career. The sort that would go in the blurb of his memoirs.

"Is there anything else I should know?" Magala asked.

"No." Lane had been lying to both him and the police consistently for days. He fully intended to lie to a judge and jury too, if it came to that.

"Alright, then. I have good news. The DPP wants to make a deal."

That should have been cause for excitement. At the very least, it meant taking up far less of his time, and so fewer bills for Lynnie to worry about. But he only felt numb.

"Can I ask you a question? It's about self-defense—"

"You had him at gunpoint, after kidnapping him and driving him across the state. Him swinging the shovel was self-defense." The words were harsh, but Magala's tone was cheerful. Starrett had been wrong. This defense lawyer wasn't excited by an inept opponent. He was completely enchanted by the complexities of Lane's case, and the attention it would bring.

"So," Lane said, "if I'd shot him without kidnapping him, then it would have been self-defense?"

"Given that his attack was directly linked to your kidnapping, it's a moot point."

"But what if, say, someone else kidnapped him and—"

"Was there another person involved?" Magala leaned forward, clasping his hands together on the table. "Because that was definitely something to mention when I asked earlier."

"No. I just mean hypothetically. If I hadn't kidnapped him. Say I was just one of the hostages . . ." Lane pressed his lips together. He was wandering into dangerous territory now.

"If you want to discuss hypotheticals, I suggest you try Reddit's legal advice sub. If you want advice from your lawyer about your actual situation, it's this: self-defense is messy even at the best of times. Even cases that seem justified to the man in the street can result in conviction because deadly force was excessive, or the supposed attacker was trying to escape, or the shooter ignored better options in favor of violence. Take the plea."

Something loosened in Lane's chest. Taking the blame for the shooting had been a panicked, adrenaline-fueled decision, but it was the right one. No matter what, he'd have had to face the music for abducting his father, and if they'd told the truth, Mina risked at worst being charged as a coconspirator and murderer, and at best living under a new cloud of suspicion for the rest of her life.

He had set the events in motion that left Mina with no choice, and so really he had killed his father.

"The plea offer is generous," Magala said. "They're willing to kick it down to manslaughter, and let you serve that and the two kidnapping charges concurrently."

"Concurrently?" Lane repeated. He could barely believe that he'd heard that right.

"That means you'll receive multiple sentences but serve them at the same time. It's much better than consecutive sentences, where you would have to complete them one after the other."

"I know, I'm just . . ." Lane waved a hand, trying to convey his complete bewilderment. It meant that he could end up serving the same amount of prison time for the kidnapping and the murder as he would have on the kidnapping alone.

Which gave him the one thing he never expected: confirmation he'd made the right decision in taking the fall for it.

"Honestly, your real risk is the sentencing judge squelching it for being so lenient. But the victim impact statement—"

"Mina wrote a victim impact statement?" Lane interrupted.

"No." Magala looked uncomfortable. "Your sister wrote a statement, as the deceased's next of kin. She expressed her forgiveness, and a strong desire for you not to receive a custodial sentence."

Lynnie hadn't told him she was doing that. Probably because

he'd have told her not to. It had been the main theme of their relationship for days: him telling her to stay out of his mess and her telling him where he could shove that idea. It was hardly surprising she'd gone behind his back to try to help him; she'd learned from the best. "Surely they're not going to take that seriously?"

"Everything is taken into consideration." Magala started ticking off on his fingers. "There's also the fact that you turned yourself in. Your good character, and your history. Public sentiment is strongly in your favor. But if you want the judge to sign off on this, you need to show an appropriate amount of remorse." The look Magala gave him made it clear that he had noticed Lane's giddy reaction, even if he was misinterpreting the cause.

"Then I'd be lying," Lane admitted. "This isn't what I wanted. I wanted him alive. I wanted him sitting here, not me. But it doesn't matter. If I go to prison, I go to prison. Lynnie is safe. Mina has her answers. Liam McCreery finally has a body to bury. I can live with that."

Magala paused, frowning at him. "Have you not seen today's news?"

Lane shook his head. He avoided the newspapers, and kept out of the TV room. It was disturbing, seeing his own face plastered everywhere. Seeing talking heads picking over what he had done, and arguing about it.

"Phew. If I knew that, I would have told you as soon as I came in. The DNA test on the female remains found at the scene showed no relation to Wilhelmina or Liam McCreery. There is no chance you found the body of Evelyn McCreery."

Lane looked up, dizzy with shock. "Then who?"

"Further testing will take time," Magala said. "But based on an examination of the remains by a forensic anthropologist, the body is consistent with another cold case from the state. A girl named—"

"Christa Rennold," Lane said. As one final, sick joke his father had taken them to the wrong body.

Lane sat back in his chair. In a way, it was a relief. It had been keeping him awake, trying to figure out why his father had actually taken them to the body. If his plan had been to attack Lane and escape, then why not just take them to a random spot? "God, poor Mina," he said. "Is she okay?"

The lawyer's smile dropped. "I'm not going to pass you information about your victim."

"Of course," Lane said quickly. "I didn't mean it like that."

"Do you regret the distress you caused Wilhelmina McCreery?"

"Yes," Lane said immediately.

"Try to lean into that, then. As for your father, the general consensus is still that he killed Evelyn McCreery. It was likely a strategy—he knew that he was caught, and was going back to prison for life, so his plan was probably to hold the location of Evelyn's body back as a bargaining chip."

"I doubt it," Lane said.

"You doubt it?"

"You're a brilliant lawyer, and so you're imagining what a brilliant lawyer would have done. But my father didn't bargain, or plan, or strategize. He just hurt people. If you're trying to figure out why he did anything, ask yourself: where's the pain?"

"He pulled off a plan elaborate enough to get away with Evelyn's murder for twenty years."

"No, he didn't." Lane drummed his fingers on the table. "Everybody acts like it took a mastermind to avoid leaving any evidence. But what was he trying to achieve? Imagine: he's in the pub. He's mad as hell, because he's been fired and he's forced to hide and depend on his wife and son. Then he overhears two blokes arguing about how they've left their wives and two children all alone on a remote property, no neighbors for miles around. He probably wasn't even thinking about avoiding getting caught, just boiling over with rage and presented with a great target. He already had form as a car thief; he knew to wear gloves to avoid leaving fingerprints."

Magala looked thoughtful. "He may not even have known about DNA. It was 1999—we didn't even have a national database until, what, 2001?"

"Exactly! So he steals Hendrik's car, finds the address in the glove box and drives out there, planning to smash his way in and . . ." Lane faltered, acid rising in his throat. "And he doesn't have to do that. Because Evelyn was just out there, alone."

He fell silent for a beat, and swallowed against the nausea. "Then he drives back to town, puts the ute back, and slides back into his life like nothing happened. He gets to watch it blow up into the case of the century. The press talked about him as if he were a genius."

He could see it. Everything slipping into place perfectly, like an evil miracle to protect him. He'd have felt like a god. "Maybe the constant press coverage was enough to keep him satisfied for years. Then, when he decides to kill again, he tries to recreate it. He overhears Gunther in a pub, ranting about the government stealing his children. How they're alone with a foster mother. He took Gunther's car because it was part of the ritual for him. Then he tried to pull it again on Alexandra's parents, and his luck ran out."

Magala shook his head. "You're starting to sound like one of those forum guys now."

The laugh that punched out of Lane actually hurt. "You're right. But my point stands. Don't start from the assumption he was working from some kind of master plan. Maybe you had it, maybe he hoped to cut a deal. Or maybe he wasn't thinking straight after what I slipped him . . ."

Magala cringed. "Please don't confess things to me that you don't have to."

"Sorry." Lane rubbed his forehead. His thoughts were churning faster than he could handle, and he was going to end up laid out on his cot with a monstrous headache. "Has Gunther come forward, now that he has proof of his innocence?"

Magala shook his head. "No sign of him."

Lane ached for Alanna. Within weeks she'd gone from her sister miraculously alive to definitely dead, and odds were good that her father was dead too. Probably one of the country's five hundred unidentified bodies.

It was too much. He needed to get out of this room, go stick his head under his pillow and squeeze his eyes shut against the pain. "Okay. Tell me about the deal."

"Eight years," Magala said. "Eligible for parole after six."

Lane leaned forward, gasping like Magala had punched him in the solar plexus. "Six years?"

"That's a lot less than fifteen to twenty. You would be what, forty? You would still have time for marriage, a family, another career. My dad was that age when he had me."

Lane could barely hear him. Six years was a lifetime. It was the same amount of time he'd spent raising Lynnie. This was supposed to be to protect her, to set things right, but what had he really done? He'd abandoned her.

FORTY-ONE

HERE'S A STORY. A little girl slips out of her house at night. The door locks behind her, but the lock is fifty years old and she knows it will open again if she jiggles the loose brass handle just the right way. She walks along the path, sweeping the light of her torch in front of her, looking for snakes attracted to the warm bricks. When the path ends she avoids the sticky mud, stepping on tussocks of grass and flat patches of bark instead.

Does she reach the windmill? Does she find out that, no, she can't see the lights from the top? Where is she when she hears the hum of a familiar engine returning home unexpectedly, and turns in excitement?

* * *

Tea glugged from Mina's thermos into the lid, and she breathed in the sweet steam. Down below the searchers were spread out, yellow hi-vis vests popping in and out of stands of trees.

Following the coroner's ruling that Evelyn could be presumed dead, the state government approved funding for another large-scale

351

search of the property, the area between it and Christa's burial site, and a few kilometers on either side just for good measure. Mina's confession that she had always known Evelyn wasn't taken from the house had barely made a ripple in the press, outshone by more sensational details, but it caused a great deal of excitement inside the investigation. Between that, the knowledge that Holland had likely buried her body, and advances in technology and ground penetrating radar, there was a strong chance of turning up something they had missed on previous searches.

If the search was unsuccessful, there were talks of conducting one around the Wentworth Showground, which had been the Holland family's next stop after Nannine, but that was proving tricky due to how close it was to the Victorian border.

Mina had offered to help, but Starrett had tactfully steered her away. Her argument had been that Mina needed to take care of herself, but she suspected they didn't want rumors circulating that Mina had interfered with the search again.

In the distance, one of the dogs from the canine units barked. She had dropped Echo at Alanna's house the night before, so he wouldn't go crazy with all the strange dogs and people in his territory. She took a little comfort in the fact that if Echo couldn't be there to help her, he could help Alanna instead. She'd tried to be there for Alanna after the truth of what happened to Christa came out, but their friendship was still frayed and complicated. The comfort Echo could offer wasn't.

* * *

The windmill creaked under the weight of someone climbing up. She turned, and a strange part of her expected to see Lane Holland's head pop up. But he was gone, and would be for years. They'd offered her a form she could sign, to be notified of where he was every year and any time they moved him, but she'd thrown it in the bin.

"Hi, Mina," her dad said, hauling himself up onto the platform. She felt a flash of gratitude for his good health, even at his age. She wondered briefly which parent they had inherited their health from, if the life stolen from Evelyn would otherwise have been long or short.

"Hey, Dad," she said, shuffling over. "Any news?"

"It's barely started."

A group down below were spreading out a blanket, and one of them had a picnic basket. The search for her sister was doubling as their family day out. Her father followed her gaze and said, "They're volunteers, love. They've got to eat."

"I know," she said. "It's still weird, though."

There was another group at the edge of her field of vision, wearing matching white shirts, the backs screen-printed with the MyMurder logo. One of them turned to point something out, and there was a slogan printed on the front. She was glad she couldn't make out what it said.

"You don't have to stay out here and watch, if it's too much. They'll radio with any updates."

She nodded, staring out at the expanse of the paddocks. "If they find her, will you want to sell?"

Her father made a thoughtful noise. "I wouldn't do anything you weren't ready for."

"Not until you're ready" and "no" were very different answers. He hadn't moved back into the house, and she didn't think he ever would. She didn't know if he would see Hendrik again, wherever he went next. They'd always kept secrets from each other, and even after they'd cleared the air, new ones had taken their place. Sometimes she tried to imagine telling him what she had done to Lane's father, but she couldn't picture a good outcome. Either he would pressure her to confess, or he would be pulled into keeping her secret. It would be unburdening herself by passing half the load to him.

"Even if we find her, I don't think I could stand to see it bulldozed," she said. "The conservation work we've done here, the replanting . . ." It was nothing against the land clearing going on around it. Like throwing water drops on a bushfire. But it was the closest thing she had to a life's work.

"So we put a conservation covenant on it," he said with a shrug.

"And tank the value."

"There's no rush. Take some time and think about what you really want. Let's not talk land prices right now."

Mina had thought a lot about what she wanted. She certainly had plenty of offers on the table. The publishers were after her to write her own memoir now. Three of the major networks had extended offers for her to do interviews, especially if she was willing to talk about what happened that night, and during the hour and a half it took for the police to find them after she called. She'd declined every time.

"How would you feel about me taking your campervan for a while?" she asked. She could do her job from anywhere with a secure internet connection.

One of the items entered as evidence in Lane's aborted murder trial, and then in the coronial inquest into Evelyn's missing person's case, was a map collected from Lane's flat. It was a map of his lifelong obsession, tracing the path his father took around the country, with dates and possible nearby cold cases. The users of MyMurder were beside themselves trying to get their hands on a copy. It was the new holy grail for amateur investigators. But as a member of Evelyn's immediate family, all Mina had to do was fill out a form.

She didn't delude herself that she could make a go of investigating them herself. But she did have the ability to throw a spotlight on any of those cases. If they wanted it.

Down below a volunteer emerged from the trees. She stared up at the windmill, like she was searching for Mina.

"She's going to regret not wearing a hat," Mina said. The woman had her honey-blond hair pulled up in a ponytail, and nothing protecting the top of her head or her face at all.

The woman stood awkwardly down below, her hands jammed in her pockets, and Mina stood up with a sigh. "I'll go see what she wants."

The woman definitely wanted to talk to her. When Mina reached the bottom of the ladder she jogged over, then stopped short a few meters away like she was unsure of her welcome.

"We're not giving any statements to the media today," Mina said.

"I'm not from the media," the woman said. "I'm Evelyn."

For one beautiful, absurd moment Mina was confused. Then the fog cleared. "Evelyn Holland. Lane's sister."

"Yes, apparently that's what I'm known for now."

That will never go away, Mina thought, but she wasn't cruel enough to say it. "It took me a moment. He always called you Lynnie."

"Yes. He's the only one who calls me that. I guess I know why, now."

Mina tried to relax, tried to pull her shoulders back and down, because they were trying to crush her neck. Here it was, the other shoe dropping at last. She waited for Lynnie to tell her what she owed in exchange for Lane covering her tracks.

"I promise I'm here off my own bat," Evelyn said. "I wanted to . . . He doesn't know I'm here, I swear."

Mina blinked. Part of Lane's sentencing had included a non-contact order, and if Lynnie tried to pass on any messages Mina could get him slammed with more time in a heartbeat. If Lynnie thought there was any risk of that, it meant she didn't know. Mina breathed in, and out, counting her breaths, and asked, "How are you?"

"Managing." Evelyn looked over Mina's shoulder at something. She turned to look, but it was just a group of searchers passing by.

"I'm sorry about the money," Mina said. "That must have been rough, on top of everything else."

The court had ruled that the advertised reward for solving Christa's murder could not be paid to Lane or his family, as it would be the proceeds of crime. While Evelyn had been declared dead, the coroner had returned an open finding about who had killed her, meaning that the NSW Police reward would not be paid out. The additional reward offered by Mina's mother had stipulated that Evelyn must be found.

Several interesting articles had come out from lawyers arguing that if Evelyn's body was found, and the coroner revised her findings to name Lane Holland Sr. as her killer, then perhaps the reward could be paid out, because Sergeant Starrett had opened an investigation into Lane's father as soon as Lane brought him to her attention. This meant that, assuming the Rube Goldberg machine of justice eventually came to the same conclusion, he had already met the conditions of the reward before he committed any crime. It was an interesting question, and one that Mina was glad would be decided by the courts and not her.

"It wasn't a shock; William told us to expect that," Evelyn

said. "It's been okay. I have a job now, and I'm pretty good at eating cheap. I've, uh, had some offers to give interviews."

She looked at Mina, the question obvious in her silence. But Mina just shrugged. She honestly couldn't tell her whether to do it or not. It was probably more money than she would see all year working behind a bar or waiting tables. And interest in her would likely fade fast, after the initial flurry. But once she'd made herself a public figure, it couldn't be undone.

Evelyn gave a little nod, and looked down at her feet. "Anyway, I wanted to thank you. William—I mean, Lane's lawyer—said that you must have asked the prosecutor not to put you through a trial. They wouldn't have been half as willing to plead him out otherwise."

"I just told the truth," Mina said.

"The truth can be told in a lot of different ways."

Mina smiled at her. "Have you thought about making that your family motto?"

Evelyn frowned, which was fair. Lane would have laughed.

"Mina!" her father shouted.

She turned around and looked up at him, shading her eyes against the harsh glare, expecting to be scolded. But he was pointing past the trees, at somewhere he could see from his vantage point and they couldn't.

Something was happening.

* * *

They waited for an eternity at the bottom of the windmill. Other people arrived long before Starrett did. When the first group emerged from the trees Mina felt a surge of anger, thinking they were ghouls wanting to be where the action was when it all finally happened. But the group resolved from faceless figures in yellow vests to people she knew—Mrs. Gilligan, and Neil, and some girls she'd gone to school with, Meryl and Sandra. Cherise from the real estate and Marc from the takeaway. People from the town, who needed to know almost as much as Mina and her father did.

When Starrett appeared, Mina knew, just from the look on her face.

"Have you found her?" her father asked.

Starrett nodded. She took her hat off and tucked it under her arm. "Liam, I'm so—"

"Take me there," Mina interrupted. She needed to know where. Starrett had come on foot, so it wasn't far. A horrible suspicion had taken root.

"I think it would be best if—" Starrett began, and Mina started walking. Starrett didn't stop her, just fell into step beside her as she stormed down the road.

The air hummed, a steady *thwap-thwap-thwap* like an emu's warning hum. It was a strange comfort to look up and actually see a helicopter hovering in the blue, a news channel logo splashed across the side. She took a deep breath and let it out slowly. It didn't matter. Nothing mattered except the walk ahead of her.

Starrett didn't have to tell her where to go. It was obvious, from the crowd of volunteers that had gathered around the fallen spotted gum. The police had pulled them back, cordoning off the space where a grid had been staked out with string to guide the forensics team buzzing about in white Tyvek suits, bagging up samples of the soil and plants, the white fuzz of fallen gum blossoms. A crime scene photographer was snapping away at something blessedly hidden by the trunk. He had one knee up on it so he could get closer without losing his balance, pressing against the worn-away patch of bark where she had sat so many times.

ACKNOWLEDGMENTS

I WOULD LIKE to acknowledge the Ngunnawal people, on whose lands I lived while writing this book. Nginggada Dindi dhawura Ngunnawalbun yindjumaralidjinyin. I pay my respects to their elders past and present.

Nannine is a fictional town in a real part of Australia. I would like to acknowledge the Barkindji people as the custodians of the land on which this novel is set and pay my respects to their elders past and present.

Thank you to:

The amazing team at Hachette: Rebecca Saunders, Fiona Hazard, Lee Moir, Melissa Wilson, Emma Dorph, Sarah Brooks. My editors, Emma Rafferty, Samantha Sainsbury, Ali Lavau, and Meaghan Amor. Debra Billson for the cover of my dreams.

The amazing team at Hodder and Stoughton: Eve Hall, Jo Dickinson, and Melissa Dagoglu.

My extraordinary agent, Sarah McKenzie.

Nicholas Cole, lawyer and the best money I ever spent.

The Crime Writers' Association of the UK, and the judges of the Debut Dagger and the Bath Novel Award for their feedback.

Kill Your Darlings: Rebecca Starford and Alan Vaarwerk. My fellow shortlistees for the *Kill Your Darlings* Unpublished Manuscript Award: Matt Millikan, Sam van Zweden, Lisa Emanuel.

Varuna the National Writers' House and the Copyright Agency. Particularly the national treasure Sheila Atkinson for all she does to nourish Australian literature, and Dr. Carol Major for expert advice.

ACT Writers and Hardcopy. Nigel Featherstone, Claire Delahunty, Katy Mutton, Sophie Mannix, Nadine Davidoff. Kylie, Karen, Sky, and Steve for your thoughtful and generous feedback. Elle the ML, who warned me during NaNo 2017 to go for Hardcopy now and not wait until I felt ready, because funding is tenuous for arts programs. Sadly you were right.

My family, who were not the inspiration for any character in this book.

All my friends for their endless support, motivation, and patience with my whining. Lana, Abra, Amelia, Bea, Claire, Deb, Ella, John, Maree, Mick, Maureen, Natalie, Craig, Patrick, Jordan. Marita, and Nick. Nikki and Chris. Sarah. Emma. Gill and Jeff. Rosalind. Sue.

Every group chat that I crashed into with straw polls about random regionalisms.

The crew of the Westpac Rescue Helicopter, for coming to my rescue when I was the one who walked through long grass without checking for snakes.

My English teachers. Ms. MacNaughton, I'm sorry for all the times I skipped class during the Extension 1 Crime Fiction unit to spend time with a cute boy.

That cute boy. There were times when you were the only person who believed in this book, self included. For every Sunday in the park so I could have a quiet house to myself. For every note in the margins of a draft. For every conversation in the kitchen. Here's to many more.